KT-512-353
47218000032559 0

Christobel Kent was born in London and educated at Cambridge. She has lived variously in Essex, London and Italy. Her childhood included several years spent on a Thames sailing barge in Maldon, Essex with her father, stepmother, three siblings and four step-siblings. She now lives in both Cambridge and Florence with her husband and five children.

Also by Christobel Kent

The Crooked House
The Loving Husband

THE DAY SHE DISAPPEARED

Christobel Kent

sphere

SPHERE

First published in Great Britain in 2017 by Sphere

1 3 5 7 9 10 8 6 4 2

A CIP catalogue record for this book is available from the British Library.

Hardback ISBN 978-0-7515-6242-2
Trade Paperback ISBN 978-0-7515-6243-9

Typeset in Bembo by Palimpsest Ltd, Falkirk, Stirlingshire
Printed and bound in Great Britain by Clays Ltd, St Ives plc

Papers used by Sphere are from well-managed forests and other responsible sources.

Sphere
An imprint of
Little, Brown Book Group
Carmelite House
50 Victoria Embankment
London
EC4Y 0DZ

An Hachette UK Company
www.hachette.co.uk

www.littlebrown.co.uk

For my father

Acknowledgements

I'd like to thank the two editors, outgoing Jade Chandler and incoming Maddie West, both unimpeachable, who helped get this book as good as it could possibly be with their taste, brains and forbearance. My thanks too to Sphere supremo Cath Burke for her unflagging support, to Kirsteen and Emma for getting the books out there into the market-place and the sales team for putting them into the hands of the readers, which is what it's all about. To the brilliant Thalia Proctor for leaving no loose end flapping anywhere, ever, and to my husband for doing everything else.

Evil is unspectacular and always human,
And shares our bed and eats at our own table

Herman Melville, W.H. Auden

He did it quite quickly, before she opened her mouth to start again.

It had started in the kitchen. He'd thought they could have sex first so he had started that way, looking into her face and touching as she talked. But then she kept on talking, *You didn't think*, her voice hardening, *you never thought this was*— slapping his hand away then her voice rising until the sound of it set up a vibration in his head that had its own momentum, that he knew wouldn't stop until he put an end to it, and it was simply there as the solution. There was really very little in that moment to be said against it.

He had smiled down at her then. He had never seen what other people saw: good-looking, ugly. In the pub he listened to what the others said about women, looking at the images on the big screen high in the corner, a woman under a shower with her head back and water running down her, they talked about the shape of her arse. He had a different range. He saw things they couldn't see.

Then as he walked her backwards through the door and – registering her expression changing, her eyes going flat in the made-up face because she thought she knew why he wanted her in there, thought she could handle him – it occurred to him that the bedroom was a better place to do it, anyway, because the window looked out over the fields, and it was less likely that the neighbours would hear something. Although not impossible: he knew they heard things, it just hadn't been of interest to him until now.

They had got as far as the bed so he let the body fall there, a shine on her legs from the window. As she went down in all the bedclothes there was a wet sound from her throat and for a flashing red second he thought maybe he hadn't done it properly so he waited. But he considered that it must have been just air forced back out of the lungs somehow, perhaps as the body folded on itself, because she was certainly dead.

Her bedside table was dusty, and the bin in the corner was overflowing. Dirty. Lazy. On the bed now her face was half hidden in the duvet and he leaned over her, he knelt astride her breasts, looking down, and carefully he moved the fabric out of the way so he could see. He stepped back off the bed. Her legs were open and between them the dark. They could have gone on, another month or two at least. She'd been stupid, that was all. He began to consider that: how stupid?

Coming around the bed to the window he looked for a second: the meadow was uncut and shaggy as far as the tidal river. It had been hot a month now, a heatwave across

Europe, it said on the news, five thousand dead although most of them old people. The grass was turning to straw.

He drew the curtains, then he turned to go into the kitchen. He was going to need a knife.

Chapter One

'No,' said Nat, turning on her side in the bed, bleary. Pleading. 'No, Jim, for the five thousandth bloody time. I can't talk to you any more.' And losing patience, 'Go away, Jim. Leave me alone.'

She stabbed at the phone with her finger to end the conversation and dropped it with a clatter on to the side table. Feeling all sorts of things, mostly guilty. The longer you stayed, the worse it was when it ended. She'd always known that, probably. Loving someone wasn't everything, she *hadn't* known that. Jim, Jim, Jim. He needed help. She should be helping him, not hanging up on him.

The last time she'd seen him he'd cried: she'd let him put his face on her shoulder, she'd patted, helpless. 'I can't do this,' she'd said. Coward.

It was hot in the room: the boxes sat there still unopened, the big suitcase, crowding the small space. Although the window had been open all night Nat – Natalie only to the older generation, to her mother, who had for four years lived a thousand miles away in a cheap bit of Spain – felt suffocated suddenly, and struggled upright. A green light filtered in past the curtains but no dawn chorus, it was too hot even for the birds. She sank back on the pillow; she buried her face. Six thirty and it was only going to get warmer.

There was a reason Jim called at the crack of bloody dawn, although sometimes it was midnight. He never actually came out with it but the question hovered. *Is there someone else there?* Opening one eye Nat monitored the bed beside her, although she knew already. *Of course there bloody isn't.* She was alone.

On the bedside table the phone rang again. Sitting up furiously, arms folded across her chest, Nat stared at it. One of these days, Jim, please, Jim, don't . . . Only it wasn't him, this time. *Janine*, said her screen.

As usual, Janine was already talking, before Nat even got the phone to her ear. Voice lowered. Steve must have got in late.

Nat waited. You had to do that with Janine: every fifth word might be useful, if you were lucky. You had to let the rest of it go, or your head would explode. Now she was addressing Nat, halfway through a sentence, hissing for her attention.

'Sorry, Janine,' Nat said. 'What?'

'Not coming back, is what she said.' And Janine came to an expectant stop. Nat could picture her, half out of bed, rumpled cleavage, big hair askew.

A shaft of low, white-bright sun had got around the curtain. On the pillow, Nat shifted to get out of the dazzle and saw herself in the low dressing table mirror across the room. A fierce line of eyebrow, short dark hair sticking up. 'It's so hot,' she said, disbelieving. Then, feeling it with a thud. 'Hold on, did you say Beth's—'

'Late night?' said Janine, impatient. 'Have you been listening to a word I said, babe?' In her fag-fuelled husky voice. 'Look, I know the Tinder was my idea, you needed to move on, but—'

'Janine, I don't . . . there's no one . . .' Forget it. She started again. 'What did you say?'

'Beth's texted me. She'd met some bloke up there and she's not coming back.'

Up there, where she was supposed to be looking after her poorly mum.

'Not coming back?' Nat repeated stupidly and it was as if the air had been knocked out of her. She could hear her voice, sounding like a kid. 'But she—'

The Bird in Hand without Beth? Beth winking across at Nat behind Janine's back, a quick squeeze round Nat's shoulders when Janine had just told her to cheer up, it might never happen. 'But there's . . . she's supposed to be . . .' She stopped. Beth hadn't told Janine, had she? She's got a doctor's appointment next week. Hospital.

Just routine. Bound to be nothing. Just a check-up. It had been Nat had said that to Beth, just to get that look off her face.

Nat started again. 'She said she—'

Hold on, what had she said? Sorry babe no signal really up here see you soon.

Janine rattled on oblivious. 'She said she's met the love of her life, not coming back after all.' Impatient. 'Whatever.'

'Love of her life?' Nat put a hand to her hair, feeling how short it was, feeling naked and exposed suddenly though she'd had it cut a month ago. She'd thought she was getting used to it, too.

'Ergo she won't be opening up today, and there's a brewery delivery scheduled for nine.' Janine was working up a rage. 'Dumped me right in it, bloody typical.'

It was sinking in but it didn't feel any better. 'I . . . you want me to come in and open up?' said Nat, trying to think.

Wheedling now. 'I wouldn't ask. Only Steve's turned up, worn out, bless him, needs his kip. You know how he is.'

Did she? Big Steve, hardly opened his mouth to say a word and Janine made it quite clear it wasn't his mind she was after.

'All right,' said Nat, not paying attention now. Thinking instead, her heart pattering, it'll be one of her adventures, just some bloke. Janine must think that too or she'd be pulling her hair out. Because Beth might come in late more often than not with last night's make-up on and spend the first half-hour cramming toast into her mouth but she was the reason half the punters came in.

But Janine was back in there. 'Look, love,' she said, confiding. 'You've seen as many barmaids as I have, you know the type. She's all lovey-dovey and your best friend – and she *was*, I know she thought a lot of you . . .' Nat wanted Janine to just shut up, now, but of course, she didn't. 'But when a certain kind of bloke comes along, well. We might as well not exist, not her mates, not her job, nothing. Here today, gone tomorrow.'

Nat wasn't going to say *She wasn't like that*. She said nothing.

'You can stay in the cottage,' said Janine, hearing the silence, wheedling again. 'All right? As long as you like.'

Nat had been supposed to be finding a new place to live next week, Beth covering for her. Never mind that now. Things went round in her head.

What about the punters who'd been asking when Beth was getting back from her mum's? What about her boots in for reheeling in town?

What about Beth's hospital appointment? Next Monday, half past three. Dodgy smear test, she'd said with a scowl, stuffing the crumpled piece of paper into her pocket when Nat caught her in the kitchen staring at it, asked her what was up. Abnormalities, said Beth, not looking her in the eye, hand still in her pocket.

And then Nat had remembered a doctor's appointment, weeks before, because she'd heard Beth ask Janine for the time off. Poor old Dr Ramsay, she'd thought, with patients like Beth and Nat on her books, women and their insides.

Nat lay there another five minutes, the sheet over her face. When eventually she got up she meant to put the kettle on, but found herself at the window instead. She pushed the curtains out of the way and leaned over the sill, into the air. She could smell it, the dark smell of things stirred to the surface in the heat. The river.

Chapter Two

They'd started missing her even before she jumped ship for good, Beth's fan club. A man had come in to the pub – the Bird in Hand, hidden up a meandering overgrown green lane from the river – a bit more than a week after Beth had first gone, disappeared up north after an afternoon shift with only a midnight text to Janine to say where, and why.

His name was Jonathan Dowd. A tall man Nat didn't remember ever having seen before, who said, a bit shy, he and Beth'd been seeing each other only he hadn't heard . . . she'd . . . she wasn't answering his calls. Good-looking, she supposed, dark eyes, lean but broad-shouldered, he was having difficulty getting the words out. He must have known he wasn't the only one, Nat muttered to herself, having to go back into the kitchen so as not to look into his mournful face. *Ah, shit.* Janine had patted him sympathetically on the shoulder for a good five seconds before asking him if he'd like to order.

Beth. Lovely Beth with her eyeliner and her almost perfect skin; you had to work with her, up close, to see the faintest stippled trace of acne scars, under the make-up. Very good at avoiding every job – crisps, mixers, changing the barrel – that she didn't like, but even better at charming the punters which was why Janine turned a blind eye. Party girl Beth.

Nat had texted Beth the day after she went off to see her mum, got a text back hours later telling her there wasn't much signal, See you soon. Fourth of August, her phone told her. The next message Nat had sent, a couple of days later, just checking in – How you doing, how's your mum, get back here Janine's doing my head in – had been delivered because Nat's phone told her so. But wasn't answered. Too busy, or no signal, or nothing much to say: Nat had shrugged that one off. She and Beth didn't really text, what with working together.

Don't forget your hospital appointment.

Nat felt like her mum, fussing. Big sister: neither of them had ever had a sister. It had been Beth held Nat's hand when she needed it, and now it was Beth's turn Nat was helpless.

Would Beth have made another appointment, up there wherever she'd gone? Hard to imagine her getting on to that straight away, not with the love of her life turned up, if Janine was right. As she pressed send, staring at her phone, Nat had felt her heart pattering in anxiety. More likely that was why Beth had gone. Running away, forgetting she'd ever had that letter. Abnormalities.

Nat had told herself, here today, gone tomorrow, over and over, till she almost believed it.

It was a busy week, though, even for August, and maybe Beth wouldn't have been in her element anyway, her favoured method of serving a punter being to set her elbows on the bar lazily either side of her assets and deliver a slow smile while she worked out if he was worth her trouble or not.

Nat had never had a sister, and never had a friend like Beth. Someone who knew you, without you having to tell them, even if they were so different. At school Nat would have been the one who sat in the front row with her head down, and Beth arriving late and smelling of fags. But they hadn't gone to school together, had they? From different ends of the country, Nat having grown up on the edge of this very village, done her time at the high school in town, then college. Beth, four years younger though you wouldn't know it sometimes, was from somewhere up north and had left school at sixteen.

'What good is fecking school anyway,' she'd said, without bitterness, or so it seemed, cool, agreeable. 'Flipping teachers after you every five minutes. What they gonna teach me?'

And then that smile, that big lazy smile that drew people to her. 'More to learn other places. Right, Nat?' And she'd give Nat a shove with her shoulder, that shoulder always peeling brown after hours staked out in the sun. She knew Nat had played it by the book: college, sleeping on sofas in London for a year trying to get jobs before ending up back here anyway. Both of them behind the bar of the Bird.

Nat had never had a friend like Beth, who'd step in front of her if a punter started something. The bloke who'd tried to climb across the bar when she'd just cut all her hair off back when . . . well, back then. After she'd left Jim. The bloke drooling, 'You a dyke then?' The hair had been down below her shoulder blades before, when she let it down, which mostly she didn't. 'You two? I'd like summa that.'

Beth had reached across her with a firm brown arm and pinched him somewhere at the base of his neck, then with the other hand shoved him so he ended sprawled on the floor. By the time Steve had walked through from the back at the sound, Beth had been leaning back frowning over a torn nail while Nat unloaded the dishwasher.

August was always busy. Was that why she'd chosen to jump ship now?

And what with schlepping in and out of the scruffy beer garden with trays while trying to keep her own smile in place and only Craig, the pub's potboy – a lanky overgrown kid gone silent lately as if his mind was on other things: girls was Janine's diagnosis – to help, Nat told herself she didn't have too much time to think about Beth and why she'd done a runner. Or about her own future, and finding a place to live – which suited her fine. It didn't get any cooler, though. It got hotter.

There was a film crew rumoured – Craig had mumbled something about it as his mum worked at the hotel they'd been staying in, ten miles inland – to be working no more than three fields away, some historical spine-tingler or other, murder in corsets. Wilkie Collins? One of those. They were supposed to be over in the direction of Eastcote where the sea wall snaked around the marsh, and the possibility of someone off the set straying up to the Bird kept Janine applying the slap every morning. Nat hadn't been down that way to look but she had seen the glow of arc lamps above the hedges one night, so she assumed it was that way, where the river widened to meet the sea, grey and silver. She hoped they weren't too pampered, because no hotels in a sixty-mile radius had such a thing as air-con.

The news had spread, though, it was why the caravan site – Sunny Slopes, as old-fashioned as it sounded but people obviously liked that – was so full and plenty of the visitors found their way along the footpath or the long way round up the lane to the Bird, the only pub in walking distance from that bit of the estuary.

Nat found herself missing the water: too full-on in the pub to get out there, away from the land, from the narrow landlocked river. The small sound of waves against wood and the caravans dotted across the slope. She missed her regulars in the Bird too: with the extra bodies they ended up squeezed into corners or staying away all together. Old Victor from the caravan site – her total, one hundred per cent favourite customer – had appeared in the door for his Tuesday night drink and she'd seen him think better of it and back out again apologetically, his bobble hat (whatever the weather it was bobble hat weather for Victor) hanging off the back of his old bald head as he disappeared.

That Friday – the day Beth went off radar, as they thought of it later, the day she disappeared – Janine had clattered down at midday. Made-up, hair fluffed and very pleased with herself, as usual: behind her Nat had seen Steve letting himself out the back door.

Steve had just walked in one spring evening, a customer like any other, a good-looking truck driver scanning the bar to check out the barmaid – Beth had been in the back, invisible, his eyes had met Janine's and that had been that. Love at first sight, Janine purred: chemistry. In the six odd months he'd been around Janine spent the whole time bustling proudly in and out of the bar preening like she was the main attraction. Nat had to admit, Janine looked good on it even if the last thing on Nat's own agenda, Tinder or no Tinder, was sexual satisfaction. The last bloke she'd gone for a drink with (two nights ago? Three?) had been lucky to get out of there without an axe in the back of his head.

So why was she doing it? She didn't know. Never again – but she'd said that before.

'Thanks for coming in, babe,' said Janine, all fluffy angora and boobs as she slung an arm round Nat's shoulders and squeezed.

'S'all right,' said Nat, distracted still by the thought of Beth. 'I could do with the cash.' Which was true. 'And I get the weekend off, right?' Janine had pretended not to hear that one.

Craig had looked relieved when he peered inside half an hour later and saw that he'd got Nat instead of Beth, maybe because he knew he wouldn't be sweating it up and down from the cellar every five minutes. Craig was nineteen and monosyllabic. He had used to gaze at Beth as if she held the secrets of the universe for a while, but working with her – or something – seemed to have rubbed the edges off that.

'I don't understand though,' she said to Janine as they dried up. 'Beth. Texting you, like, six hours before she's supposed to be starting back at work?'

And not a word to me.

'You know our Beth,' said Janine, eyeing a glass critically. Someone came through the swing doors, letting in the warm dusty air.

Nat stopped with her arms full of glasses. 'But what about what's-his-name, then? The guy who came in asking for her?'

'And the rest,' said Janine, scanning the room.

Beth didn't talk to Nat about her love life, just came in humming to herself some mornings, in the same outfit she left in the night before. 'Only causes trouble,' she'd said once. 'Falling out over blokes. Not worth it.'

'The rest?' said Nat warily now to Janine. Not wanting to think Beth would have told her what she didn't tell Nat. Janine only shrugged, inscrutable. 'No law against it,' she said. 'Keeping her options open; not old yet, is she?' Then moved past Nat to serve the customer.

Nat felt a stir of something, discontent. Was she worried, or jealous? She'd have liked to be reckless herself, once in a while; she'd have liked not to worry about consequences. But she'd had a mum to do that for her, and Nat's rebellion had been to stick to the straight and narrow. Lying in a field with Jim when they were both seventeen and talking about getting married and buying a flat. Coming back had just been temporary, just while she applied for more jobs, internships, a bit of money and the river to sail on. Jim had been waiting, of course, like she'd always been going to come back. She loved him. Of course she did, how could she not – he was like family. She would never hurt him if she could help it. Thirteen years together. Sometimes you couldn't help it.

In the corner sat three girls from the caravan site with fluorescent scrunchies in their hair, each one staring down at a mobile screen. Long fingernails painted individually with stars and flowers, crystals and stripes. Nat got a good look at the nails, tapping out an irritable rhythm on the bar when she asked for the lead girl's ID. Close on nineteen (if the ID wasn't fake) and wearing pigtails – they made Nat feel old, what with one thing and another. They were, she overheard, in a tent there for a month in the hope of catching sight of one of the actors on the film set, some good-looking stubbled bloke whipping off his wig in the heat. No one Nat had ever heard of, but there it was. Past twenty-five was old. Bet they knew how to make Tinder work in their favour too: she heard a squeal and laughs of derision as a profile did the rounds.

Beth, Beth. The day of Beth's appointment at the hospital came and went and Nat's anxiety didn't go away, it hardened, sitting there like a lump in her belly. It was mixed up with something else, too. Beth had sat next to her in the pub's back garden with both arms around her, telling her everything would be all right. And that they'd be friends for ever. That hadn't been her imagination.

Janine's view was that it was typical, she'd seen Beth's type before and they let you down, every time. She didn't know about the hospital but maybe she'd still think, typical. Beth had just dropped everything and walked, a different part of the country, a new bloke, clean slate, pure and simple.

Would Beth's mum tell her to make a new appointment? There was no way of knowing, because Beth had never talked about her.

Then, Thursday night and busy, in she walked, planting her forearms heavily on the bar. Mrs Hawkins, Beth's landlady. Ex-landlady.

'Where is she?' she said. A woman of seventy-odd who looked, on balance, more grumpy old bloke than female, square and unkempt. Beth hated her, Nat knew. 'I've left notes. Three weeks overdue with the rent and she's not answering the door.'

'She didn't say anything to you?' said Janine, all innocence.

That was when Nat, reaching for the beer pump, felt the first whisper of something not right. 'She's gone, hasn't she,' Janine informed the woman stiffly, turning back and pushing the drink down the bar to Paddy. He raised his head a moment to look past her at Nat. A sad smile: he knew how Nat felt about Beth. Tall and kind, Paddy was a quiet presence at the bar most nights, but he was shy: he took his pint and retreated from Mrs Hawkins into his corner. 'Up north to her mum's.'

The woman's old prune of a mouth worked away as they watched her. 'Well,' she said finally, having settled on something that satisfied her. 'If she thinks she'll see the deposit again she's got another think coming. The state she's left it in.'

She went on for a bit longer, to anyone in earshot, but Nat wasn't really listening. There was a flutter set up, a buzz in her head, something to do with the nasty old woman running on, complaint after complaint, *filthy*, more to do with Beth.

It was the thought of Beth gazing abstractly into the spotted glass of the mirror in the back as she applied make-up to that little rash of bumpy scars you had to get close to see. The thought of her tugging carefully at her skirt to get it sitting just right, then leaning forward to smile across the bar – and with a dull thud Nat thought, all over again, Come back.

And then the room felt full, hot, the sound of voices was too loud and there were too many faces she didn't know. Where were they, the familiar ones? Paddy, Victor, Mary from the shop with her two glasses of port, and Beth's lager-drinking admirers. Crowded out. Gone.

'You all right?' said Janine, frowning. And the door was swinging shut behind Mrs Hawkins and there was Paddy after all, looking at her, sorrowful, along the bar. 'You should get home early, Craig can come in.' Worried now, guilt poking at her, Nat could see; Janine got bad-tempered when she felt guilty. An explosive sigh. 'Go on then, take tomorrow morning off.'

But Nat stood still, unable to reach for her bag and go, because she felt that thud all over again, the same one she'd felt when Janine first called her to say Beth wasn't coming back. Because it didn't make sense. Just didn't.

When Nat had left Jim she'd come for the key to the cottage and Beth had been standing behind the bar, getting ready to open up. 'Oh, love,' she'd said, watching Nat pile her bags and boxes inside the door. Then she'd shoved up the counter and come through it and hugged her, long and hard.

And now she was gone and with her the sense of something gone for ever: Beth wouldn't have wanted that, not to just – disappear, not for things to move on without her. But she was gone. And the prickle of something else, moving in.

The feeling lasted, long after she turned out the light. She tried saying, over and over, 'She's gone, get over it,' but however many times she told herself, it didn't sound right. Nat lay in the dark with the window open, watching the last glow leave the summer evening; listening for the river. If you waited it always came, the trickle and rush of the weir.

Chapter Three

Friday

There was a little twinge, the old ache, as Victor climbed out of the narrow bed and headed for the stove. You couldn't keep every little complaint on the radar but he was so used to this one he might even miss it if it disappeared. Lower right quadrant, somewhere deep inside, not muscular. Somehow he knew it would not disappear. He need not fear.

It wasn't the bed: he rather liked the bed, and it wasn't uncomfortable. It made him think of the navy, and the war, and the narrow bunks on the *Belfast*; he could even persuade himself the walls of the tin box that now was home were like a ship's steel bulkheads. Not, of course, that wartime had been congenial, nor the RNVR either for an eighteen-year-old volunteer, but the older you got the warmer memories felt, and Victor didn't have any terrible ones. He hadn't forgotten for one minute what it was to be young, and the twinge didn't have any effect on that.

He lit the gas, set the kettle on to boil, and opened his little door.

Victor had never been a big man, and he'd got smaller. A caravan – he never called it a mobile home, it didn't have the right ring, to him, 'caravan' at least spoke of nomads and the wide desert – suited his proportions pretty well, all things considered. Sophie, of course, had paled at the idea when it had become the only option available. She couldn't offer to have him, he'd always known that. Richard wouldn't allow it. Richard was never asked, but he wouldn't have it.

Where the twinge barely touched Victor, the thought of Richard weakened him, it turned his knees old and feeble. Steadying himself he reached for the bobble hat Sophie had knitted him and adjusted it carefully to sit above his ears, then put a hand to the frame of the miniature door and took a deep breath of morning air. Heat, stubble, a holiday family cooking bacon on the far side of the site and the river underneath it all. Cautiously, Victor lowered himself to sit on the step, mug in hand.

Sunny Slopes was full, it being August. More had rolled up last night, cheerful parent-voices at two in the morning. Victor didn't mind that: there was very little left that he allowed himself to mind and he decided that sleeplessness, at his age, was a chance to prolong life, or expand it. Time otherwise spent dead to the world. He missed his drink in the pub, his favourite corner too full this week with teenage drinkers, but the sleepy chatter of small children, car doors closing, the sounds of tired tearfulness and consolation, the memory of Sophie – *the Sophy, my little sophist, my sophisticate* – as a tiny creature, were all soothing. A round pale face looking up at him in wonder, or trust.

He didn't know how he could have let it happen. Let *him* happen: Richard. And now the baby cemented it, where once it might have been loosened. And Sophie nearly fifty and crying with happiness.

Had it been his responsibility to step in, to say: Sophie, may I inspect this man before you ally yourself to him? His duty to say: Sophie, this is not the man for you? Tender-hearted Sophie, rescuer of spiders, Sophie of the stout little legs who cried over a rabbit dead in a field? He turned that idea over and over, not being one for regret but sometimes regret was appropriate. In this case, Sophie could have done with his intervention. Would she have listened? He would never know, now. He, her father, came on the scene too late, when Sophie's head only turned to follow Richard around the room, to gaze at Richard as he held forth.

Her mother, her mother now. She wouldn't have let this happen, but Sophie's mother was long gone. Joy, dead of cancer at fifty-one, in five minutes flat. One day she was frowning over her cookery books and the next she couldn't form words. The girl he married.

Victor got to his feet, creaking, the tea half cold. Better to do something than sit and turn it over and over. He tipped the tea away, washed the mug, frowned at the brown ring inside it he never seemed to be able to get rid of as Sophie could, with her dishwasher and her array of products. She had been once to the site, pregnant, dismayed, newly powerless. After that he had travelled on the train to meet her, halfway between here and there.

But Victor loved it here. It might, to others – to Richard – be a seedy caravan park but to Victor, with dreams of boyhood sailing adventures, it had a particular magic, the place where the sea turned into a river. Turn one way and it opened out grey to the horizon, turn the other and it narrowed, secret, blurred with nodding bulrushes, with hedges crowding the water. The sound of the weir hidden from sight.

A walk. Down to the river, on the way to the red telephone box that still, against all the odds, stood and functioned in the lane. Richard would be at work, it was after nine, Sophie at home with the baby. Round-eyed, downy-headed Rufus who looked nothing like his father, who was all his Sophie, utterly his grandchild. Nearly three.

Victor sat on the bench, in the sun that stood high now in the sky, so slowly had he made his way up from the site with the scent of the tide behind him.

The bench had been cemented into the verge where the footpath came up from the river and joined the lane, out of sight of the water, inland. Victor could see the red flash of the phone box from where he sat, or could before he closed his eyes better to enjoy the warmth on his face. He didn't object to this heat, not at all, it was being old. Among the many things he hadn't known about being old was that it made you grateful for every heat source, like an old lizard he liked to bask against hot stone, drawing up the warmth, breathing slowly, conserving energy. The hat comfortable around his ears. He could tell from the raised voices on the site that it didn't agree with everyone, by no means, tempers frayed at night. The children liked it, running around till midnight and no reason to go to bed. Rufus: she could bring little Rufus here.

There was a sound, down below him, down the path, the whisper of grasses parting. Take away one sense, the others sharpen. That was a thing about age, too: capacities were removed but shyly, apologetically, others tiptoed up, offering themselves. He might forget what whiskery Mary at the post office had said to him yesterday morning but he could remember Joy's face as she leaned back against the pillow in some foreign hotel room. The light from the window, reflections of water on the wall.

Eyes closed, Victor could hear the crunch of footsteps on the hard dry ground: slow, methodical steps. There was something, something that he hadn't remembered. Was that a gift, a mercy – or the opposite? To know that something had struck you as worth remembering yesterday, the day before, two weeks ago, but for the life of you, you couldn't lay your hands on it when you tried.

A man's footsteps.

Richard. Richard. Victor had seen cruelty before, it wasn't new to him. The pale-eyed lieutenant on that beach in Anzio, kicking a frightened man. Getting out his pistol. Seventy years ago but he hadn't forgotten that. Men in pubs, in offices, the occasional careless, shocking female. It was there if you looked, which he did not. He should have looked, and then he might have saved Soph.

Eyelids trembling, Victor performed his favourite trick for soothing himself: sit quiet and think of all those you are fond of, have loved, felt affection for, been grateful to. Love must become an elastic thing, find it more readily, feel it more often, as it is more necessary the older you get, not less: you can love whiskery Mary because she remembers without fail to put your newspaper aside, and will post a parcel for you if you arrive before the counter opens. Soph sat comfortably top of the list and Rufus still a part of her, nestling in the crook of her arm, beaming.

Then something altered in the air around him, and Victor found himself staying very still on his bench.

Go away, Richard.

He kept his eyes closed. Old man snoozing in the sun:

old man playing dead. And then the warmth diminished, as though he was sitting in someone's shade, there was a dimming through his papery closed eyelids. The memory swam, mysterious, a pike through the weeds: he let it. As with the pike, an encounter might not be desirable. He was holding his breath. He was afraid.

The air hummed with it: danger, he knew it of old, like cruelty, there was no mistaking it. Victor sat for as long as he could, to let it pass, but he felt a strangeness creep up through his body and it seemed suddenly urgent that he open his eyes. He didn't want to sit there, in his own dark, and wait for it. So he opened his eyes, and there was no one there. He looked up at the sky, for some fugitive cloud, but it was clear.

Sitting up on the bench, Victor cleared his throat carefully. He stood and turned carefully to keep confusion at bay but there it was, down at the bottom of the lane, the dark shape of a man. He shifted so his back was to the lane, turned towards the telephone box as if he'd seen nothing.

That was it. That was what he had forgotten, the thing he had seen, the feeling it had given him: a man walking up that lane towards him. How long ago? He waited, for the small pleasure of remembering to spark but something wasn't responding.

The phone box seemed a long way away now, and he did feel distinctly odd, but he would get there. He needed to talk to Soph. There were things he needed to tell her.

The wind picked up only when she got past the big old mastless yacht that had been wedged in the mud for twenty years, a good gust that filled the small square sail and Nat settled back in the stern as she felt the small boat tilt and gather under her. It had been early when she'd called Paddy and he had mumbled into the phone so softly she couldn't hear him, then he shifted the phone to his good ear. Funny old Paddy: she'd noticed that habit. When he couldn't hear, his voice dropped too, as if fearful of giving the wrong answer.

'Can I borrow her for an hour or so?' she said, again. 'Catch the tide.' High tide at midday, and she had to be at the Bird for one. Out here, though, it all fell away. All the worry.

She came past the yacht, the *Sweet Breeze*, settled long since into the silver-grey mud on a tilt, and the sweep of the site came into view.

How old was Paddy? She squinted up at the cloudless sky, feeling the burn on her cheeks already. Could be fifty. Older? More likely younger, given he'd worked outside his whole life. The back of his neck was burned dark, his eyes crinkled but nicely, the creases came out with his rare smiles. A thatch of hair, unruly. Only a sprinkling of grey.

'Sure, sure,' he had murmured, 'why not?' as he always did. Nat had felt a little prick of guilt then, feeling like she was taking advantage. Was Paddy too much of a gentleman to expect anything in return for the loan of his battered little boat? And as if he knew her thoughts: 'She needs taking out,' he said vaguely. 'Day like this.'

He worked for Jim: that was what made Nat uneasy, taking advantage. Though Jim needed Paddy, a master craftsman who could replace a stanchion or patch a bit of decking in his sleep, more than Jim needed him. Jim had inherited the yard from his own father when Nat had been at college and had been out of his depth trying to make it work from the beginning, wanting nothing more than to be an apprentice himself, not responsible for paying business rates and drumming up business. He hadn't been in the shed yet when Nat had come down to the front this morning for the boat. She didn't know when he did get in, these days. No longer any of her business.

Talking of gentlemen. Nat put in a tack and let the sail out to run down closer to the campsite: the tide was only half up so there was a hundred metres of mud keeping her at a distance. The grassy slope was pale from two dry months, the neat rows of mobile homes were on the eastward side, at the other end a patchwork of tents where it flattened upriver. The black clapboard hut. She could make out figures clustered round the door to a big trailer two up from Victor's, women with arms folded, gassing.

Had it all started when Jim had insisted on buying the flat? Waterside new-build, balcony, mod cons, too much money. A mortgage he could only just afford with Nat paying rent too – she'd told him they'd be better off renting together but he wouldn't listen. Then he'd got into trouble borrowing more when a job went bad and the customer refused to pay, stuffing bills in the bin so she couldn't see them. And when she found out, he'd gone out and got so pissed he slept in the shed.

Nat had given him her savings, to bail him out. But it had changed things: there'd been a grimness to it after that. He needed her. She had to stay. And then – it happened. She got pregnant. And then she knew she couldn't stay.

The boat Nat borrowed was called the *Chickadee*, and she was probably older than Paddy. Nat offered Beth a sail once but Beth had made a face. 'I get seasick on the dodgems,' she'd said. 'Dunno how I ended up in a place like this.' Smiling, fond, like what she was really saying was that she was happy, in a place like this.

Nat was getting too close to the land. She still hadn't spotted Victor but she put in another tack and headed off downriver, the site behind her.

The wind slackened and the boat turned heavy, the water gurgled lazily against the bow. The open sea and the chance of more of a breeze was five miles downriver; where the *Chickadee* drifted it was so still there was a heat haze across the far bank, dusting the familiar outlines of trees, a row of cottages, a big house with its veranda. The golden sweep of a cornfield. Behind her the estuary narrowed below the little tumble of the village's roofs, hidden by trees it as it wound its way inland.

Would she have missed this, would it have been in her dreams? Should she have left, long ago, before Beth turned up at the Bird in Hand? Told Jim back then, I want to see the world?

In the meantime, getting out on the water was compensation. Maybe one day she'd have saved enough for her own boat, though not any day soon on what Janine was paying. And she had rent to find now. A deposit, eventually.

She wasn't going to think about Jim, or the flat, the bedroom with the massive bay window, the tiny kitchen so small she could feel the warmth of his body if he came in while she was cooking, or vice versa. Nat shoved the tiller harder than she'd meant to and had to correct it. That was the trouble with getting out of the pub, out here under the big sky, it got more difficult to keep certain thoughts out. The boat swung and the campsite came back into view. She took a breath and scanned it for Victor. Her all-time favourite human being, full stop.

Victor, quiet in the corner of the pub, lifting his schooner of sherry with care. Victor, a steady presence, the old sloping shoulders under a ridiculous charity shop coat he wore with dignity. Beth had loved Victor. Everyone loved Victor. Victor, they all agreed, would live for ever.

What was that? She squinted, nudging the tiller with her knee so she could use the hand to shade her eyes. Something flashed in the trees at the top of the site, coming down the lane that wound off up and eventually reached the Bird, a mile on. Something catching the light. Her eyes travelled back down, to Victor's caravan, door closed, she could even see the little table where he sat for his breakfast on a fine day, folded and leaning against it, the chair flat beside it.

Victor had come into the pub the day after, when Nat was still sore in her belly, her legs still shaking with the shock of it but she'd said to Janine she'd work because there was no way, no way on this earth she was ever going to tell anyone what she'd done. Bad enough that Jim had to know, that the nurses had to know, that doctor whose face now she had turned to a blur. Victor had looked up from his table and in some trick of the dim light of the saloon bar she had felt his eyes rest on her, and she'd wanted to cry. I didn't mean to. Like a kid. Close on thirty and not grown-up after all.

Beth had been in that day. Back in May, a beautiful day, maybe the beginnings of the weather that had stretched into August, but in May the air had been crystal clear and perfect. Nat blinked, trying to remember, and the campsite lost focus.

Beth, coming out of the pub kitchen, humming to herself.

Nat's face so pale it was almost transparent in the mirror over the toilet in the back, but at first she thought Beth, coming in behind her, hadn't noticed a thing. Her mind elsewhere. In fairness, Beth's mind usually was. If she closed her eyes she could still remember what Beth had been wearing. Striped top she tugged down to show off her shoulders, high-waisted jeans that showed off her backside. She had breezed in then stopped, her face in the mirror beside Nat's.

Nat's face, green and ill.

'You sick?' said Beth sharply, and her hand was on Nat's shoulder, pulling her round so she could see, not trusting what there was in the mirror, for once. Beth who loved her own reflection so much she turned in front of it, blowing kisses. 'Hey?' Scrutinising her. And that warning note in her voice, as if Nat was a twelve-year-old come off her bike and Beth, *Beth* of all people, her mum. Angry and fearful and something else, something that came unwillingly with the hand she put up to Nat's cheek, sorrowful. 'What've you done?'

Nat rubbed at her eyes in the fresh wind, trying to see Victor's back door, half a mile away across the grey water.

He would have gone out for a walk. She swallowed. Victor didn't like to just sit there: he'd said that to Nat probably the first time she served him. It was what had started her sailing again, a year ago, if she was honest. 'When in doubt,' he had said, slightly out of breath as he reached the bar and she'd asked him if he was all right, 'just get outside a bit.' He had looked just a bit down in the mouth then, as if he wasn't so sure any more, but the large sherry had perked him up.

Not a big man but upright, and neat in his movements so that you couldn't see until he got close how old he was. Very old. Janine said she thought he was ninety. Frowning, because that was the effect pity had on Janine, it made her uncomfortable. 'Ninety and living in a caravan. I mean.' Although Victor never mentioned where he lived to begin with. He had asked her about herself, and against all the odds Nat had found herself answering.

Nothing big, nothing – she didn't want to tell. Not that there was much, anyway, not then, just the underwhelming truth. Where she was from, family. Although she had the definite feeling he worked things out, from the way he nodded, or frowned, or winced. Victor came in regular as clockwork twice a week and they always had a conversation but she only ever learned snippets about him. A widower, he'd worked in books somewhere, one daughter. A listener rather than a talker; the most unlikely people found themselves talking to Victor, she'd seen them. Tucked in his corner while he nodded, sipping his sherry.

It only came to her then, why it seemed important to see Victor. She wanted to ask him about Beth.

She didn't know what it had been that had made her turn wordless in front of the mirror and butt her head, just for a second, into Beth's neck. And Beth's arms coming around her, firm and warm and steady. ''S'all right, darling.' Not letting go.

Holding on until she knew Nat was safe. Without her it would have been like falling into a deep dark hole, Nat not knowing where, who, *what* she was. What kind of person has an abortion? What kind of cold bitch leaves the boy she's known since he was a kid, leaves him alone to cry? 'It's all right,' Beth said, into her hair, as if she knew what Nat was thinking. 'Sometimes you got to do something horrible, sometimes you got no alternative.'

Five months ago. It seemed like a lifetime.

Had it been a week later, or more? Nat had sat down beside Victor at his usual spot and together they had contemplated Beth up there behind the bar, big gold hoops swinging and an inch of belly exposed as she reached for an optic, Janine eyeing her from the other end of the bar. They had been talking about home: coming home. She had told him about London.

'When you're young,' Victor said thoughtfully, 'yes, of course. You need to see a bit of the world.' Pulling his hat straight, the way he did when he was thinking, and watching Beth exchange glances with Janine. 'I think it's rather nice to find a place to stop, though, too. A home, if you like, wherever that is.' And Beth had smiled across at them.

Nat came about again, and headed for the jetty that ran off the far end of the campsite because with a bit of luck there would be enough tide by now for her to get there. She was so focused on the tide, though, and the rickety little jetty and how high the water was that it wasn't until she was pulling down the sail to drift the last few metres that she saw it. Standing there trying to see round the canvas as she took it up in her arms, although all her life Nat had felt safer in a boat than out of one, suddenly the boards under her feet felt unsteady and she had to grab the mast.

An ambulance was parked at the top of the site, its blue light revolving, and a small crowd gathering.

Chapter Four

Nat ran, jerky, up the spiky stubbled grass between guy ropes and trailers, and holidaymakers turned to see her go. They stepped back to let her past. A toddler let his ice cream cone drop, top heavy into the dust.

Why should it be him? It could be any of them, a kid fallen from a tree, a dad hit his thumb with a hammer, asthma attack. She felt sweat drip from her forehead. She knew it was Victor.

Something to do with wanting to ask him if Beth had said anything to him about leaving – but mostly because Victor was ninety, after all. Over ninety. Not that he gave any sign of being afraid of anything – always merry, always interested, asking her about her mum in Spain and how she managed for marmalade – but that didn't mean it wasn't there. So there were nights when Nat saw the pub doors close behind Victor as he set off on that dark walk back to the site, the vulnerable look to the back of his old neck below the bobble hat, like a tortoise's, and the thought popped into her head that, at ninety, it's right there. Death is right there, not a surprise, long overdue. It's going nowhere.

And it *was* him. Stretchered out, two ambulancemen in fluorescent jackets were loading him into the back of the ambulance. She could see his proud beaked nose, dark nostrils, hands folded on his chest.

'Can I, can I—' Nat was out of breath. She kept going almost till she could reach out and take one of his hands but the near ambulanceman already had a warning hand on her arm.

'You related?' he said.

'Victor?' Ignoring him, she leaned closer. 'Victor? What happened?' His mouth moved, lopsided, but no sound came out. Alive. Alive.

'He can't talk.' Another voice, from behind her.

A paramedic was inside the ambulance, stooped over some machine or other, as they continued to slide him in. Nat turned to see who'd spoken. It was a stocky man in shirtsleeves, dusty colourless hair sticking up. 'What happened?' she said, and as he opened his mouth she did know who he was, he had been into the pub once or twice. Owen something: Victor had told her. Had stuck up for him, even, a graceless man, no eye contact as he ordered his drink. Owen Wilkins, manager of the campsite, sandy-haired and short-tempered.

'He collapsed,' said Wilkins. 'They found him beside the telephone box.' Impatient.

A bookish man, Victor had said, an exile from the modern world, that's Mr Wilkins. I sympathise, he'd said, though Victor was in fact very interested in the modern world.

His one wish to have the funds for a mobile phone, one day, when the pension allowed. He took the bus to the library to use their computers once a week.

All this raced through her head. Victor Victor Victor. Don't go. *I need to ask you.* Because Victor would know. He had the vigilance, which went along with having someone – something – at his shoulder waiting. He noticed, all sorts.

Victor was inside the ambulance.

'I'll come with him,' said Nat but Wilkins shook his head, his pale mouth set in a line.

'It's my responsibility,' he said, and he was already climbing in.

The driver had closed one door and the revolving light gave a whoop. 'It's sorted, love,' the paramedic said. 'Quicker we get there . . .' He didn't finish the sentence before the other door closed on them.

'Where are you taking him?' Nat called after the ambulance, but they were bumping off, across the dusty grass.

Nat turned, feeling as though she had cement in her chest.

A girl said, 'Raynwick casualty, it'll be. My nan got took there last year when she had a turn.' The three of them were there, the film-set groupies, all tanned dark, their hair blonded at the hairline, all in short shorts. One smaller than the others, like a little doll, one had boobs and was proud of them, and the one who'd spoken was the tallest and skinniest.

'Who found him?'

'Kirsty did,' said the little one, elbowing the tall girl – Kirsty – who shifted from one foot to another, uncomfortable, carefully taking gum out of her mouth as if Nat was a teacher. Rolling it into a ball between thumb and finger with her fancy nails catching the light. 'We were right behind her, though,' said the small one.

'Did he say anything?' Nat asked, the cement in her chest seeming to rise up her throat. 'Victor. What happened?'

A fidgeting like Chinese whispers. 'We was talking about the dead body,' said Kirsty. 'In the weir, drowned.' Darkly. 'He'd bin in the water *days*, someone said.'

He. Nat felt her heart disappear, then it was speeding up.

'Who?' she said.

'Some kid,' said Kirsty, sticking the gum back in. 'Police car come up the site, late last night, asking if we know him. We was talking about it up the lane and he – Victor did – he made like to turn round, just ahead of us on his way to the telephone, but he looked all funny. He . . . he started to ask us about it then he just went over. He like just fell right over.' She looked sulky and scared at once. 'I run for Mr Wilkins.'

'What kid?' said Nat, running out of breath. 'The body. Do they know his name?'

But they just shrugged, turning away, parting to release her, she didn't know if they'd lost interest or they'd had enough of answering questions. She watched them go.

There'd been a drowning a year or so ago, further upstream, a teenager pissed on alcopops from some booze factory in the town. It didn't have to be someone she knew, but Nat's heart was pounding all the same.

She was inside Victor's caravan thinking she could bring something with her to the hospital, his pyjamas at least, a toothbrush, when the girl with the cleavage stuck her head round the door, eyes bright and round. Nat had only taken a step inside, got as far as scanning the photographs on a shelf in frames that looked like silver, her eye travelling over the neatly made bed to stop and wonder why a drawer was already open and its contents turned over, when she heard the sound behind her, and her heart was off again.

'Did you see anyone come in here?' she said. The door had been unlocked. The silver frames were still there, though: if someone had thought to take advantage.

The girl shrugged. 'No one would nick off old Victor,' she said, after a moment's thought.

'What did you come for?' asked Nat, trying not to make it sound like an accusation.

'They're saying it was Oliver,' said the girl and for a moment the name meant nothing, Nat just stared. 'He's one of your regulars, isn't he?' the girl said. 'I seen him up there, up the pub. Oliver, his mate works there, tall bloke never says nothing, whassisname. Craig, is it?' And then, impatiently. 'The body, they're saying it's him. S'Ollie.'

Raynwick had been a Victorian hospital, now expanded with an ugly modern extension that almost completely hid the original. By the time Nat got there it was almost three.

'Never,' Janine had said, '*never*.' Then, 'I mean, someone did mention a body, I don't know, I thought it'd be some down-and-out.' Shaking her head. 'Come to think of it he's not been in, has he?' Glancing at Steve. 'Since Beth did her runner.'

Nat just stood, frozen, not wanting to think about it, at all, any of it. The girls whispering about it in the lane, excited and horrified – but did they care? Just a kid. Ollie:

she tried and tried but something had stuck in her brain, all she could picture was his mop of hair, head bent over his glass, Beth nudging and pointing, he's the shy one. That stuck in her throat. Maybe the girls did care. But then Victor hearing them talk and staggering, keeling over.

Then Janine had been concerned, in a distracted way. 'Ah, bless, old Victor. Well . . .' She tailed off before she could say something about a good innings, which was just as well as Nat might have lamped her. Janine had a good heart but she just didn't bloody think, sometimes. She'd rolled her eyes when Nat had asked if she could get off early – *again?* unspoken – and distinctly put out when Steve had said he'd give her a lift to the hospital, but Nat wasn't going to think about that.

She could see Victor from the corridor through some curtains, still motionless on his back under a sheet. They'd said to wait a bit, the consultant was in there. Did all hospitals smell the same? It made her uneasy, to remember sitting on the bed, behind the curtain, taking the pill the nurse had given her. 'That's done with,' she told herself. 'This is urgent. Come on, come on.'

Owen Wilkins was still there: she saw him on his phone at a window, looking down into the car park. Geography teacher trousers, and as he turned at the sound of her, the same look most of Nat's teachers had had, exasperation at everyone else's stupidity. He was here, she supposed, which was something. Victor had stuck up for him, but then Victor was kind.

Wilkins hung up, frowning at her.

'What's the news?' she said. 'What do they say? Is he going to be all right?'

Wilkins cleared his throat. 'They're still assuming it was a stroke,' he said, Welsh somewhere faint in his accent. Eyeing her, hostile. 'What's your connection with him?' Rude. A pause. 'If I might ask.' Still rude.

'I'm his friend,' Nat said. 'I expect you'll need to get back sooner or later, won't you? To your caravan site.' She was angry now. And blurting, finally, 'I don't like to think of him being alone.'

Wilkins pursed his lips, but before she could get angrier the curtains around Victor's cubicle opened and a consultant emerged, gave them a look and turned to walk off. Nat had to hurry after him, practically tugging at his sleeve, but when he did stop he was patient. 'Is it a stroke?' she said.

'It could be just a TIA, transient ischaemic attack, meaning it will pass without effect, or it might be more serious,' said the doctor, shoving his glasses up his nose to look at her.

'I'm a friend,' she said quickly. 'He's . . . he's got a daughter, I know that. Sophie. His daughter. They're very close.' How did she know that? She knew how Victor's voice changed, down a register, tender, when he talked about Sophie – which was rarely. 'Should I contact her?'

'Mr Wilkins has offered to do that,' said the consultant. A laminated tag round his neck had a photograph, and his name. Mr Paget. He was maybe fifty and wore a crumpled shirt and tie. 'Have I got that right, is he called Wilkins?'

Nat turned but the site manager wasn't where she'd left him. 'Yes,' she said, 'Owen Wilkins.'

'He . . . is he the manager of the . . . wherever Mr Powell lives?' Obviously Mr Paget had not quite got his head around a man like Victor living in a place like the Sunny Slopes, in a mobile home.

'It's a caravan site,' she said, feeling the need to be blunt. 'Victor's pretty happy there, as a matter of fact.' She didn't know if she was sticking up for the place or for proud Victor. He *had* seemed happy.

'Well, yes,' said the consultant dubiously, 'I don't know if we can take your word for that. Anyway, we have his daughter's number too, now.' It sounded ominous.

He made as if to turn away, frowning, but she said quickly, 'Can I . . . talk to Victor? Or just be with him for a bit?'

Paget regarded her. 'We'll be taking him for more tests very soon,' he said. 'But in the meantime . . .' He shrugged. 'He'll be glad of the company, I'm sure. No dramas, though.' He leaned down to look into her face. 'All right?'

Pulling gingerly at the cubicle curtain Nat half expected to see Wilkins in there, but there was only Victor, his old hands folded together on top of a clean blanket. For a second all she could think was that it took this to get him properly looked after. *He shouldn't be on his own, he shouldn't* – but then he made a sound. His breathing seemed quick to her and she remembered, no dramas.

'It's all right, Victor,' she said. 'It's just me. Nat.' She swallowed. 'Natalie.'

She couldn't ask him anything. She didn't want to be the one who disturbed whatever equilibrium he'd arrived at. His head turned, minutely, one hand strayed towards her, no more than a centimetre, and without thinking she took it. It was warm, but she could feel the bones under the papery skin. She held it between her hands.

He was trying to speak, his mouth still lopsided and his tongue working in one corner. His hand fluttered between hers. 'No, no,' she said. 'Don't, Victor.' Trying to keep her voice calm. 'We're here. I'm here. And your . . . Sophie's coming.' She pulled the chair closer, to see his face. There was an awful slackness to it that made her heart race, so unlike Victor was it, but then she saw his eyes, soft, brown, searching. Alive. He was trying to communicate something to her urgently, something was in there.

She came even closer, leaning across him a little he could see square into her face, so there could be no mistaking what she was saying. 'It can wait, Victor.' Enunciating carefully, watching for him to understand. 'Whatever it is, it can wait.' For a second everything in him seemed to strain, without actually moving, then relax, his head tilting back. 'Victor?' she said, alarmed. 'Victor?' But he was breathing, he was breathing still, no alarm sounded.

Then behind her the curtain rattled back and a nurse was coming round her and talking as she came, leaving no pause for an answer, 'All right then, Mr Powell, are we ready, is this your daughter, well, that was quick.' And Nat stepped back.

A porter came around the curtain to the head of the bed. Nat shook her head when the nurse addressed her directly, asking if she was Sophie, and then the woman, leaning down to shift some lever under the bed, said briskly, 'Well, we'll take it from here then, love. Visiting's five till seven.' Dismissing her.

Nat watched the nurse's broad behind retreating down the corridor alongside the wheeled bed, her hand on Victor's blanket, tucking, patting, rearranging, her head moving up and down, mechanically reassuring.

He's in good hands, Nat told herself, he's in the right place. But her heart fluttered on, like a bird in her chest. *What was it? What did you want to say?*

The pub was buzzing when Nat climbed out of the taxi, and cars lined both sides of the lane. Squeezing through the punters she didn't have to wonder what had brought them all out for a drink: she lifted the flap and got the right side of the bar, breathing a sigh of relief, for once. The buzz was all about Ollie.

'You all right, love?' said Steve sliding someone's pint across the bar. 'How was he then? Poor old sod.'

She shrugged, not really able to say anything that mattered. 'They don't know yet,' was all she came up with and Steve just nodded, kind. 'I'll get off then,' he said. 'Madam's on her way down, she retired to repair her face. Kid's out the back, it's heaving out there.'

Craig. She grimaced at the thought: Craig had known him. Ollie.

'All right,' was all she said, though, and Steve reached for his jacket. For a second or two she wondered where he was going but she didn't even need to ask the question. Anywhere but here, on a night like this, after a day like this, somewhere cool and quiet, where you could hear yourself think.

Just a boy. Ollie. Off to see bands with Craig on a Friday night, crawl home stinking of booze in the early hours, still too young for hangovers. It wouldn't be the same, would it? Not for Craig, for whatever other mates he had. Not for Ollie's parents. Not ever again.

Janine clattered down the stairs to catch Steve, planting

a lipsticked kiss as he headed out the back before turning, pleased, to Nat. She sobered quickly at Nat's expression. 'I know, I know,' she said. 'But it's an ill wind, or whatever. Look at the place.'

Keeping her voice lowered, though, and just as well because although Janine couldn't see him Craig was coming through the side door from the garden with a tray loaded with greasy glasses. He looked shaky: catching Nat's eye on him he ducked his head.

'I'm worried about Beth,' Nat muttered, and she saw Janine's face set, sulky, as if Nat was out to spoil her night.

'Beth takes care of herself,' she said, reaching for the tray from Craig, dumping the glasses noisily in the sink below the bar and handing it back to him. He retreated the way he'd come but not before Nat had seen his face, pale and sweaty and frightened.

'Seriously,' said Janine, reaching up to pump a double vodka for someone. 'Do you need me to say it again? It's par for the bloody course, isn't it? Beth was never exactly Mrs Commitment. Lads all over the place, she'd follow her fanny to the Outer Hebrides.' Hand out for the punter's cash, she didn't bother to keep her voice down now. She slapped the money into the till and folded her arms across her front. 'I admit going to see her mum was out of character – but stopping up there for a bloke and dumping us all in the shit weren't.' She leaned in. 'You know what? What surprised me is why she bothered to let us know at all.'

But the more time passed Nat thought maybe Janine was more put out than she let on. That evening when Victor had said that about settling down, watching Beth and Janine behind the bar for a moment there they'd felt like a funny old sort of family: Mum, Dad, big sister, little sister. Victor could even be Granddad in the corner. None of them having the conventional sort of home to go to.

Wish fulfilment, pure and simple, even if it looked like Janine had fallen for it too. And now where are we? Little sister's disappeared and Granddad's in the hospital.

There was a little stir somewhere in the corner of the room, over by the juke. Still frowning over what Janine had said – because it *was* surprising, given she hadn't told her landlady, and what about her stuff – Nat shifted, half unconsciously, to see what it was about. She spotted Kirsty over there, with her mates, a head taller even sitting down, and they were all straining to see someone who'd just come in, the door still closing. Then they hunkered down over their mobiles, busy. Nat tried to see who it was but the room was full of strangers.

Craig was back with another loaded tray. Janine was already at the other end of the bar, chin up and taking an order for five pints and a blackcurrant shandy, so Nat took it off him this time, cornering him by the sink. 'You all right?' she said in an undertone. 'He was your mate, wasn't he? Ollie.' Craig shifted.

'Yeah,' he said, then cleared his throat. 'Not so much lately.'

Nat supposed that was true. Always a bit of distance between them in the pub, what with Craig being at work, and collecting pots not being a job you could show off with. Craig was the quiet type too, and if anything quieter when Ollie was around. Ollie would just sit in a corner waiting for Beth to notice him, drinking Red Bull.

'Do you know anything?' she said. 'About what happened.'

Ollie *had* been in since Beth went off, Nat remembered now. It seemed important suddenly to get the times straight. Beth had gone on the third of August, and it had been the following week so it would have been around the eleventh – no, the twelfth, because it had been a Friday. Two weeks ago. He'd sat in his corner, frowning down at his mobile, and Nat remembered feeling sorry for him. She'd had to tell him, she's gone to see her mum and he'd looked crestfallen then tried to cover it up by ordering another drink, like he'd never come in for Beth. He'd been tipsy when he left, a little guy, two halves his limit.

Craig rubbed his eyes furiously and she put her arm round his shoulders: she had the distinct feeling he wanted to pull away from her but she held on. 'Sorry,' she said. He ducked his head.

'I don't know,' he said in a grim monotone. 'It felt like we weren't mates any more, that's all.'

She could see him, little Ollie at the table two weeks ago, frowning down at his mobile the whole evening. 'Was it a girl?'

Craig shrugged again, stiff and resistant under her arm, and reluctantly she let him go. She turned and Craig grabbed the tray and was gone. Janine was at the other end of the bar on her knees ferreting about for crisps while her customer wound her up over what flavours he was after.

'Any chance of some service?' She whipped round, ready to snap, but the voice had been quiet and the face – she liked the face. A big bloke, brown eyes, smiling. Older than her, but not old. 'Half of Guinness?' Mildly. 'When you've got a minute.'

Out of the corner of her eye Nat saw Kirsty nudging, signalling. She sighed. 'Sorry,' she said, reaching for the pump, sticking the glass under it. 'It's bloody mad in here tonight.' She frowned. 'Does she know you?'

An elbow on the bar, relaxed, he turned an inch to examine the girls in the corner, and winced. 'Well, in a manner of speaking,' he said. 'It's not me they're after. They're wondering if I've got anyone better-looking waiting for me outside.'

Nat slid his drink across, not understanding. He elaborated. 'I'm a cameraman,' he said, sighing. 'I'm working on a production a couple of miles away. I've seen them there, they just want a look at our leading man. Just my luck to pick their local.'

'Autographs?' said Nat, raising an eyebrow.

'And the rest,' said the cameraman, wearily. He held out a hand over the bar. 'I'm Bill, Bill Sullivan.' The gesture was so old-fashioned she almost laughed, but instead she shook his hand quickly. Over in the corner the girls' heads bobbed, but she couldn't see if they were cracking up.

'How did you find this place?' Nat said, hands safely back behind the bar. 'It's not exactly on the map.'

'That's what I like,' he said. 'I did think it might be a bit quieter.' He slid his money across. 'As a matter of fact I came because I heard the Bird in Hand had the best-looking barmaid in the county.'

'Oh, that's Beth,' she began to say, 'she's—' and then she stopped, because he was looking at her quizzically. And felt herself blush, furious. Her hand went up to the short hair at the back of her head as she looked down at the drink she'd poured.

Bill didn't seem to notice: he lifted the glass, wiped his lip. 'Cheers,' he said. 'Can I buy you one?' Politely.

'Not right now, thanks,' she said. 'It's been a long day.'

'Another time, maybe?' he said.

The blush evaporated abruptly. Nat didn't know why she was angry suddenly, but she was. Bloody punters, barmaids fair game. She was thinking, if Beth was here, you wouldn't be chatting me up. Thinking, you came for her, and you got me.

'I don't think so,' she said, stiffly, knowing she was over-reacting, wishing for Beth there to create a diversion, take the heat off her, make a joke, and she saw his face change, hardly at all but enough. He nodded, tilting his head, watching her a second, then he raised his glass again and turned, into the packed room.

Chapter Five

Saturday

In the white morning light Victor rehearsed the words. *I've never been in a place like this before.*

They'd been round with breakfast, a middle-aged man shuffling with a trolley and asking Victor questions he couldn't answer. Because however much he rehearsed them, the words wouldn't emerge from his mouth.

Ninety-two, and I've never been in a hospital before. What he was trying to say, of course, was that he didn't belong here, even now, even at ninety-two. But perhaps he was wrong about that.

There was a smell of boiled coffee, and canteen food, there were sounds all the time, bleeps and alarms going off and murmuring voices, the occasional louder voice. An officer's voice was how he thought of it, overriding the others. Funny how, seventy years away from the war, certain aspects of it were clear and bright and sparkling as a newly polished glass. That would be the consultant, he assumed, talking louder than the rest. Victor's senses were sharpened, the present was sharpened as though now was all there was. The now.

They had left a tray beside his bed: a carton of juice, a plate with toast now cold, a tiny packet of marmalade he couldn't have opened even before this happened.

But he could remember the consultant, now he thought about it. Had that been yesterday?

A nurse appeared, leaning over the bed, looking into his face, a round anxious face, and another thought sprang. The dark barmaid, the older one, the sadder one. He felt his body rise to alert as he reached for her name, she had said it to him but he couldn't remember now. Was that all that was frightening him? And all at once the absolute hopeless failure of his body rose to overwhelm him, everything crashing at once, memory, muscle, nerves, words.

The nurse understood: she knew what was happening. He could see it reflected in her face. 'It's all right, Victor,' she said and her hands were either side of him, holding his arms, gently.

Don't give up now. Not now. Don't panic. There were strategies. Victor felt his body settle back under her hands. He felt as though he'd strained every sinew to rise and nothing had happened. He knew what it was that had frightened him although he couldn't see it, didn't want to see it. Didn't dare. A dark corner in the corridors of his rattled old brain. It was where this had started, the dark that had crept up as he sat on that bench in the sun. He had been going to tell Sophie.

There was a man with blood on his arm, coming out of the darkness. Someone sitting down to talk to him on the bench in the sun, girls chattering like birds about a body in the weir. A boy's body caught in the sluice, like a rabbit.

There was the ambulance ride. Victor had lain as though in a box, feeling the bumping underneath him, his body shifting, a strange man sitting beside him, and the last he'd seen of the real world was her face through the ambulance doors. Natalie. Nat. In his chest something swelled, released, joy, at remembering. The strange man wasn't a stranger, either, was he? Owen. Wilkins.

He tried to sit up, but her hands were still there. Something did move, though, something quivered, the right arm, tired but willing, and he saw surprise in the nurse's face. She sat back, releasing him. Her name was on a tab on her breast, he stared but the letters jumbled. An S, an A. Laboriously he focused. Lisa. Lisa frowned at the uneaten breakfast, and made a sound of exasperation; she said something under her breath.

'We'll get you something you can eat, Victor,' she said. 'When the consultant's been round, when he's said if you need . . . more tests.'

I can't eat if they're going to operate, Victor intended to say, to stop her worrying. *I've watched enough telly to know that.* No words came out – but he could see, she knew. If he could only smile at her. He was smiling as hard as he could but all that happened was that one corner of his mouth trembled, there was a trickle he couldn't dab away. He closed his eyes to stop the feeling that gave him. He tried to focus in the dark on that shining point.

Where was she? Where was Sophie? Victor didn't want to cause her trouble but somehow he felt she should be here by now. If she knew, nothing would prevent Sophie from coming, his kind, small Sophie. A trembling set up somewhere deep inside him, that he tried, and failed, to subdue; it was as though the man with blood on his hands and his Sophie were in dangerous proximity, there in his muddled, misfiring brain.

'It won't be long, Victor,' said the nurse, as if she knew. 'Not long now.'

Thank you, Lisa, he said, in his head. *You're very kind.*

But then her meaning broke free and floated, translucent in the white light of the hospital morning. I may die, thought Victor, before I see my Sophie again. For a second he felt perfectly calm.

And then he thought, No.

It was in the paper.

He stood in the newsagent's shop on the concourse with it in his hands, reading the front page. He could see the tiny tremor he transmitted to the pages, excitement, not nerves. The rush, and 'rush' was just the word, he could feel it in his veins, fast water through a sluice. Roaring. No one else could see it, and he liked that. He turned for the cash desk because the fat jobsworth behind the till would say something if he stood there reading for free, and he didn't know what he would do then. His hands at her fat throat.

Took his time, selected the exact change, smallest coins he could find, standing between the chewing gum stand and the special offer, bar of chocolate plus bottle of water one pound. The fat woman eating chocolate bars when the customers' backs are turned, you can bet on it, breaking out in spots. A line of acne on her cheek: the memory of that and he felt a sound in his throat, waiting to be let out. And all the time the headline sat between them on the counter. He had turned it so the fat woman behind the till could read it. A secret sign: he willed her to look but she was punching the computerised till with her pudgy fingers, peep, peep, ping. The drawer opened, the cash went in and then he saw her pause, saw her look.

BODY FOUND IN LOCK. LOCAL YOUTH IDENTIFIED AS VICTIM. Smaller lettering. *'Not misadventure,' says DI.*

He would have liked something bigger, bolder, a screaming headline. The photograph showed a police tent among the dusty reeds, and he would have liked to have seen the body – to make the fat woman look at it. I did that. The ankles tied, the swollen face. He felt her look up but he just turned the paper slowly, folded it and only then did he raise his eyes to hers, smile, take the receipt she held out.

I got him down there. The bloody rags for tying him kept safe, folded carefully in plastic in his pocket, her DNA on another one of her men. Just what the boy had always wanted, and a little hint they'd be too stupid to understand, into the bargain. The stupid police.

'Cheers, darling,' he said, to see the shadow cross her face, to see her unsure. To see her understand something, without knowing.

Their bodies in his hands. *I did that.*

She had sold herself to him as a loner, no ties, no obligations, free agent, here today, gone tomorrow. She had had a friend, though, hadn't she. And walking back out of the door with the newspaper in his hand and knowing the fat woman was watching him go, he let the friend materialise behind his eyes, growing, as he stared down at the headline. She was smaller, darker. Quicker on her feet maybe. But not quick enough.

The pub was quiet. It was early still, but Nat could tell it was going to be one of those days, the morning after the night before.

There'd been too much going on for closing time to come easily, the feeding frenzy that wasn't all to do with some kid's body found a mile away. Janine had spent twenty minutes bellowing, turfing them out of their dark corners. *Haven't you got homes to go to*, and sometimes that phrase had a nasty ring to it, sometimes it made Nat think, no doubt, I've got to get out of this place.

Some of them had hung around smoking in the garden, on the doorstep, even once the doors had been bolted on them: teenagers from the campsite, barely old enough to drink, some bikers from up north, a handful of Dutch students off the ferry. There had been no sign of anyone she recognised as a friend of Ollie's. She'd caught Craig standing in the door into the bar's kitchen, swaying with tiredness, scanning the room, hollow-eyed. Janine had packed him off at ten, even she could see the lad was shattered.

Now Paddy was in, drinking bitter lemon in the gloom and reading the local newspaper, but otherwise the bar was empty.

Nat had her laptop on the counter next to a mug of coffee and was googling, her search terms all the names she could think of for Beth's mum, plus Otley. It was at least half about finding Beth, although the search seemed redundant this morning, the whole village having more to think about. A mile-wide radius around the house where

Ollie had lived with his parents – two villages away, inland – might as well have been radioactive, no one would be going that way any time soon.

The other half was diversionary tactic. It nagged at her: this isn't about her, it's about you. You've messed up, not just your life but Jim's too. Sooner or later, you're going to have to face it. Get things straightened out.

The doorbell had rung at seven thirty, not the kind of ring the postman makes, either, nothing polite or tentative about it but someone standing on the bellpush until it shrieked, and with no intention of getting off. Nat had known who it would be, even before she leaned out of the window, wrapped in a sheet. Oh, Jim. And it came down on her, like a great crushing weight, sadness all mixed up with anger. I can't. I can't.

Not content with phoning her at crack of dawn to see if she'd dragged someone home, he wanted to see for himself. As she clumped down the stairs the anger came to the fore, anger like a child's. And she felt like telling him there *was* someone in her bed. With tattoos and a shotgun.

It was only as she reached to unlatch the front door that Nat, with a small shock, remembered the cameraman. *She could have, they could have.* Then she saw Jim's face and she felt it all depart like air from a balloon. 'For Christ's sake, Jim,' she said, unhappily, as he almost fell into the hallway, reaching blindly with his head for her shoulder.

'I'm sorry,' he said, his eyes red. 'I'm sorry.'

He wasn't exactly sorry, though, like people often aren't. There was a thin layer of sorry laid over something nastier. There had been a moment as she stepped back into the hall to let him in, a moment when she got a whiff of that, sweat and desperation, and she had to tell herself, this is just Jim. Jim you've known since you were a kid, Jim you woke up next to every day for five, nearly six years, it's OK. Just Jim. Poor Jim, not all his fault.

Nat had made him coffee in the kitchen, making him sit down. She told herself, if he starts on about it, he's out.

He started on about it.

'I didn't give you the space,' he said, staring down into the mug. His hair was standing up stiff like he hadn't washed it in days, weeks. 'Now it's done, I think, we could have made a go of it. I mean, people do. Does anyone think they're ready to be a parent?'

Nat felt it sour in her throat, she felt it hammer at her head, there, where the bone was thin at the temples. She wanted to scream, *You don't know what you're talking about. You don't know how this feels. I can't undo it.* 'No,' she managed, rusty-voiced. 'No. I know.'

But it's too late. It's too late. We didn't understand. I didn't.

Jim looked up at her, his eyes sore-looking, red-rimmed, bright blue, his hands cupped round the mug. And then he said it. 'You've moved on, though.'

It wasn't so much the words, though she could have laughed at how far they were from the truth. It was the undertone: ragged, gravelly, on the brink of rage. He never used to be angry. She held herself very still, on instinct. This could go wrong. She knew he needed her to tell him it was all right, to tell him they could try again. But she needed to save herself.

'I haven't moved on, Jim,' she said. 'But that doesn't

mean I'm coming back, either. I can't be near you, I can't—'

And then, jerkily, Jim was on his feet; Nat had stepped back quickly on the same instinct that had kept her still. The mug tipped and rolled on the table, the hot liquid spreading, dripping on to the flagstones.

She hadn't dared even say it, she'd just crossed her arms across her body to protect herself and somehow the gesture had stopped him in his tracks then turned him around and he was gone, the door swinging behind him. And Nat had stood there alone in the green shifting morning light, knowing that it wasn't sorted, not by a long long way.

How did you leave someone you'd known since you were twelve? When you could see how much it hurt. She had no idea. She was going to have to find out.

By eleven thirty things had livened up a bit, half a dozen customers and another few outside in the lane. Nat had shifted the computer under the bar because Janine was downstairs and breezing in and out, singing under her breath. Steve had gone off somewhere for the night but wherever it was hadn't been on Janine's radar as a cause for concern and anyway, he'd be back that evening. That was why she was singing.

A car pulled up outside the pub, something with a big engine. Paddy, in for light refreshment and a bit of silent company, raised his head from the paper a moment. He ran a hand through his rumpled hair and darted a glance at her, his blue eyes, surprisingly bright in the tanned face, lingering then looking away.

Paddy knew what she was looking for: he knew the questions she'd been asking about Beth. Probably most of the punters did, the regulars, anyway, she supposed she'd mentioned it to anyone who'd listen. And one or two of them had asked even that morning, where's the one with the big . . . the big brown eyes? Not even using her name, just the old joke about her boobs.

Unless it was Jim he was thinking about; Jim who could have turned up at the yard in any kind of state this morning. No wonder he was up here to read the paper.

Outside, a heavy car door slammed, and before Nat could look up from the computer screen Jonathan Dowd was in the bar. He looked, if anything, even more unhappy than he had the previous week, when Janine had patted him briskly on the hand and told him never mind, plenty more fish in the sea, and what was he drinking.

Janine had expected him just to suck it up, move on. Not all men did move on, though. Jim, for one. Jonathan Dowd walked heavily up to the bar, and after a bit of frowning, as if he wasn't quite sure what he was doing there, settled on an orange juice. He seemed to have got thinner since she last saw him, the regular features she'd thought handsome turned gaunt. He hesitated as if about to ask something but then Janine breezed back inside and instead he dodged across to the table where Paddy sat. They nodded to each other then both made that little shift on their stools that would allow them to ignore each other.

A dad came in with a little kid and took her out to the garden at the back. Two of the previous night's bikers, bleary-eyed and wanting a hair of the dog, shambled through the door. As she pulled pints and loaded trays and filled the dishwasher, Nat kept looking across at Dowd: his orange juice barely touched, he sat with his hands loose on his knees. Then there was a lull and Janine was upstairs doing something in the bedroom and on impulse Nat slipped over to where Dowd was sitting. Paddy shifted, further down.

'I do think there's something funny about it,' Nat said, launching straight in. Dowd raised his eyes to hers, wary. 'About Beth disappearing,' she added, and he nodded as if he'd known. 'She left her stuff behind. The landlady came and told us.' She saw him go still, unhappiness turning into something else, more like panic. He put his head in his hands.

'What is it you do, um, Jonathan?' Nat asked, more in an attempt to comfort him than anything else. 'You're camping down the estuary, aren't you?' She had some idea – from Beth? – that it was some eco-project.

'Living off-grid,' Dowd corrected her, saying dully, 'I'm collecting samples from the water. Monitoring the algae—' He broke off then, with a slightly impatient look, at having to explain. 'I can get . . . closer, that way. To the work, I mean, to the river. I'm not so keen on . . . well. Campsites are noisy. I've got a generator, for the refrigeration. The samples need refrigeration.' Brushing her off, he was a funny mixture, she'd seen it before. On the spectrum, was that what they called it these days? Arrogant and shy at the same time, anyway.

'Look,' said Nat, on impulse, 'come on.' She took hold of his arm, feeling him stiffen. 'I'm trying to find her mum's number. At least it's doing something, you can help me.' Reluctantly he got to his feet and followed her: him one side of the bar, her another, and the laptop between them. At midday Craig came in, slipping past Nat into the kitchen to get started on making up rolls for lunch, just giving them a nervous glance. Janine's footsteps audible overhead

– what was she up to? Scattering rose petals on the pillow? All sorts of pampering went on now Steve was on the scene, at all hours, like she had turned into some film star. At one point she called down to see if she was needed but the bikers had drifted off, the dad in the garden was making his pint last.

''S fine,' Nat shouted back up, but the bubble bath was already running.

They were trawling through online search results when they got somewhere finally – because Dowd said Beth had told him once she had a cousin who ran a florist's in Otley. 'Called Gorgeous,' Dowd muttered, sheepish. 'Beth liked that. It was what the cousin's boyfriend called her.' Nat gave him a sidelong glance, wondering how that came up in conversation; she couldn't imagine him calling anyone gorgeous, or darling, or sweetheart for that matter. He avoided her eye. She called the number.

Even though Nat realised – as the phone began to ring – that she had no name for the cousin beyond gorgeous, they hit lucky.

'Mimi,' the shop's owner said, promptly, as if customers phoned asking her name all the time. 'Michelle. What's she got up to now, then?' She sounded amused, fond. 'Little Beth.'

'Just . . . well, we're not sure,' said Nat. 'She's done a bunk. We're trying to get hold of her mum.'

'On the run again, is she?' said Mimi, and before Nat could reply, she bellowed something – *No, cellophane, they want cellophane* – before returning to the receiver, impatient. 'I haven't seen her, if that's what you're asking. Not in five years.'

'Did you fall out?'

'What? No, no – she never gave you a chance to fall out, she'd just disappear, off to pastures new.' There was a tiny pause, and when Mimi spoke she was almost wistful. 'I don't know that I'd be helping you if you were a man asking. Always hiding from some bloke or other. Kiss the boys and make them cry, that was our Beth.' Then she sighed. 'Hold up. I've got a number somewhere. What's she called these days, Jackson, Johnson, something like that?'

Beth's mum was called Johnson at last count, and she lived in Cornwall. Truro.

'Cornwall?' Dowd's head jerked up, at the sound of Nat's voice, perhaps. She could hear the fear in it herself because why would Beth have texted that she was up north, then? She was thanking Mimi when Janine finally emerged, in a warm cloud of bath bombs and scented candles. Something about the sight of Nat and Dowd, flushed and either side of a laptop, made her eyes narrow.

'Can I see those texts?' Nat said quickly. Janine frowned. 'The ones from Beth? Saying where she was going.'

Janine reached up and took her phone down from the shelf above the spirits. 'What's up?' she said. 'Who was that on the phone?' She stared down at the phone for a bit with pursed lips then looked up and said, 'I must have deleted them.' Apologetic, then defensive. 'Well, I was pissed off with her, wasn't I?'

Nat sighed, looking down at her own phone, where she'd tapped in the number Mimi had given her. 'All right,' she said, and taking a deep breath, she dialled.

Listening to the phone ringing, did she have an idea of what Beth's mother was going to be like? Some kind of old hippy chick like Nat's own mother Patty off sunning herself in Spain, laughter lines from her hairline to her cleavage but happy enough. Nat felt her shoulders sag a little at the thought of her mum, painted toenails, going round the supermarket in a kaftan. 'Come and visit,' she'd say gaily. 'What you waiting for?'

Waiting for the latest bloke to be off the scene, maybe. Waiting to have some good news like, I've got a proper job, I've got my own place. Not, *I think it's over with Jim, Mum*. Not, *I've done something, Mum . . .*

'Yes?'

Beth's mother, Melissa Johnson, Maxwell as was, didn't sound anything like Patty. Melissa was nothing like her name, she was sour and hard and gravel-voiced.

'No,' she said, straight off, then laughed, harshly. 'And I'd have sent her packing if she had turned up on my doorstep. Do I sound like I need looking after? Like you'd leave her in charge of a fucking cat.'

She sounded so flatly hostile all Nat wanted to do was hang up on her. She managed to ask if there was anyone else, anyone Melissa could think of, though she knew it was hopeless. Beth's mother didn't care, hadn't cared for years, if ever. 'Her father?' Then Melissa Johnson laughed again and she was the one who hung up. Nat set the phone down on the counter and pushed it away.

Stupidly, all she could think was, She's not going to make Beth sort out another hospital appointment, is she? Even if Beth had turned up on her mother's doorstep. Nat felt her heart speed up.

They were looking at her, Janine and Dowd, Janine with her mouth set in a line, and Dowd pale and anxious, staring at his feet. 'Well?' he said, and Nat just shook her head, still hearing Beth's mother's voice in her ear. For a second all she wanted was to back out of the door to somewhere no one could overhear, no one could look, and phone her own mother, phone Patty in Spain. Phone her and tell her everything.

'She wasn't there,' Nat said with dull fear. 'Hasn't been there at all.'

Where is she? It hammered at her. Where is she? She thought of those abnormal cells multiplying, faster and faster. What have I been doing? Not bothering her. No signal, she'd said.

'We should go to the police,' she said, out loud. They stared. She swallowed. 'I mean, isn't she missing, now? She's missing.'

'Missing?' Janine folded her arms across her body defiantly. 'She's a piece of work, is what she is.'

'But you don't know,' said Nat urgently. 'There's . . . she had—' Would Beth have wanted Janine knowing? No reason for shame, smear test, everyone had them – but she couldn't quite say it. It was private.

Dowd raised his eyes as if he hadn't heard what Janine had said. 'Something *has* happened to her,' he said dully. 'I thought it was just me.' He stared back down at the bar top, not meeting her eye. 'I thought she wasn't picking up because she could see it was me calling. Just didn't want to answer my calls.'

And then, as Nat stared at him, watching the painful-looking Adam's apple bob as he swallowed, she thought of something so obvious she almost laughed. All this texting. You just didn't call any more – unless you were Jonathan

Dowd, obviously. Crazy: she could have done it weeks ago. It hadn't occurred to her: she wondered if she was even thinking straight.

'Hold on,' she said, dialling with one hand, holding the other up to Janine and Dowd to make them wait. 'Hold on.' She held the phone to her ear, listening. Of course, if something . . . it could just . . . but it rang. It rang. Beth's phone wasn't dead. It was 27 August and she'd been gone since 3 August: three weeks. Three and a half weeks, to be precise, her friend had been gone. More than gone, now: missing. She felt cold with the sound of those words in her head. My friend's missing. If anything had happened to Beth, if she was lying in woodland somewhere waiting to be found, if she was in the river, weighted, waterlogged . . . Why was she thinking that? Thinking those things? Why? You always thought of the worst case scenario, didn't you? But her phone was ringing.

If she was. That phone should be long dead. But it was ringing.

It rang, and rang. And then there was Beth's voice, as the answerphone cut in. Nat's hand flew to her mouth as she heard it.

'*If you're getting this message, I'm too busy having fun. But I'll get back to you.*'

She hung up, and suddenly the phone rang. For a split second something released inside her, euphoria. It'll be her.

It was the hospital.

At the foot of the stripped bed Mo Hawkins was on her knees in her pinny with two bin bags at her side. She had two piles: one for the bin, one for . . . well, she called it compensation. Not that that little madam had that much she'd *want* but Mo liked a bit of eBay, pennies here and there and sometimes a windfall – much as anything else she liked seeing the watchers mount up. Watching and waiting to press that button, not that Mo ever bought, only sold, stuff from charity shops, jumble sales, surprising how they didn't know gold from gilt, the occasional find left behind by a tenant. This was a windfall, all right. Plenty out there liked this tarty stuff.

It was only payback, three, four weeks' rent she could have had. A nice little place, quiet, good neighbours, views. Tutting, Mo peered at a peach-coloured blouse to see a rim of foundation round inside the neck; dirty, with it. Glad to see the back of her. There'd been notes, about the noises, through Mo's door, as they'd given up having a go at Madam. She leaned down for the next item, it was stretchy, green and glittering, looked like a vest.

Under the bed something caught her eye in the dust and she hooked it out with a coathanger – not the first time she'd found one of *those* left behind. Deftly she flicked it into one of the bin bags and sat back on her haunches.

Somewhere, a phone began to ring. Not Mo's, which was on the chair beside her. For a minute or two she thought it was coming from next door, someone out along the back gardens or in the meadows but it was the wrong direction, it was too loud. It was inside the house; then she thought it would stop, but it kept on ringing. Mo shuffled out of the bedroom into the hall, the green sparkly top forgotten in her hand, peered into the bathroom, kitchen. It was muffled, like maybe it had been dropped behind something. She opened the door to the hall cupboard just as the ringing stopped, and the little screen died into darkness.

There. *Got you*. There.

Walking slowly back to the bedroom Mo puzzled over it, in her hand, still on its charger; pausing a second, she dropped it on top of the selling pile. Then she heaved up the rest of the stuff – torn jeans, a shirt with underarm sweat marks, dusty shoes and toiletries and dog-eared paperbacks – and dropped it in the bin bag. She pushed open the glazed doors.

The incinerator was all set up, rolled newspaper, can of meths. Mo just had to set a match to it.

Chapter Six

'We've got your number and Mr Wilkins' number, and Mr Wilkins isn't answering. There's been some improvement in Victor's condition.'

Nat let out a shaky breath. When they'd shown her in here – the relatives' room – she'd feared the worst.

The nurse looked harried. Lisa, it said on her name badge. 'The scan showed a small area of concern, as the doctor will have told you,' Lisa went on. 'And he's most certainly not out of the woods yet.' She hesitated. 'We really do need a next of kin, though.' She pressed her lips together, anxious.

'His daughter hasn't been in touch yet?' A knot formed in Nat's stomach. What if . . . what if . . . she thought again about the way he talked about his daughter. Fond, tender. He talked about her as a child, more than anything else. How long was it since he had actually seen her?

'Mr Wilkins did assure us that he was taking care of it,'

said the nurse, and she shrugged, helpless. 'The manager of the caravan site? I called myself this morning but there was no answer. We're run off our feet, and in the meantime he has no one. He needs someone. I thought perhaps you—'

'Of course,' said Nat, already at the door.

Steve had been walking back into the pub as she ran out. As she stood back in the doorway he smelled of clean clothes and aftershave and she felt a momentary, irrational stab of envy for Janine, and a bloke who made an effort, and all things normal. Even the bloody rose petals on the pillow.

'Where you off to in such a hurry?' he said and she had told him.

'Need a lift?' he said without missing a beat.

But before she could answer Janine had called over from the bar, 'She's got a cab coming.' Just a hint of shrill in it. And not to leave anything to chance Janine was round the bar and at the door with them, beaming at him.

'You just look after old Victor, Natalie,' she said. 'I can manage with Craig, now Steve's back.' Eyes only for him, turning to address him without pause. 'She's given our Beth a call and her phone's still on so I don't know what all the fuss was about, good riddance leaving us in the shit like that.'

Steve nodded slowly. 'I suppose that figures,' he said, though he hadn't sounded convinced, not to Nat.

Then the taxi's bonnet slid into view through the doorway and Janine practically pushed her out the door.

As she came around the curtain Nat couldn't see the improvement they talked about: Victor was still motionless on his back, hands blue-white and thin at his sides. But when she spoke his head turned. His mouth moved but no sound came out.

'I'm back,' she said and she saw him breathe, deliberately, effortful.

Then he said, slurred but deliberate, an unmistakable two syllables, 'Sophie.'

'It's not Sophie,' she said, sorrowful. 'It's Nat, it's Natalie, Victor,' but she could see that he knew that already, he understood.

'Caw,' he said. 'Caw—' and his eyes clouded, as if with pain or frustration.

'Do you mean you want me to call Sophie?' she said, her face so close to his she could feel his breath, light as a feather, on her cheek and smelling thin and chemical.

He struggled, chin coming down, trying to nod. When he said yes it sounded more like choking. 'I'll phone her right away,' she said, 'I'm going to do it now,' and he sank back down, exhausted.

They gave Nat the number at the desk, and she walked outside to make the call. There was something about hospitals: people everywhere, wandering the corridors looking frightened, whispering into their phones. Noises, alarms, heads turning to eavesdrop. As a taxi pulled up she walked away from the entrance, past a sign telling people not to smoke, then past a grey-skinned man on a drip, tucking a lighter into his fag packet and taking a deep drag on the cigarette he'd just lit. The number the nurse had given her was a landline, a London number.

Dialling it Nat turned around and looked up at the windows, trying to work out which one was Victor's as she listened to it ring.

A man answered, irritable, and there was something so coolly hostile in his voice that for a second she held her breath then she thought: Saturday, of course, it'll be her husband home from work. 'I'd like to speak to Sophie,' she said.

'I'm sorry,' he said, unhesitating, 'she's busy.'

'Is that Mr . . .' She searched her brain for the name because she knew Victor had told her it, once upon a time, and as she remembered it she found she also remembered the note in Victor's voice when the subject had come up. The husband. *A mistake, I fear,* Victor had said sorrowfully, with foreboding. 'Richard? Is that Richard?'

A child made a shrill sound in the background.

'That must be Rufus,' she said, placatory, trying to establish her credentials. 'Victor told me about him. I'm calling for Victor, he's not well, he's—'

The room's sounds went muffled as if his hand had gone across the mouthpiece: the child crying, another voice, a door closing.

'Hello?' she said. 'Hello?'

Then he was back. 'Yes, yes,' he said. 'Thank you, I'll pass on the message.'

'No,' she said, 'you don't understand, he may not . . . he needs to see her.'

A silence. 'I assure you,' he said, and his voice was only calm and measured but for some reason Nat felt herself go cold, stupidly fearful. 'I do indeed understand,' he said, enunciating carefully, 'and I will pass on the message.'

'You need to take down the address of the hospital,' said Nat, stubborn, and then he did make a sudden sharp sound of impatience.

'Right,' he said. 'Just a moment.' But when she told him the address – all of it, the ward name and the road and the telephone number – she was speaking into silence: he didn't ask her to repeat anything or spell it, no questions about directions, she might even have thought he had already hung up on her except that, leaving it a beat after she had finished speaking, he just said, brutal, 'Yes.'

And then he did hang up.

Bless her. Bless her.

Bless you, Natalie, Victor would have liked to say, but in the event he could only hope that she already understood. Nat seemed to him eminently capable of that.

They had managed to get him a little more upright – it seemed that was a triumph, a step forward, and he had nodded to congratulate them – he could see through the big grubby hospital window that it was almost dark. Behind rooftops the sky was the electric blue of a long summer evening, although shortening, night arriving with a rush that whispered to Victor of autumn. He felt a surge of something – he wouldn't call it loss, not yet – but longing, perhaps, for the endless luminous evenings of June as he sat in his small folding chair and looked down the green slope across the water. The sensation was not familiar to him, he had never minded autumn, nor even winter, there always seemed a next stage to look forward to. Victor lay still, propped on clean pillows: there was no struggling with the sensation, wherever it came from. He would not call it mourning, because there *was* something to look forward to. There was Sophie.

Natalie was sitting beside him looking out of the window

and holding on to his hand. She had been there for more than two hours now, through the administration of supper. Tomato soup, bread and butter, lukewarm tea. He had managed to sip, he had managed to chew, he had managed to swallow, and she had helped him, showing no sign of impatience. Bless you, Nat.

When her cropped head had appeared around the curtain – it *did* suit her, though he had been uncertain, shocked even when he'd first seen it, he had wished for the thick dark pile, the softness of it, but perhaps he should accept that young women needed more than softness, in this day and age, more than hair to hide behind – he felt as though he had willed her back with the urgency of his need to know if she had succeeded, if she had kept her promise. If she had got through to Sophie.

Scrupulously Nat had told him the truth, he could tell: better that way. He steeled himself although his courage flickered when she mentioned Richard's name. She knows, he thought, his heart sinking at the thought that he had been right about Richard. She knows what kind of man he is.

'Well,' she said uncertainly, 'I did tell him twice that Sophie has got to come. I mean, she really *has got to* come. And I read him out the address, all of it.' She took his hand, not squeezing it, just holding it calmly. 'I think I'll give her another ring,' she said. 'Perhaps I'll get her next time, then we can be sure.'

Bless you.

He didn't know when she left, only that when he woke at some unrecognisable hour of the night, his curtains had been drawn back so that he could see the long ward twilit with things glowing and blinking, and the chair beside the bed was empty.

He'd seen the old man there on the bench in the sun and remembered, maybe in the same moment the old man did, that they'd looked at each other before. This time, of course, no blood on his arm; this time he had only been down there to look at the river, to look into the backs of the houses, to examine his own trail. Crouching to look how the grass stayed crushed in the heat, to be sure he'd left no trace in the gap in the hedge he'd slipped through. No shred of fabric. No blood.

This time he had been just a man, out walking. Not against the law, was it.

But the old man on the bench had raised his head and looked and gone quite still. That had been when he knew, the old man had seen something, would remember something. The old man's mistake.

He had walked on, slowly, watching as the old man got up from the bench and tottered, took two steps then fell. Walking past unnoticed as the girls clustered around him, on, on to the caravan site. To find his van and walk right in, to examine the photographs in silver frames, pull open a drawer because he could, feeling the hum inside him of power when no one challenged him, no one saw. Only the old man saw, and he was lying back up there on the road. His thin old ankles awkwardly crossed, his old man's feet in shabby shoes.

Of course, he had known they would come into her place. The old bitch sorting rags. It was why he had left certain things there, and taken others away. Lay a trail and see them frown over it: it always took a time for them to understand and that he found enjoyable. He could follow and watch, to see what they would do next.

A woman on her knees in the same room he'd done it, going still with her head down, wondering. So many steps behind him that by the time she raised her head to look at where he had been standing, in plain view watching her, he would be gone.

Chapter Seven

Sunday

It was Sunday.

Victor knew this because the elderly man opposite (less elderly than me, he had to remind himself) had been brought a Sunday newspaper by his wife. The newspaper lay untouched on the bottom of the bed. Even in a hospital, there were Sunday mornings.

Once there had been roast lamb for lunch and Joy in an apron. Victor had not thought of this for years: he had not thought it wise. But now he lay here immobile in Sunday sunshine he found there was no terror left in the memory, no dark crevasse of grief waiting to swallow him whole. It felt closer, more present, as if a lifetime was not, after all, so much a trainline with stops as an ocean dotted with ships, some visible, others out of sight, a world you could sail around and find yourself back where you began.

Even if he could make himself understood it would probably be wisest, thought Victor, to say nothing. The odd thing about a hospital was that it turned you into someone else, even if you were feeling yourself when you entered. Which he certainly had not been.

It felt like a long time ago, now, that hot morning he'd been wheeled in on his back, following the striplighting down corridors and in and out of lifts – and cautiously Victor interpreted that feeling positively. He had in the interval adjusted to what he could and could not do, and thought that he could do more, not less, as time passed. He could, for example, raise both arms, he could hold a pen, he could say thank you quite clearly. Whatever it had been was in retreat – for the moment. It seemed safest, though, not to express that to anyone, either. Because the truth was, Victor was not at all sure that he was amongst friends here, on the sunny ward. He wasn't at all sure that whatever it had been hadn't followed him here.

It was distinctly quieter today. All the same, thought Victor, on balance, he would not wish to spend more than one hospital Sunday morning. There were other Sundays he wanted to experience.

It was important to adjust to circumstances, to the most pressing circumstance of all, that his own death was closer than it had ever been. Closer even than in the last surge of his landing craft as he brought it up on the beach with the din and crackle of artillery in his ears, aged nineteen years and one month, the crash and thump of bombardment, sand flying. Then Victor had experienced it as a fierce chemical sensation he could still remember seventy years on; then he had been able to turn to Corporal Tunstall (Joseph, known as Joe, born and bred in Kent among hop fields) next to him leaning against the metal bulwark with his lips pressed to the barrel of his rifle and see the bottomless black-eyed look that mirrored his own. Then, they had been brothers all fighting the same fire, the same blistering devil. Now Victor was on his own – that was the thing they didn't really dwell on when talking of old age, wasn't it – it wasn't all to do with infirmity, joints and eyesight, it was the aloneness, he wouldn't call it loneliness, the being alone you should guard against. On his own and the fierce black gaze was dulled, blurred. He was alone and hearing it walk behind him on soft feet, hearing the flame crackle in corners, and so he needed to be circumspect. Victor eyed the newspaper – and then she walked into his line of sight. Lisa. Nurse Lisa.

As though she could read his mind she leaned in one quick movement and picked up the newspaper. It was a broadsheet.

'I'll put it back,' she said softly, holding it out to him. 'When you've had a look. Poor Mr Saunders is in for respite, hasn't been able to read a newspaper in eight or nine years, but it makes Mrs Saunders feel better to bring him one.' With an effort he raised both arms to hold it, trembling, in front of him and Lisa gave a little gasp. 'Victor,' she said, 'well done.' But she moved discreetly to hold the thing with him, and when he turned his head, the newsprint blurring maddeningly, she understood that as well and reached for his spectacles.

Home news. Boy's body found. A small paragraph, but suddenly the newspaper felt heavy, or Victor felt weak, and he lay back on the pillow, helpless. He closed his eyes.

In the dark he saw a man's arms, streaked in blood as he walked up the lane to Victor, from the shadow into the light. He tried to think: when? The newsprint blurred again. In the water at least a week. Drowned. Another moment and the walking man would raise his head in the dappled sun and Victor would see his face. He waited, he waited, he heard the nurse murmur, anxious out there in the light somewhere, and he thought, he knows I saw him. He knows where I am.

Upstairs she could hear Steve and Janine, talking over their full English. The fry-up was their Sunday ritual, and the oasis of peace in the bar that was a by-product as much of a luxury for Nat as for them, if she was truthful. Especially on a day like this with the doors open front and back and the sun, still low in the morning sky, shining right through from the garden to the lane as Nat swept out. The pumps gleaming, bar top polished and clean towels laid out on it.

When she'd started, aged, what, fifteen and collecting glasses and washing up, strictly-behind-the-bar work, the smell in the pub first thing had been very different. The first job had been to empty and wipe out the ashtrays, so it was dregs and fag ash mixed. Duster in hand Nat paused, trying to remember when Beth had turned up. A year ago? Two? She calculated.

Two and a bit, not long after Nat's return from London, really. Turning up in the doorway one autumn morning as unlike today as could be, soaked to the skin in a tight croptop and with a shiny bag festooned with glitterballs and furry pompoms over one shoulder, that turned out to contain everything she owned. She hadn't said much about where she came from beyond a few careless mentions of backpacking, a stint in a bar in Ibiza, some guy who'd disappeared overnight and turned out to have had a wife. Nothing about home, not then and not much more later. Nothing about a father long gone, a mother who'd kicked her out.

Janine, of course, with her sharp eye for what the punters liked, had seen it in her straight away, seen past the hair plastered down with rain and the streaked mascara to the party girl not so dormant beneath, and had practically offered her a job before she'd set her belongings down in the doorway. And then, looking down at Beth's wet feet and the underwear spilling out of the top of the bag, a place to stay – to seal the deal, quickly followed by Janine's usual, 'Strictly temporary, all right? While you sort yourself out.'

Before Beth had set her bag down Janine had enquired, unashamed, about relationships – 'No husbands coming out the woodwork, I hope?' – and Beth had just laughed.

'Did have a *relationship*,' she said, mocking, of herself as much as anything, once Janine was out of earshot. 'Ibiza. Not a lad, older bloke. Near on a year, Christ knows why. "It's not you, it's me," he kept saying. Meaning the opposite, giving me a look like, just change your hair, just wear the right thing, *say* the right thing.' Her jaw set.

'Not you it's me ?' Nat hadn't understood.

Beth had smoothed her top, carefully, lovingly. 'He didn't want it. Sex. Couldn't get it up was the truth. But you know what? What he wanted was to see my face, trying to get it right, turn him on. Wanted to see me squirm. So now – I just like to have my fun. I don't want to hold on to anyone, if you get what I mean. Don't ask for something I can't give you, and I won't do it to you.'

She'd leaned back against the wall in the kitchen, staring off somewhere for a minute, then she'd clicked back to the here and now and smiled. Leaned forwards and put her arms round Nat and gave her a bone-cracking hug.

'That's blokes though. You don't want to take sex too serious. I'm holding on to you, mate, don't you worry.'

Don't take sex too serious: easier said than done. Nat had turned that over in her mind afterwards, and again when she'd seen Beth the morning after some bloke now and again since; a little ruffled, needing to reset, moving on. Is it what she wants? How can she make sure?

What with pub shifts it had been hard for them to go out together, her and Beth, but they'd managed it a few times. They'd been to see a movie with Ryan Gosling in, a big box of popcorn each and wine and Beth saying as they left, yeah, well, he's all right, I suppose. Take him or leave him, and them laughing so hard Nat fell off the pavement and Beth had to yank her back out of the way of a passing car.

That was before. Before Nat found out she was pregnant. Jim looking at her expressionless when she came in after that night at the movies, she had forgotten about that. It occurred to her for the first time, remembering, that it was possible Jim hadn't been all that happy about her being friends with Beth.

And then. Did he think her leaving him had something to do with Beth? Men did think that, didn't they? Though Beth had never said anything bad about Jim. She'd only sighed, once or twice.

There was a sound from upstairs and Nat tipped her head, listening for what was going on. She could hear Steve's voice, deep and steady and reasonable, Janine's sharper, though she couldn't hear what they were saying. She went into the kitchen to fill the bowls with peanuts and crisps and little cubes of cheese: only on a Sunday, a treat for the punters. Janine's idea of generosity, a Sunday tradition to keep them here while the roast cooked, though Nat couldn't imagine anyone doing roast dinner on a day like this. She thought of Beth's mother on the phone and found herself giving an involuntary shiver, despite the heat, at the memory, *little bitch*. Nat should have known: Beth wouldn't have wandered into the Bird in Hand in the rain if she'd had a home to go to, would she? Even Patty out on the Spanish costa represented home, of a sort.

She'd tried, Patty had. To make a home, to be a mum. Laying the table, putting up curtains. And she was all heart, was Patty, her face crumpling if she saw anyone hurt or unhappy, anyone or anything, dogs, cats, birds. Nat – and Nat's dad, too, soggy-faced, hung-over, repentant. It was watching Patty at the breakfast table hovering round him, not sure if he was going to hit her or cry on her shoulder, Patty ready to fly back to him and say, there, there, you never meant it – that had taught Nat to keep quiet. Because by the time she was five Nat had been able to see – or hear, Patty crying behind her bedroom door, a sad, ugly sound – that there was only so much a heart like Patty's could take, and Nat had better stay in her room and look after herself.

It had taken a while – it had taken maybe till May this year – for Nat to see that she wasn't as unlike Patty as she thought. She'd always hated to see Jim unhappy.

The fallout from the fry-up was all over the kitchen counter. Frying pan, grill pan, toast crumbs, open bottle of ketchup. Janine had been taking the tray up in another new dressing gown when Nat arrived and had said, careless, 'Just leave it,' but Nat knew what that meant. She was wiping down the surfaces when she heard Janine at the top of the stairs, talking back into the bedroom over her shoulder. 'I don't know why you're so bothered,' sharply, 'it's not like she'd been making the effort any more.' To Steve.

From the sharp clop of Janine's footsteps on the stairs Nat could tell the day wasn't off to a good start and she tugged off her apron to get out of her way but not quite fast enough, and Janine brushed impatiently past her in the door. Even the sound she made surveying the kitchen at Nat's back was dissatisfied, but Nat didn't have time to wonder because as she came through to the bar there was Mrs Hawkins, Mau*reen* as Beth used to call her, sardonic in cod Irish accent, and Mo to her friends. Of whom there were few.

In a grubby peach tracksuit that looked like it had been lifted from a younger woman Mo Hawkins was tapping on the counter, not with a coin as had been known among impatient punters (Nat had never smacked one of them for doing it, but her day would come) but her mobile. She was turning it on end and back again, and something about the picture stopped Nat in her tracks.

'Sorry, Mrs Hawkins, we don't open for another twenty minutes,' she said, but the hair was rising on the back of her neck already. She wasn't here for a drink. Tight-fisted and teetotal: Beth had had a theory about that, and Nat could almost hear her say it. *Ol' frickin vulture. Likes to keep her wits about her in case a bit of roadkill turns up.*

The mobile tipped again, screen at the bottom this time, and Nat stared, down to the bar top then up to the old woman's face. 'Yes,' said Mrs Hawkins. 'Reckernise it, do you?' Nat reached out a hand for it and Mo snatched it back.

'What's all this?' Janine's voice was sharp from the kitchen doorway behind her.

Nat saw a sullen look come into Mo Hawkins' face. 'I found it, didn't I,' she said, sullen replaced with self-righteous. 'Cleaning up her mess. Just trying to be helpful.'

'You mean you thought about flogging it then even you worked out that could get you in trouble?' Janine was steely. Nat's hand was still held out.

The old woman didn't look so certain, suddenly. 'I don't know why she would've left it behind,' she said, and she pushed the phone at Nat abruptly. 'It was in a cupboard, plugged in. She could've just forgot it – but then—'

Janine laughed scornfully. 'Leave her phone behind? Beth? I remember when she got it, you'd have thought it was her firstborn she was that proud.' Folding her arms across her. 'And who charges their phone in a cupboard?'

'She'd have been back for it before now,' said Nat, but she wasn't sure they heard her, she spoke so quietly. The messages, though. Beth had sent messages.

One to her: Sorry babe no signal really up here see you soon.

Had that sounded like Beth? No – but Beth was too big to squeeze into a text message.

The phone had been in a cupboard all along.

She tried to make it work. To make it make sense. Beth, hiding somewhere, sneaking back into that ground-floor flat, opening a cupboard and swooping for her phone, laughing as she pressed send. As a laugh? No. She'd have had to have lost her marbles to be playing this kind of silly beggars. She had friends here, she had lovers. She had a hospital appointment.

And with that realisation, for a plunging black second Nat knew – *knew* – that something had happened to Beth. Something bad.

'We're going to the police,' she said. Out loud.

Mo Hawkins' mouth fell open and Janine leaned in, triumphant, and snatched the mobile from her. 'I'll have that, thanks,' she said and was on the stairs by the time Mo had moved, fast for an old biddy, to the flap in the counter to get after her. Nat blocked her.

'*No*,' she said. 'It isn't yours, Mo, is it?' From upstairs she heard Janine's voice, Steve's raised in surprised answer. 'Is it?'

Mo Hawkins eyed her, venomous. 'I'm owed rent. And what's she mean, anyway, get me into trouble? She left it behind, didn't she? Not like she left no forwarding address.' Hunching her shoulders. 'And it's Mrs Hawkins to you, missy.'

Inside Nat something snapped. 'Something's happened to her,' she said, grabbing the woman's peach velour sleeve. 'Don't you understand, you . . . you . . .'

Mo Hawkins' eyes were sharp and brown and beady, gleeful for the fight. 'You what? Calling me names, is it?' she said, tugging her sleeve out of Nat's grasp. With a huge effort Nat slowed, stopped herself.

'I'm sorry,' she said, hearing her voice uneven with the strain of not shouting into the woman's face. 'Mrs Hawkins, look, I'm sorry. I'm just worried about my friend. Was there anyone . . . was she seeing anyone we might not know about? Who might have come over to the flat? Was she seen leaving with anyone?'

Mo Hawkins' mouth pursing. 'Neighbours?' Nat persisted. 'Anyone who might know where she's gone?' Pleading now, and all the time the stony-faced cow staring back at her like she was enjoying it. 'Because it's not normal, is it? Leaving all your stuff behind?' Beth's stuff, all those outfits, the shoes. 'Someone must know something.'

Mo snorted. '*Normal* you want, is it?' Pronouncing the word with relish. Nat faced her down until eventually she shrugged. 'Your guess as good as mine,' she said. 'Special friends, get yourselves in trouble, you girls, with yer special friends, she had 'em all right but she was careful not to let no one see 'em. Hear 'em's a different matter.' Nat swallowed, but Mo was still going, the bit between her teeth. 'Din't she say where she was off? You said her mum's.'

'You don't understand.' Through gritted teeth. 'That message – I don't think it was . . . that was . . .' *That wasn't her.* Nat stared at Mo Hawkins' wizened old face but her gut churned with the implications. Someone. Someone with her phone, winding them up. Lying to them. And where was Beth? What had happened to Beth?

It was like coming up against a wall. If she'd gone off without her phone, if she'd lost it, she'd have got a new one. She would have been in touch. She would have called, and at the thought of that, of Beth's actual voice, rough and sweet, a big sigh and saying *you missed me, then*, Nat put a hand to her mouth. Then dropped it. 'I spoke to her mum and she hasn't been there, so that was a . . . well maybe a misunderstanding.'

'She always was a little liar,' said the old woman, almost wistful and Nat seized the moment.

'I'm worried about her,' she said quickly and she saw

Mo's eyes narrow, suspicious. 'I think someone's been using the phone. I think someone wants us to think she's just gone off.'

'She coulda, coulda bin coming back an' . . .' but Mo ground to a halt and slowly Nat shook her head.

'So as to get out of paying rent, or what?' Incredulous. 'No.' She tipped her head back to listen. 'Janine?' she called. They were still talking up there. Then stepping back from the bar and catching sight of Mo Hawkins as she turned to look up the stairs, seeing the old woman's face sagging into lines and pouches: afraid.

'Janine?' Then the voices stopped overhead and the two of them were on the stairs, coming down, Janine first with the mobile in her hand and frowning and Steve behind her, patient as ever. He wore a clean shirt and his jeans were ironed, Janine the domestic goddess these days, thought Nat, distracted.

'I think we should take it to the police,' she said.

Janine looked back at Steve, anxious; he set a hand on her shoulder, tentatively. 'I think she could be right, babe,' he said, clearing his throat.

Janine thrust it out at Nat. 'It's been wiped,' she said. 'More or less. Messages and that.'

'I could've told you that,' piped up Mo Hawkins and they all turned to look at her. She shrugged. 'Come off it,' she said, 'anyone woulda looked, wouldn't they? Girl like that.' Back to plain nasty – but there was still a trace of fear, the beady eyes darting.

They all looked at Nat now, expectant. 'Even if it's been wiped,' she said, taking the phone, 'the police'll have ways of finding stuff, won't they?'

Standing at the foot of the stairs where the landline sat, pride of place and barely used, these days, as she waited to be put through Nat could hear the murmur of voices. Janine trying to get rid of Mo Hawkins, who was dead set on sticking around, a free place at the bar, at the centre of things, and not even the need to buy a drink. Should feel sorry for the old cow, lonely, maybe, but Nat had no room for pity. *Find her. Find her.*

Then there was a harassed-sounding DS on the line, maybe her own age by the sound of her voice. DS Garfield: she repeated it as Nat itched with impatience. Donna Garfield. 'We're a bit busy, just now, don't know if you've heard.' Sarcastic.

Nat felt her blood rise, she had to work hard to keep her voice even. 'I'll try not to take up too much of your time,' she said.

'Miss . . . ?'

'My name's Natalie Cooper. It's . . . I'm worried about my friend, that's all.'

A pause, then the DS sighed. 'Well, tell me again,' she said. 'She's left her stuff behind and disappeared.'

'She left her *phone*,' said Nat. 'Messages were sent on it saying she'd gone to her mum's but her phone's still here.'

A silence. 'And you last saw her—'

'We last saw her on August the third.' Nat hurried on, trying to detain her. 'She worked the afternoon shift, went off at four, five.' Had she said what she would be doing that evening? No. She had been the same old Beth, same old secret smile. 'She knew him. The dead boy, Ollie. We all did.'

'Go on,' said the policewoman warily, maybe all sorts of

people had turned up saying they knew him, wanting their fifteen minutes.

'He would come in the pub,' said Nat. 'He fancied her – well, most of the punters did – but he didn't come on to her, just looked.'

'And her? Did she give him any encouragement?'

'No. No.' Nat was uneasy. How could you explain what she was like, Beth? 'She didn't tell him to get lost, exactly, but you have to understand she got it day in day out, part of the job, she couldn't be slapping them down every five minutes, and he was only a kid. She just thought he'd grow out of it.'

There was a silence. Were they both thinking the same thing? Ollie wasn't going to grow out of anything now. Nat cleared her throat. 'How . . . how long had he been in the water? Do you know yet?'

'A while,' said the DS shortly. 'We're working on that.'

'So, does that make it harder – I mean, evidence on the body will have been lost?'

DS Garfield cleared her throat. 'Look,' she said, a warning note, 'I thought this was about your friend? I can't talk to you about an ongoing investigation: what we can say will be released through the usual channels.' Nat fell silent and she heard the woman get impatient. 'Someone will come over and get your friend's phone off you. If we can spare an officer – well, it'll be me – we'll check out her flat, too.'

'Thanks,' said Nat, wanting to shout at the woman. *For fuck's sake.* Was this how it worked, with the police? Treating everyone like a time-waster? It was what it felt like. But if she started yelling now . . .

Garfield sighed. 'I can tell you it won't be today, though,' she said. 'Sorry. I'll be in touch.' And hung up, leaving Nat to crash the receiver back down in rage.

Mo was still there, triumphant on her bar stool; she'd even managed to get a tonic water out of Janine, who was standing at the far end of the bar, drying glasses savagely. Steve seemed to have done the sensible thing and gone out for some fresh air, or maybe he had a job to go to.

'I would leave the place as it is, if I were you, M— Mrs Hawkins,' said Nat. 'In case the police . . . you know. Want a look around.' She had no faith they would, but it didn't do any harm to put the wind up Mo Hawkins. She could have already flogged half the stuff on eBay.

As if the thought had occurred to her, the old woman eased herself painfully off the bar stool and defiantly drained the tonic water. 'It's all there,' she said. 'Far as I can see she didn't take nothing with her. Can't blame me for doing a bit of tidying, can they?' Nat took the glass, Janine came up beside her and after a moment's aggressive staring at them Mo Hawkins made her way towards the door, just in time to meet a stream of pensioners elbowing their way inside, all walking sticks and pakamacs.

'Jesus,' said Janine, shading her eyes. 'I'd forgotten. Daycare centre in Leigh, ploughman's lunch and strawberries and cream. Eighteen of 'em, so you'd better get plating up.' She tugged her blouse into place as the group's leader approached, a red-faced man with a gleam in his eye. 'Shandy or a glass of house white each, and no more,' she muttered to Nat.

Then Janine picked the mobile up off the counter and set it carefully on top of the racks of spirits. 'Keep it safe,' she said. 'Cos that's us for the day. They would be bloody early, wouldn't they.'

Nat took the tray full of shandies Janine shoved at her and turned and walked out to the garden and the tables of old biddies all yattering like birds. She walked and listened and answered and handed out drinks mechanically but she was thinking about that night at the movies and Beth pulling her back on the pavement: Beth, Beth, Beth. Her whole insides hurt her, right up to her heart.

A big hard fist of fear.

Chapter Eight

The light was going, at last, in the London street, darkening door after door stretching away down the hill and the sky a bright deep blue over the rooftops. She couldn't think of him, of where he was, what the light was doing, what he could see.

Turning from the window Sophie locked the door carefully, quietly, and turned to Rufus who was sitting patiently in the bath waiting for her to soap him. The bruise was low on his back, a little to one side, at the dark stage. She tipped water over him gently.

If Richard tried the door she would think of a reason as to why she had locked it. To keep us safe. Not that reason, perhaps. Because she *was* safe, they were safe, of course they were. The house beyond the door was quiet, it was peaceful. The clock ticking in the hall, Richard at his desk. He wouldn't try the door.

She had asked him about the telephone call last night,

of course, how could she not? 'Was that Daddy?' she had said straight away, Richard's head turning as she said the word, his mouth scornful. 'No,' he'd said, 'not him. Just someone . . .' irritable with her, for guessing correctly, she knew that. 'Someone from the campsite, some girl, saying he's . . . oh, something and nothing, I'm sure. Taken a tumble, soon be back on his feet, nothing to worry about.'

Lying awake last night she had been reduced to guessing, increasingly urgently. She could hear Richard say, You've always been a panicker, and she had, a worrier, a worst-case scenario person since her mother died – and he had always been very understanding. She had seen him begin to write something down with the receiver under his ear, pretending, dropping the pencil.

A chubby, shy child who grew into an awkward adult, Sophie had always believed Richard loved her. Why, otherwise, would he have married her? In this day and age, getting pregnant, even at forty-eight, didn't mean you had to marry someone (although in Richard's world, said the inner voice, she supposed it did, and she had been determined to have him, Rufus, obstinate at last over that). Her best interests at his heart. He decided everything.

'Come along, darling,' she said, getting to her feet. In the bath Rufus tipped his head back, trusting, looking into her eyes, and she reached for him with the towel, warmed on the radiator. He set his small soft hands on her shoulders as she held out the pyjama trousers for him to step into. She led him, buttoned up and teeth brushed, to his room, pulled the quilt up to his chin and held a finger to her lips.

Richard was working on a big contract case in the sitting room: had been there all day. He didn't like to be disturbed.

But the sitting room was where he answered the telephone.

He had laughed at the idea of her having a mobile phone: why on earth? He had pointed out to her that she would need to give bank references for a contract. But Sophie happened to know that there were mobile phones you could buy for almost nothing, topped up in cash. She thought perhaps she would get herself one. Richard might disapprove but . . . but . . . She swallowed at the thought of his discovering her with such a thing.

She would be brave. She left Rufus in his bedroom and went down. Supper to be made, the vegetables were chopped and laid out. All she needed to do was find the piece of paper. She came into the sitting room and Richard's head turned, briefly. He looked back at the page but she could tell from the set of his shoulders that she had irritated him just by entering the room, just by her continued presence there. She walked to the wastepaper bin and swiftly picked it up.

'What are you doing?' he said sharply.

'Empt—' She had to catch her breath, turning for the door so she wouldn't see him, the basket still in her hand. *My father, he's my father.* Be brave. 'Emptying the bins, darling,' and the door closing, closing behind her. 'Supper in ten minutes,' she called back over her shoulder.

It had been a knackering day. Nat felt as though she'd been running on adrenalin and it had used her up, she was twitching with tiredness but she couldn't stop. From where it sat behind the bar Beth's phone sent out a signal, the steady pulse of a message just for Nat. *Find me, find me, find me. Keep going.*

In the fading light she stood at the turning into the little modern close where Beth had rented. She'd been on her feet seven hours, and she swayed. It was silent in the dusk, some curtains drawn, no lights visible. She hesitated. In her pocket, though, she had the keys. Two keys on a greasy strip of ribbon, given to her by Mo Hawkins.

Craig had remembered about the daycare centre lunch, even if Janine hadn't. His trailbike had hurtled into the car park ten minutes after their arrival and he had run into the kitchen pulling off his helmet just in time to garnish the plates, and have his head tousled by half a dozen old ladies, all high as kites on a hot day out and two sips of house white, as he did the rounds with their ploughmans'. There had been gales of laughter coming from the garden all afternoon. Some of them had circumvented the group leader to get a second glass, and by the end of the day they had got through a bottle and a half of port on top.

Craig hadn't been himself, though. He had tolerated the old people's jokes about gherkins and questions about girlfriends, he had nodded and been polite, but barely: Nat could see he was on the edge. Ollie. Nat had cornered him in the kitchen to ask if he was OK, and he had just mumbled, avoiding her eye.

'You go,' said Janine, hanging a damp dishcloth over the pumps at seven. The minibus had come back for the old folks at six thirty and there was a brief respite. If anything it had got hotter, and no one normal wanted to sit in a steamy little pub till a lot later, when a breeze might come up from the water. 'Steve's said he shouldn't be much longer, anyway, he was only over to Ipswich in the rig.' Something else had come into Janine's face then, thoughtful.

'He's talking about moving in,' she said. 'Says he doesn't want his name over the door or nothing, just . . .' and the frown, Nat could see, was just her pretending to weigh it up. 'He wants to see more of me.' And then Janine couldn't disguise it, the broad grin spread and spread.

Be happy for her. Not that hard: Steve was a good guy. Quiet, responsible: Janine's adoring face as he took over some task. He'd been clearing the drains for her a week ago.

The close where Beth had lived was still quiet, just the odd murmur in a back garden, a bit of barbecue smoke from somewhere. In her pocket Nat's hand curled around the key. There was another one out there somewhere, because Beth hadn't returned hers.

'The latest one, then,' she had said to Janine, who was shaking her head trying to remember. 'That last message, saying she wasn't coming back. What time did it come in?'

'It came in late, yes,' Janine said, screwing up her face in an effort to remember. 'One, two, maybe. Woke me up.'

Somewhere between Thursday night and Friday morning, Friday 12 August. Nat tried to rerun the conversation she'd had with Janine. Bad temper, woken up in the middle of the night and Steve needing a lie-in. Two o'clock in the morning of that Friday sixteen days ago, someone, if not Beth then someone, had held her phone in their hand, composed the message. Someone who knew a bit about her but not enough, that she had a mother but not that her mother was in the West Country and they hated each other. Knew where she worked, and who her friends were. If you had someone's mobile you knew a lot about them.

She tried to think of what she knew, about mobile phones, what the police could do. Two young girls had been murdered, a hundred miles away and ten years ago, and they traced their last whereabouts through the mobile signal. How old had they been? Ten, eleven years old and already with their own mobile phones, back then. Nat took out her own and looked at it. It couldn't save you, could it? It could get you into trouble, was all she knew. She'd ended up deleting the dating app because just looking at it made her feel sick. All those blokes.

Beth hadn't really bothered with online dating, she had laughed when Nat had got the app. What had she said? Barmaid was one profession where you had cut out the middle man: you were already in the pub with blokes. But then Beth could find a boyfriend just walking to the bus stop. Nat's argument had been that she didn't want to go out with anyone she'd seen propping up the bar day in, day out. After . . . after Jim, she had wanted someone who knew nothing about her. She shoved the phone back in her pocket.

So. Beth's phone, sitting in the pub up there above the optics would tell the police where she'd been. Where it had been. If the phone had been here all along, someone had been here to use it.

It wasn't safe there. The thought sprang into her head. Janine shouldn't have put it there, it was practically on display. It would have been an automatic response, it was where they put stuff people left in the bar: an umbrella, a lunchbox. Victor's bobble hat had found its way up on to the shelf one time.

Victor, Victor. The thought of him rose unbidden, and with it the tide of formless anxiety. He's safe, he's safe, he's in a hospital: Nat pushed the thought into that box.

Janine had put it up there like it was lost property, and Beth'd be back for it.

Someone else had been using it, though. Here, in Beth's place. The thought that was forming wasn't welcome, particularly not where she stood, with night falling visibly, softly, like a blur in the evening air. Nat turned into the close. It was quiet. She wondered if you could access the house from the rear. She tried to assess where the river lay. The close was a small loop of seventies' semis, a circle of ground planted with ornamental trees in the centre, for privacy, she supposed. So that everyone couldn't look into everyone else's front room. The soft twilight blanketed everything, it was so still, so quiet. Then something altered and she moved her head, trying to trace it. Something . . . and there, she saw behind a curtained window a fine crack of light had appeared. She approached the front door. Along a window sill this side of the curtain she could see a row of ornaments. She stopped, turned, gauged the distance from her to number six, where Beth had lived. Line of sight: yes.

Unless he came in at the back, to send those messages. He or she? Whoever. Someone had sent them.

She stepped up to the door and pressed the bell.

The woman didn't open the door more than a crack to start with, all Nat could see was heavy framed glasses. She was sourly pleased about Beth's disappearance: she didn't seem interested in why Nat was asking, she was itching to dish some kind of dirt. 'Yes, I knew her,' she said and the door opened an inch or two more. Hefty, dark perm, in big slippers, maybe seventy. 'Well, to look at. She did shout to me now and then but I never answered.'

She spoke with satisfaction, and Nat stared back at her, feeling her jaw rigid.

'When did you last see her?' she said quietly. 'Do you remember?'

The woman leaned against the door jamb, examining her. Monkey-brown eyes calculating. 'Month back?' she said eventually. 'Beginning of the month. Hanging out her washing, didn't see that often, neither, so I remember. Tol' her, you can hang your knickers to dry inside, it's not decent.'

'In the back garden?' The brown eyes stared, hostile, and Nat persisted. 'Is there a back way into the gardens?'

'No gate, if thass what you mean,' said the woman, without interest. 'There's just the field behind, and the river. I seen her come up that way now an again.'

'Not lately,' said Nat, her heart in her mouth suddenly, please, please, let Beth walk up there now, through the grass from the river, but the woman shook her head.

'Foxes is all,' she said. 'Disgusting what they bring up.'

'Foxes?'

'Doing their dirt. Scrabbling around.'

'Late in the night?' Nat held her breath. 'Any particular . . . a couple of weeks ago, did you hear . . . around one, two in the morning? Say, Thursday eleventh, that night?'

The woman's face screwed up, leaning forwards into the crack. 'Could be,' she said. Then with relish, 'Good riddance, I say. She had no consideration.' Examining Nat. 'There was noise.'

'What kind of noise?' said Nat, 'Mrs—'

'What d'you need my name for?' said the woman suspiciously, then, relenting, self-important suddenly, 'Margaret, then, if you like.'

'What noise, um, Margaret?' Nat had the idea Margaret and Beth had never been on first name terms. Or any terms at all, but that didn't mean they hadn't known all about each other. 'Like, loud music, you mean?'

'And the rest,' said the woman. There was movement inside the house and the shape of a man appeared behind her in the hall, Nat could see wisps of hair on an almost bald head, shining in the hall light. Margaret snapped at him to go back in, and he lumbered off meekly. 'She didn't care who heard,' said Margaret. 'It upset my husband.'

Nat knew she was talking about sex. Margaret's face was pressed to the crack now, obscuring everything behind. 'Come a cropper, has she? About time. They need to learn, women like that. Old enough to know better. Only ends one way.'

Nat wanted to shove the woman backwards into her hallway and throttle her till her little eyes popped but instead she stood very still. One last try. 'Did you see—'

'Nothing,' said Margaret, and she was savage with disappointment. 'I never saw none of them. I jus' heard 'em.' And the door snapped shut.

For a second Nat stared at the closed door with loathing, behind it the woman shuffling after her husband into the curtained front room, a row brewing. I could just go, she thought, sod it, what am I doing here? But she didn't turn for home. She crossed the road.

The upper storey of number six was dark; she'd already ascertained from Mo Hawkins that the house had been converted to two flats but she hadn't had a tenant above Beth for a year. She thought of a man, in the shadows, of all those men out there, online, in clubs, at bus stops. A man letting himself in and out, after dark, at two in the morning when no one can see.

Why would he do that? The messages. Covering something up? Wanting us to know, stringing us along.

Or maybe she's OK. Alive. The spark sprang, as she hoped, fervently, unable to stop herself, hoping against hope. Please. Please.

In the deep quiet she fished the key out of her pocket and let herself in. There was a smell, immediately, in the narrow carpeted hallway: faint, fusty. Was that just the smell of a fridge gone stale, unemptied bins somewhere in the heat? It wasn't the smell of Beth, perfume and foundation. Beth's smell was musky, sweet. Nat swallowed, painfully: you couldn't bring a smell back, but she'd know it if it hit her. She groped for a light switch. There was a crack and flash above her head and for a second she had to hold very still, fighting panic. A blown bulb, that's all. She made herself walk on, feeling with her hand along the wall for the next switch. There.

The hall ended in a kind of lobby. She'd been here once or twice, fish and chips from the van in her kitchen, sunbathing on the patch of grass beyond the window, but Beth never took pride in it like it was a home, never showed her around. Half cleared, the place contained nothing that spoke to Nat about the real Beth, the woman she'd worked alongside for nearly two years. It was dismal. Bad carpet, worse wallpaper, an open door into a kitchenette, another closed, the third door, on her right opening on to the front room was ajar. She pushed at it gingerly and saw two bin bags. She stepped back again.

In the lobby she saw now there was the shape of a

walled-in staircase that must lead to the upstairs flat through a separate entrance, and a cupboard set in under it. She looked at the bin bags, back to the cupboard door. It was open a crack. This must be where, thought Nat, didn't Mo Hawkins say a cupboard? She pulled it open with a fingertip and there was a socket, inside the cupboard. Otherwise it was empty, furred with dust save a smudge, mobile phone sized, on the floor.

Deep in the night, everyone asleep, coming inside on soft feet to send a message on Beth's phone. She envisioned a man. Because every time she closed her eyes and thought of Beth, there was a man's arm around her, a man staring at her, watching her backside move, looking down her front.

A sleaze off Tinder, some heavy breather, a lecherous punter following her home, had her locked in his cellar or . . . or worse.

Would the neighbours have seen him coming in here, so late? A man, young, old, married, single, did he drive, did he walk whistling into the close? The possibilities multiplied, teetering, dangerous. Nat backed out into the lobby.

The black plastic bin bags sat there in the door to the dark front room: she could see straight off how Mo Hawkins had divided the stuff. Rubbish in one, the other one full of clothes, for flogging on eBay. Would the police go through the rubbish? Should she touch nothing? In one rash movement Nat upended the bag full of clothes and it all came tumbling out: crop tops, the favourite sequinned mini, the wedges, the sandals, jeans, jeans, more jeans. The pair she never washed, she was wearing them in to the perfect colour, Beth said, the perfect jeans, *moulded to my arse*, and slapping her own backside, friendly.

Mo Hawkins wouldn't have given it a thought, why a girl like Beth would leave it all behind. It wasn't like she could splash out on a new wardrobe, on what she earned – or maybe Mo thought Beth would be looked after, a sugar daddy, taken round the shops. Not likely. Beth wasn't that girl. Beth wanted her freedom. Party girl Beth wasn't going to be locked up in a carpeted pink pad or a chrome and glass high rise.

Hold on, hold on, thought Nat. Those were the jeans she'd been wearing when . . . and she tugged them from the pile and held them up. She could see Beth's shape in them and for a moment the sight stopped her. Then, tentative, she put a hand in the back pocket, not expecting it to be there still, but it was. She fished it out. A crumpled page on hospital letterhead, she scanned it but it told her nothing she didn't already know, did it? An appointment has been made for you with Mr Sarafidis, clinic 1A.

You liked it here, Beth. I know you did. We were friends.

That morning in May, she'd heard Beth sigh as Nat turned quickly in front of the toilet mirror, not wanting to see herself, turned to hide her face in Beth's hair. 'We've all been there, love,' Beth had said. 'They tell you, get it done quick and it's a missed period, nothing more. Don't feel like that, though, does it?' Giving her a little shake, her arm round Nat's shoulders. 'Come on,' she said, in her rough kind voice, *coom on*, 'we'll be all right.'

We.

Nat set the page aside on the carpet and stared down at the heap, moved her hand through it, sifting. Something. Something was missing. She sat back on her haunches, staring, then stood. She went into the kitchen, but it was still buzzing at her, knocking from side to side inside her head like a trapped fly.

She felt apprehension creep in from the corners, the shadows. Staring into the narrow room, she walked up to the glazed garden door at the far end and looked out through the glass. The light was almost gone but you could see the long grass of a meadow, silver in the dusk, the shape of a clump of willows. The river must be down there.

The kitchen was unused, not even dirty, bar a film of dust on top of the toaster and a scattering of crumbs. Beth was not a cook, you couldn't trust her even to warm up a pie for a punter. She lived off crisps and wine gums like a kid, that was why she was still breaking out in spots at closer to thirty than twenty and she knew it, but she didn't care enough: Beth was never one to stare at herself and find fault. Nat didn't expect to find herself thinking of Beth in a kitchen of all places but suddenly she was everywhere, a whispering presence.

It was here you'd expect the smell, if things were going off, but it only smelt a bit fusty. Nat decided not to look in the fridge; she walked quickly back past it and out. Bathroom.

An old-fashioned bath with limescale following the drip of a tap. Bottles of cleaning products stacked in a bucket, a cloth hung over its lip. The toilet was clean, but that was probably Mo Hawkins, never happier than chucking bleach around, and you could smell it. The door on a mirrored cabinet above the sink hung open, the shelves half cleared. Painkillers. Tubes of make-up, foundation. Nat stood closer. Roaccutane She frowned. Acne medication. She remembered Beth saying how hard it had been to get that out of the doctor because of the side-effects. The foundation was expensive stuff, by their standard, anyway, hers and Beth's, on barmaids' wages. 'Should be tax deductible,' Nat had said to her one time and Beth had only snorted uncomprehending because, of course, it was all cash in hand. 'Joke,' Nat had said.

She wouldn't have left it behind, anyway, no more than she would her jeans. Not the make-up, not the medication. Nat added it up in her head, ready to take it to the police.

What was the alternative? That it might be Beth herself sneaking back under cover of darkness, sending the messages, hiding out for reasons of her own. Nat strained to think what those reasons might be and came up with nothing. And then the smell drifted back, it was here beneath the bleach and the disinfectant, whatever it was, something sweet, something sickly. Nat swallowed: the light, suddenly, seemed bright. Bedroom.

The bed was stripped, the drawers all pulled out of the chest, empty, and a poster was peeling off from the wall by a corner. She pulled the wardrobe door open, setting wire hangers clattering. There were no curtains at the wide plate-glass window. Feeling exposed, Nat turned, slow, forcing herself to look harder, in the glare of the overhead light. A wastepaper basket, emptied. A varnished dressing table, old-style, low, with a bevelled rectangle of mirror, one earring settled in a crack in the veneer, gilt tasselled, and she remembered it swinging against Beth's cheek. She picked it up.

Under the bed? She lowered herself to look and in that moment she caught something out of the corner of her eye and without thinking she straightened, went for the light switch by the door and dropped flat, in the dark.

What was it? She had heard something, had she? Seen something? Had it been her own reflection in the wide dark expanse of glass, or was there . . . was there? She listened.

The faintest sound of music, far off, a burst of distant laughter that stopped. And in the quiet something else: an engine running, steady, close by. A car with its engine idling. Nat waited for the engine to be switched off, for a door to open and slam, for voices, someone walking up next door's path or across the road. But it was still running.

Someone was waiting in a car, outside the house.

Just a car. Just someone waiting, picking a teenager up, taking five minutes before going inside. But in her head another story fell softly into place like a child's game, like marbles running, the logic of it, click, click, click. Was he coming back for the phone?

The engine turned, and stopped. Silence. She waited, waited. Out there someone sat in his car. A minute passed, another. Five minutes. Crouched, stiff, Nat began to unbend.

Then, so soft, so careful she hardly caught it, the sound of a car door opening. Closing. The faintest rasp of a footstep on tarmac.

Nat was bent over in the dark, following the sound. Closer – closer – the crunch of footsteps on the gravel footpath. Coming up the path towards the front door, there was something about the footsteps – slow, deliberate – that brought the hairs up on the back of her neck. *As if he knew she was there.*

A key. A key. Did he have a key? Her body was cramped and stiff and at the centre of it her belly felt hard, like a stone: she couldn't move.

Get up, she ordered herself, *run at him, whoever he is, shout and scream so everyone can hear, don't just sit here waiting*— then suddenly someone *was* shouting, somewhere along the back gardens, next door. Something smashed. A woman's voice, muffled then louder as if a back door had been flung open.

Not a young voice. Ranting, nasty. It was Margaret from next door, shouting at her husband. Nat could hear him murmuring.

Standing with her hand against the wall in the dark, Nat heard words, identified a row. *I've told you fifty fucking times not to*— The swear words so shocking in the old woman's voice that they shook Nat out of whatever state she'd been in.

And then as suddenly as the row had broken out, it stopped: the door closed, she heard it slam, for a second muffling the voices then silencing them.

As the sound died away she heard the feet on the gravel, going back the way they'd come, quick now, though, a car door slammed.

A breath, held one beat then Nat moved. She charged, blundering through the flat's narrow hallway and out into the road, because she would batter on the car's doors, she would press her face against the window, she would haul him out.

The car was gone, the red ghost of tail lights through shrubs at the entrance of the close the only sign it had ever been there. And Nat, alone on the pavement in the warm dark with the sound of footsteps in her head.

Chapter Nine

Monday

'It's disgusting.'

The six-bed room where Victor lay was directly behind the nurses' station. The double doors that might have separated them had been open all night and were still open now, so he could hear their conversation. They didn't really lower their voices: it made Victor feel odd, as though he had already passed beyond civilised society, he wasn't fully alive any more. Or was it something else making him feel odd? Best not to think, best not to wonder.

They were talking about Sophie. They hadn't used her name, but they were talking about her, or people in what they assumed was her position.

'They just dump them. Nothing we can do.' Someone clicked their tongue, someone exhaled disapprovingly. He hoped it wasn't her, Lisa. 'You'd think. I mean, what's a ninety-two-year-old doing living in a caravan?'

I like it there, he wanted to say. It liked me. Among friends. Until he wasn't, any more. Until that man walked out of the shadows. I couldn't live with her. She'd love to have me but she can't.

Victor had known Sophie's telephone number by heart since she had first bought that tiny house in London, twenty years ago. Richard had moved in with her, not she with him: he had taken over the mortgage, although she had assured him the house was still in her name. But now it seemed that his tired brain had dispensed with that information, he could assemble four, five of the digits but they wouldn't stay in the right order. The screen he could use to make a telephone call or pay to watch television on, was attached to a mechanical arm about ten inches from his head on the pillow, dark. No use to him anyway, until he could remember, until he could locate money and numbers and make his body work.

He couldn't tell, now, if he'd spent the night asleep or awake. He remembered someone filling his water jug. He remembered sitting up to take a drink. Or had that been a dream? He didn't seem to be able to sit up now. Yesterday he had thought he was improving. This morning there was a sheen on everything, a silvered edge, it all looked as though it might shift and slide, like mercury.

It was just after seven, the clock told him that. Abandoning the telephone number, he decided to put something else in the right order. The breakfast trolley would be round at seven thirty, pushed by a man called Emile who had been born in the Philippines. Emile was allowed to open his sandwiches for him but not allowed to help him sit up. The nurses' shifts changed at eight.

And as if the thought brought her to him, Lisa walked in from the corridor past the nurses' station right up to his bed and smiled. 'I'm finishing up,' she said, a hand on his arm. What was that look? Searching him. He felt muddled, fuzzy. There was something he needed to say.

Beside the bed on the cabinet was the jug of water. He looked at it and back to Lisa. Police, he wanted to say, but the word wouldn't appear. His lips felt dry and cracked: his tongue moved cautiously to wet them, an effort, but it felt as though that jellied muscle was the strongest in his body. Victor could see himself as if from above, so old, so helpless. So close. So close to something that appeared to him as a dark doorway, that led down into the earth.

Police. His lips trembled as he tried to press them. Plosive. The P sound is a plosive. Nothing came out. Her hand on his arm lifted, hesitated, patted.

'Back this evening,' she said.

His eyelids fluttered.

He was woken by the sound of a chair being scraped across the lino. Whiskery Mary was dragging the chair up to the bed, knitting spilling from her bag and a packet of the cheap biscuits from the shop parked on the bed on his abdomen.

'Oh, Victor,' she said consolingly, asking questions and answering them herself as she always did. 'Oh, Victor, this is a bad lookout isn't it, isn't this a bad lookout? Isn't it.'

His eyes followed her as she settled back in the chair with satisfaction, but as she began to talk he closed them again. Weary. He had never felt so weary.

Nat was running, running, down a lane between high hedges at night when the river opened in front of her, wide and dark, she smelled the weed, she saw dead things floating. She sat up with a start, with the sun hot on her face.

Last night she had run. Without even taking a breath,

it seemed, her sandals flapping on the tarmac loud in her ears. A car had passed her, but it had been going the other way, it didn't come from behind her. A dark car with mud on the wheels, she had not looked into the windscreen as it went by.

If that row hadn't broken out, if she'd just waited, he might have come in. If she'd had the balls to go out when she first heard the engine running, she'd have seen his face. She needed to go to the police but she could imagine the questions they would ask her. Incredulous. *You what? A suspicious engine running? Footsteps? And what did you think you were doing there? How can you be sure it wasn't your friend, trying to avoid her landlady, some ex—*

Because I'm sure she's missing, she heard herself insist. It came to her that this was a game, to the man whose footsteps she'd heard on the path. The man who had sat at the kerb in his car. He could be patient. That was what this was to him, coming back to the close late at night, returning to the scene of . . . whatever. To send a message he knew no one would believe, in the end, a tease. A game.

Next move.

Had he seen her go in there? Had he seen the lights go on? Had he seen them go off again? Might he have thought whoever was here had gone, out of the front door? Might he have assumed it was Mo Hawkins and Mo Hawkins was of no interest to him?

Had she walked past him on her way in? That thought stopped her in her tracks. She scanned her memory, but came up with nothing. The close was quiet, dark, innocent, the safest dullest place in the world – until Margaret started shrieking.

If she had run out sooner? Shouting the odds at some bloke in his car. Old Margaret shuffling out in her slippers with her husband cowering behind her in the doorway. Or was it none of their business, heads down and turn up the sound on the telly?

It had taken her to get within a hundred yards of the cottage, before Nat had slowed, those red tail lights in her head, the sound of those footsteps in her ears and as the adrenalin ebbed she felt the other thing return. Fear. *Shit, shit, shit.* She looked up, and there was a pickup parked outside her cottage, and a man standing beside it.

It was Jonathan Dowd, Beth's ex, and he stared. Coming close to him she was aware of her own breathing, sweat down her back in the heat. 'Are you all right?' he said, taking a step towards her, concerned. He put out a hand, touching her on the arm. Then he stepped back abruptly, awkwardly respectful. 'Something's happened,' he said. 'You've found something. It's her, isn't it? Something's happened to her.' Breathless.

Nat began to shake her head, not even sure what she was going to say. 'Her clothes,' she began. 'I went to her flat. She's left them all behind—' There was something, though, wasn't there? Something wrong, something missing. It was as if the run had momentarily deprived her brain of enough oxygen, she couldn't think straight. 'What are you doing here?' she said. Then, of course, the most important thing. 'He came. *He* came, while I was there.'

In the yellow streetlight she saw him grow pale, open his mouth, hesitate. 'He? Who's he?'

She shook her head to clear it, aware she sounded like a crazy person. 'Whoever has been sending those messages.

He came back for the phone, maybe he was going to send another message, maybe—'

'Why would . . .' Dowd swallowed, and his Adam's apple bobbed. 'Why wouldn't – he, if there is – why wouldn't he take the phone with him? Why risk coming back?'

Nat stared, trying to construct her theory. 'Because . . . I don't know.' Tried harder. 'The police can track phones, can't they? Say where they were when messages were sent, that could lead them to him? Wasn't there . . .' She searched her memory. 'When those two girls were killed, years ago, that school caretaker, they got him because their phones were traced.' She stopped, stubborn, chin in the air.

Dowd shrugged, uneasily. She felt impatience rise at his refusal to understand.

'Or it could be just his game, don't you see? Or wanting . . . wanting—' She broke off, feeling her own reluctance suddenly. 'Wanting to be there, right in there with all her stuff.' Beth's clothes, the jeans moulded to her arse, the smell of her perfume and the phone, her phone. Like her firstborn, wasn't that what Janine had said? 'I don't know. A sort of . . . trophy.'

She didn't like the word even as she said it. It meant something terrible. She shut up.

'I'm not sure I understand,' said Dowd, looking pale, defeated. 'You're sure it was . . . him.' Frowning. 'But did you actually see . . . him? A man.' Cleared his throat. 'Did you see anyone at all?'

Nat felt herself sag: if she couldn't explain herself to this harmless streak of nothing, how was she going to be able to talk sense to the police? His hand was back on her arm, though. 'No, I didn't mean—'

He squeezed. 'I believe you. You know I do. You know I think something has happened to her.'

She began to shake her head, somehow it wasn't helping. Dowd was an obsessive – if she involved him the police would see that straight off, a failed relationship with Beth, a loner, a loser.

'I just want to help.' His voice was resigned, as if he was used to people thinking the way she was thinking.

'I know,' she said. 'I – I think . . . thank you. Yes. I need all the help I can get, don't I?'

'I'm spending most of my time on the river,' Dowd said, calm. 'I need to make the most of these tides. Early afternoons I get back.' Holding his ground.

'All right,' she'd said then, awkwardly. 'Maybe I'll come and find you one afternoon.' It wasn't till his lights had disappeared round the corner at the top of the lane that she realised he hadn't said what he'd been doing there.

Letting herself in she had stopped, registering something she hadn't really thought about before. She had left the door unlocked – half the time she did, the village being the village, and she had nothing worth nicking. That was going to have to change.

She'd locked and bolted it behind her.

The sun seemed too hot now. Looking at her phone on the bedside table Nat saw that it was late, almost ten. How had she slept so long? All that adrenalin, perhaps. And no wake-up call from Jim, either. That thought bothered her, even as she hauled on her clothes, flew downstairs, gulped cereal – milk on the turn, she hadn't shopped in weeks. Can't have it both ways, tell him to leave you alone then miss him when he does.

Running again, up to the pub and mercifully shaded by hedges, Nat knew it wasn't that she missed Jim, except it made her feel uneasy. Wondering where he was. The thought of going back and starting again made her feel sick, the cereal churning. Think of something else: Dowd. She could sail there, to where he was camping.

Early afternoon.

She would ask Paddy.

Chapter Ten

Just the door between them: he'd sat out of sight and watched her go into the close. Wait, give her time, talk to the neighbours. Play detective if you like, go on, knock on doors.

She had never minded the neighbours hearing them at it. *Not against the law, is it?* Not like they were doing it in the back garden. But it had got on his nerves, the old bitch next door banging on the wall, that had set something up inside his head, irritating him. She wouldn't have cared if they'd seen him come and go – but he didn't want that. So he took care not to be seen.

Or not so as anyone would know, anyway. Other times he could be anyone, couldn't he? Passing her in the street, walking into a bar as she walked out, standing in a corner of the pub. Opening a door for her.

He was sure he'd got away in time, last night; the key was to stay calm, don't speed off, keep her guessing. She'd known he was there, waiting for her on the path, just a door between them. She'd known he was waiting for her. That was what mattered.

The pub had a tiny car park to the side, tucked in under overgrown hedges. Steve said he'd trim them but he hadn't got to it yet. As she approached it Nat saw Craig standing next to his trailbike, slowly pulling off his helmet.

There was the sound of a car coming up the lane and he shifted, stepping closer in under the straggly hedge.

'What kind of time d'you call this, Craig?' she said. 'You're almost as late as me.' Then, peering closer. 'You all right?' she asked, abrupt. His eyes looked red.

'The police called me.' He was staring, unfocused.

Behind the pub door she could hear glasses being put away, the murmur of Janine's voice. 'You talked to them?' she asked.

His hand went to his mouth and she could see his nails bitten down and raw. He nodded.

'Did they tell you anything?'

He hadn't shaved recently, his chin dark, his eyes deep-set. He looked like he hadn't slept. Would they have treated him as a suspect? They start with the people you're closest to, if you're murdered, she'd read that somewhere. Most women murdered by their husbands, or their fathers. But teenage boys?

They'd been less close lately. Had they actually fallen out? She hadn't seen that. She'd been too busy thinking about her own shit, hadn't she?

'He'd been in the water for a long time,' he said and she saw his eyes dark with horror. 'A week. Maybe more.'

His head bobbed, he seemed to be having trouble getting the words out. 'They want me to come in,' he said, blurting. She gaped, then he said, before she could even process that, 'His wrists were tied up in a rag. Ollie's were.' And Craig was staring; he was crying. She put an arm round his shoulder, helpless. Ollie. First time he came in the pub he'd barely started shaving, that sprouty chin boys get, but already he had a way with girls, the fast nervy way. Had he made someone jealous? Craig jealous? She couldn't get her head around it.

'Tied up?' That was where that picture was wrong. A loose punch, maybe, she'd seen that happen outside this pub and plenty of others. But to tie someone's wrists? 'I don't understand.'

Craig's head was shaking too, side to side, his black hair lank and greasy. 'No,' he said. 'There was blood on the rag, they said, not his blood.'

'They told you that? Why would they tell you that?'

'They want me to give a DNA sample. I don't know if they think . . . if the blood—' He stopped, then started again. He was trying so hard to keep calm but she could feel him trembling under her arm. 'They were trying to scare me, I think.' A kind of shudder, then he was still. 'It's not my blood, I know that, so there's no reason for me to be scared, but . . .' And when he looked into her face she thought, You don't get over this. Shit like this. Suddenly he looked lost, like a great overgrown kid, stumbling over his words, holding everything inside. Too young for this.

'I mean, we were mates, what if I, you know, borrowed his sweatshirt and gave it back, it'd have my DNA on it, right?'

Nat exhaled. 'I don't know, Craig,' she said. 'I doubt it,

you know?' He was in the water a week, she didn't say. 'And if there's a reasonable explanation . . . anyway. Just . . . I would just go along.' She tried to smile at him, to look reassuring, but he stepped back, stumbling.

'I dunno,' he mumbled. On the other side of the hedge the car pulled up and she heard the voices of cheerful punters piling out of their cab. *All right, mate? Nah, keep the change.*

Janine called through the open door, 'That you?' Exasperated.

'Come on,' she muttered, tugging Craig's sleeve, turning him and pushing him ahead of her into the pub.

Blood on a rag. Not an accident. Someone had murdered him. Something occurred to her, it sickened her, she felt stiff with horror. Had he been alive, when they put him in the water?

Ollie, full of life, full of the future.

When she thought of him it was sitting there in the corner, following Beth with his eyes.

First chance she got, Nat called the police.

When she finally came on the line DS Donna Garfield no longer sounded annoyed, exactly, more frantic. Nat, hiding behind the shed at the pub garden so as to keep out of Janine's sight, started talking straight away, tripping over herself. Not making enough sense.

'Craig told me – he works here – he told me you're sure Ollie was put in the water by someone, he was tied up in some kind of cloth.'

'I can't talk to you about that.' It sounded like the woman was going to hang up on her. 'Look, if there's nothing concrete—'

Nat just blundered on. 'Her phone. It's connected, I don't know how, but it's connected. Ollie was really smitten with her, she disappears and now we've found her phone—'

DS Garfield cleared her throat. 'If I'm honest, love, you're not making much sense. We've got no reason to think there's any connection between your mate doing a runner and Oliver's death. None. As far as I can tell all you've got is he fancied her.'

Nat felt herself tremble with frustration. 'That's *not* all. Not all. Something has happened to her too,' she said, enunciating it as clearly as she could. 'Something bad. That's the connection. That's the connection.'

A silence.

'She's gone. Someone sent a message saying she was going to see her mum, but her mum hasn't seen her.' Desperate. 'She's missed a hospital appointment. She left her stuff, everything. *She left her phone.* It's been wiped.'

A sigh, reluctant. 'I can give you her mum's number,' said Nat, flailing now. 'She'll tell you, they haven't spoken in years.'

Why had she said that? Because now Beth's mum would be badmouthing her to a policewoman. She'd just wanted the nasty old cow to know, this was serious. The police were on it.

'All right.' Donna Garfield had sounded weary. 'All right. I've got all that, Miss, ah . . . We'll . . . we will certainly follow it up. We will.'

When she hung up, though, all Nat felt was boiling rage. Donna Garfield might be going to follow it up – eventually. She had no sense that the woman took her seriously. But there *was* a connection. Ollie's death, and Beth's disappearance: there had to be.

Her back against the shed, she squeezed her eyes shut, trying to think of what might have passed between them, but all she could come up with was Ollie gazing like a puppy, Beth giving him no encouragement. Had Ollie been in Beth's flat? Nat couldn't imagine it. Beth wasn't interested in young lads, she had always kept them at arm's length – lads, she had confided more than once, were always going off on one. Talking about you after, smashing stuff up when you dumped them. Topping themselves. Ollie hadn't topped himself. Ollie had been murdered.

'Oi!' Nat's eyes snapped open and she peered around the shed. Janine was at the back door, hands on hips, frowning. Hastily, Nat got the tray she'd stashed under her arm and began clearing the tables. Janine turned and went back inside and following her with her eyes Nat saw Craig hovering in the doorway.

They'd asked him for a DNA sample. Setting glasses on the tray in a trance, scraping plates, half-eaten ploughmans', all she could think was: that's what she should have told the police, shouted down the phone. She should have told them to get into Beth's flat, before it was too late, before Mo Hawkins got her rubber gloves on and scrubbed the place down.

Because that's where it happened.

She lifted the tray and began to walk, one foot behind the other, towards the pub's back door but she was somewhere else. In that flat. And she knew with a sudden suffocating certainty that he'd been there, he had been *everywhere* in there. Nat could see him, in her head, the man whose heavy tread she'd heard outside, she *felt* him. He was looking through Beth's most private things. He was choosing what to take and what to leave – and there was nothing Beth could do about it.

And it was as if Nat saw in infrared, or something, the walls of that little box where Beth had lived – and they were splashed with blood.

Chapter Eleven

The lights ran over his head like the white lines on a motorway, as he was wheeled down the corridor.

'There's something we're just not quite sure about,' the new consultant had said, a pretty girl with a mass of curly hair tied back and glasses, not what the word consultant summoned up to him but all the better for that. 'Your readings are a bit off.' In his old life he would have made a joke with that term, but now he simply wondered what on earth she could actually mean by it. He felt life slipping from him. 'So we'll just try to clear it up with a scan, is that all right?' Victor managed something like a nod.

Lisa, Lisa. She was gone, of course, she was coming back later, she had told him that. He had no real idea of the time. There was another nurse with her hand on his arm as he was wheeled down the corridor: looking down it appeared to him as the arm of someone he didn't know, someone terribly, terribly old. What had the nurse said, though, as she bent to release the wheels on the bed and began to push?

He didn't know if he had imagined it, dreamed it, wished it. 'Your daughter telephoned,' she said again.

At that moment he heard someone say his name, 'Mr Powell?'

The rolling bed slowed. 'He's on his way for a scan,' said the new nurse.

'Victor?' Victor found he could turn his head towards the sound and for a moment he just stared, trying to recognise the speaker. Once he had had radar, social radar, Sophie used to call it, fondly, and everyone he knew was there, a small blip, a big blip, an MFV or a warship, someone he'd met once in the queue at the post office or someone dear, someone close. Sophie. The fog shifted, a window opened. Owen. Owen Wilkins, the site manager. A surge of relief allowed him to nod, the tremble of a smile. He formed an O, for Owen, and he saw Wilkins frown, which he also knew was Wilkins' standard response. The site manager had a different kind of radar, he intuited.

'Just . . . came to see how things were going,' he said. Victor could sense the nurse's impatience, some senses had become keener, hadn't they? When had he that thought before? In another life. Wilkins had a . . . what was the word? An aura.

Not that Victor believed in the aura, though Sophie sometimes had confessed to it, in her old life as a parole officer, his soft Sophie leading criminals by the hand. She had developed a belief that you could sense a bad man from a good man before you looked at his notes and knew what he had done. It hadn't helped her, had it? Not where

Richard was concerned. Victor could feel his thoughts scattering, like rabbits. He chased them down. Wilkins was a severe man who offended people sometimes – but try as he might Victor could not work out if Wilkins was good or bad. He was here, wasn't he? He had come in the ambulance with Victor all that time ago, the day the old life slipped.

The nurse began to push again, slowly, and out of the corner of his eye Victor could tell Wilkins was walking alongside them. He closed his eyes and there was the caravan site, the long sunny slope down to the water, he could smell cut grass and the river, light glittering on the grey water. Wilkins bending to help him unfold his chair, standing back stiffly as he sat, Wilkins poised and waiting for something. Then the man's voice sharp, turned on some teenagers as music blared, two pitches away.

The rolling bed was moving briskly now. At his side Wilkins cleared his throat. 'I'll wait, then, shall I?' he said, more to the nurse than to Victor, and Victor opened his eyes in time to see him step back and let them move on. A lift, a change of light, the hiss of a pneumatic door. Imagine if these were the last, the last sensations. The last sights.

The world was turning, beyond the lift, beyond the corridors, people were doing their business out in the sunlit world and he let whiskery Mary, gossiping, come back into his mind. She had been talking about the film crew, all crowding into the post office and buying every ice cream in the freezer cabinet. A nice man taking the time to chat to her, not a film star. The girls hanging about outside the post office giggling, asking for ice creams, and the crew's big trucks full of equipment on the pavement.

That was the world, the world outside.

The lift's brushed metal doors slid open and they turned a corner and were in a large room, a warm room where lights blinked and Victor could see the mouth of a tube, a tunnel; there was a hum in the air. A woman in a white coat turned from a monitor, smiled and stood. Curly hair, tied back, *blip* went the radar. *Consultant.* 'Mr Powell,' she said, kindly.

I want to see Sophie.

He had to lie very still in the white tunnel. He refused to think that this was what it would be like to be dead. He thought about Sophie.

There were strangers at Victor's table, in the corner of the pub. If Nat stood at the pumps she could always get a clear line of sight to Victor and she always knew he knew she was looking, that little ghost of a smile, his old head, polished brown by the sun, lifting to acknowledge her.

It was as if her whole body was humming, now, with certainty. She'd tried calling the police station again but she'd been told no one could talk to her. She had left a message: Beth's address. She'd left a message for Mo Hawkins too: don't touch anything. No one answered.

If Victor was here, he would listen, his clever old eyes understanding. He would believe her. The fact that Victor wasn't here felt like it meant something, too. He should be here.

Two hefty blokes in cycling shorts were at his table instead, drinking lager and eating crisp sandwiches, talking with their mouths full. Nat watched them, just a couple of overgrown lads was what she told herself but the truth was, one of them might have known Beth, mightn't they? Heard about her, followed her out here, muttered conversations in the garden, arranging to meet one evening when he was supposed to be working late. They both had wedding rings on, she'd seen that when they stood at the bar ordering, but that meant nothing. Behind her Janine made an exasperated sound, and Nat moved.

'I miss Victor,' she said, the words not enough for the feeling she had of dread, and Janine sighed.

'How's he doing?' she said reluctantly: Janine was funny around illness.

'Holding his own, that's what they said.' Nat had a knot in her stomach at the thought of that. 'But something's worrying him, I don't know if it's his daughter, or what. I don't know how he came to have his funny turn, even, if it was a stroke or what. Something.' It came to her, and tentatively she said, 'What if something frightened him?'

Janine gave her a sceptical look. 'He's bloody ninety-odd,' she said. 'I mean, it wouldn't take much, would it?'

'It would take something, though,' said Nat, urgent. 'Didn't smoke, hardly a drink, Victor was healthier than I am.' Janine shrugged and the gesture infuriated Nat.

'I'm going to go to the police,' she said and she saw alarm come into Janine's face. 'What happened last night, at Beth's place. The phone plugged in there, all her stuff left behind, and then . . . what I heard. I was scared. I was scared, and you know me, Janine, I'm not the nervous type.' Wasn't she? Well, if she was, she wasn't going to confess it to Janine. The door opened and someone came in. 'They weren't listening on the phone. I've got to go there.' She didn't mention Craig, and the DNA test.

Janine fidgeted. 'I don't like it,' she said. 'It's not good for the pub if . . . something's happened. Something else. I don't want people thinking—'

'Thinking what?' said Nat, bitterly. 'Do you think custom is going to fall off?'

'You think that's all I care about?' said Janine, tight-lipped, stepping stiffly away from her up to the bar, and Nat relented.

'No,' she said. 'But there's nothing you can do about it, one way or the other, is there? I'm going to talk to them. As for business, the place is rammed since Ollie died. There's a queue for the pool table, have you seen it?' Bitterly.

And when she turned there he was, Bill the cameraman, two broad hands flat on the bar, smiling at them. It must have been him just come in.

'What can I do you for?' said Janine, almost elbowing her out. His smile followed Nat, lopsided.

And then Craig was coming in from the back, a tray loaded and wobbling in his hand. His face was drawn and anxious.

She took the tray and steered him back outside. 'Are you going to see the police?' He looked frightened, staring back at her as if she had hypnotised him. She gave him a little shake. 'If you do—'

A child ran, squealing, between them followed by its mother and they stepped back, under the old plum tree that leaned against the garden's fence. The plums were almost ripe and something came back to Nat then: she remembered Beth picking them – this time last year? – and taking them to make jam. She'd been living in the cottage then, and she'd brought Janine a jar of the jam a few days later, ruby red. They'd gawped, Nat and Janine, tasting it, because it was delicious. 'Thought I'd have a go,' Beth had said, shrugging. She'd never done it again.

'If you do, you have to think of anything – *anything* – you can tell them.' He was still just staring and she tried to pull him closer. 'Like . . .' She wasn't going to mention Beth. 'Like, girls. A girlfriend.' The focus in his eyes changed. 'There *is* something, isn't there?' Slowly he pulled his arm away, rubbing at it where she'd held him.

'I saw him with some lads in town, I dunno, a couple of weeks ago?' He spoke slowly. 'They were winding him up.'

'Think,' she said. 'When? Was it . . . was Beth still here, for example?' He was shaking his head. 'What lads?'

'Just lads, they'd got hold of his phone, lads we were at school with. Saying he had an imaginary girlfriend, she was one of those Russian scambots, you know, wants money, they get your mobile number from somewhere and try to get pin numbers or whatever. So I thought it was some online stuff.' He swallowed, and then looked at her. 'I thought, serve him right.' Blinked. 'I shouldn't have thought that, should I?'

'Serve him right why?'

He just shook his head. 'Nothing.'

'Did you fall out over Beth?' He didn't answer, just turned away. Another shrug. 'Look, Craig,' she tried to explain. 'It might have seemed . . . well, it was Beth's way. I think she probably was trying to save you the misery. Both of you. But you need to tell the police – about these lads, the scammer, the girlfriend.'

Craig nodded, his back to her, refusing to look. 'You don't think they'll – the police – they won't—' Mumbling.

'It's all right, Craig,' she said, to his tall stooped back and for the first time she thought with a shock how young he was, the things that happened to lads in custody. They took the laces out of their trainers. 'No one's going to lock you up, they just want to ask you a few questions.' Surely that was true? But Craig didn't answer, just stood aside for her to go ahead of him into the bar.

And when Nat shouted out the back for him half an hour later Janine raised a weary eyebrow. 'He's gone,' she said. 'Said he had something urgent to do.'

It wasn't just summer, and the weather, it was everything: it was Ollie, it was Beth, and this lot like flies to a carcass. Rubberneckers. Nat kept her head down and just worked, slapping on a smile, trying not to think, while Janine, sweaty and defeated, waiting for Steve to reappear (voluble for once, he'd even told them where he was going, a Harwich pick-up, toys from China to be dropped in Birmingham) had been up and down the stairs four or five times to reapply her make-up before he eventually walked in the door at eight, fresh and cool and easy-going as he always was.

Unlike Janine, Nat hadn't looked in a mirror since she'd left the house, but Steve's expression said it all. 'You get going, girl,' he said, carefully hanging his jacket behind the bar. Nat could see Janine opening her mouth to object a second before softening, and she took her chance.

Outside, the evening was soft and blue and sweet-smelling: warm grass and hedgerow. Nat shouldered her bag and was turning up the lane when someone stepped out behind her.

Bill, the cameraman, leaning in the shadow of the pub's

side wall and smoking. Nat had forgotten about him. Halfway through the afternoon she'd remembered and wondered what kind of look she must have given him at the bar, that he made himself scarce so efficiently, but wherever he'd disappeared to, he had come back. She stopped.

'Walk you home?' he said, pushing himself off the wall and standing there, hands in his pockets, keeping his distance. How old was he? Forty, maybe, square and solid and unthreatening. She sighed, too weary in that instant to wonder what he was up to.

'Didn't it work out, then?' he said.

'What?' she said, and felt the weariness shift, clear.

'I was trying to remember where I'd seen you before,' he said. 'And then I did. You were on a date, a couple of weeks ago, a pub in town.'

A date: that stupid Tinder experiment. It seemed like another life.

He smiled a little, head on one side and something fired, something sounded, a little ping, ping of alarm. Nat held herself still, asking herself, quiet, how she felt about this level of interest. But he seemed only relaxed, well-intentioned, holding his position. 'Look, I don't want to muscle in,' he said quietly and then he did step into the light, she saw his face, earnest. 'I mean, if you're with someone, but maybe we could go for a drink some time. If you're not.'

She stood, examining him, making herself take her time. 'No,' she said finally. Tired. 'Not just now.' Sighed. 'There's too much going on—' she began to explain, but then she stopped herself, no. Then began again. 'Thanks but no thanks,' she said, and there was a tiny pause before he nodded. And smiled: that smile again.

'I understand,' he said. 'Sorry.' Blowing out smoke, stepping back to the outside table to stub out his cigarette on an ashtray, carefully. 'We won't be here for more than another month anyway.' He seemed resigned.

Turning to go, she paused. 'How long is it, then?' she asked. 'How long have you been around?'

The look he gave her was steady, as if he didn't need to ask why she wanted to know. 'Two months?' he said. 'Maybe a bit more.'

Nat didn't turn to look back until she was at the bend in the lane but when she did he hadn't moved. He did then, though – he walked out into the light and climbed into a car. She heard the engine fire but he must have driven the other way, inland, because he didn't pass her in the lane.

Had she wanted him to? She liked him, was the truth, that calm, still quality appealed to her. She fancied him, to take it that step further and actually be honest. But that didn't mean she thought it was a good idea, any of it. It pinged to and fro in her head as she walked so that she was right at the cottage and in the porch before it registered, the outside world, some change, something wrong, something.

The door as locked as she had left it. The green of the overgrown garden was deep blue dusk, and quiet, the birds sleeping.

But inside, a light was on. And in the tiny kitchen a place had been laid at the table.

Someone had been there.

She stepped back quickly into the doorway, her back to the wall.

Hold on, hold on. What was this? What did this mean? Hold on. Was he still there?

Nat made herself wait one heartbeat, then another. Silence.

'Hello?' Her voice sounded scared. She cleared her throat. 'Who's there?'

Nothing: no answer, no sound, no movement. With trembling fingers she pulled out her mobile, and dialled the number Donna Garfield had given her.

Chapter Twelve

The ward was dark again, though it was barely past nine. Already Victor had learned that in here the days passed quickly, the nights seemed to last for ever. They had closed the double doors to the nurses' station tonight, which meant perhaps that he was more likely to sleep – but he wouldn't hear anything, either. They were his conduit to the outside world, the nurses grumbling about the vending machine and the lack of spaces in the car park. Those frightening coded terms, dosage and pain thresholds and DNR orders. Do not resuscitate.

Sidestepping the steady beat of anxiety those thoughts set up, Victor retraced his day. What have I seen, today? I have seen new things. The lift doors, the white tunnel. He had not imagined that it would be so noisy, in the scanner. You lay, as still as you could manage, and above you, around you, it ground and creaked and rumbled like some great clumsy piece of Victorian engineering. It could only mean you harm: he had brushed that thought away too, to focus on Brunel instead, on sounding arches and soaring girders. And then at last it had been over and they had eased him out, blinking, pale, into the bright lights.

The door swung open, soft, and she came in, a silhouette familiar now, the wisps of hair, the comfortable rounded shoulders. She came up to the bed, hesitating. He tested his voice, his tongue. 'Lisa?' he said. 'Is that you?'

She came closer, half perching. 'Just checking on you, Victor,' she whispered. 'Takes it out of you, that machine, doesn't it?'

It *had* exhausted him, he had not expected that. She had something to say, though, he focused on that. 'They told you, your daughter phoned, I heard?'

Ting, ting, ting, went the fear, *daughter, daughter, daughter.* 'Is she all right?' he said immediately, astonished that the entire sentence emerged more or less whole, if a little blurred at the edges.

Lisa cleared her throat. 'Well,' she said and at the sound of her equivocation he struggled on the bed. She set a hand on his arm and he felt despair that he didn't even have the strength to resist that gentle pressure. He sank back down, his breathing shallow.

'She's fine, but . . .' She hesitated again, her voice was soft. 'It wasn't actually Sophie who called, in fact, it was her husband, Richard. She's hurt herself, nothing serious, a sprain to her wrist, he said, I think. She needs to have it dealt with and as long as there's nothing more serious—' Feeling him struggle again she patted, warning. 'I mean, as long as there's no fracture, then she will be up to see you, just as soon as she can.'

At the sound of her attempt to reassure him, with that undertone of resignation – *these relatives, excuses, excuses* – his anxiety set firm, into certainty. 'He's hurt her,' he said, and there was a pause, a tiny intake of breath, from Lisa. She leaned in.

'I'm sorry, Victor?' she said and he froze at her warning tone, he groped for the right thing to do.

'I – I don't know,' he said. 'I'm worried about her, Lisa.' His speech was ebbing now, he was mumbling.

She sighed. 'I'm sure she's being looked after, Victor,' she said, then, 'I tell you what, I'll call her myself in the morning, I'll talk to – is it Richard? – if need be.' She sounded tense, wary. 'But a sprain really isn't something to worry about.'

'There's a child,' he said, fumbling for the right words, to make her understand: he felt her resist, but he didn't know why. 'Rufus. Grandson.' She patted his hand again, something distracted in it now. She would be wondering if he was losing his marbles, was that it? He subsided, not hopeless, not quite yet, feigning calm. Closing his eyes.

'That's it, Victor,' said Lisa. 'That's it. You get some sleep.'

The downstairs bathroom window was open a crack: dubiously the policeman prodded at it with a pen. The window wasn't much bigger than a laptop screen. Nat couldn't make herself believe an adult could have squeezed through it.

'Well,' said the PC, shrugging. He seemed a nice enough bloke, tired, stubbly, fortyish. 'Depends, you'd be surprised. Burglars – well, generally the skinny lads, if I'm honest – you know what they say about mice, can get through a crack the size of a ballpoint pen? A bit like that.' He frowned. 'But nothing was taken, you're saying?'

Nat shook her head.

They'd turned up in a squad car about twenty minutes after she called, no sirens but the light flashing toward her as she stood in the quiet lane, the stubbly bloke climbing out followed by the driver, who looked on the verge of retirement and said nothing. They stood there in fluorescent jackets, taking what felt like an hour to understand what she was saying to them.

Ducking their heads to get under the low lintel, they came inside. They looked around respectfully, and she saw it through their eyes for a moment: Janine's ancient sofa, the dust on the shade that hung low over the table, her books stacked sideways on a shelf, temporary. She saw the older bloke tilt his head sideways to read the spines.

'Right,' the younger one said eventually. 'So the light was on and the table was laid, for one. No damage, no theft, no signs of forced entry.' A sideways glance at his colleague. 'I dunno if forensics . . .' and he was back looking at Nat, tailing off.

They expected Nat to look sheepish, to say, she over-reacted, she could tell. 'I didn't lay the table,' she said. 'I never lay the table.' There it was. Knife, fork, spoon, glass, one of the blue flower-patterned plates she'd brought from Jim's.

What had he thought she was going to eat? There was no food in her fridge. Was that the point? Sad loser with empty fridge and no one to eat with?

'Boyfriend?' interjected the older bloke. It was the only word he uttered. His colleague raised an eyebrow, expectant.

'I haven't got a boyfriend,' she said, steely. 'I live here on my own.' She opened her mouth then closed it, changed tack, thinking, *Jim*, thinking, is that fair? Send a patrol car round to Jim's? 'Look,' she said, choosing her words carefully, 'I think there's someone following me – I think it's to do with my friend going missing. I spoke to someone, a woman, a DS.' She searched her memory for the name. 'Donna,' she said finally. 'I told her this morning.'

They listened as she went over it again and the lead officer took notes, laboriously. Finding herself telling them more than she would have liked about Beth: about the plum jam, even. Beth's phone in her pocket. She'd been about to get it out and give it to them when a radio crackled urgently and as his colleague disappeared off outside to talk the older bloke stifled a yawn, apologetic. Nat forced herself to let him off, thinking of Ollie, of them on duty round the clock, but her hand tightened round the phone in her pocket. Hand it to some dozy bloke, who thought this was all just a prank? 'She knew Ollie,' she said, finally, when the other policeman came back in tucking the radio inside his collar. 'Oliver Mason. The kid that was . . . that they found in the river.' Taking the plunge then. 'Have they . . . there was blood, he was tied up, I heard. Do they know whose?' The younger man snapped his notebook shut then and frowned. Nat held her ground. 'I mean, do they know if it's a man's or a woman's?'

He gave her a hard stare, not unfriendly. 'I can't tell you that,' he said briefly. He glanced around the low-ceilinged room one more time then stepped over to the table and looked down one more time at the place set for one. She could see him frown, then he sighed and looked up.

'I think under the circumstances we've done all we can here,' he said. 'There's no evidence of someone intending you harm. No evidence of a break-in. This stuff about your girlfriend, it's just – well it's a bit random, a bit . . .' he searched for the word, 'conjectural. I think you need to sleep on it and if it all makes a bit more sense in the morning then come in and make a statement. It is of interest that your friend knew the dead lad, Oliver Mason, of course it is. But she was a barmaid, wasn't she? Not exactly a special relationship.' The two men exchanged glances then.

'Barmaids fair game, are we?' she said. 'Or what?'

The policeman cleared his throat nervously. 'I just meant – you work in a pub, you come into contact with all sorts.' When she said nothing he made something out of looking around as he put his notebook away. 'You'll come in to the station tomorrow, then?' he said hastily. 'All right? And needless to say if anything else happens, anything at all, get straight in touch.'

Nat stood there a good five minutes unclenching, staring blindly at the books the older man had looked at. Making herself see it their way. A book of poems Jim had given her one Valentine's; he'd probably bought it at random, she couldn't see him reading a poem.

Jim. They always suspect the boyfriend first. Grudgingly, she considered that there might be a reason for that. She should have said something, she knew that. But Jim – poor bastard. She could phone him herself, if she wanted to know if it was him, she always knew when he was trying to hide something from her. When he wrote off his car and told her it was in the shop. When he said, we can keep it, if that's what you want, keep the baby, all the time pleading silently with her to let him off the hook.

She weighed the phone in her hand, but she didn't call him. It wasn't a coincidence, was all she knew. Sitting in the dark on the floor of Beth's bedroom and listening to a car's engine idling patiently beyond the front door. Walking into her own place and finding someone had been there. Plus if she called Jim he might think she needed him.

Beth had lived here once, for eight, ten months, hadn't she? Nat stopped on the tiny dark landing upstairs and put her fingertips to the wall, as if it might tell her something. If these walls . . . there was a phrase. A fly on the wall.

She went round the whole house again before she went to bed. Everything locked and bolted, and nothing missing. *Why, why, why?* She stood behind the closed front door. Fuck off, she mouthed at it. Whoever you are, fuck right off. I'm not scared. I'm angry.

Outside he was watching, in the dark, out of sight of the house. He saw things other people didn't: the way she moved signalled to him, the sight of the back of her neck. He saw where she was vulnerable, looking down at her mobile with her lip pulled in between her teeth, turning suddenly, pulling a curtain closed. Walking easily up to the house, stepping closer until he was behind the window: he wanted to be so close she could hear him breathe, standing back, watching for a sliver of her through the glass, through the crack in the drawn curtains. He stayed there until she went up to sleep. In his head he could see her, the sheet over her slipping free as she slept.

Lying in the long grass he had seen them arrive, through the tangled hedge, the smell of the river in his nostrils even from up here, the dark water was slow, slower and slower in the heat. He was perfectly still, he had that ability, nothing startled him, he didn't waver, he didn't shudder. Not like her. He had waited until they left. He played their conversation with her in his head, he saw her clench her fists, he saw her angry, he saw her tremble.

He had seen what she'd been up to. He thought of his treasure, his store, packed into dark places, stored for when he wanted it found. He got hard thinking of that, of the shock, the gasp, taking her breath away.

Quick on her feet, but not quick enough.

In his head, he took her apart, joint by joint. He felt her slippery between his hands.

Chapter Thirteen

Tuesday

It took Victor a little while to understand, bleary as he was, that the alarm he could hear was coming from his own bed. Even when he saw them converging on him – Lisa first, panicked, then a junior nurse dropping a drip on the bed opposite to head across to him and even Emile, alarmed, peering round his breakfast trolley –Victor couldn't make sense of it.

'It's your blood pressure, Victor,' Lisa was saying, taking hold of his hand, leaning back to drop the tilted bedhead, he felt himself laid back. 'There's been a sudden drop . . .' and she turned, calling for someone else and didn't finish what she had been going to say. He did feel distinctly strange, a different kind of strange.

Someone had come in the night, late in the night, or early in the morning perhaps, and filled his glass, had raised him to sip. Or had he dreamed that? She had had to lower his head, Lisa had, so it had been raised. His brain was soft as mush, he couldn't make things stick together. There was something he had to remember, Lisa had told him.

They blurred, moving swiftly across him, calling more

urgently. *Let them*, something whispered in his head, *let them.*

Victor could see slanting sunlight down the lane, and the man walking up. The sun fell on him in stripes, and he kept moving, arms hanging by his sides. He was walking up from the weir, where the water rushed and burbled and floating things snagged and caught. There was blood streaked up one of the young man's arms. The boy lay and drifted, sinking, rising, turning, that boy. The days were a river, running into each other, things Victor had seen bumped up against things he only feared.

Something she had told him. As long as it's nothing more serious, she had said, Lisa had said. Sophie's sprain.

'Sophie. How is Sophie?' It came out as mush.

When Nat woke again, it was after eight.

The phone had rung at five. Reaching for it, Nat had not even thought it might be Jim, too early for her to make that connection. Instead her mind had chased in panicked circles, police, hospital, Beth, Mum, *who*. Him.

'Hello? Hello?' *He had her phone, so he has my number.* There was a crackling, a heavy breathing, a ragged whispering, sinister in the grey light. *He hasn't got her phone any more, though.*

Then there was a sharp high-pitched cry and Nat sat up, it was so unmistakably distress she could hear, that high wail – then the line was cut. Her heart pounding, running, tripping, she stared at the screen, only imagining the worst, thinking of Beth, in pain, Beth hurt, Beth calling for her help – and she stumbled out of the bed, catching her foot in the tasselled coverlet and landing, painfully, on her side.

Stop. Nat turned on the light, she listened: it was quiet. Her hands trembled as she held the screen, went to recent calls, searched for the number.

She knew it. She recognised that number.

Staring again, Nat ran down the list, red numbers were missed calls, those she had made had a tiny arrow one way, those received another, there, there. There it was. A London number, no name, it wasn't in her address book. She stared, blinking, at the arrow: she had called that number, Saturday. Saturday.

And then she knew, she had leaned back against the bed, tangled in the coverlet, feeling the pounding behind her ribs subside. Victor's daughter. The child, his grandson, must have been playing with the phone, dialled by mistake.

After a long five minutes staring, waiting for her body to catch up and realise they were safe, she and it, Nat had climbed back in bed. And she had slept again, the moment her head hit the pillow, like a log, like a dead thing.

Now she climbed out, groggy, her mouth dry and sour from adrenalin or the glass of wine she'd had from the fridge last night, from no food. Hungry. She padded down-stairs and put some bread in the toaster.

As it browned she looked around, her back to the kitchen corner, facing into the small, low-ceilinged sitting room. There was something about someone coming in, uninvited, that shifted everything out of whack, it all looked different. A black beam, the little stove that smoked, the bookshelf. Beth had lived here too, and remembering that she walked into the room. On the bottom shelf were a few dusty books that had been here since she arrived, hers on their sides on the top: she went over and knelt to look at them.

A self-help manual, a DIY manual, *Joy of Sex*. Janine, not Beth.

Smelling the toasted bread Nat got back up and retrieved a plate, knife and fork, the ones, no doubt, that she'd put away last night. She should have pushed it: she should have insisted on fingerprints being taken. They'd made her feel foolish, though. Nat imagined, in the pale greenish light of early morning, that they thought she was an attention-seeker, or drunk. They hadn't asked about Beth's phone, still sitting above the optics in the bar, and she wasn't going to offer it. It was too precious, she didn't trust them not to lose it, or forget it, or wipe it. She'd give it to the woman, Donna Garfield. Could Nat trust a female officer not to have a laugh over Beth's selfies, her emojis, her shopping apps? Candy Crush for quiet times behind the bar.

Finding, looking down at the place laid, that she didn't want to sit at the table, after all, Nat walked through the room, toast in hand, trying to catch something, a scent of something. A scent of Beth. She'd lived here, after all. *Come back.* There was an old wooden chest: she raised the lid but there was nothing but dust and a film of cobweb. The toast was finished, and she was in the hall, that's better, she told herself, but she wasn't sure, it was going to take more than a bit of toast to get rid of this uneasy feeling. She had not, after all, imagined it, last night. The same feeling as she'd had crouched in Beth's bedroom, but this was more than a feeling. Knife, fork, plate.

There was a cupboard under the narrow staircase, a panelled door that Nat had never, to her knowledge, opened before. She opened it now. A narrow black coat hung there.

Reaching to touch it Nat was startled to realise that it was made of fur, which meant it wasn't Beth's because she'd always said she hated fur, gave her the creeps more than anything, the thought of something killed, wearing another animal on your back. Soft where animals were concerned, she always looked sharply away if there was a thing dead in the road, don't we all, maybe, Nat thought, reflecting, but with Beth it was different; once Nat had actually seen her turn away, stiff and awkward, so as not to be seen upset. It was like that single batch of jam she'd made: sometimes you saw there was another Beth, gentle behind the foundation and the careful cleavage and the determination to Just. Have. A Good Time.

Did she know, even before she saw it? Part of what she knew in her gut, part of that picture that had appeared in her head of the man sorting through Beth's things, leaving traces of himself, and her, spattered invisible on the walls. Choosing something of hers and taking it away.

As she tried to get a purchase on it the coat swung under Nat's hand, turning towards the light from the hall, and Nat saw what was inside it, slung over the hook and hanging. A black bra.

Now that, now that. Nat reached out a hand to grab it, scratchy lace, a tiny pink satin rose that sat where the cups met, she saw the label grubby, without considering what she was doing she pulled it, held it to her face, breathed in. *Now that. No.*

That.

It was Beth's bra. Even if the little rose – that Nat had seen a hundred times, visible, and intentionally so, down in the V of certain tops, sitting there to catch some punter's eye, anyone's eye – hadn't done it, the grubby label had, Beth who boasted she washed her bras twice a year. 'Whether they need it or not,' winking at her audience the other side of the bra. 'Blokes don't like you too clean,' she'd confided airily to Nat afterwards. Shrugging. 'Don't ask me why, chemistry or something.' She'd paused then, thoughtful. 'I suppose they might want a clean girl for something.' Musing, as if she really couldn't work it out.

It smelled of her. It was still pressed to Nat's face and suddenly, feeling the toast churn and rise inside her she dropped it and shut the door on it as it swung there against the dark musty fur.

And then it came to her: she had seen him in her head, sorting through those things because something had been missing from that bin bag full of Beth's stuff. The jeans, miniskirt with the frayed edge, the shoes – they'd all been there, but there'd been no underwear. Not a pair of knickers, not a bra. Beth had been all about the underwear, coming back from town with another plastic bag stuffed with it, strappy bras, lacy stuff, slips, suspender belts, you name it. And standing there with her back to the cupboard door trying to keep her breakfast down Nat knew for absolutely certain that it wasn't that old Mo Hawkins had chucked it, no, she'd have liked to hang it out for all to see. Nor that she'd stashed it elsewhere, greedy old cow that she was, she hadn't been a size ten in decades, nor a 32D, and she must know there's no cash to be had for second-hand underwear, well not unless you know your market – Nat put a hand to her mouth, horrified. *Not funny.* Not funny, no.

Behind her, behind the cupboard door, that fur coat

swung, the bra hanging down, enfolded in it. A kind of Beth, someone had put her there, in the dark, someone had wrapped her in a dead thing and left her to be found.

By me, thought Nat.

In that moment she felt it, suffocatingly close, in the walls: Beth.

A din in her ears, *Help me. Answer me.* Find me.

And eyes closed she saw him again, padding through an empty house, opening cupboards, she heard him, heard his breathing, heard the low throb of an idling car waiting just where she couldn't see it. Beth's soft underwear in his hands.

A man moving through an empty house in the dark – only now the rooms aren't in Beth's flat, with her phone gone from the cupboard, and nasty Margaret screeching next door.

The blood that only Nat could see, those walls speckled with her traces.

Now *this* is the house.

The ward was busy, but Victor saw it all play out in a thin grey light, fuzzed at the edges, as though a soft mist had crept in through the open window, under the doors. His attention was turned carefully inwards, following his own inner workings, looking for the source of the trouble. He didn't like it – the insides, he thought, were a mystery like the deep sea, that was best not investigated. Low blood pressure, well, that sounded manageable, benign, even. It didn't feel it, though, it was unsettling, inside him things were thinning, slowing, losing power; as though part of him was escaping to float upwards. Victor didn't think his daft old weakened body was whispering to him about heaven as he did not believe in God. That, he thought, was perhaps unfortunate under the circumstances but it couldn't be helped.

In the corridor there was a burst of laughter, and Victor felt himself turn towards it like a sunflower. Only the able-bodied laughed like that, with energy to spare.

A man had been wheeled in whose leg had had to be amputated. Another man was being prepared for dialysis. Victor had taken careful hold of these pieces of information, gripping as though they were a rope that would stop him falling.

He could hear Lisa's voice: she had stopped to talk to someone, just out of sight, glancing back at him. Was he imagining things? He drifted, sleep lapping softly at him. He felt someone raise him up on the pillow to drink again, went back to sleep. When he woke the next time he was foggy. Lisa came in: he could barely make her out. Someone to see you, she said, like an angel.

Then her face came closer, and she called for help.

Chapter Fourteen

Nat was in Paddy's shed, and rooting around. It was chaotic, with buckets full of junk and a row of drawers overflowing and hanging open, but – tucked away behind Paddy's tidy little cottage – it felt about the safest place she'd been in days. She had more or less found everything she'd been looking for: a hammer, nails, even two little bolts that would probably do the job.

Paddy came into the doorway, lean and brown and weary, and cleared his throat apologetically. 'Give me a couple of hours, I can get over and do it for you,' he said. 'Whatever it is.'

She hadn't told him why she wanted the stuff, of course. Paddy would quietly do anything for anyone, which was why you couldn't take advantage, and she didn't want him worrying. It was too complicated. Once she started unpacking it all, following the thread of her thoughts, she'd look like a nutter – or feel like one. It was still hanging there, inside the cupboard. The police would have a laugh, wouldn't they? She straightened, and smiled at Paddy's anxious frown.

'I can manage,' she said. 'I think I can, anyway.'

'Jim's . . . not right, you know,' said Paddy, and there was the little cough again.

Nat sighed. 'Oh, yeah,' she said, head down and sorting through a box of screws.

'He's drinking too much,' said Paddy, and she looked up. 'I saw him in town the other day, and he was out of it.' Paddy drank himself, his nightly couple of pints consumed in solitary silence.

'Well,' she said, 'I don't know that that's any of my business, any more.'

Paddy looked at her. 'If you say so,' he said mildly.

She sat back on her heels, irritable. 'There's other . . . Look. Jim can look after himself.'

'Beth,' he said. 'That it? You think she needs you more?' She stood, clutching her handful of bits and pieces. How many nights had Paddy and Beth occupied opposite sides of the bar, exchanging not a word? No point in snapping at Paddy, he didn't deserve it.

'What do you think, Paddy?' she said, and he thrust his hands down in his pockets.

'Beth?' he said. 'I miss her.' His jeans stiff with paint. Paddy deserved a bit of looking after himself, didn't he? 'Reminds me of my sister,' he said. 'I used to watch her there and think, there goes Moira.'

'Moira,' said Nat, in surprise. She'd never heard Paddy mention a sister before.

'Tough as old boots,' he said. 'Loud. Wild. Party girl, if you like. But underneath it – she had something. She would give you anything. Kind – somewhere no one ever saw it, you had to know it was there.' Nat's mouth was open. He was frowning down at his hands, black under his nails. His eyebrows were fierce and bushy.

'Where is she now?' Nat said and he looked up, startled. 'Moira?' she said.

He shook his head. 'Dead,' he said and the word drew something tight inside her. 'She's dead. Tough as old boots, only it turned out she wasn't. Never complained, she was a big woman but nothing left of her by the time she died.' A silence. 'Cancer. Years back now.'

Nat pondered. 'Beth —' and she realised she was about to use the past tense, shifted. 'Sounds like Beth,' she said. 'I didn't know.' Didn't know about Moira. Didn't know he'd spent those evenings working Beth out, either.

Paddy smiled, gentle. 'You better get going,' he said. 'You want to catch the tide.'

It was hot and windless, and Nat had to row a bit just to get off the mud. She had heard Jim's radio on inside the boat shed as she crossed the shingle to shove the *Chickadee* into the rising tide and she didn't want him to come out and see her there drifting, sail flapping. She knew what Beth would say – had said – about having a reason to come down to the water this often, where Jim just happened to work, but sod it. The *Chickadee* felt like her lifeline sometimes. Get away from it all.

By the time she'd got out into the fairway though, she'd worked up a sweat, but she'd persuaded Janine to let her come in late, and she didn't want to push it. She couldn't just drift. She thought of London, for the first time in a long while. The smell of the Underground, walking over the big grey-brown river, the lighters passing underneath. A bright office she'd temped in. How much she'd like to get back there.

Chance would be a fine thing. She hauled up the sail, then settling back on to the stern thwart she thought about Janine, instead. What did she think, exactly, about Beth? She just wanted rid, was how it felt. Beth had ended up more trouble than she was worth. Nat supposed Janine knew more than most about flaky barmaids – but she had the feeling there was more to it than that, however hard Janine tried not to show it. A nervousness. The sail flapped, filling briefly, then slackened again. She adjusted the sheet, shifted a little off the wind and it filled again. She could see the clumped trees where she supposed Dowd's camp to be. A little dinghy hauled up on the mud.

What was it she'd said exactly, hissed to Steve upstairs, yesterday, the day before? Nat couldn't remember, but they'd been having a row, and it had been about Beth.

The light was hazy, heat glittering off the flat grey estuary. Someone had emerged from the trees on the far bank: she couldn't make out more than a white T-shirt, the smudge of a face, but it had to be him. He stood there quite motionless, waiting; it wasn't till she was almost at the rickety jetty that he raised a hand. He was there taking the painter, his hand under her elbow before she even had a chance to notice the slime on the old wood, let alone slip on it.

Dowd's camp was very neat and orderly, a top-of-the-range tent tucked in under the trees, a fire pit kept neat with a small stack of wood beside it. He showed her around, nervous. It wasn't till she'd seen his generator (for the fridge, to keep samples cold); his stove; his equipment (some weird little knives and scrapers, flat glass dishes and test tubes, a contraption like a small hoover); and even his latrine – that he fished out his mobile. Nat realised that she could have asked him before, couldn't she? To see it.

'She had an appointment at the hospital,' she said. 'Monday before last. She missed it.'

He stopped, pale. 'She was ill?'

'She didn't tell you?' Feeling guilty, of course she wouldn't have told him.

He flushed, biting his lip. Shook his head.

'It was just a . . . routine thing,' said Nat. 'That's what she said to me.' Wanting to put him out of his misery. Something occurred to her, though. Someone she could ask, about that hospital appointment. It would be confidential, but . . .

Dowd made a quick nervous movement, tugging at his collar, and she refocused.

'I know I was just . . .' He hesitated and she saw the flush rising higher at his neck. 'An occasional shag.' Blurting that out, not able to hide the bitterness that was sadness, too. She resisted the urge to put a hand on his arm: she wasn't sure what his reaction would be. He might cry, or he might hit her. He was frowning down at the mobile now, scrolling through messages until he found what he was looking for and thrust it at her, holding it out till she took it from him then stepping back away from her so hurriedly he almost stumbled. Thrusting his hands in his armpits, shoulders hunched.

How about next week?

Dated 2 August, the day before she sent the message to Janine that Nat had never seen but said, Mum's not well, off up north for a bit. 'Something like that, anyway,' Janine had said, twitchy. 'How was I to know? Not to delete it. Silly cow.'

'I know it doesn't look much,' he said, defensive, looking up at her from under sandy eyebrows. His wrists, bent where his hand disappeared under his armpits, were bony and thin. Poor guy, she thought, poor guy. 'But that was her being keen. We'd only . . . I'd only seen her the week before and if she wasn't in the mood she could not bother to answer at all and I'd wonder if she'd got the message or should I turn up.' He faltered, then pulled his hands out from under his arms and let them hang by his sides, waiting for judgement.

A little string of emojis, pink hearts, stars, a martini glass. That was Beth, all right, she was addicted to them.

Nat stopped. She took out her phone, because she'd kept that message, of course she had.

Sorry babe no signal here really see you soon. No emojis.

She'd bet the texts Janine had deleted didn't have any either.

Blokes wouldn't know where to find an emoji, would they? Let alone which ones to use. Babe was as far as he'd got in trying to make it sound like Beth. She called everyone babe. He'd only have had to sit in the corner of the pub to know that. She handed Dowd's phone back to him, and stashed hers.

'So,' she said. 'Yes – I mean, I've never tried to fix a date with Beth, thank Christ—' Pausing then, because that was something too, wasn't it? The number of times Beth had hinted she swung both ways and Nat never had worked out whether it was true, or just for the benefit of the lads. 'But – yes. That's her being keen.'

He stared down at it a moment. 'Would you like some coffee?' he asked abruptly.

'Sure,' she said, taken aback. He busied himself with his little stove and she could see where he had everything stashed, safety matches in a tiny plastic container for camera film, a stack of aluminium camping pots all scoured, snap-lock tubs of coffee and sugar. He handed her the cup and she sipped: instant, hot, tasteless.

'What if . . . well,' Dowd said, the flush gone. 'I mean I wonder, now, if she'd had someone else and ditched him and that was why she was available.'

'Maybe,' Nat said slowly, 'or maybe she was planning to ditch him. A . . . say a day or two later.'

'There was someone,' he said slowly.

'What?' said Nat, setting down the cup carefully. 'You knew?'

The flush started up again at his neck and she saw him go still, fighting it. His Adam's apple bobbed. 'Every Monday,' he said. 'She could never see me Mondays, she didn't mind me wondering either, she liked looking mysterious about it.'

'She didn't work Mondays,' said Nat, trying to remember. The second of August had been what day of the week? When she'd sent the message to Dowd. Nine p.m., on a Tuesday. And she had jumped ship – what day? 'We last saw her the next day, the third,' she said, working hard to think. 'She sent the first message to Janine in the middle of that night, saying she was going to her mum's. I texted her the next day and got a message back saying she didn't have signal. Thursday.' That Friday and Saturday short-staffed and Janine grim-faced and furious.

Nat tried to make that work, but it didn't. 'No Mondays between Tuesday and Friday,' she said. 'But maybe she'd have made a special date, to ditch someone. Maybe something happened the day before, that particular Monday, August first, she made up her mind, sent you the message the next day, maybe went round to see him again—' She stopped then, because of the misery on Dowd's face. And this wasn't a game. 'Where did she go, on those Mondays?' she said. 'You know, don't you?' He was staring down at his hands, where the skin was flaking over his knuckles.

'Did you follow her?' Nat was gentle. Poor sad Jonathan Dowd. Unhappily he shook his head. 'I don't know where she went,' he said. 'But I know it was someone she had to dress up for. Lipstick, high heels.'

'How do you know that?' she asked, faltering. Dowd was still looking at his hands and when he spoke it was a mumble so low she could hardly hear it. 'I watched her,' he said. 'Through the window. I went round there and watched her.'

Something gripped inside Nat. 'You didn't follow her, though,' she said, trying hard to keep her voice gentle, level, calm.

He shook his head slowly, then looked up into her face. 'I went before she came out of the house,' he said. 'She was ready, and I saw her pick up her mobile phone and start to dial, and I left.' The Adam's apple moved again as he swallowed. 'I didn't want her to see me.'

'Was she phoning someone to come and get her?' Nat was trying not to think of him out in the patch of garden behind Beth's flat, hiding, watching.

He shook his head stiffly, his hands jammed back under his armpits. 'Like I said.' He was watchful now. 'I left. I didn't want her to see me.'

She nodded. 'I'm going to go to the police this afternoon, Jonathan,' she said, and he leaned stiffly to pick up her cup, then his own, then went and rooted behind his fridge, extracting a plastic washing-up bowl. 'Shall I tell them what you told me?' Giving him the option. 'Shall I give them your number?'

Dowd stood there with the plastic bowl in his hands. 'I have to get things washed up straight away,' he said. 'I get inspected, you know. And you can't be . . . living like this, you have to be organised.' She nodded, but said nothing. 'You can give them my number,' he said, holding the basin against himself. 'You can tell them what I think.' He swallowed. 'You can tell them I think someone's hurt her.'

And they stared at each other then, because it was the first time it had been said, out loud, by someone else. Then at last Nat turned away, feeling her throat tight. 'I'd better . . .' she said. 'The tide.' She realised that she was *more* afraid, now, she understood that the fear had crept outwards, not just her imagination. Whoever those footsteps on the gravel outside Beth's flat had belonged to – he was real.

She could have passed him in the street, she could have talked to him in a shop. He could be someone she knew.

They walked down to the water. Nat didn't dare speak. The tide had come up a bit but Dowd didn't try to help her on the slippery surface of the jetty this time, keeping his distance, though she had the feeling he would move fast, if he needed to. And when they got to the *Chickadee*, bobbing in the wavelets, he did hold out his hand. She stepped in, feeling the bones in his hand, the strung tendons.

He coiled the rope for her, holding it while she settled herself, kneeling to set it on the thwart neatly, taking hold of the *Chickadee*'s bow ready to shove her off, but not quite ready. She held herself steady, waiting. 'I can give you a lift in the pickup,' he said then. 'I could get to you around four. Take you to the police station?' Swallowing.

She looked at him, not knowing, not knowing. He wanted to help. He wanted to be trusted. She saw his hand holding the bow. 'Thanks, Jonathan,' she said, hesitating. 'That . . . sure. That would be great.'

He rocked back on his heels and pushed her off, standing in the same movement, and he was walking away from her. As she watched him, stiff-legged, crossing the marsh she could only think, But you spied on her. You watched her.

She came about, the boat swung and when she settled back on her course there was no sign of Jonathan Dowd.

Jim's shed was locked up when Nat brought *Chickadee* up on the gravelly mud behind it, the radio was silent and there was no sign of Paddy. He should be working – lunch maybe, she told herself. She stowed the sail and sluiced the mud from her feet; it was close to one and she had to hurry, her heart thumping. Things were rocky enough with Janine as it was and when she turned into the lane and saw a straggle of cars already parked outside the pub she began to run.

The saloon bar was empty, though, and to her relief only Steve was behind the bar, polishing glasses. 'You're all right,' he said. 'She's gone to the cash and carry and whatever she tries to tell you, we've not been run off our feet.'

He set the glass down. 'There is someone in the garden, though,' he said. She stopped in the doorway, feeling the sweat bead on her forehead after the run. Hearing something in his voice.

'Someone who wants to see you,' he said, and leaning down he released a cloud of steam from the little dishwasher. As Nat slipped past him he was unloading it. She pushed open the door out from the kitchen into the little garden, she took in the warm smell of earth and the big rustling canopy of leaves but all she could think was, It won't be her, *let it be her*, Beth, Beth, Beth. Dowd's words still in her head. I think someone's hurt her. He was very sure, wasn't he?

Let it be her.

Nat didn't see the woman at first, because she was kneeling behind one of the wooden tables. She saw a small ginger head tipped and looking down at something at his feet solemnly, a little boy of about three with hair that reached to his collar. He turned to look at her and she saw a trace of something, someone, she knew, then a woman straightened and stood. A plump, anxious woman, about Nat's mother's age, a bit more than fifty, and all Nat thought was, Victor must have been a redhead, once upon a time when he had had hair – because apart from that all she could see in the woman's face was him.

'Are you Natalie?' the red-haired woman said, tentatively, and all her inflections, old-school soft posh, were his too.

Nat registered that she had her arm in a sling. She nodded. 'You're Sophie,' she said.

Chapter Fifteen

Was there a word for it? thought Victor. If there was a word for it and he could think of that word then everything would be all right, that awful tipping to the world would be arrested. Already, since they had begun the new drug, cautiously he thought he could detect things settling, returning to focus.

Triangulation? Setting up a stable system, bringing three points into relation with each other so you could work out where you were. He couldn't remember who had taught him the word, of course, but that had not been part of the bargain he had made with his memory. Victor, Nat and Sophie.

'You gave us a bit of a shock,' Lisa had said, comfortably.

She was used to it, he supposed. He wondered how many of the patients on her ward didn't get back up and take their clothes out of the little cupboard and go back out into the sunshine. Enough for it to be as much a part of her job as Special Delivery is part of the postman's.

Mr Hesketh. Who had, like all Victor's teachers, worn a mortar board and gown every day in the classroom. Had taught him about triangulation.

Lisa had been smiling and he had wondered why, weak as he was. He had just emerged, blinking and nervous, from an awful dream state that might have lasted moments or hours, he couldn't tell, in which lights had gone off and on and alarms had sounded and a trolley with a huge and terrifying machine had drawn up alongside him, humming with menace. They had hooked something new up to the drip beside him, then they had hauled and rubbed at him.

Now he was sitting up on his pillows, feeling like a newborn, blinking in the sunshine. Outside in the corridor he heard a scuffle, a little high cry of protest.

'There's someone here to see you,' Lisa had said and Victor remembered then that that had been what she had come in to say before, before all the fuss. Cautiously he waited for the word to have the same effect, but nothing happened. Well, something did happen, a little warm pulse of hope that, try as he might, Victor could not subdue, and then there she was, in the doorway.

'Daddy,' she said, a hand coming up to her mouth and tears glistening in the corners of her eyes, his little round-legged tender-hearted Sophie. And then Rufus barrelled past her and flung himself forward on to the bed, giving it and Victor a jolt, Sophie gasping and laughing and seizing him all at once.

After they'd sat and she'd hugged him silently and Rufus had been given a stethoscope to play with by Lisa – no, she had told Sophie, I haven't got any children, looking wistful and Victor thanking God, or someone, that whatever else Richard had brought into Sophie's life, they had Rufus – he told her. Had Lisa gone, by then? He remembered her explaining to Sophie that they thought his dramatic dip in blood pressure had been down to a reaction to one of the drugs they had been administering, and that they felt they had managed to identify and correct it, and the consultant would be along later and would 'talk her through it'.

On reflection, Victor thought Lisa *had* gone, because he remembered waiting for her to go. Wanting it to be just them, safe and tight, and no danger of any chilling hospital phrases on anyone's lips. Sophie had eventually gone out to talk to the consultant, and he had heard them in the corridor while he sat with Rufus stretched out beside him on the bed asleep, the little warm head under his hand. He hadn't heard the words: the tone, though, had been reasonable, a murmur which he supposed was as much as he could expect.

It had taken him a little while to steady himself to speak. He didn't want Sophie to hear anything that would frighten her, no mush, no gibberish. Don't tell about the man with blood on his arm: what's important is that she stays, that she thinks it's safe. That it *is* safe – how to make sure of that? Then Rufus had laid his head down and the moment had come. Victor had opened his mouth and one precise perfect word had emerged, intact.

'Darling,' he said, and he saw Sophie's eyes widen, grateful.

He had told her to go and find Natalie.

In the end Dowd turned up at the pub earlier than he'd said, closer to three than four. Ducking his head to come through the door and seeing Nat was still working, he got himself a drink. Ginger beer: he was one of those non-drinkers who didn't trust booze, or didn't trust themselves, but then she told herself off for thinking that way. He was going to be driving her, of course he wasn't drinking.

Steve had brought her out a sandwich in the garden when he came out with crisps for Rufus, winking.

'Ten minutes,' he said. 'She just called to say she's on her way back from the cash and carry.'

There was something about Sophie that bothered Nat.

'Just a hairline fracture,' she had said, nervously, when Nat had stared at the sling, the cast on her wrist. 'You won't tell Da— Victor, will you? I told him it was a sprain, and they did think it was a sprain to start with, so stupid of me—'

And the little boy's head going still, Rufus, there where he crouched under the plum tree trying to run his toy car up the trunk – still and listening as if he'd picked up on something, there was a key word in there, something he'd been told not to say, not to tell about.

Stop it, Nat told herself now, watching Dowd sip his ginger beer in the corner. Think you're a flipping amateur psychologist, just because you got an A in Biology GCSE? But still. It was all she had, it was all she could do, standing behind that bar day in, day out, was watch people. Try and work it out. Which was why now and again she jumped into the *Chickadee* and shoved off, no matter how indebted it made her to Paddy, because she'd had enough of watching people. Couples picking fights, lads getting pissed and loud and leery, parents kicking back a bit too much and kids getting slapped. She wished Victor was back.

'You don't get to see your dad much?' she'd said to Sophie, tentatively, and Sophie's face had drawn tight, pink and painful. She had pulled Rufus on to her knee and hugged him.

'I'd love to see him more,' she said with a catch in her voice, then impulsively, 'I'd live with him if I could. Me and Rufus, we could get another caravan,' jogging him on her knee, 'couldn't we, Rufie?' The little boy wriggled back closer into her body, frowning down at the car in his hands, and Sophie sighed. Her blue eyes were faded, looking into Nat's; not a scrap of make-up, hair pulled back, a few broken veins here and there but sweet, pretty. All the same Nat wanted to take hold of her, make her stand up straight, look in a mirror.

You're a fine one to talk, she told herself. When was the last time you looked? She put a hand up to her hair, self-conscious, short but clean at least. Pulled her T-shirt straight.

'London's not so far away,' she said. 'Is it? I mean, it's holidays?' Rufus was tugging at his mother's sleeve, pulling her down so he could whisper in her ear. Sophie hugged him closer, nodding, yes, to whatever he'd asked her and seeming to find it difficult all of a sudden to meet Nat's eye.

'Well, yes, I . . . there's my husband, of course,' breaking off, trying for a laugh that didn't come off. 'I can't see him in a caravan, can you, Rufie?' The little boy just examined his toy with fiercer attention and Sophie looked up, brightly, aiming at Nat but in fact looking over her shoulder. 'So it's just a day or two, until . . . well. As long as we can. You're right, it's holidays, and Richard might be glad of the peace and quiet.'

'You can stay with me, if you like.' Nat hadn't known

where the invitation had come from exactly, she just knew she had to keep them here. For Victor.

'Oh, no,' said Sophie, 'I want to look after his place for him, he was worried—' She frowned. 'I don't know exactly what he was worried about. Someone. Something. He couldn't quite—' She broke off, blinking back tears.

'How is he?' Nat said. 'You saw him this afternoon?'

Now Sophie could look her in the eye, it seemed, now she was talking about her father and not her husband. But her face was pale and set. 'There was—' and on her knee Rufus made a sound of protest, she loosened her grip and he wriggled free. She cleared her throat, straightened up. 'They said there'd been a setback, his blood pressure had dropped very suddenly and they thought it might be something to do with his salt levels.'

'What's the prognosis?' said Nat, wanting to take it back straight away, trying to soften it. 'What do they say—'

Sophie's hand was at her mouth. 'I don't . . . I can't . . . he's so . . . he's such a . . .'

'What a great dad he must have been,' said Nat, out of nowhere thinking fiercely, I wish he'd been *my* dad. If he'd been mine . . .

But Sophie's face, so suddenly soft and lit with something, love, she supposed, took all the bitterness out of it. 'He *was* great,' she said, simply. 'He still is. I used to feel sorry for everyone else at school, not having my father.'

'You'd better stay as long as you can then,' said Nat. 'Don't you think?'

Sophie blinked again then, getting to her feet, and Nat saw an overnight bag tucked under the table. It didn't look big enough to last two people more than a day or two.

'If there's anything you need,' she said, and Sophie had turned to her.

'He told me to come and find you,' Sophie said. 'He thinks very highly of you. His speech is getting better, it must have been awful when he couldn't . . . he's such a . . .'

'Yes,' said Nat, and she found herself putting her arms around Sophie. 'He is, he . . . yes.'

'Go and see him, anyway.' Sophie was rubbing her eyes now, pulling away, tugging her clothes back into place, putting her hand out to reel Rufus in. 'He . . . it would help if you would. He wants to see you.'

Janine had been arriving as Sophie and Rufus's taxi pulled off, scrambling the gravel in the ugly tank of a four-by-four she'd bought to impress Steve, and Nat had ducked back inside hastily to clear tables. Craig hadn't turned up: Janine just shrugged when Nat asked where he was. Run off her feet trying to make sure she could get that hour off, all the time she was hoping. That Craig wasn't there because he had remembered something useful and was telling it to DS Garfield right now.

Unless he'd just done a runner last night. Back home to his mum's, to hide? The police would find him there. Anxiety ticked, ticked. Too many dangers.

Dowd's pickup was as neat as his camp, the footwells so clean it might have been hoovered in her honour. The interior smelled of diesel and the woods. He had sat in the corner patient and wordless until she had finally, after muttered negotiations with Janine, stripped off the heavy apron and gone over to him and said, brusque, 'Let's go.' As an afterthought, 'All right?'

If Beth had had a car, it would have been full of sweet wrappers and crumpled cans and scarves and fag butts. They did say opposites attract but it was still a stretch to think of her with Jonathan Dowd. 'Where did you think it was going?' she said on impulse, after five minutes of silence as he drove – careful, full use of mirrors, proper deceleration into the narrow bends – out of the village. 'Jonathan? You and Beth.'

He snatched a sideways glance then looked back at the road ahead. His hands were the regulation distance apart on the steering wheel and his narrow shoulders contracted, uncomfortable. 'I didn't think about that,' he said, eventually. 'I knew . . . well. She had to settle down sometime, I thought. I thought she might . . .' His Adam's apple bobbed and Nat took pity.

'All right,' she said. 'I get it.'

She supposed she'd had the same thought, on and off. Something would happen, Beth would hit a bump in the road and she'd take the safe route, for once.

They didn't speak again until they were at the police station. Dowd fretted over where or whether he was allowed to park and she just climbed out in the end, leaving him to it. 'I'll ask inside,' she said.

Inside though, a lot seemed to be going on. It was a scruffy, seventies building backing on to the canal in the town, seven or so miles inland. Nat supposed the canal was the same one as stretched all the way to the weir upriver from the pub, where the estuary split and dwindled, divided between a sluggish river and the black manmade watercourse she could see beyond the station. The weir where they'd found Ollie. As she walked through the dusty glass doors two police officers were half running down the stairs, pushing their way past her and outside. A patrol car pulled up beyond the glass doors, then roared off again. The last thing, Nat decided, that they were going to be bothered about was where Jonathan Dowd put his pickup.

In the event he came through the doors after her before she'd got a chance to talk to anyone beyond the duty sergeant. A chunky woman looking sweaty in her uniform collar buttoned to the neck, who'd listened impassively then told her to wait. There was no sign of Craig.

'I've asked for her,' Nat said. 'Donna Garfield, the woman I spoke to before.' Bypassing the two policemen who'd come to the cottage last night, on instinct.

She hadn't told Jonathan about last night, not in his camp, not in his pickup on the way to the station: she wasn't sure why. She'd shot a look at him as he drove and wondered, but put the thought out of her mind. Best not to say anything. How to explain it? And her reaction to it. And who could she trust, after all – who did she feel safe with? Victor, and look where he was. Beth, once upon a time.

Looming over her Dowd was jumpy, shifting from foot to foot; he wouldn't sit down. It occurred to her what weird places police stations were. But he had agreed to come, he had wanted to come. He paced a bit then headed to the glass screen where the desk officer sat. She didn't hear what he said – he leaned forward over his elbows on the counter. When he turned back to her he looked calmer. By the time he had sat down beside her there were footsteps on the stairs and a young woman in uniform was eyeing them. She was small and neat: she looked to Nat barely out of school but that couldn't be true. Twenty-five?

'Miss Cooper?' she said, warily. Nat jumped up.

'This is . . . Jonathan Dowd. He was – is – he's a friend of Beth's too.' Donna Garfield looked him up and down, and sighed.

She showed them into a side room; it was bright, at least. A big dusty window overlooked the canal: Nat caught a glimpse of it before Garfield gestured to her to sit. 'I understand you spoke to some of my colleagues last night, Miss Cooper?' she said. 'Called them out?' and Nat caught the look Dowd shot her.

Heat prickled at the back of her neck: she didn't want him knowing, didn't want any of them knowing, how afraid she had been. She wished she hadn't brought Jonathan with her: she wished he hadn't had to come into the room with them but it was too late now. She made her voice calm. 'Yes,' she said. 'Can we just talk about Beth for the moment? Beth Maxwell. I want to register her as a missing person, officially.'

When she got to the part about being in Beth's flat and getting the feeling someone was watching her through that big window – out of the corner of her eye she saw him shift in his chair and Donna Garfield paused, her pen hovering over the notebook a second, before methodically she went on writing. And Nat went on talking, telling her everything, about the phone, the underwear, about Ollie fancying Beth. She even told her what Craig had said he'd overheard, the lads in town teasing Ollie about his imaginary girlfriend. At that point Donna Garfield frowned hard and held up a hand to stop her while she scribbled fiercely, dropping the hand to allow her to continue. Nat hoped she hadn't dropped him in it, somehow. It was only when Nat finished that Donna Garfield addressed Jonathan.

'And you, Mr Dowd?'

He coloured. 'Well, I'm mostly just the chauffeur,' he said, but it fell flat: they both just looked at him and his shoulders dropped. 'I haven't seen her in a month. We had an . . . on-off thing.' Donna Garfield's mouth twisted, but he went on, bravely, Nat thought. 'She wasn't serious about me – but that doesn't mean I can't worry, does it? I'm here because I think Nat is right and no one seems to be listening to her.' He avoided Nat's eye.

'Jonathan thinks there was someone else,' said Nat. 'She was seeing someone else.'

Donna Garfield looked at him a moment then nodded. 'Well, that happens,' she said. 'Any idea who?'

He shook his head unhappily. 'Monday evenings,' he said. 'She went out somewhere every Monday, that's all I know.'

'Yoga classes? Zumba night?' The policewoman's head was on one side, sceptical. Nat wanted to stand up and shout.

'I don't think so,' said Jonathan.

'She wasn't the yoga type,' said Nat, angrily. 'Look, don't you . . . don't you understand—' Her voice rising, uncontrollable.

Donna Garfield's palm went up again to shut her up, not looking at her, just going on making notes. Finally she looked up. 'And what about the phone,' she said, and when Nat stared. 'Miss Maxwell's mobile?'

Shit. Oh, shit. 'I'm sorry,' said Nat. 'Shit. I should have picked it up I was . . . we were—' In too much of a bloody hurry.

'It's all right,' said Garfield, cool. 'Someone will be coming over. Now.' Expressionless. 'I'll pick it up when we've checked out your story.'

'Check out . . . as in . . . ?'

'Verify.' Nat opened her mouth then closed it again. As in, make sure it's true. She nodded.

'So,' said Donna Garfield, closing her notebook. 'Her mother hasn't seen her?'

'No one's seen her,' said Nat. 'And someone came to her place that night, while I was there, I'm sure of it. I think it was someone who'd been using her phone to send messages. I don't know if he—'

'Or she?'

Nat held the policewoman's gaze as she tried to think clearly. 'I don't know,' she said eventually. 'I heard . . . I heard a car.' The woman stared at her, flat-eyed. 'Parked outside, just waiting, I think he . . .' Garfield's eyebrows lifted just a little bit; she pressed on. 'I think he knew I was inside. I think . . . I think . . .' And she stopped then, cold suddenly. 'This morning I found a . . . a piece of Beth's underwear in the cottage I'm staying in. She used to live there, but I'm sure . . . I'm sure it was put there by someone.' That sceptical look, it forced her on. 'I think . . .' But it wasn't that she *thought*. She knew. 'I think he's hurt her.' Or worse. Nat didn't say that, and the more she didn't say it the harder it grew, at her centre. Killed her. 'Whoever he is. And he wants me to know it.'

'You.' That flat-eyed, disbelieving look.

'Yes.' Staring back.

And now he wants me. Now he wants to hurt me. Tell them, tell them, tell her. But she couldn't: she didn't like the way it sounded. Pathetic, frightened. 'This is about Beth,' she stated. 'This isn't about me.'

Donna Garfield leaned back in the chair and Nat couldn't

believe she'd ever thought she was young, her level gaze, the grime visible on her collar, her indifference, all said she knew too much about the world. 'If you say so,' she said. 'Have you got a picture? Of – ah – Beth?'

On the low chair beside her Jonathan Dowd dropped his head and drawn by the movement she saw him look pale and shaken. Feeling sorry for him then, she patted his shoulder and caught Donna Garfield's eyes narrowing, just for a second. She took her hand away and pulled out her own phone from her bag. Under Donna Garfield's eye she scrolled through her pictures. Flowers, a cloudscape, the estuary, she couldn't remember having taken half of these, what was she, an idiot? Jim. Jim smiling. Jim half asleep behind a newspaper. Jim sailing. There. She held up the little screen.

Beth's wide mouth, lopsided smile, the stippling on her cheeks so light you'd only see it if you knew. Beth's blue-grey eyes, narrowed, watching, laughing.

'Where was this taken?' asked the policewoman. The pictures on the walls in the background, the useless little balcony, the shiny new kitchen.

'Somewhere I used to live,' said Nat. She couldn't take her eyes off the picture. She'd forgotten that, how Beth's eyes could look, like metal, silvered and reflective. She'd forgotten that evening altogether. Beth had come over for a meal, with Nat and Jim playing at grown-ups, and they'd all laughed, like something off the telly, trying to impress, a dinner party. Nat had found out she was pregnant three days later. Was that why she'd forgotten? Sometimes life divided: that bump in the road. You had to choose which way to go.

With Beth, what had it been? That hospital appointment, had it made her do something reckless? Say something? What had taken her away from them?

Donna Garfield was telling her the number to send the photo to and Nat remembered Beth liking the photo, asking her to send it so she could put it on Instagram. Nat didn't do that stuff. The picture sent to Garfield's number, she put the mobile back in her pocket, feeling Jonathan's eyes on her. And then it seemed to be over, then they were outside, and Nat had to stop herself gulping the air, clean fresh air, it seemed, after the inside of the police station, for all they were just off the ring road and you could smell the canal.

'Jesus,' she said furiously, both hands clutching her head. Dowd had looked alarmed, hurrying round to the other side of the pickup.

He had dropped her with barely a word and roared away. Not at the pub: at the little modern building half a mile outside the village that housed the GP surgery. They'd thought maybe the village would expand but it hadn't and the building sat lonely in a field. 'This'll do,' she'd said. He'd opened his mouth then closed it again, at the warning look she'd given him. You don't ask, do you? Why someone needs to see the doctor.

Seven o'clock, and the surgery was dark, or mostly. A light around the back and a couple of cars in the car park, including the one Nat wanted. Dr Ramsay drove a battered Opel, twenty years old, orange. Nat stood in the fading light, aware of the emptiness beyond the building as she waited. The receptionist emerged, giving her a funny look as she got on her bike and cycled away. Maybe she knows, thought Nat with resignation, all about my fucked-up life. Sod it.

There was the sound of the key in a lock from the back of the surgery and Dr Ramsay came around the side of the building and stopped. Sighed, pocketing her keys. Her name was Jane, Nat knew that. Nat had sat there in her consulting room, not able to look her in the eye, heard her sigh. Heard her say, reluctant, *I can refer you for a termination.*

'Natalie,' she said, weary. Pushing sixty: she must be looking forward to retirement. She wore a wedding ring.

'It's not about me,' Nat said, stepping forward, quickly. The sun was close to the horizon across the empty fields, the light uncertain. 'It's about my friend Beth, she's a patient too. Beth Maxwell.'

'Yes,' said Jane Ramsay, wary.

'She missed her hospital appointment.'

Ramsay hesitated. 'Yes . . . I assumed she—' Stopped. 'Why are you here?'

'I'm worried about her.' Nat stood her ground, blocking Ramsay's path to her car.

'Worried? There's no need to—'

'It was a smear follow-up,' said Nat. 'I know that, she told me. Abnormalities, if she doesn't—' There was something odd about the way Ramsay was looking at her. 'What?' said Nat. 'What?'

'It wasn't . . . you don't need to—' Ramsay broke off, started again. 'I can't talk to you about another patient,' she said carefully. 'You do know that?' But she didn't make a move for her car. 'Are you all right, Natalie?' Concern in her voice.

'She's my friend and I'm worried about her,' Nat said.

Keeping her tone steady, patient. 'She's supposed to have gone off to her mum's but she hasn't. She's left her phone behind. I think—' She stopped. 'Would you know, for example, if she had registered with another doctor? Can you tell me that much?'

She felt Jane Ramsay studying her in the fading light. 'I would know, yes,' she said finally. 'And she hasn't gone to another practice.' There was a silence, and Nat felt it filling up with fear. Beth's gone nowhere.

'Can't you . . . can't you tell me *anything* . . .' She felt her voice break, she saw herself through the doctor's eyes. 'Can you tell the police, at least?'

'Natalie . . .' Nat backed away, stumbling in the low sun, only wanting to get away from the pitying look in the doctor's eyes. Bumping into the thin hedge surrounding the car park, around it, into the empty road, the doctor standing there watching her go.

It was almost dark in the road and she had to hurry to get back to the pub in time. Something weird, she thought, about the way the doctor had responded. Like she didn't believe Nat? Like Nat had got it all wrong.

What had the doctor's name been? Something Greek. Clinic 1A. She should have kept the piece of paper.

A car came up behind her, slowly. Too slowly. Barely moving so Nat turned to see his lights on full beam and dazzling her and then speeding up so she had to jump the ditch to let him pass. Nat could feel her heart thumping as she stood, pressed into the hedge on the lonely road. She ran, after that, awkward and sweating in the humid twilight and her sandals rubbing and flapping, slowing only when the edge of the village appeared.

Behind the bar Janine and Steve were all loved up, so much so that as Nat slipped in, breathless, they hardly noticed her. So much so that she wondered what they'd been up to all afternoon. So much so that she felt faintly nauseated, her heart still pounding. She couldn't turn around behind the bar without coming across them stroking or nuzzling each other.

She got to work straight away but the fear didn't go away, the queasy cocktail of fear and panic and anger that sent her up and down the bar, jittery and careless with filling drinks, in and out of the garden too fast until Janine did notice, frowning, and she had to make an effort to pretend.

The police needed to know, she's gone nowhere. Not registered with another doctor, didn't that mean something? And those Monday evenings. Beth all dressed up, locking her door behind her, never knowing someone was watching her, Jonathan out in the garden. Beth in high heels. When that thought came to her Nat happened to be reaching up to the optics for someone's last drink, close to closing time and already she was thinking ahead, fearful, to the dark lane and putting her key in the lock of the cottage. She stared, frozen.

And there it was, the taxi firm's card, stuck in above the optics alongside the postcards people sent, thinking there was nothing a barmaid liked more than to be reminded that other people got holidays. Nat reached it down. She'll have got a taxi, she thought. To wherever she went every Monday night. Still staring up at the ranked bottles she saw Beth's mobile and in a swift movement grabbed that too, and pocketing it she heard Janine behind her. 'What the . . . what—' and thought she'd been caught red-handed. But then the door banged and Nat turned around and stared: Craig's mum was in the doorway, white as a sheet. A widow and a home bird, plump and kind with only a trace of Craig in her dark eyes, the only time she came near the pub was when his bike wasn't working and he needed a lift home. She came towards the bar. As she got closer Nat saw she was trembling.

'He's not here, is he?' she said, trying to keep her voice steady.

Setting the customer his double Scotch down and leaving his money where it lay, in his palm, Nat lifted the counter, came round to comfort her.

But Steve was there ahead of her. 'What is it, love?' Big and easy, his arm around her shoulders. 'You after the lad? Craig?'

'He went to the police,' she said, her chin wobbling, hardly able to say it. 'He went like they asked him and they kept him in. They wouldn't . . . wouldn't let me . . .' She was staring, the tears streaming now. The pub had fallen silent. 'My Craig couldn't . . . he wouldn't hurt anyone.'

'But they let him go?' Her head raised, trying to nod. 'This morning, they said. But he never came home.'

There was a silence then, everyone waiting for someone, listening and then Nat heard it, a sound that had been there off and on all evening, just on the edge of the pub's noise. The sound of a helicopter, circling in the dark.

Chapter Sixteen

The helicopter had been there since Sophie got back to the caravan site, moving up and down the river, shining its light down on to the water and across the sloping fields, the black clumped trees. Rufus had asked what it was looking for and she had told him she didn't know, shutting the flimsy little door behind them. And she didn't know, in fact, it was only some aberrant thought pattern that made her connect the helicopter with her father, lying in the hospital, trying to tell them something. Aberrant: a favourite word of Richard's.

There she was, on the little veneer flip-up table edged in aluminium, laughing in a silver frame, aged four and half. Sophie could remember the dress, remember the photographer with hair greased flat on his head, she could remember her father doing silly voices to make her smile for the camera. And there were his books, along the bookshelf above the bunk where Rufus lay, curled like a dormouse with the ragged piece of blanket pressed to his upper lip, fast asleep. The navy blue cloth-bound Oxford poetry collections, a dictionary with a torn binding, an ancient set of sailing tours, dark red with gilding on their spines. There was his old candlewick bedcover. It felt like home, the only real home there ever is, it felt like her childhood. There was only one thing missing. He was missing. Her father was lying in the hospital.

He was alive. Sophie sat very still, concentrating on that fact and what needed to be done. Carefully she set the shiny new mobile phone down on the table, given to her by Richard before she left, the account in his name. 'So I know where you are,' he said. His smile. 'So I can always get hold of you.' She looked at it with apprehension.

What absolutely needed to be done, before it was too late. She was going to bring her father back here and she was not going to leave him. No matter what. No matter who.

'Another number for you to learn, Daddy,' she'd said, showing him the phone. 'That way, it's . . . easier.' She should have got her *own* phone. She should have got two. One for each of them, her and Victor, the thought of her failure made her clutch at her blouse, wanting to sob.

How could she? The joint bank account and Richard's frowning face if he saw anything on it he didn't like, or hadn't approved.

As if someone was listening to her thoughts there was a loud rattle, shockingly loud, and she jumped to her feet. On the bunk Rufus stirred in his sleep, his face contracting.

Him. It's him. She stood, between Rufus and the door. Had she locked it? Rufus was still again.

'Mrs . . . Mrs Powell?' Not him. Stupidly, all she could think was, not Mrs Powell, that was my mother. It's Cameron, now. 'Yes?' she said, not opening the door.

'Are you all right, Mrs Powell?'

'Oh,' she said, recognising the voice. She fiddled with the door: she *had* locked it. Good, she thought, and opening it she saw the manager of the campsite. She couldn't remember his name – then she could.

'Mr Wilkins,' she said. She could hear girls' voices, raucous.

'I was just checking you're all right,' he said stiffly. 'Your father . . . well. He seems to think you need keeping an eye on.' He was not exactly friendly. He was frowning, and for a second – aberrant again – she thought she saw Richard in him.

'I'm fine,' she said, making herself smile, fighting the urge – not polite at all – to shut the door. To shut it on him and lock it and set her back against it. 'Thank you, though. It is kind of you.'

The girls teetered past in a huddle, five or six of them all with their mobiles held up in front of their faces. 'They said ten minutes,' Sophie heard. 'He'll take us all for twenty quid.' One of them looked across at her in the lighted doorway and said something. Owen Wilkins held his ground, even when a burst of laughter came from the group and they began to run, shrieking now, high heels sinking in the grass.

'Well,' he said, turning stiffly to watch them climbing into a taxi that was pulling up at the top of the site. 'If there's anything I can do.'

Sophie made herself wait until he'd turned his back but then she was quick, and quiet. She turned the key and slid the bolts shut, top and bottom.

It was partly to distract herself from the fact that she was walking home alone that Nat called the taxi firm. They had music on in the background: she knew where the cab office was. Not far from the hospital, where all the customers were, she supposed. Cheesy music, twenty years old. Thirty.

Out of breath as she was hurrying in the dark, half the words she had to repeat. 'Every Monday. Picking up from Meadow Close.'

The man sounded tired and fed up and – eventually – suspicious. 'Look,' he said, 'I can't go giving out information about customers, can I? Be reasonable. And I've got two paying punters on hold right now, chucking out time, isn't it? So if you don't want an actual cab . . .' Another solution occurred to Nat, and abruptly she backed down, apologising, thanking him.

The cottage was dark when she got home. Nat found herself walking more softly as she approached it, then standing inside the hedge for a good five minutes before going in. Just waiting. Listening: nothing. Not even a rustle, not even a cat slinking out of the bushes.

The cottage felt as she'd left it, just stale from sitting in the heat with all the windows tight shut. No lights on. She made herself get Paddy's bits and pieces out of her bag, fixing another bolt to the door, another on the bigger ground-floor window. Carefully she closed the curtains, upstairs and down. Then she flopped into an armchair, dead tired suddenly, and pulled her bag on to her knee.

She needed to run a bath, but she didn't have the energy. She was sick of being on her own, doing all this shit on her own. Something made her think of that picture of Beth, the three of them eating shanghai noodles and pretending it was a dinner party just because they'd folded paper napkins into nice shapes. Three – and now there was one.

Don't call Jim. Don't send Jim a text, just because you're knackered and you're lonely and you're frightened. She got out her mobile.

There was a message on it, from an unknown number.

Sorry, I know this is a bit underhand.

She stared at the number, at the words, and made herself go on reading.

Subterfuge but I asked your boss for your number. Boss? He must mean Janine. Her heart still bumping in alarm she tried to think back, the looks Janine gave her today. The message was from Bill Sullivan, the cameraman. She sat up straighter in the armchair, and frowned down at the screen.

It's Bill. I won't contact you again unless you get in
touch, but I heard you were having some trouble.
Might need a friend? With a car, even.

Slowly she stood up, the phone in her hand, and went over to the kettle. She set the mobile on the counter as she filled the kettle and set it on to boil, took a mug down, got the milk out of the fridge. Sniffed it, poured.

Then she looked back at the words again and forced herself to go down a gear. Take it easy.

There was a line, wasn't there? A line you drew around yourself, this close, no closer. A line between eager and stalker, between friend and intruder. *I won't contact you again, unless you get in touch.* OK, OK. The danger receded, the buzz in her ears receded.

Beth hadn't believed in that line, not really. Or rather – she liked it to be breached. She liked that sensation, of someone stepping inside her space, she liked the danger of it. Nat thought of Beth's mother, hard-voiced, full of dislike, cold. She thought of Beth putting herself out there, like bait, to get inside the circle, to feel the heat of another human being. Why not? It was what life was all about. Nat knew why not. Because it was dangerous.

It came back to her then, one morning leaning against the sink in the pub toilet while Beth put on her make-up. 'There's something about it,' she had said, dreamy at the mirror after a one-night stand with some guy. How long ago? Nat couldn't think. 'About finding out the things you only know if you're close up.' Raising her own forearm to her nostrils and breathing in. 'What someone smells like. What they're scared of, when they take their clothes off.'

Now Nat raised the mug to her lips, sipped cautiously. Hot.

'Scared of?' she'd said, warily to Beth, though she knew exactly what she had been talking about. It was why she'd gone back to Jim after London, why Tinder made her furious and jumpy. Scared to take your clothes off in front of someone new.

'Everyone is,' said Beth, matter of fact, narrowing her eyes to apply eyeliner. 'It's why you have to watch yourself.'

'What are you scared of, Beth?' Nat had said, and Beth had turned that look on her, silver-eyed, and said nothing.

Now, gingerly, Nat put the phone down on the arm of the chair. All she had to do was delete the message and Bill Sullivan was out of the picture, but she didn't do that. She thought of his nice square face, his smile. His eyes moving round Janine to settle on her.

Still, though. Janine shouldn't have given him the number. She pulled up Janine's contact details. Any chance of coming in late again tomorrow?

If she went on like this Janine might just give her the push, now Steve was around more. Fuck it, though. Maybe it was time. And was it underhand of Bill Sullivan, really? No. Not really.

Overhead the helicopter was restless, moving away, coming back, looking for something. It should have made her feel safe, but it didn't. She thought of Victor, in hospital, of Sophie in the caravan, of Paddy alone with his piles of newspapers and tarnished photoframes. She thought of Beth, getting dressed up and taking a taxi and never coming back. But it was thinking of Bill Sullivan that she fell asleep, to the sound of the rotor blades, thrumming in the dark.

Chapter Seventeen

Wednesday

The taxi driver was chatty, smiling, breaking off only to pick up his radio. *'Don, you got time for Mrs J, needs picking up from the GP in Church Lane in five?'*

Nat opened her mouth, wanting to ask something only not sure what but Don was leaning forward to pick up the handset, clicking through to answer. 'Sorry, on a run to the hospital, Linda,' he said, smiling back at Nat between the seats. 'No can do.' Nat couldn't remember the last time she'd taken a taxi. Jim always used to drive her. She was relying on this guy not having been the grumpy bloke on duty last night, taking calls, but that seemed to her a pretty safe bet. A careful driver, hands on the wheel, talking to himself more than to her because he didn't bother to seek her out in the rear-view mirror.

Casually Nat steered him round to other fares, regular bookings, mentioned the pub. Eventually mentioned Beth. 'My friend recommended you.' Cautiously.

'Sure, Miss Monday nights, I do that run sometimes. Haven't seen her in a while, come to think of it. She on holiday?'

Nat made a non-committal sound, then quickly, running out of caution, 'Where was it you used to take her?' Hearing herself use the past tense.

Slowly, Don made the turn. Nat watched him in the rear-view mirror but he didn't seem suspicious, not flicking a look back at her. 'Up Brandon,' he said promptly.

'Brandon,' she repeated, nonplussed. She knew the name, but it meant nothing to her. She'd never been there.

'Eight, ten mile fare?' he said. 'Halfway to Harlow. She'd always get me to drop her at the church, I used to joke with her, was she seeing the vicar, she'd always look so done up, high heels.' Chuckling. 'The vicar, imagine that. Brandon vicar's about seventy, but they're randy bastards, aren't they?'

The hospital loomed and Nat undid her seat belt, edging forwards on the seat, suddenly eager to get out. She tipped him too generously but he still didn't take an interest, only quickly stashed the money away before she could change her mind.

Coming past reception she saw a sign to Clinic 1A and hesitated – 1A OBSTETRICS AND GYNAECOLOGY, and the words stopped her in her tracks, of course it had rung a bell, *of course*. They kept terminations in a separate ward, but close enough. Nat had been on the same floor as Clinic 1A. In a daze she walked on and then the name came back to her, the consultant's name on the piece of crumpled paper. Greek. Sarafidis. What use was that now? He'd tell her nothing, like Ramsay. And she was here for Victor: she turned towards his ward.

Standing in the doorway Nat did a double take, wondering if she was in the wrong place and then steadying herself against the door jamb when she realised she wasn't: his bed, though, had been stripped. It suddenly felt horribly hot in the room, she smelled old flowers, disinfectant, something worse. A nurse bustled past her with a heap of laundry then stopped, and turned. Her mouth was drawn taut and Nat began to shake her head. 'Is he . . .'

The laundry went down on the bed and the nurse came up close to her and put a hand on her arm. Blue eyes, worried creases at the side even though she smiled, at last. 'No, darling, no . . . no he's . . . we're very pleased with him, as a matter of fact. He's in the sun room.'

Walking her down the corridor the nurse – Lisa, her name was, on her badge – was upbeat, but with reservations. 'It wasn't a stroke, so that's the good news. It was what we call a TIA, transient, it passes off. His speech is back to normal.'

'I know what that is,' said Nat. 'It means he's going to get better.' A bit too prickly but the place – and Victor being here – put her on edge.

Lisa sighed. 'We are just a bit worried, you know, about discharging him, at his age.' Lowering her voice, slowing as they approached a door through which sunlight flooded. 'Ninety-two, and living in a . . . a mobile home, I mean—'

'He likes it there,' said Nat and she stopped, alarmed, and the nurse gave her a sharp look. 'I mean, do the district nurses . . . will they not go to caravans, is that the problem?'

Lisa took her hand away from Nat's arm, looking troubled. 'Well of course they will,' she said. 'It's just . . . do you not get the feeling that there's something he's not telling us? Something he's . . . anxious about. Older people, well, they often disguise problems. They don't want . . .

interference. They have a fear of being institutionalised but sometimes—'

'What kind of thing?' said Nat, sharply. 'Has he said anything?'

'He . . .' Lisa frowned. 'He's . . . he has ideas,' she said slowly. 'The kind that can be a sign of . . . well. He wouldn't drink the water in his jug this morning.' Her face was pouchy, anxious. 'He thought . . . he asked if we administer drugs without him knowing.'

'I see,' said Nat. 'So you think he might be, what? Paranoid? And that's a sign of . . . ?' She left the question hanging. She didn't want to say the word. Not Victor, no. *Dementia.* 'I'm going to lose my marbles before he is,' she said, stoutly. 'Or you. Or any of us.' Lisa's face closed then. 'Thanks, though,' Nat said, and walked away from her through the door.

The room was long, with glass down one side and low padded chairs, a big central table with flowers.

Victor sat there bathed in sunshine and quite still, a hand on each arm of his chair, eyes closed. As she stepped up beside him they opened, and he smiled, a proper smile, perhaps the hint of a tremble but not lopsided. 'Ah, beautiful Natalie,' he said, beaming now, and he flapped a hand towards a neighbouring chair. Nat pulled it up, feeling relief flood her system.

'Looks like you're on the mend, then,' she said and the hand flip-flopped, his smile rueful.

'Well,' he said, and his voice was rusty but clear. 'I do feel rather tired but so far so good.'

She leaned forward on her elbows so she could look into his face. 'The nurse said you thought they were putting things in your water,' she said, straight to the point, and Victor looked back at her quite calmly.

'I could just be old and . . .' he cleared his throat, 'failing. In my mind. I know that.' A little shrug. 'There was someone, though. Someone came in the night. There's often someone in the corridor. I can't see his face.' He spoke in short sentences and she could hear him getting breathless, anxious, she began to shake her head and he stopped, breathed.

'All right,' she said. 'This someone. Let's look at it another way. Why? What does he want?'

'I saw something,' he said, his light eyes quite clear and searching. 'I saw a man coming up from the river. He knows I saw him – he had—' There was a sound then, of voices in the corridor, Lisa's comfortable voice and another, higher, anxious one.

'It's Sophie,' said Victor and to Nat's horror his eyes brimmed, his hand reached out towards her. She took it and he sank back into the chair. 'I've done something wrong,' he said in an undertone, the words tumbling, and his head dipped, hiding from her. In the corridor, the advancing voices had stopped, they had lowered. Lisa, giving Sophie the same words of warning she'd given Nat.

'I should never have allowed her to marry him.' Victor's head was shaking, side to side. 'I should have been a better father.' He was talking as quickly as he was able, agitated. 'If he comes, Natalie, if he comes from London to get her back, you have to—' But then he stopped, looking past her, and she saw him fight to shape his trembling mouth into a smile and then he really was smiling, he couldn't help himself.

Sophie stood there, hesitant, in the doorway, then Rufus

hurtled around her into the room. Nat looked at her, a small plump fiftyish woman with frizzy hair, hands clasped and blinking in the sunshine. The expression on Victor's face said that wasn't what he saw at all.

'Don't go,' said Sophie anxiously, as Nat stood to leave, and actually took hold of her to keep her there so she sat down again, Sophie pulling up another chair beside her as Rufus hurtled the length of the room, up and down. Kids, Nat found herself thinking, curiously unbothered considering how they could drive her mad in the pub garden – she knew the look Beth would have given her, wry. And something closed up, inside her: she looked away from Rufus. She felt Victor's dry soft hand on hers, tapping for her attention.

'Your friend,' he said. 'Beth. What's the news? Has she . . .' There was a look in his soft bright eyes, a searching look. 'Has she popped up again?'

Nat cleared her throat. 'No,' she said, warily. 'Nothing yet.' He continued to look at her, though, and she sighed. 'I'm worried about her,' she said. 'I want to find her. If . . . well.' She changed tack. 'You used to talk to her. I know you did.' She could see Beth leaning over the table to take his glass, asking him if she could bring him another. 'Not that I'm a waitress,' she'd say, looking round haughtily in case anyone took advantage. And Victor would pat the seat beside him.

'There's Jonathan Dowd, who she went out with off and on, he's worried about her too.' Nat hesitated. 'Says there was someone she used to see on a Monday night. In Brandon? Taxi firm said they used to drop her at the church there.'

Victor sat back. On his far side Sophie was sitting up in the chair, had been distracted by Rufus, who was pressed against the glass and making shapes on it with his mouth.

'I – I don't know . . .' and to her alarm Victor did seem to be wandering a little, uncertain. 'Well, yes I did know, she did talk to me about . . . I'm not sure if I should say. It was private, you see, a confidence.' Sophie was poised to go after Rufus, both hands on the chair's arms.

'Was it a man she was seeing?' Nat was leaning forwards, urgent, 'On Monday nights?' but Victor began to shake his head, she saw a kind of panicked confusion and changed tack, on to firmer ground. 'The man you saw coming up from the river,' she said, trying to keep her voice as calm as she could. The last thing she wanted, the very last thing, was to upset Victor. 'What was it about him,' speaking low and even, 'what was it that . . . alarmed you?'

His head turned, slow, and his mouth opened but at that moment there was a colossal crash and before they could see what it was Sophie was up and barrelling the length of the room. A nurse they hadn't seen before appeared in the doorway and behind him Lisa again, hands up and running: at the centre of the room a puddle was spreading below the table and the vase of flowers had disappeared. Sophie whisked Rufus out of the way and all Nat could see of him was his small head buried in his mother's blouse. The male nurse hurried past them to the door, calling, 'Emile!' She turned back to Victor but he looked suddenly exhausted, eyelids trembling.

'Victor,' she said and he hardly seemed to hear her. The aproned man who pushed the trolley came back in bearing a mop and bucket and joined the little group at the table, kneeling to retrieve glass from the floor.

More urgently. 'Victor. Victor.' The eyes opened. 'I'll make sure Sophie's all right,' she said and she was suddenly seized with a panic. How? How to keep him alive? It wasn't within her power: he was ninety-two. 'What's going to keep her here is you, Victor. You. Stay with us.' And slowly, very slowly, he nodded, ran a tongue across his dry cracked lips.

'Her brother,' he said. 'You should talk to her brother.' Then. 'She wouldn't have left him.'

'Whose brother?' said Nat and she could see Sophie looking at them from across the room, Rufus pinioned against her. 'Left who? Victor?' But he just shook his head, despairing. Nat felt in that moment that she wasn't good for him, she was draining the strength he needed. 'All right,' she said. 'Rest, Victor, they're clearing it up, it'll all be fine.'

But crossing to Sophie she saw that it was going to be a long job: there were tiny pieces everywhere. 'We'll have to move him back out of here now,' said Lisa, a pained look on her face. The mess had put her on edge: that was the job, Nat supposed, grateful for once for the general chaos she worked in. 'Health and safety,' Lisa continued. 'It's why they don't allow flowers on the wards.' Then, seeing Sophie's expression, 'It's all right, love,' she said, with an effort. 'Not your fault.'

'I'd better go,' said Nat, turning for the door, and Sophie started after her.

'No, don't, please – I need . . .' She seemed suddenly so desperate that in her arms Rufus squealed and struggled and she had to loosen her grip.

‘I’ll be back,’ said Nat. ‘I will, honestly, Victor’s told me about—’ She stopped there, knowing somehow that she mustn’t say anything about Sophie’s husband.

‘What?’ said Sophie, breathless.

‘Have you got a brother?’ Nat said and Sophie stared, shaking her head.

‘I’m an only child,’ she said. ‘Mum – like me and Rufus, she had me very late. Why?’

‘Nothing,’ said Nat, ‘nothing.’ She swallowed. ‘Don’t go anywhere, Sophie, OK? He needs you.’

As she got to the other end of the corridor she turned to look back and Sophie was still standing there, looking bewildered.

Emerging from the hospital’s grim concourse of fast-food outlets and newsagent into the gaggle of gowned smokers lurking on the pavement outside (beside the no-smoking signs, just out of sight of the receptionist), someone called after her. When she turned she saw Steve. He was ditching a crumpled paper bag in a bin, looking grim. For a second it was as if she was seeing him for the first time, not strong, silent, helpful Steve, but a stranger.

‘What . . . ?’

‘Mum,’ he said, and jerked his head back to indicate an upper floor. ‘Cancer. She’s not got long to go.’ He shrugged, uneasy, at her questioning look. ‘Not nice,’ he said, groping for an explanation. ‘It isn’t something you talk about.’

Cautiously, Nat nodded. Thinking of Sophie, thinking of her own mum, crossing her fingers inside her pocket. ‘Good she’s got you close,’ she said, and he just nodded.

‘Anyway,’ he said, looking away from her, off past the

ambulances ranged in front of the A and E entrance. 'You want a lift, or what?'

He watched Sophie come towards him across the hospital's canteen. She had tried to hold the tray but it had wobbled and a man had jumped up from a table to help her carry it. 'I don't think, darling,' he ventured once she had sat down, the good Samaritan gone back to his plate of baked beans and sausage, 'I don't think it will bear any weight, not if it's broken. Didn't they say that?'

'It's just a hairline fracture, is what they said.' Her head was down as determinedly she unloaded the tray. He couldn't help but recall her laying out her tea set for her dolls, always scrupulously fair, *One for you.* Always careful.

'But still . . .' She wouldn't look at him, and he faltered.

On the table she set out a little carton of juice for Rufus and a pot of tea for two. To cheer her up in the queue Victor had asked for his old favourite, two poached eggs on toast, and he eyed it now. *Their* favourite: after her mother died he had used to make it for her every Sunday morning. He pulled it towards himself – his hands felt weak and frustratingly disobedient. He focused on the plate and the implements in his hands, not looking at her. 'You haven't said,' knife across the fork, sawing laboriously, to his surprise the eggs perfectly done, 'how you broke it.' Keeping his eyes down.

'Oh, so silly, nothing really, just a silly . . .' She was sounding breathless, panicked and he raised his head to look at her.

'An accident,' he said, 'was it?' Looking at her and for a second only she held his gaze, looking back at him with those limpid blue eyes, mesmerised. Sometimes, he thought, sometimes you simply have to say it. 'Because if someone did this to you then you must tell me.' What he wanted to say was tumbling too quickly out of him. 'Sophie, Soph, my little . . .' And she bent over the teapot, her fingers trembling on the lid as she poured. He steeled himself.

'Because if he . . . if Richard is not kind to you, Sophie, then . . .' There was a scrape on the far side of the melamine-topped table as Rufus turned his chair so the back – his back – was to them. There was a gurgle as he slurped the juice, defiantly loud, his little shoulders drawn together. 'Then you don't have to stay with him.' There: it was out.

Sophie went on pouring, slow, steadier. Her cup, his cup. She pushed one across to Victor. 'What was it you were saying to Natalie?' she asked, quite calm, to his face then away. 'About seeing a man with blood on him? About a girl who has disappeared? Is that it?'

Something occurred to him then, as he looked down at her poor wrist in the cast. The police occurred to him: they could involve themselves. 'A girl,' Victor said, tentatively, uneasy. 'Beth, yes, a nice girl, lively, full of fun, she's . . .' He frowned. 'I think . . . we, Natalie and I, we think that perhaps something may have happened to her, some man she had been seeing—' He broke off. He could ask the police, *What did one do if one suspected* . . . There were helplines, he had heard them announced after radio dramas.

Delay her.

'How long can you stay?' said Victor, before he no longer dared say it. 'I would like you to stay with me, Sophie, darling.' He would never have dared say it for himself, because after all he was quite content, well, almost, most of the time, almost entirely happy. 'Just for a while. They say . . . well, there are places, and I'm not saying, for ever, but just that they might release me from here, there has to be someone—' And then he did stop, distress muddling his words again, at the thought that her heart might indeed be sinking at the thought. The caravan, the noise at nights, the thin walls, the damp.

On the other side of the table Sophie seemed paralysed. Her mobile telephone sat on the table top between them and with what seemed an effort of will she reached for it, pulled it towards her. 'Richard says,' she whispered, 'Richard says perhaps we could afford . . . says there are homes. We should drive you around, take you to look at one or two. The best option, he says.'

Victor couldn't speak. He can't say, couldn't you have me?

I have nothing to offer her, he thought. He just nodded.

Chapter Eighteen

'But Janine knows? About your mum?'

Steve was driving with both arms straight out in front of him, as unrelaxed as she had ever seen him.

'She don't like hospitals,' he said. 'Who does?'

True enough. 'Has she even met your mum?'

He shrugged uneasily. 'I didn't want to do anything to upset things,' he said, not meeting her eye. 'It's hardly first-date material, is it?'

Nat stared straight ahead, mulling on that. She'd never known a bloke who was bothered enough, to think ahead that way. One in a million, Janine was always saying proudly: well, maybe he was.

She'd asked Steve to take her to the police station: he seemed to know the way. The streets were bleached out in the heat, front lawns dried to straw, and bungalows with their blinds down. He wove through them expertly, but Nat had no idea where they were.

Abruptly Steve's arms relaxed on the wheel, and he glanced at her. 'Sorry, love,' he said. 'Look, just forget it, all right? No need to tell her.'

'Sure,' she said. 'Sure.'

'You found anything out about the kid?' For a second she didn't know what he meant. 'Kid? Oh. Beth.' She frowned down, examining her hands, and felt him watching her.

'Did she ever confide in you, Steve? Like, about who she was seeing? Someone in Brandon, for example?'

He let out an abrupt laugh. 'Me? You're joking.'

'Why?'

He turned fully from the wheel to look at her then, disbelieving. 'You saw her around blokes. Come on.'

She didn't understand. What Beth was around blokes was flirty, full-on, big smile.

He kept looking at her, then he shrugged. 'She doesn't trust us further than she can kick us, love, plain as the nose on your face.' His eyes were back on the road. They were on a main road now, rows of double-glazed villas, a teenage girl standing at a bus stop – left behind for the holidays, her shoulders rounded with disappointment – watching them pass. Steve's sunburned arm resting on the wound-down window. There was no smell of summer here, only diesel and hot tarmac.

'It's why she never stuck with one. Brandon? Dunno. Old, young, fat, skinny – she'll take 'em for a ride but she makes sure to kick 'em off at the end of the line. And she's not the girl to take advice, is she? Not the girl who takes to being looked after.'

The speech took her aback. Steve still had his eyes on the road, chin up and defiant.

'You take Janine,' he said. 'She acts tough as old boots but one cuddle and she's helpless. It's why you *got* to look after her.' Nat opened her mouth, closed it again – because he was right. It was just that she hadn't ever credited him with trying to work any of it out, what was inside people. 'Beth – well. No one tells her what to do. Free spirit, isn't it? That's her theory, anyway.'

His chin went down again and he sighed. 'I don't know that it did her any good, though. I don't know if she had the right . . . radar, if you know what I mean. I think she thought she had all the power, and she . . . she might not have seen something coming.'

'What do you mean?' She felt breathless, constricted.

'I think she might not have known. What some blokes are like. She's worked pubs, sure – but that place, the Bird, well, it's bloody Disneyland compared with some I've seen, on the road. I'm talking . . .' He hesitated. 'Blokes turning nasty, if they don't get what they want. You can't always see them on the outside, they might be the one sitting quiet in the corner all night.'

His face was pale and she could see a sheen of sweat on it. He hadn't talked like this with Janine around and she could see why. Nat stayed silent, thinking. They were driving alongside the canal now: it was just visible through some drifts of town weeds, buddleia waving purple spikes. The water was a lazy dark green, the surface dusted with pollen. The foliage gave way to an iron fence, Steve swung the wheel and suddenly they were in the police station's car park.

'You talked to her mum,' he said, pulling up at the canal end of the car park, where it was overhung with trees.

'Didn't she know anything?' His face set, uneasy. 'Not a single name, like friends from the old days or whatever, somewhere she could go if it all went tits up? Someone to . . . talk to?'

'She . . .' Nat hesitated. 'I don't think she cares.' The light shone low and shifting through the spindly trees. Motes of something, pollen or dust, hung in the green light, and she could see detritus caught in the undergrowth, an old crisp packet.

Steve grunted. 'What,' he said, 'no one? No friends from school? No relatives?'

'I got the impression she didn't give a shit if Beth was dead or alive,' said Nat and with that she shoved the door open with her shoulder.

He drove past her as she approached the building and she heard him rev behind her, a small screech of tyres as he pulled back on to the road. Not keen to stick around any longer then he had to, but who would? Not Nat.

She paused outside the door watching him disappear and when she put her hand in her pocket there it was, Beth's mobile. She took it out and scrolled through the numbers, nothing jumped out at her – they could check through the names, anyway, couldn't they? The police could. But then there it was, the taxi firm. She dialled.

'Hello, stranger.' The voice on the switchboard was cheerful. Yes. 'Long time no hear, eh? He'll be wondering where you've got to.'

She didn't say, I'm not her. *I'm not Beth*. 'Pick us up at the . . . at the Canal Street police station, in an hour, will you?' she said, trying to sound a bit like her. Trying to sound tough and sweet together.

There was an intercom crackle, voices in the background. 'Been up to no good again, have you, love?' A woman's chesty chuckle. 'No worries, sweetheart. Glad to have you back.'

A fat bloke was reclining in the waiting area, his belly proud and his legs stretched out so she had to walk around them. She could see a bit of tattoo and three chins; he looked at her from under heavy lids with steady unsmiling hostility. 'Donna Garfield,' she said, and the desk sergeant shoved a signing-in book at her. She sat two rows away from the fat bloke but she could smell him.

Donna Garfield, when she came, had a different energy about her. She jerked her head for Nat to follow her, without a word, and Nat had to hurry to keep up with her. They ducked down a corridor and into a small bare room, no comfy chairs like last time, a chipped table and hard chairs and a stale smell. 'It's all there is at the moment, sorry,' said Donna briskly, 'and I've not got a lot of time, to be honest. We're pushed, but there was something about . . . well. Try telling the lads, this barmaid's got a funny feeling about her mate, you know?' Nat wasn't sure whether this was about female solidarity, or a game was being played, so she kept quiet. 'So tell me. '

'Has something happened?' Nat said.

'We've talked to the lad,' said Donna curtly. 'The one works with you. I'm sure you know that.'

'Craig,' said Nat. 'You'd talked to him when I last saw you.' Garfield's mouth tightened and Nat went on. 'I know his mum hasn't heard from him since you released him.' Keeping her voice level. She felt in her pocket and laid the mobile on the table. She didn't want to let it go. She pushed it towards Donna Garfield. 'I brought this.' She hesitated. 'Was it his blood, then?' she said, and she saw the policewoman's eyes narrow. 'On the rag? Blood on the rag, Ollie's hands were tied up in.'

Slowly Donna Garfield shook her head and she almost knew, Nat almost knew before she said it. 'The blood doesn't match anything on the DNA database,' said Donna, 'but we knew from the off it wasn't his, we didn't need to take a sample, not unless Craig Jackson started out as Christine.'

'You mean . . .' Something felt numb, her lips, her jaw solid. She couldn't say it.

'I mean,' said Donna Garfield softly, 'we're thinking perhaps we would like a look around your mate's flat, after all.' Putting out a hand she drew the mobile towards her across the ugly little table. 'The blood on the rags used to tie Oliver's hands came from a woman.'

The taxi pulled alongside Nat as she came out through the car park.

Down in the basement room she'd told Garfield about Victor.

'He saw someone, he's not clear when, a couple of weeks ago, maybe more, maybe less.'

Garfield saying nothing so she elaborated. 'It could have been around the time Beth went. A young man, he said, although he's ninety-odd so maybe they all look young to him.' Swallowing. 'A man, with blood on him, coming up from the river.'

Donna Garfield had leaned across the table to her then,

listening at last. 'Go and see him,' said Nat, urgent. 'Send someone. He's old, he's . . . he might not . . .' Then the thought of the danger Victor was in overcame her, and she put both hands up to her face, squeezing, hurting herself. Donna Garfield pulling back, fastidious, and Nat pulled herself together. 'He needs looking after. He's got all his marbles.'

But the policewoman's face under the bleak lighting had been elsewhere, following a scent. Nat had to actually touch her. 'Go carefully with him, will you?' And then the policewoman had nodded.

Now as the the taxi came to a halt beside her, Nat leaned down to look through the windscreen and nodded to him, yes. It was Don again, frowning up at her, quizzical bewilderment on his face.

'Hang on,' he said, 'they said it was—'

'I want to go to Brandon,' she said, cutting him short. 'Is that all right?'

He shrugged, smiling, and leaned to open the door for her. 'You're the boss.'

They were on the edge of the town where the fields began when she saw him – or saw his trailbike, half hidden in undergrowth. 'Stop,' she said, urgently and Don swerved, making a noise under his breath, to pull in a little way ahead. A car behind them blared its horn and roared past. 'Wait,' she said, flinging open the door and she ran back. *Please, please, please* pattered her heart, panic rising. What if he's what if—

She saw his head, bowed. And then she was on her knees in the long grass beside him.

* * *

Victor had certainly been interviewed by the police before, but not since 1958, in London, when he had lied to them. A small matter of covering for a friend, accused of an immoral act in a park. Victor had been surprised then by how simple it had been to lie, you only needed to be consistent. And the immoral act in question had not seemed to him anything terrible, not with the war still sharp and clear in his mind, and men sobbing in each other's arms.

You also needed not to be afraid, because fear was the thing that would give you away. It had occurred to him then, that a man could get away with anything, if he felt no fear, or shame, or guilt. Victor was not that man: remorse tagged him, it wouldn't let him go.

He was back in bed: the slow journey to the canteen had worn him out. Softly, softly. Back to bed, take it slowly.

Police procedure was probably not what it had been then, Victor read the newspapers – but there was something about the heavy-footed approach of the two uniformed men that was familiar. Could it be all that time ago? Half a life. More.

Perhaps it took so long to understand what immorality was, perhaps that was why one was shocked at how young policemen looked. Richard: his mind settled on Richard. Richard was a bad man. Sophie and Rufus had gone to find something to eat: Victor tracked them in his head, two little soft blips on his radar.

One of the policemen was what he called too young, the other had some grey at his temples. Victor smiled at the younger one who was holding his peaked cap awkwardly across his groin. The patient in the bed next to Victor, a younger man, with diabetes, turned and gawped as they approached, and Victor began the laborious process of raising himself in the bed.

Lisa was bringing up the rear. She came alongside the bed to help him upright, and sharply tugged the curtain between Victor and the gawper.

'These gentlemen—' she began but Victor raised his hand.

'I know what they're here for, Lisa,' he said, taking care over his words, speaking gently, and the two men came around her. They drew the other curtain themselves.

They showed him pictures on a computer device Victor knew to be a tablet: you could see children huddled over them on the caravan site, oblivious to the estuary and the sun until a parent would come and snatch it away and they would disperse, wheeling and shrieking like birds among the tents.

The pictures were mugshots, some just blurred street photographs, the young policeman holding the tablet upright on his lap facing outwards. One was of a young man he knew from the pub – he put out a hand when he saw it and the older policeman made a quick movement forward saying sharply, 'It was him?'

And Victor sank back on the pillows, overcome suddenly, feeling weakness rise from his trembling hands. 'No – no. I don't . . . I don't . . .' He waited, instructing the fog to disperse, the weakness to halt its progress. He began again. 'I couldn't be sure, you know, unless I saw the person walk up that path again. It was so much to do with the way he walked and how the light is there. How it falls.' The two men watched him, waiting, frowning: he could hear his voice failing, slurring. They didn't understand him. Be patient, he told himself. Try again. 'Might that be possible?'

It's someone, he rehearsed in his head, *it's someone I've seen, I just don't know when, I don't know where. It could be him. It could be that young man.* He knew, though, that once he opened his mouth to say this, they would seize on his words. They might misconstrue.

The policemen looked at each other, the older one shrugged. 'A reconstruction?' And he looked around the room dubiously. 'Well, it's more to do, sir, with whether you would be fit enough to attend one yourself.'

Gently Victor smiled, let the smile flutter there. 'Well, why don't you let me deal with that aspect,' he said, carefully, trying to subdue his misgivings.

A clatter and a squeal came from behind the curtain and Sophie's face peered in, small, round, paling visibly at the sight of the policemen. She pushed in. 'Da— I'm sorry, who . . . it isn't about social services, is it?' Looking from one policeman to the other, bewildered at the tablet with its screen now dark on the younger man's lap. 'He will be in safe hands, you know, I – I – I can stay as long as he needs me.' He saw them take in her dishevelment, the wince as she leaned down to restrain Rufus, and the cast on her wrist.

'Soph,' he said, then, steadying himself, 'it's all right. Dearest girl. Can we have a minute more?'

When he was sure she was gone, out of the ward, he asked them. Again, they looked at each other, passing questions silently between them. *What's all this? Is this a waste of time, is he gaga?*

'I am worried about my daughter. I thought perhaps you might – at least – advise me? She has a broken wrist and her account of how it happened is really very . . . vague. Her husband is not . . . not the man she thought him to be. It isn't my imagination. Her wrist is broken.'

He reminded himself, he was not gaga. He waited for them to respond. Although it was, he had to admit only to himself, about a feeling. An instinct.

'We can get some leaflets together for you,' said the older policeman. 'There are helplines. There's a website.' He listed some names, then, 'You don't have a' – waving the tablet – 'a laptop? There's the library in town.' Looking around the ward vaguely as if the limits to Victor's web-browsing or helpline-calling were only just dawning on him.

Victor sank back on the pillow again, nodding. 'That . . . leaflets, perhaps. That would be helpful.' The important thing, he understood, was that they should believe in him. He should be credible, because if he was not, if he didn't manage to impart his information before he . . . well.

The urgent thing was Sophie. He must find a way of communicating that to the police. *He may hurt the child*; the little red-headed boy whose hair felt as soft as silk under Victor's hand. He didn't want to think of that man in the shadows down the lane again. Mightn't he after all have been a hallucination, generated by his misfiring brain; had Victor in fact been very wrong to mention him at all?

As the policemen shifted, impatient, on their plastic seats, Victor gazed at them. He had to believe that Sophie and Rufus were safe here, no men waiting under trees with blood on their skin. And Natalie must be safe, too, and there was Beth, of course, she was safe elsewhere, wasn't she? He gazed at the policemen. Please let it be so.

Only the insistent, awful voice that said, You must make sure. The voice that said, A boy, not much more than a child, a boy who has sat at your table and smiled at you – that boy is *dead*.

But they were on their feet and going, exchanging glances. 'We'll be in touch,' said the younger man, hopefully, but as they left all he saw was their discomfort, here among the sick and old and failing, the unreliable witnesses. Victor thought of his books, his photographs, his small pile of napkins and linen, the counterpane, worn thin, that had covered his marriage bed – he reached for them, he told them, I haven't gone yet.

Then a nurse, not Lisa, was there wheeling something alongside the bed, another machine. But Victor wasn't looking at whatever it was she was reaching towards him to do, because over her shoulder, where she had drawn back the curtain, he glimpsed a flash of Sophie, her face quite white and turning away to look where someone had walked into the ward.

And then there he was, smiling steadily.

It was his son-in-law. It was Richard.

Sun on his closed eyelids, he breathed steady, in and out.

The boy had not been the same. He turned the feeling over, the one act set against the other. Putting his hands to her throat, hearing the clotted sound of the life squeezing out of her – that had been the purest feeling, sap rising inside him, joyful. The leisure to examine her afterwards without her eyes following him. And then keeping her, what was left of her, for himself.

The other one – the boy – had been a necessity, which made it different. Stopping him in the street and saying, I know you. I know you. I've seen you with her.

What have you done with her?

Not even knowing how close he was to the truth, not then. *Where has she gone?*

There'd been entertainment to be made out of it, of stringing the boy along with the messages. He had pleased himself, learned the pleasure, in fact, that was in it, it had pointed him in the direction of the next game.

Sitting perfectly still, anticipating the moment when he would lift his hands and the boy would stare just like she had, not knowing, not believing. Yes. Days could pass like this, in perfect calm as far as the world was concerned, carrying out the tasks expected of him, smiling, being agreeable. No one ever knew, what went on inside. He did. He did.

Women thought they knew, didn't they? There was a look on a woman's face, as if they had the measure. Oh, he's one of those, they thought. He's one of those that likes her kneeling, pleading up at him, or legs behind the ears, a doll bent in half, *yes*. One who wants her to talk, or be quiet. He wanted her to be quiet.

Thinks you're a child, or her father – and either way, thinks she can handle you.

She thought she had the measure of him, did she? *Natalie*. She was the one afraid to climb the stairs at night. Had she found it, yet? The little surprise he'd left in the under-stairs cupboard, more than a week ago now, back when he could walk right in unnoticed with his little trophy, her dirty underwear hanging in black fur, his little joke. Before

Natalie realised that she should be afraid, that her doors needed locking.

You can't handle me, however short you cut your hair, however hard you frown, nails bitten down. You're all the same, inside. Red, inside, because he has seen it, he has seen.

Chapter Nineteen

As she shoved Craig ahead of her into the back seat, bringing a sharp metallic smell with him, of sweat and unwashed skin, Don gave Nat a questioning look in his rear-view mirror, but she shook her head quickly, just once.

'Where to, then?' he asked, shifting out of her line of sight as he engaged gear.

'Like I said,' she said. 'Brandon.'

'Outside the church, then?' Head half turned.

'Please.' They moved off.

Craig seemed to fill the taxi's hoovered, pine-scented interior, crowding it out with his long legs and his lank hair and his prison smell. Could she handle him, if she had to, if she was alone? Probably not. He was restless, he was angry. She turned on him, tough.

'Where have you been, Craig? Your mother's terrified something's happened to you.' she said. He mumbled. 'What?'

'I called her,' he said. Nat leaned back in the seat, exhaling angrily. 'They talked to me,' Craig said, his voice dead. He seemed older, by years. 'The police.'

'I've just come from the police station,' she said. 'They told me. They said they're going to look for Beth. They said it's a woman's blood, on those rags.'

'*Her.*' His voice was level with anger. 'It's him that's dead,' he said. 'It's Ollie.' His chin thrust towards her. 'This is all down to *her.*' He was unshaven, his eyes bloodshot. She felt herself push back into the corner, trying to get as far away from him as she could. The driver was still there, though, in the mirror. She forced herself out of the corner.

'Something's happened to her.' Her voice shook.

'What if that's all in your head?' muttered Craig, savage. Avoiding her eye. 'She sent him those messages.'

'What?' She heard herself as if from a distance, whispering. 'They were from Beth?' she said, incredulous. 'It wasn't her, it can't have been her.' Hardly even knowing what she was saying. 'She's . . . the police have got her phone now. She left it behind.'

He turned towards her and his face changed, stiffened into something else. 'What?' Then shaking his head. 'Nah – I'm talking, from way back. Way back. A year ago.' Staring at the back of the driver's head, Craig wouldn't look at her: she could see him thinking, though.

Eventually he spoke again, in a monotone. 'He showed me them. The texts. It was her, all right, it was Beth, you could tell it was her, I know her style. Suggesting stuff, you know, hinting. There was a picture . . . well, he said she'd sent him a picture.' His face was drawn. She remembered Ollie, that boy's face, a quiff sticking up, lovely skin.

A smile that could get any girl, if only he knew it. 'He never showed me the picture. But every time he thought he was in there . . .' He smacked his palms together. '"Oh, no, it's not real. Just having fun." Or "Not tonight, not this weekend, I've got someone coming over."' He drew a breath, bitter. 'Or, "*My mum's sick*."' In a nasty little whiny voice that shocked Nat.

'You sure we're talking about Ollie, here?' she said, and his head whipped round and the look he gave her told her there had been something. 'Since when did you hate Beth this much?' she said.

'Since he got hurt.' He sounded on the edge of tears now.

'Was there something between you and and Beth, too?' Her voice quiet. Because you didn't hate someone this much if there was nothing.

He didn't answer.

'You want to sort yourself out, Craig,' she said, weary. 'Are you surprised the police want you for it?'

'I didn't like her messing him around,' he said in a low voice. 'That's all.'

The taxi turned sharply and briefly they rolled together for a second before she pushed back, hastily, Craig reached for the strap above the window and they were apart again. She registered that they had left the town: they were driving through high hedges, dark with the end of summer, she could smell grass and hot earth through the driver's window.

'He stopped showing me the messages months ago,' Craig said, and the anger was gone from his voice. 'But not long before he . . . disappeared, he did say he was going to London to look for a job. And yesterday afternoon

I went riding round town, looking for those lads, the ones I saw having a go at him in the shopping centre, the ones that had his phone off him that time. I found one of them in the end and he said he'd looked at the message and as far as he was concerned anyone could see they were fake, a wind-up. "When can we meet, I've got to see you."'

'No emojis,' murmured Nat.

'What?' said Craig and she just shook her head.

'You told the police about the messages.' She stated it.

He rubbed his arms, as if he was cold. 'They said, could he have been making it up. If we hadn't seen the messages, it could have been a cover for some other plan he had, or just . . . bigging himself up. Or *I* could've been making it up.' Disbelieving.

'He never got to London, did he?' said Nat, thinking of the weir, and of Ollie's carefully gelled hair, the fluff on his chin. 'Perhaps he got a message telling him to meet her there. At the weir.'

'They never found his phone,' said Craig dully.

'Why did they let you go in the end?' she said softly and he turned his eyes on her, red-rimmed.

'I don't know,' he said, his voice rising. 'Because I didn't do it?'

She saw Don glance in the rear-view mirror again, but she wasn't scared of Craig. With the hair out of his eyes she could see he was on the verge of tears.

'They thought we fell out over something, maybe over her. They thought we had a fight and I smacked him, or whatever.' He was staring at her. 'Like I could do that. And tie him up and fucking drown him?' His voice rose, disbelieving, challenging her. Then he sat back. 'But they had no evidence. Nothing. No DNA. Nothing.'

And the taxi swayed again as they rounded a bend and there was the long slope of a field, stubble glittering, running down to a cluster of houses and the grey spire of a church rising out of them, before the tall hedges closed in again. She hadn't been this way before. The hedges rushed past, silent and dark beyond the windows, a smell of summer in them, of warm foliage.

They pulled up outside the church but before Nat had even got her purse out Craig was already fumbling with the car door, as if he was suffocating

Don stashed the notes in his holder. 'You want me to wait?' he said, glancing over at Craig who stood under a row of pollarded limes along the churchyard wall, hands shoved down in his pockets.

'Did she want you to wait?' The driver looked up at her a moment, then he shook his head. 'Drop off here, then you had to be back three hours later. Same place.'

'You never wondered what she was here for?'

'You mean if it wasn't the vicar?' Winking. 'Not much mystery about it.' He had a nice smile, sunny, open. 'I mean, there's what he was in for – well, he or she, but you don't put on make-up and heels for your mum or your sister, do you?'

'In for?'

'Most fares to Brandon are for the Hall,' he said, patiently. 'They take all kinds, I believe. There's a drying-out centre, a rehab place, spinal injuries, there's residential care, dementia and what not. I don't know which she was visiting.'

She stared, and he engaged gear. 'So no pick-up, then?'

He tilted his head to look at Craig through the window. 'You all right with that one?' Craig looked very tall, suddenly, and angry, as he stalked away.

'Yes I . . .' she said, distracted, but she took the card he gave her. 'I'll call.' Just as well, too, she realised as he disappeared down the lane: she'd got the number from Beth's phone, and the police had it now.

It was only when she caught up with Craig at the far end of the churchyard wall under the heavy-headed trees that it occurred to her to wonder why he was still with her, and hadn't taken the cab back somewhere else, to find someone to haul his trailbike to a garage. He set off walking: he seemed to know where he was going. They turned a corner and there was a set of iron gates at the foot of a wide drive stretching up a lawned hill. Nat could see some low buildings dotted about among trees, and a big, pillared, grey-brick house at the top of the hill. They stopped.

'Brandon Hall,' said Craig.

'How come you know about this place?' she said. 'Did you know she came here?'

Craig looked up the hill. The sight of the building seemed to have calmed him down. 'I grew up out this way,' he said, simply. 'It's the nuthouse, isn't it?' he said. 'Every kid knows where the loony bin is. We used to come out here on our bikes, hide behind the wall looking out for them. We thought we'd catch them wandering around like zombies in their straitjackets.' He gave her a sidelong glance. 'Never saw 'em, but that didn't stop us.' He looked different, his face was sadder, more grown-up. 'I think they moved the psych unit into town, so it's not the loony bin any more, is it?'

'Why are you still here?' she asked. 'I mean, now, why did you stay?'

He shrugged, uneasy. 'I thought you might . . . I dunno. I thought you might want someone with you.' Nodding. 'Up there.'

They started walking, up towards the big pillared house. They passed a big well-tended shrubbery where they saw two women in tracksuits sitting quietly on a bench. Further on there was some kind of a ball game going on among the trees and Craig slowed. 'I never knew she came up here, no. Beth, I mean. Visiting someone.'

'Nor did I,' said Nat. 'But then – plenty she kept quiet about, isn't there? Ruin her image maybe, hospital visiting.'

Craig's mouth set in a line.

'She was *kind*,' said Nat. 'A good friend.' He snorted and she took hold of his arm. 'She shouldn't have messed about with Ollie's feelings, but maybe she had her reasons for being like she was with men. Maybe she'd have liked to be different.' Nat had never thought this before. 'We all make mistakes. We all want to be better.'

Beth sticking up for her, Beth laughing with her on a night bus home, Beth hauling her out of the way of a car. Beth's sigh, standing behind her at the mirror in the pub toilets, examining her green-pale face and knowing what there was, inside her. Emptiness. *Oh, love.*

Out of the blue Nat felt tears spring to her eyes, and angrily she dropped his arm and turned away so he wouldn't see. 'You lot, you just saw this brassy barmaid, behind the bar with her boobs out. Did you think you could do what you wanted to her, nothing was going to hurt her?' Her back was still to him when she heard him clear his throat.

'Hold on,' he said, his voice brittle and angry, 'hold on, who said anything about wanting to hurt *her*?' And his hand was on her shoulder, big knuckles.

And as if on cue, in her pocket the phone blipped and she pulled away and took it out. Craig turned to watch her.

Can you come back please

It was from Sophie.

The nurses were talking about Richard at their station: Victor could hear them.

'Ah, bless. And so good with the little boy, you don't always see that, look how—' They broke off then and one – not Lisa, Lisa had gone home, gave them half a glance backwards, Victor in the bed and Sophie perched on it, holding his hand. The nurse's voice lowered a little. 'So well behaved now his daddy's here.'

Victor had to close his eyes. He felt Sophie's hand squeeze his, he felt the warmth of her close to him through the blanket, her comfortable weight on the bed. He had seen her, her eyes darting from Richard to the nurses, he had seen her formulating a plan secretly, fearfully, knowing she wouldn't dare carry it out.

They meant that Rufus had not been well behaved before. Victor would have liked to disagree with that, to point out that he was only three and that small boys needed to run about. But with Sophie's hand in his he didn't need to: she, of course, would have heard the words and understood them too. Sophie had been such a clever little girl, most particularly where understanding what went on between other human beings was involved, who liked whom, who was telling lies, who would be faithful and true. He had been exceptionally proud of her when she completed her training and became a parole officer, it seemed so brave, he felt that her parolees were very lucky to have her, she was so kind and clever and sensitive. Richard – she'd met him through the job, of course, a solicitor – had not wanted her to continue but she had done, until she got pregnant.

Victor had trusted her understanding of human beings too much: he had trusted her to marry a good man.

'I've asked her to come back,' she said and he opened his eyes. 'Your friend Natalie.' She glanced over to make sure Richard wasn't back. At their station the nurses had moved on to a different subject.

Richard had started to talk about Victor being put into a home within about ten minutes of his arrival. He had managed – Victor didn't know how, or whom he had bullied – to get hold of the curly-haired consultant who appeared, and bring the senior nurse who was not Lisa to his bedside.

'Well,' the consultant had been hesitant, 'whenever possible, we like to return the patient to his or her own home, assisted living.' She looked dubious then, looking from side to side, was this, Victor wondered, even her job? 'Assisted living is the gold standard, really, we do find patients respond best to their own—'

'Of course, of course.' Richard was earnest, he was reasonable. He smiled at the consultant, then at the staff nurse, then back at the doctor. 'But these circumstances are . . .

well, they're tricky. Goodness knows, we'd love to have him with us. Love to.'

Was it Victor's imagination or did the consultant's eyelids flicker at this, did she see how flagrant was his lie? Perhaps she had heard it before, perhaps it was so universal that it was allowed to pass, a convenient, a necessary lie.

'But even leaving aside my father-in-law's reluctance to bother us . . .' a kindly smile now for Victor, 'it's just . . . well, London houses, we haven't the space since Rufus was born.'

A guest room, with its own bathroom, occupied the top floor of their house in London: Sophie had shown it to him, hurried and anxious, when he had visited almost a year ago. She had said, *I wish, I wish, maybe one day he'll . . .* And Victor had squeezed her hand and said, 'I'm really so happy where I am.' He felt Sophie's eyes on him now – was she willing him not to challenge Richard? He tried to smile at her, but his mouth wouldn't obey, it only trembled.

'And he's so . . . determined,' said Richard. 'Really very brave of him, I'm sure he doesn't understand . . .' Victor struggled, *I do understand, I do*, but no one turned to look at him. Richard lowered his voice. 'He doesn't grasp the fact that his insistence on independence . . . that . . . it only causes more trouble.'

'It's rather lovely, actually, darling,' said Sophie bravely. They looked at her, Victor with love, as she quailed, but kept on. 'The caravan, it's very nice.' Looking around for Rufus. 'Isn't it, Rufie? It's a lovely place to live. Everyone's so friendly, and the . . . the caravan is really very comfortable.'

The consultant looked down at her own feet at the word 'caravan' and Victor closed his own eyes but then he heard her speak, holding her line. 'We do encourage independent living, or within the family environment, if at all possible.' And Victor opened his eyes just in time to see something dawn, in Sophie's face, a little spark of hope.

And then he looked at Richard and Richard looked back at him like that pale-eyed lieutenant on the beach, so many years ago, the man he'd seen drawing back his boot, white-lipped, to kick a subordinate on the churned and filthy sand. Richard looked at him with such loathing that Victor knew that his son-in-law wished quite simply that he would die: if a button could make it happen – within the law, of course – Richard would press the button without hesitation.

Then Richard had knelt and said to Rufus, in the move that brought the nurses to his side but that had been to disguise his rage, 'Let's get something to eat, shall we, old boy?' Rufus had just stood there still and straight, hands down at his sides, his head bowed, and again Victor was reminded of that white-lipped lieutenant on the beach, so many years ago.

'So.' Richard's voice was quite different, now the consultant had gone, and it was just the four of them in the cubicle. His voice was pushing, it held a threat. Beside him Rufus looked unhappy: there was a damp patch on his T-shirt where something had been spilled or scrubbed.

'Daddy says we're going home now,' he said to Sophie, his small voice high with anxiety.

Richard's hand settled heavily on Sophie's shoulder. 'They'll keep us informed,' he said, turning her so she had to look at him. 'And you haven't forgotten that my mother's coming for lunch tomorrow?'

'No, but . . . surely . . .' Sophie pulled away in alarm. 'Surely . . .' She even put her hand up to detach his from her shoulder.

But he ignored her. 'And there's the dinner on Thursday, clearly there's no question of cancelling with two of the partners coming.' Not once did his eyes stray to Victor – it was as though he didn't exist, had already vanished. Only Rufus dared a glance up at his grandfather, a small pleading look.

Victor saw the hand on Sophie's shoulder relax its grip and he thought, it's done. It's all done, but she shifted, just enough. 'I'm sure they wouldn't mind, under the circumstances,' she said in a calm clear voice and then Richard did look, his eyes slid across to Victor. His voice was quiet, velvety, a lawyer's voice but his eyes were hard.

'This is a very important dinner,' as though speaking man to man, although Victor knew he had only contempt for Victor's life as a man, muddling along fuelled by sentiment, making no provision for himself or his daughter. 'They say you're doing very well, that there's no cause for concern, none of this bedside vigil stuff.' The harder edge entering his voice there. 'None of that's necessary, and, I know,' the voice used never to being contradicted, 'I know you wouldn't want to keep Sophie from her family.'

Her family. Her family. Victor was winded by the cruelty of it. *Just die, just die*, said another voice that whispered just on the edge of earshot, but then Sophie's hand was in his.

She held on, tight. He didn't want to put her in danger, that was the very last thing he could allow, and so he cleared his throat. 'It's all right,' he began to say. 'You must . . . if . . .' And Richard was nodding, he moved round to take her from him, he was about to claim her. But then someone had arrived, someone was talking to the nurses at their station. Her voice stopped Victor finishing his sentence, completing his surrender. Natalie.

Chapter Twenty

Another cab would take twenty minutes, so they walked on up. The wide-pillared doorway had hidden an institutional reception area with linoleum floor; this wasn't a private clinic. This was NHS. There was a reception desk with computer monitors and arrowed signage, pointing down a corridor, up the scuffed stairs. REHABILITATION UNIT; PSYCHIATRIC OUTPATIENTS; physio upstairs. RESIDENTIAL UNIT, MOORSOM HOUSE, pointing back out the way they'd come.

A youngish woman with a thin ponytail peered around one of the monitors. Nat and Craig stepped back in the doorway hastily. 'She came every Monday? Maybe she was seeing someone,' said Craig, shrugging. 'Physio.'

'In heels?' said Nat. 'In the evening?'

Craig ripped at a hangnail with his teeth. 'Psychiatric outpatients?'

'You think this is a joke?'

'Can I help you?' The receptionist's voice was reedy and insistent: reluctantly they approached the desk.

It could only be, thought Nat. 'A friend of mine,' she said, 'used to come here every Monday evening to see someone. A relative, in the residential unit.' She ignored the glance Craig gave her. 'Moorsom House?'

'And?'

Nat went through it, keeping it as low-key as possible, apologising every other word, no confrontation, no demanding. Whenever the receptionist frowned Nat gave her a pleading look but when she'd finished the woman just pressed a buzzer before she said anything, leaning down and muttering into a microphone, 'Someone asking about Moorsom.' Nat kept her head down, and the woman sighed. 'We can't talk about patients, you know. Not without their permission.' An older woman appeared at the end of a corridor and walked towards them with an awkward, lopsided, unhurried gait, assessing them, Nat could tell, as she came.

'That's Mrs Walters,' said the girl with the ponytail. 'She manages Moorsom.'

She had a nice, weary manner. 'Dodgy hip,' she said. 'On the waiting list.'

She gave Craig a long look, head on one side, and he shuffled a bit then said, 'I'll be outside.'

Mrs Walters sighed. 'So what can we do you for?' The girl ducked back behind her computer.

Nat went over it all again and when she'd finished Walters said, 'So what'd she look like?'

Describing Beth, Nat had to clear her throat a couple of times. She knew too much, it was like when she'd talked to the police, she could have gone on, stories tried to creep in. The time Beth tried to do her own highlights and her fringe fell out, where she'd bought her favourite high heels, they were striped wedges. Turquoise toenails. It was only when he finished that she thought to show the woman the picture, on her phone.

Walters just nodded. 'Sure,' she said, but she had a guarded edge. 'She has a brother in Moorsom. But she hasn't been in three, four weeks.' She looked out through the door to where Craig stood. 'It happens. People . . . lose interest.' Then she frowned. 'I didn't think she was the type – she was good about coming. It was disappointing when . . . well. *He* was disappointed, that's the main thing.'

'Can we see him?' said Nat, quickly. 'What . . . what is his condition?'

The woman gestured towards the door and they took a few steps back into the porch. Craig was a little way down the hill now, his hands in his pockets. He was angry. Did that make him dangerous? Mrs Walters nodded to the side and Nat could make out a low building behind young trees where a group of people were throwing a ball to each other: she heard a shout, happy.

'I can't talk about patients,' said the manager. 'I can't tell you his name.' She tilted on her hip and winced. 'Moorsom is mostly Down's patients who can't live on their own, there are a few others, but—'

'Can you ask him?' said Nat. 'If I can talk to him? I mean if he can . . . if he . . .'

'You're worried about her, aren't you?' said the woman. 'I don't . . . he doesn't need to be upset.'

'I would try very hard not to do that,' said Nat, simply. 'I think if I don't talk to him, it will be the police.' Not quite true, not yet, but she couldn't wait for them to get interested. 'I've known Beth a long time,' she added, trying to keep her voice steady. 'And her disappearance is . . . uncharacteristic.' Whatever anyone else might say. 'She's my friend.'

Then Walters had given her a long look. Finally she had nodded.

'I'll talk to him.' She'd looked at Craig, standing with his back to them. 'Making no promises. But I'll ask him.'

It had been a different driver, on the way to the hospital: an ancient bloke with a greasy bald head who kept silence and besides, she no longer needed to know where Beth went. Craig had asked to be dropped on the edge of town. She turned to watch him as they pulled off again. He had said he need to get someone to fix the bike, but he just stood there, waiting for them to disappear.

Walking in to the hospital ward and seeing them there, Victor so pale and still on the bed between them he was almost a part of it, for a flashing moment she saw how a dead person looked, as dead as the sheets and blankets. Only when he moved his head to her did Nat look around the bed, and work it out. Sophie holding her dad's hand, the little boy downcast, his lower lip stuck out – and the man. The husband, with his hand resting on Sophie's shoulder. *Don't like him, don't like him, don't like him*, it was like an alarm going off. Nat stepped through them – between the husband and the boy – up to the bed and caught Sophie's glance, pale with relief.

'Victor,' said Nat. 'All right?' The husband cleared his throat behind her but she didn't turn to look until Sophie said, high and bright, 'Richard, this is Natalie, she's been so good. So good.'

The little boy – Rufus – had sidled away from his father, into the corner beside the bed. Sophie must have been old when she had him. There must have been risks: she must have really wanted him so badly. Nat thought of Beth's brother, in Moorsom House. The supervisor's strong hint had been that he had Down's. She thought of Beth's mother, hard as nails. You never knew, did you, where that hardness came from?

And of course there would be a dad, somewhere, maybe two, one for Beth, one for the boy in Moorsom House. She'd never asked Beth what had become of her dad – but then Beth never asked her where hers was, either. Fucking dead and good fucking riddance.

Nat could still remember when Mum had kicked him out. She had been eight years old, a bruise on her thigh from the last time he'd kicked her a week earlier – the last time he ever would – and a bubble of jubilation in her chest so huge it hurt her, she had to go up to her bedroom and let it out in a weird shouting laugh. Mum had come up and put her arms around her so Nat could feel her shaking, trembling, could hear her whispering something Nat as a kid hadn't understood, about her being sorry. And when she'd let her go there'd been just a big shaky smile on Mum's face. He'd hung around the house some nights, shouting, cracked a window pounding on it with his fist but when Mum had called the police on him he'd disappeared. The next they heard was five years later and he was dead in a car crash, drink-driving. Hit a lamp-post. Nat remembered feeling sorrier for the lamp-post.

What had been in her head when she'd done the

pregnancy test, Jim waiting outside the bathroom door? Sheer bloody blind panic.

Sophie's husband was looking at her and although his expression was only a sort of smile she could tell what was behind it. Resentment, dislike, a kind of itching hatred – for her, or all of them. He wanted his own way, and they were standing in it.

'I'm a friend of Victor's,' she said, staring back. 'It's great he's doing so well, isn't it?' Richard cleared his throat again, dismissive, almost embarrassed. *Not great, not doing well, not if I can help it.*

She could see it right there: he wants Victor dead. He wants to be on his own with her and the kid so he can stand over them and tell them how it is and they'll never escape. For a second the feeling was so strong she thought it was a mistake, she was confusing this man with her own dad, but it was different. He was a different kind of bastard: and he did want Victor dead. It came to her. She took a breath.

'Can I have a word with you and . . . Richard?' she said to Sophie, trying to make it sound earnest, serious, glancing into the corridor. 'Just a quick one?' The look went round them, to Sophie, to Richard, to Victor.

'Rufus, can you stay here and look after Grandpa?' Sophie spoke quickly. The boy nodded warily, but brightening. They walked to the sun room, Nat leading them, Sophie hurrying anxiously beside her and Richard upright, hands in pockets and impatient.

'Look—' he began, when they'd barely got through the door. The room was empty, and hot.

'I bumped into the consultant,' improvised Nat and saw

Richard put a hand up to knead the back of his neck, working it angrily. She went on. 'I don't know what she's told you, but—'

'She's so eager for Daddy to be back in his own home,' said Sophie, rushing in clumsily. 'The consultant is. But Richard says—'

Nat nodded, soberly. 'Yes, I expect . . . well, she was probably being as positive as possible, in front of Victor, but . . .' She hesitated, thinking, Liar, liar, then superstition rising against it but fuck it, saying it won't make it true. 'Look, he could only have a matter of days.'

Sophie gave a sort of choking gasp and Nat made herself not look because if she did she would have to recant, to reassure her. She looked at Richard instead, and saw a flicker of satisfaction, that pushed her on. 'Sophie can stay at the caravan or at the cottage with me but . . . I do think he needs her here. I do. I mean' – she stared down at her feet so as not to see him, and in case he saw what she was up to – 'it's really not going to be long.'

'But the consultant said—' Sophie said brokenly, and Nat put an arm round her, squeezing hard, harder, so she would understand. Richard stared at them both and Nat saw anger competing with the prospect of Victor gone, dealt with.

Then abruptly he expelled a breath. 'I'll take Rufus back with me,' he said. 'That caravan's no place for him.' Then, viciously, 'It's squalid.' Looking at Sophie, a look that made Nat want to punch him, on Victor's behalf too, *squalid*? But she felt Sophie only go still.

It was obvious, what he was doing. It was revenge, and more. Rufus was his hostage. But to Nat's surprise Sophie spoke calmly.

'I know, darling, it's hardly ideal.' She was sweet, she was submissive, she was reasonable. She had learned to be like this. And all the time Nat could see the trembling fear underneath, she knew that scenario. 'But there's your work. You'll hardly get anything done with Rufus, you know how demanding he can be.' Richard was quite still, watching her. Nat could see a pinched look at his nostrils.

Sophie kept going, bravely. 'I would like him to see his grandfather just for these last . . . if . . .' And then she did stop. Nat could see her staring hard at Richard's chest, his stupid button-down shirt, to stop herself crying. Why shouldn't she cry? Nat wanted to run at Richard and slap him and scratch his face but she knew she had really, really better not.

And then Sophie took a breath and went on. 'And I'll bring him back at the weekend.'

Not a crack, not a tremble. Was that what she had to do? thought Nat. She had to be obedient, he wanted to see her in pain, but she couldn't break down, she couldn't show it. In that moment Nat had the strongest feeling that if Sophie did cry, Richard would burst out laughing.

'I'll bring him back, whatever happens,' she said. If Victor lives or dies, was what she meant.

He took half a step towards Sophie and stopped. Nat could see how angry he was, he didn't have to do anything, it was in the stiffness of his movements, in the light eyes, the flush at his neck, it was even in his receding hairline, where a vein throbbed.

'I will come back for you,' he said, enunciating distinctly. He would punish Sophie, somehow. But they had won.

And now Sophie was tripping over herself, breathless,

telling him she'd brought enough clothes to last them, saying she'd apologise personally to the partners and their wives for the dinner.

'She can stay with me in my cottage,' said Nat, just wanting to stop Sophie but when Richard turned to look at her she felt a deep, horrible unease. 'I mean, if she needs to?' You have to pretend, she realised. That you don't know he hates you. She smiled.

'I'll go and say goodbye to Rufus,' was all he said.

They watched him leave the hospital from the window in the corridor outside the ward.

Rufus had stood with his head lowered as Richard spoke to him intently, out of earshot of any of them. Richard didn't speak to Sophie or to Victor again, he just walked straight-backed out of the ward.

They saw him walk across the car park below them and climb into a big expensive car. When the car door closed on him Sophie backed away until she reached the wall, and crumpled to the floor where she crouched, her face in her hands. Awkward in her hurry, Nat ran to get to her, to tell her, and then both of them were on the linoleum floor, and fuck the lot of them, nurses, doctors, fuck what anyone might think.

'It's all right,' she said urgently, trying to prise Sophie's hands away from her face. 'He's not going to die, it's all right. Victor's not. I just had to say that.' Sophie's face appeared, her cheeks red and streaked with crying. 'They're pleased with him, really. They are. I had to say that so that he would let you stay.' She was tempted to go further, to interrogate Sophie, but she knew she couldn't. One step at a time. 'Right? That's how we make sure Victor gets better. It's how we get him out of the hospital. You know that. It's why you did your bit too.' She had both Sophie's wrists in her hands now. 'You were brilliant, Sophie. You were fucking brilliant.'

Sophie pulled a wrist away to rub at her eye. 'I – I don't know,' she said, sounding frightened now. Nat persisted, helping her to her feet.

'And I meant it about the cottage.'

'The cottage.' Sophie pulled her clothing awkwardly back into place, sheepish.

Nat hesitated, thinking. The new locks: did that make it safe? In her head she saw the dark garden, out through the tiny kitchen window. Safer in numbers, though, her and Sophie and Rufus. Whoever it was wouldn't be expecting that. An instant family round the table. She shoved her misgivings to one side.

'I've got to work this evening,' she said earnestly, 'I've been off all day. But come over to the pub with Rufus, you can sit in the garden and when I'm done I'll make dinner.'

'Really?' Sophie's face, pale and crumpled with relief.

Dinner, Christ knew how that would go. Nat hadn't cooked dinner in months, not since . . . Not since. And Janine would probably kill her, too.

And then Sophie was smiling, smiling, looking just like Victor. 'Yes. Oh, that would be . . . can we just, let's go and tell them? Tell Rufus and my father.'

'Let's, yes,' said Nat and she saw in Sophie's face that for the moment, it was all right. Richard had gone.

She took the bus to the supermarket from the hospital and when she walked out, with a bag of the stupidest stuff

– sausages, chocolate mousse, crisps, lettuce, anything and everything a three-year-old might conceivably eat for dinner – held in two arms because one of the handles had bust, there was Jim.

He was standing beside his van, looking brown and thin and serious. In two days she seemed to have forgotten how tall he was, or was that just because he was thinner? It seemed to her that he had been waiting for her, or for someone.

'You want a lift?' He stepped up to her and reached to take the bag out of her arms.

For a second she resisted, hung on to it, but suddenly she was just so tired, with the whole weight of the long horrible day in every limb and a shift to do and she let him take it.

Her hands fell to her sides. 'Sure,' she said.

Chapter Twenty-One

It was busy in the pub; of course it was. As she walked back from the hot gloom of the bar into the humid kitchen with another loaded tray and smelled the steam from the dishwasher and the drains and the bins beyond the side door, it seemed to Nat that this summer was never going to end. She turned and walked back into the bar, wiping her hands on her apron.

There was a group of middle-aged men in Victor's corner this time, on a fishing trip, she had gathered from their several trips to the bar; they were on their fourth round of drinks, or it might be fifth. They were talking about women and had been since round two (two bottled Mexican lagers, a gin and tonic and four pints). Nat had been trying not to listen.

There was no sign of Bill the cameraman. Already Nat had an outline of him, stocky, dependable, certain: she would know it if he appeared in the low doorway, without seeing his face. She hadn't answered the text he'd sent, yet. He'd given her that option, at least. She felt an uneasy stirring in her gut, that she'd given him encouragement, just by liking him. Things were complicated enough as they were.

Paddy was in the corner opposite the fishermen, an empty seat beside him that he seemed to be defending against all comers, which wasn't like him. His lean face thoughtful, soft. And taking his time over his pint.

Jim had dropped her at the pub, both of them silent by then. She'd heard him out as he drove her back, more carefully than she'd ever seen him drive, eyes flicking between mirrors, long pauses at junctions, headlights on as the sun dipped, brushing the trees on the horizon. On the edge of town he had expelled a long breath.

'We can start again,' he said and she could hear all the effort it took to make his voice sound reasonable, not pleading. The low red sun hit the mirror from behind them as they turned towards the estuary, the sky streaked shocking pink and purple from edge to edge. The days were shortening: it was September tomorrow. September was when the world changed, the holidaymakers went, there would be rain. She'd been in Janine's cottage in a downpour, she knew the dripping dark, the sudden damp chill in everything, shoes, jumpers, tea towels.

'We can try again.' There was the slightest movement of Jim's head as he resisted looking at her. 'We can start again – we can start a family. I love you, no one's . . . nothing terrible has happened. Nothing that can't be undone.' He swallowed, but kept his voice level. 'I can't live without you.'

She held herself still then, unable to open her mouth because it was too complicated. *No one's died*, he'd been going to say, but had stopped himself.

I love you, Jim. I want to keep you safe. But we should never have, we should never . . . I should never . . .

You don't stay with someone just because you feel sorry for them.

You don't get rid of a baby just because you panic.

Only sometimes you do.

And then he turned and looked at her, his eyes bloodshot, his brown face too thin.

'I – I'm sorry,' Nat said. 'I'm sorry, Jim.'

For a second she felt a vibration, as if he understood, and in the next second she thought what he understood might flip him back into anger, or misery, but then he sighed, his shoulders dropping. 'I heard you're worried about Beth,' he said in a monotone, head down.

'She's nowhere. She left her phone, she left her stuff . . .' She hesitated. 'Even the police look like they might be taking it seriously now.' She went over it all and she could tell he was really listening, maybe it was a relief, to be talking about something else.

She told him about the blood on the cloth tying Ollie's hands being a woman's and then Jim turned to stare. 'They know that stuff?' he said. 'They can tell? They really think she's . . .' She could hear the panic in his voice and she felt sorry for him. She sat back in her seat and he looked ahead at the road again, both quiet. The hedges were black on either side of them now.

'You need to be careful,' Jim said, as he leaned forwards at the last junction, into the village, checking both ways. 'I mean it.' And hearing something new in the way he said it Nat sat up. His voice went lower. 'I mean, I understand, the way things were when we . . . we split up, but it isn't safe, that kind of life, Beth's kind of life, guys you don't know . . .'

And Nat had frozen then, understanding that he meant her, he meant Tinder, that it had got Beth into trouble and it would get Nat into trouble too. They'd only have themselves to blame and he was pretending to sympathise but she knew him too well, she could hear bitterness – and she felt anger boil up inside her. *Two Tinder dates? What the fuck do you know about it?* She turned to look at him, ready to say it, but she didn't. She had turned her head back, slowly, and said nothing. She could tell he was anxious, mortified, by her silence when he said, 'Nat?' fearful, coming to a halt outside the Bird, but she didn't trust herself to say anything. She got out and slammed the door and left him there.

'All right, darling?' The punter had a red face, a beard, one of the fishermen and pleased as punch with being able to hold four empty glasses in his two hands, setting them down on the bar in front of her. Nat knew the next thing out of his mouth would be, *Cheer up, love, it might never happen* and she wouldn't be answerable when it was.

'Same again?' she said, stretching a smile across her face. Not his fault, was it? Then again, it could be. Could be any of them.

His face fell, just slightly. A wedding ring embedded in a fat finger. Bluffing back up to cheerful. 'Well, if you insist.'

Holding the glass steady against the pump and looking down at the amber liquid so as not to look into the man's daft red face, something was bothering her. Something Jim had said? Something Jim had done? Something wrong, something right, what had she seen? Or heard, or remembered. It tick-tick-ticked down in her head: *What, what, what*? Something to do with Jim. When he'd been listening to her so carefully, when she'd been thinking about the cottage, their old place, Jim's flat with the big windows and rain, and a table laid. A table laid for dinner.

Could be any of them. Nat set the pint down on the bar cloth and started on another.

And then it struck her, she felt it cold at her back: these were the men Beth saw. Regulars or transients, fishermen, locals, holidaymakers, they came in here and saw her. Up here at the bar with their banter or sitting quiet in a corner, watching Beth in secret. Wanting her.

Could be any of them. It could be a punter, it could be someone working at the residential home she visited once a week, it could be Bill or Steve or Craig or Jim. Could be someone Nat had never met.

She felt her hand suddenly cold and looked down to see the glass overflowing. He could be in here right now. She set the glass on a tray, dazed.

If the blood they found on Ollie isn't Beth's. She clung to that for just a second, a tiny window of hope she tried to build on: she's just walked away, left it all behind, Christ knew, Nat had been tempted herself, since . . . since. Say it. Since the termination. Start again. And what?

The fisherman handed her his money, giving her a funny look, and took the tray. She turned to the till.

But why would Beth go? Nat tried to remember those last days. A Wednesday night, she'd disappeared, off to see her mum. Thirty-six hours earlier, she'd gone to see her brother, as usual. And said nothing, to him or the staff?

Who would she have talked to? To Victor, to Paddy, to her brother? Victor and Paddy knew nothing, nor did Dowd. And then there was the hospital appointment. Dr Ramsay had told Nat not to worry – but there'd been something weird, something shifty about her answers. Hospitals didn't dish out appointments for nothing, did they?

The car that had come up behind her in the lane on her way back from the surgery, dazzling her. Something wrong about that. Too slow, lights on full beam then speeding past, trying to scare her.

Looking across the hot crowded room it felt suddenly as though they were all avoiding looking at her. She'd drawn attention to herself, thrashing around, shouting that something had happened to Beth. Some of them were embarrassed by it, some of them thought she'd lost it, avoiding her eye. But of all of them, one of them knew she was right. The one who had walked up the path to Beth's place, knowing she was behind the door. Who had placed Beth's bra where she would know Beth hadn't left it, hanging inside a dead animal's skin.

Who was watching her.

Watching her run herself ragged here, there and everywhere, hospital care centre, cadging lifts off Steve and Dowd, paying for cabs, begging to be heard. Grilling poor old Victor. Seeing it from the outside, like that – the way the police saw it, maybe, the way all this lot saw it – Nat felt anger and frustration rise. She knew what he was up to, whoever he was. Like Sophie's husband Richard, waiting for her to break down so he could laugh, seeing her get nowhere, and he was waiting. Just waiting.

She felt a sudden rush of fear. Waiting for what?

'Jesus bloody Christ, Nat.' It was Janine, planted in front of her, a box of crisps in her arms, disbelieving. 'You could turn the milk with that face. Sort it out, will you?' Then she was looking past Nat to the door, and sighed. 'And here's another one of your charity cases. When you going to learn?'

It was Sophie, standing in the doorway, looking around, blinking, and Rufus pressed against her. As Nat's heart began to sink at the complication they represented Paddy was already on his feet in the corner and Sophie was turning towards him, not to Nat at all. They edged across to him and Nat saw Sophie register Janine, watching.

'I asked her,' Nat began. 'I know it's late, he's a good kid, though. Victor—' Janine shook her head impatiently. Not child-friendly, after eight in the evening, wasn't Janine.

'If he's quiet,' she said, tight-lipped, and she was round the bar and asking them for their drinks order.

When Nat looked over again they were settled in for all the world like a little family, Paddy's dusty grey head bent as he explained something to Rufus using beermats and then, like a token in a slot, like the three apples in a row, with what almost felt like a click, Nat knew. What it was she'd been trying to remember.

The place laid for one, at her table. Jim.

A dinner party, that dinner party, their only one, getting ready in the bright glass-walled room. Laying the table, only she'd had to go round after Jim and do it all over again. You didn't see it at first, what was wrong, you had to look a few times and that night in the cottage with her heart battering like a runaway engine at the sight of the table laid for one, she had not been looking. And had the policeman asking her about her ex just got her hackles up, stopping her seeing clearly, or had she wanted to protect him? Had she known, even then?

It was quite simple really: the knife and fork reversed,

set the wrong way round, under the low-hanging light in the cottage.

Which was how Jim did it – being left-handed.

Jim. Jim. Jim. And that face rose in front of her, thin and dark, staring at her, pleading with her – and it was a stranger's face. A Jim she hadn't known, after all. Starting backwards from the bar so quickly she almost trod on Janine standing behind her, she muttered some excuse or other, aware of Janine's stiff, angry face following her out into the kitchen, then on into the dark garden, where she pulled out her phone.

The phone only rang once, as though he'd been waiting for her.

The lights had been dimmed on the ward and they lay there, none of them asleep, most of them sedated one way or another, or just obedient. You could tell that they were awake, from the shifting of legs, the sighs, but no one would speak.

Victor was obedient too, or at least he wished to be, it seemed the best way of getting out and home again although lying awake in the dark without a book or a radio or any means of feeling as though he still occupied the world, the thought hovered, just on the edge of his field of vision, that the opposite might indeed be true. Obedience to the dimming of the lights and the removal of the world and all its entertainments might be just settling in to wait for the end, making no trouble, preparing for the moment at which one disappears.

Of course, you didn't get to his age without wondering, peering over the edge to see, what those last hours, minutes, seconds, might look like. But Sophie needed him to hang on,

Rufus did. The warmth of Rufus's small body perched unself-conscious on the bed beside him, wriggling down to find a comfortable spot, had told him, perhaps he was still needed.

He stirred, uneasy, thinking of Natalie, and Sophie. Would she understand, would she see, it wasn't Sophie's fault? She had been in love with Richard, poor trusting girl, and when she understood what he was it was too late and Victor had not trained her to assert herself, or to point out others' cruelty. He had to trust that Nat would see.

They had carried out some manoeuvre between them, hadn't they? Because Richard had come in to kneel and mutter angrily in Rufus's ear, but then he had gone, back to London in his big fast car. Sophie had been red-eyed and breathless, it had cost her something that perhaps she would not tell him, but Richard had gone.

A walking frame had been left beside the bed – for the morning, they had said. Richard had gone but something like him still hovered, in here, something sat in the dark, murmuring out of sight in the shadowy corridor. He put out a hand to feel the cool metal of the frame. The water had tasted strange, the jug that someone had refilled in the night, and then he had felt that sinking, that ebbing of his capacities that they had put down to his medication.

A nurse, or someone else? Had Owen Wilkins come in, unnoticed, was there someone else, who could walk through the wards and no one would stop him – or her? Someone who didn't understand what Victor knew, that when the body failed, the other instinct strengthened, that sensed danger like a soft shadow creeping outwards from a corner.

On the bed Victor eased himself upright, feeling his body respond, a little bit slow, but true, surely, all nerves and muscles present and correct. Trying not to make any sound. His legs over the side and the soles of his feet on the odd warmth of the linoleum. He felt for slippers, gave up quickly. Not necessary. Weight on his arms, trembling, and he was upright. Three days in bed, four, and he was down to half strength, perhaps more – but caravan living had trained Victor: the morning walk for the newspaper, afternoon down to the water, evening to the pub twice a week and almost never accepting a lift, there or back. A good mile's walk. He had the strength in him, he only needed to coax it out. Up: he was up.

There was a solitary male nurse on the night desk but he didn't turn his head to look after Victor and when Victor paused to catch his breath and fully expecting to be sent back he saw that the man had earphones in. Not allowed, of course. He didn't know the man, had not seen him before. He would have guessed him to be Filipino or Malaysian.

Down the corridor, rocking step by rocking step. He could hear Sophie, bewildered, *Daddy, what did you think you were doing?* and he wasn't sure he could have come up with an explanation except the climbing, rising feeling that if he stayed in that bed he would die. If he made no effort, they would come for him. It would come: the man with bowed head and blood on his arm walking up from the darkness would come and hold a glass to his lips and unprotesting he would sink back on the pillows and die. He reached the door of the big bathroom and with a trembling hand he pushed.

It was heavy and Victor had to inch ahead painfully. Halfway through he heard the swish of another door, down the corridor, round a corner, he heard voices – but then Victor was inside and the weighted door swung silently to behind him.

His heart pattered as he stood just inside the door. Some yellow outside light was cast through a high window and he could just make out the big open shower stalls. Nowhere to hide in here but there was one door between him and them. He heard the voices, murmuring.

If he fell, if he fainted. Down on the cool-warm linoleum, his cheek against the floor, snap snap snap would go his limbs like old dry sticks. They would push inside and take him back to the bed and there he would stay.

Balancing himself between the walking frame and the wall, Victor held steady and upright, he breathed quietly.

Polite enquiry, two men talking although he didn't know what they said. One making conversation, working his way around to something, the other responding in an accented voice that identified him as the nurse. The one probing – Victor knew him. Something in the timbre of the voice, the low laugh. Knew him, but didn't know where from.

He could come out, and identify him, the man he'd seen walking up from the river, or he could hide until he had gone. The man who had come for him.

Would he ask the nurse, *You know you've lost one? Bed number twenty-three, AWOL?* And set off all sorts of alarms, there would be running feet. But all was quiet: the hunt not worth his while, then, or not part of the plan. Or all in Victor's failing mind.

Victor stayed where he was in the dark until the voices fell silent again, and for some time afterwards.

Chapter Twenty-Two

'It was you. What did you think you were doing?'

She didn't care who in the pub's scruffy garden was listening. A couple holding hands under the weeping willow at the end, and a dishevelled mother walking a baby up and down and too knackered to pay any attention.

On the phone Jim sounded frightened, he babbled. He denied it. Didn't know what she was talking about. 'I love you,' he said, in desperation. Anything but admit it.

Nat hung up on him.

Walking back into the pub not quite in control of what she was feeling – stupid, stupid Jim, stupid and frightening too, just a bit frightening for him to have done that and then deny it. And why? To what end? Looking after her. She knew how Jim's mind worked. See. Here. You need to eat properly, you need order in your life, you need me. It was him needed all those things.

Here's a place laid for you.

The table laid just like when they lived together – only just for one, to show her how lonely she was. How lonely they both were, without each other. But as she pushed the phone back in her pocket, the thought of the flat they'd shared, the wharf development with the balconies facing a dull stretch of the canal, Nat felt like she was suffocating. She came through the back door behind the bar and there was Jonathan Dowd, waiting to be served. Elbows in, hunched, and Janine pushing him over a bitter lemon. Not another one, was all she could think, as bad as Jim, with that awful look on his face.

Janine eyed them, pursing her lips, then something broke out in the corner, a bit of argy-bargy with one of the fishermen trying to grab another's phone off him and she was round the bar to sort it out and leaving Nat and Jonathan Dowd to it.

What look did he have on his face? Cool, determined. Like he was the only one keeping his head. That would have sent Beth off on one, for sure: if there was anything she couldn't stand it was being patronised. For her five GCSEs and her ragged fingernails and her dodgy dye job and her infuriating tendency not to feel sorry for herself, ever.

'Look,' he said, leaning in over his bitter lemon, 'I didn't tell you because I didn't want you to think . . . badly of her.'

'Tell me what?' Nat kept calm but it was boiling up. She drummed her fingernails on the bar top.

'It wasn't exclusive. She was . . . she—'

'She slept with who she wanted.' Her fingers were still. 'I don't think badly of her, Jonathan.' She wondered if he could hear how angry she was. Maybe he could, for all that: he bent further over the bar, his voice going lower.

'Maybe I didn't want you to think badly of me. That I . . . tolerated it.' His voice cracked. 'It isn't that I tolerated it.' And now it was ragged, helpless. 'I didn't have any choice.'

Nat sighed, not ready to be understanding, not yet. How did you read this bloke? Or any of them, come to that; since Beth had gone they'd all started looking like aliens. Thinking of Jim on the phone, Jim losing it, Jim who'd always had plans, Jim the big kid, lower than she'd ever heard him. His plans all gone to nothing, a failing boatyard and no one to come home to.

Dowd's face was set, now. 'It's not . . . they were never my area of expertise,' he said. 'Relationships.' Angry now. His face changing, like clouds chasing over the sky, he was nervy, he was arrogant, he was insecure, he was self-righteous. She imagined the whirlwind Beth must have been in his life, scattering his charts and his test tubes. She did that: wrought havoc. Was there something he was hiding? Camped out in the woods, away from prying eyes.

'Look,' she said, 'we want to know where she is, and if she's all right, don't we? Is that why you came? Is that why you're telling me this now?'

He looked pale. 'Yes . . . I—'

'Not to make yourself look better? More . . . understanding? More the victim?'

Because she didn't need this. Him coming here to confess to something she already knew. Asking for sympathy, or to say she had it coming.

His eyes dark. 'You don't . . . I don't think you understand—' Choking up.

Nat held her gaze steady. 'It would be more useful,' she said, not letting him off the hook, 'if you knew who any of these guys were, she was seeing. Where she met them, that kind of stuff. Tinder? Here? It's not like she had a lot of nights off.' He twisted awkwardly, as if he was trying to get out from under her gaze. 'The bloke she went to see on Mondays was her brother, for the record,' she said quietly and he flushed.

In the corner Sophie was still talking to Paddy: an odd couple. Her round and nervy and sweet, him dusty and shabby. Rufus almost asleep between them.

Leaving Dowd at the bar Nat went over to Janine with a tray and took some glasses off her. The middle-aged lads were shuffling on their bench seat, with her there standing over them: Janine's tried and tested method of nipping trouble in the bud was just to stand there with her arms folded giving them one of her looks. As if on cue Steve had appeared behind the bar from upstairs, yawning, ready for action.

'Look,' Nat said, 'I know I've been off all day, but' – looking at Sophie and Rufus – 'I promised them dinner, it's been a long day for them. Victor—'

Janine looked from her to Steve, cheery behind the bar and already straightening the bar cloths, not quite listening. There was something on her mind, Nat could tell. 'Go on then,' she said, tightly. 'Not far off closing, anyway.' Hesitant. As Nat reached behind herself to untie her apron Janine put a hand out to her arm, keeping her there.

'You watch yourself, though,' she said. 'I'm not happy about this. You're a worry.' Glancing over at the bar, a warning look. 'Steve agrees.'

'What? Has something happened?'

Janine looked evasive. 'People have been talking.' She stepped away from the table with her load of glasses and from the men starting to look at them, to listen to their lowered voices. 'Half the time you're so . . . angry. Shouting the odds. Interrogating the punters. Never mind Jim . . . You're not exactly in control, are you, Nat?'

Nat stared at her. 'I'm trying . . . I'm trying . . .' she said, but what was the point? *I'm trying to hold it all together, and no one's listening.* 'I'm sorry, Janine,' she said. On the other table Paddy was still talking to Sophie, Rufus tucked under her arm now, she was listening, nodding. Watching his face.

'Apparently the police have been asking around,' said Janine. 'They've been talking to people.' And Nat was quite certain in that moment that she was hiding something.

'What people?' she said.

Janine shrugged. 'Punters. You hear stuff.'

Nat scanned the room but no one was looking her way, all of a sudden. 'What did they want to know about me?'

'Nothing, nothing much. Just . . . you know. You and Beth, what kind of friends you were, how you got on.'

'What d'you mean?' Her voice was brittle, she couldn't help it.

'Well, you were chalk and cheese, weren't you? You and Beth. Some people were saying . . . well, not me, mind, but—' She broke off and from the way Janine looked around the busy bar, not looking at Nat, Nat was pretty sure it had been her.

'Saying what?'

'Saying she were a bad influence. That since Beth turned

up you . . . well. You were a different person. Leaving Jim, and that.'

'That wasn't Beth,' said Nat. Her head on Beth's shoulder, the only one who knew what it felt like. 'That was me. She didn't tell me to do it.'

Beth hugging her.

Janine sighed, avoiding her eye. 'Them friendships . . . you know. They never end well. One girl's the outgoing one, gets all the lads, the other one—'

'Oh, right,' said Nat, dangerous now. 'So I was jealous of her, or what?'

Janine backed off, mumbling. 'Just wanted to let you know, it's not all one way. Once you start talking to the cops.' And her face closed, then, end of conversation; she hugged the glasses to her chest and turned away, searching for Steve's face. 'You get off,' she said over her shoulder. 'You get off to your friends.'

'You'd better stay, don't you think?'

They looked at Rufus, who had climbed obediently on to the sofa and promptly fallen asleep again. They were all dead tired. It had been a relief not to be coming back alone down the quiet lane: everything felt different. Nat could listen to the sounds in the hedges, smell the dry grass and warm foliage, without being on her guard. Rufus had walked unsteadily between them, footsteps weaving, one hand in each of theirs, sticky, surprisingly trusting. Nat tried to remember at what age you pulled your hand away, when a strange adult reached for it. He had walked ahead of them into the house.

Sophie pulled off his shoes and he didn't stir.

'I'll carry him up,' said Nat. 'The staircase is tricky.' He was heavy and warm, and she climbed steadily, adjusting to the weight. 'You can have my room, the sofa will do me fine.' Sophie barely protested, she looked so knackered, and Nat laid Rufus down on the lumpy double bed under the eaves, hoping Sophie wouldn't notice the unpacked boxes and the total failure to turn the place into anything resembling a home. Tomorrow, thought Nat. Wouldn't do any harm to put a few things away.

They ate tuna salad and drank some warm wine at the table opposite each other. Sophie looking around the low-ceilinged room, laughing at Janine's horse brasses, protesting over how uncomfortable the sofa looked.

'You were getting along well with Paddy,' said Nat, eyeing her over her glass.

To her surprise Sophie just smiled, completely at ease. 'Isn't he absolutely lovely?' she said. 'He said such clever things about my dad, and I felt so sad for him, his wife dying, only two years of marriage, and he would have liked children—' She stopped. 'What?'

Nat could feel herself staring. 'I never knew—' Paddy had been married? She felt herself grow warm with shame, at never having asked.

Sophie just shrugged. 'Well, we just got talking,' she said, bent over her plate. 'He's easy to talk to. He loves you.' Said quite simply, as if they both knew what she meant.

'Paddy's a good friend,' said Nat.

'That's what he said,' said Sophie. 'People you can trust are rare, he told me. He trusts you.' She could have been a different woman from the woman standing submissively with Richard's hand on her shoulder. 'The consultant did talk about a place, with residential places for the elderly,' she said then, as if she knew what Nat was thinking. 'In a nearby village. Richard thinks it's a good idea.' Brandon, it turned out, on the same site as Moorsom House. At the thought of Victor out there Nat felt a lump in her throat. Laying down her knife and fork carefully, Sophie blurted, 'I wish I could have him at home. I wish. I wish I could be close to him. But—'

'It's Richard,' said Nat. 'I can see that.'

Sophie's eyes flicked up to meet hers, didn't look away.

'There could be a solution,' said Nat steadily. 'You don't have to be rushed into things. Victor doesn't.'

'He wants to leave that hospital,' said Sophie. 'He thinks it's dangerous in there.'

'Dangerous?' Nat's voice was sharp.

Sophie moved her shoulders uneasily. 'I wasn't sure what he meant,' she said slowly. 'At first I thought perhaps he meant that people die in hospitals.' Her face was pale. 'You know, MRSA, that sort of thing.'

'He's probably right,' said Nat, wanting to be reassuring.

'Old people can't fight those things off – and he is so old, so old—'

'He's very tough,' said Nat, defensive. 'We do need to get him out of there. But you think there's something else to it? Something specific that worries him? Someone?'

'Oh, the man, the man he thought he saw.' Now she was the flustered Sophie again.

'He *is* afraid, Sophie. Of that man. He told the police about him.'

'Yes, I . . .' Sophie's face crumpled. 'You mustn't say – Richard would think . . . he already keeps hinting that . . . well, dementia—'

'If he's afraid of someone, maybe he has reason to be.' She took hold of Sophie's hand across the table. 'No one could be less demented than Victor.' Sophie nodded, subsiding, but she took her hand back and stood up. 'You need to remember that, Sophie,' said Nat. 'We'll get him out.'

'I'd better get some sleep,' said Sophie, retreating. Nat retrieved a quilt for the sofa and lay there in the dark, listening to the small sounds from upstairs, Sophie's feet padding to and from the bathroom, a little cry from Rufus, a murmured exchange, the creak of the bed. Then it was quiet, a quiet that crept around the house, up the stairs, erasing the visitors until the old sounds asserted themselves. The soft rumble of the boiler, the creaking of old wood settling. The sounds outside: a window was open somewhere, perhaps just a crack, but Nat could smell the night air and gradually, gradually, the noises. A distant car, something rustling in the hedge, something softer than a rustle, padding on grass.

And then the distinct sound of a footstep on gravel, that stopped. She could hear breathing. She strained, and suddenly her heart was thumping so hard she could feel it in her throat, in her ears. The steps again, and they were close, they were right at the back door.

'*Nat?*'

And she was off the sofa, trailing the duvet, her face was pressed against the door. A shadow moved behind the small diamond-paned window beside the door, across the moonlit washing-up on the draining board. No sound from upstairs.

'*Nat.*' The voice wandering, hopeless.

She hesitated, her fingers over the key, then she turned

it. Carefully she lifted the latch, and before the door was even half open he was through it, falling against her, clinging. She held on to the door frame with one hand.

'I've lost it,' he said. 'I don't know . . . I don't know what I'm doing any more, Nat.' So heartbroken, so sorrowful, she couldn't do anything but put one hand up to his hair, stroke it.

'Jim,' she said, helpless.

He stood there, arms hanging at his sides, while she locked the door again, the bolt too. She pulled the diamond-paned window to and bolted it as well. She saw him looking around the room: he didn't seem to be able to move. 'It was me,' he said.

'I know,' she said but he didn't seem to hear her.

'I did put the plate out. I just wanted . . . I wanted it to be—'

'I know what you wanted.' Patiently, wearily.

And knowing for absolutely certain that it wasn't the right thing to do but then maybe sometimes there was no right thing, there was only trying to dodge the catastrophic thing, the wrong thing, the cruel thing, she took hold of his hand and led him to the sofa. She took off his shoes, just like Sophie had taken off Rufus's, and she lay down beside him. And when his hands wandered up and across her body, stroking her breasts, her body slid into its old place, her belly against his, her mouth against his, and it couldn't be prevented, like breathing. You could only hold your breath so long.

'This isn't—' she tried to say at one point. 'Jim, this doesn't mean—' But he wasn't listening.

* * *

He slept as if he'd been sedated afterwards, so deeply Nat had to be glad for him. Why? Why had she done it? she pleaded with herself. So as not to send him away in the dark. So he won't think he's a fuck-up, so he knows someone's there.

When you do something – out of guilt, out of pity, not wanting to see that look on his face – that you know was a mistake, what do you do next? Beth would have an answer, but Beth wasn't there.

When he rolled away before dawn and sat a moment with his head in his hands, before fumbling for his clothes, Nat didn't move. She watched him get up and stumble to the door, let him unlock and unbolt it, she felt the rush of cool green air and heard the birds. Summer was on the way out, she thought, but still she said nothing, she didn't move until the door closed and she heard his footsteps receding across the gravel.

Then she got up and locked it behind him.

Chapter Twenty-Three

Thursday

Victor had already been up on his walking frame and to the bathroom when Lisa appeared at the foot of the bed, and though he had had moments of breathless fear – leaning against the cubicle door, lowering himself to the seat – that something would happen, he had got there and back without disaster.

Not quite daring to be triumphant, though, because the fear was still there. Was it rational? To feel his heart flutter, to be so aware of the weakness of his legs, to see too clearly how easy it would be for the whole ramshackle operation of a body nearly a hundred years old simply to fold up and put itself away, was in fact in a certain light all too rational, but not for Victor. He had never been a panicker before, he had over a lifetime rehearsed the argument that panic was not sensible, he had not been afraid of his inevitable death. But that was not quite all he was afraid of now. There was someone to be afraid of, now, and here. And there were others to consider.

'Well,' said Lisa, with a kind of gasp, surprised, pleased and anxious all at once. 'Really, Victor, you are . . . you're quite something. There are patients who'd be glad of the rest.'

He thought she looked tired herself: creases at the corner of her eyes, night shifts, he supposed, and the strain of patients like him, stubborn and foolish, falling out of bed, hiding in bathrooms, although she knew nothing about that, as far as he could tell. He murmured something about it and with a sigh she sank to the bed.

Victor wasn't sure when he had understood, or how, that women like to talk to him: the only explanation he could come up with was that he did like listening. The world of women seemed to him largely comforting, or perhaps that was his age. There was so much that was practical in it, things made or cooked, clothes chosen, philosophy unfolded, who to love? Whether to have a child, or to travel, what to cook for supper.

Lisa was talking about her husband, they never saw each other, shift work was like that, when would they have a baby, what would happen to her patients if she stopped. Fiddling with her wedding ring and half forgetting she was talking to anyone but herself.

'I loved my wife,' he said and her eyes were on him, quiet. 'We never spent a night apart, until she became ill.' She fidgeted, anxious. 'Perhaps you should change things, Lisa.'

Victor was surprised at himself because he didn't usually dispense advice so openly, but there was something about being in this bed and so close, perhaps, to seeing her again, his darling – not that he believed in any afterlife but still – that made it seem too important. He had dreamed, in the three hours or so he had slept deeply, he had dreamed of the house they had brought Sophie back to from the hospital, he and Joy. He had dreamed of the sitting room, the low sofas with dark velvet cushions and wicker arms, the windows crowded with foliage and the baby folded in a white blanket in her basket, glowing pale as a pearl in the dim green room.

Lisa bobbed her head down again and Victor laid his back on the pillow.

'A baby – a child – a child is . . .' What was it that he wanted to say? A child is everything. He didn't have the energy to bring out the qualifications he knew good manners and kindness required: one can have a good life without a child, of course one can. One can fulfil oneself, one can look after others, one can . . . He closed his eyes. 'My Sophie – when we knew we were having . . .' And he found he perhaps should not say anything else, because if he dwelt on Sophie he might quite possibly tremble, or cry, and Lisa might worry about him. She might find reasons to keep him in.

Had he made a mistake in bringing Sophie out here? And Rufus? They were in danger from Richard, was that it, the nagging guilty anxious feeling that thoughts of Sophie trailed behind them? Or from something else? Or were the two connected, Richard and the man not Richard, walking up into the light? Shorter than Richard? Victor couldn't be sure, from the angle he had looked, down the slope. More hair, a different set to the shoulders?

Of course, he had always known the man in the lane with blood on his arm was not Richard, who had been a hundred miles away at the time, possibly even in a court-room, hadn't he? They only made him feel the same way: afraid. But the exercise of analysing why he knew this man had not been Richard had sparked something, had restored the image, given the man more shape. He could see him a little more clearly now.

Short-term memory's a luxury, at your age. Victor opened his eyes: who had said that? Lisa was on her feet, looking worried, so he smiled at her. It had been the accident and emergency registrar, when he had first been brought in, hadn't it? Victor's smile broadened, not because the remark had been funny – on the contrary, it had struck him as careless, although he hadn't been able to say so – but because again he had reached for the information and there it was. Remembered.

'It's all right, Lisa,' he said, reaching at random for some phrase to calm the waters. 'It'll all come out in the wash.' And she nodded, relieved. She stood up.

Short-term memory. How could he recognise a voice, through a door in the dark in the night, and yet not be able to place the speaker? A change of tack was needed, one should not try too hard to remember, that way blankness lay.

'The consultant's doing his rounds,' Lisa said comfortably, nodding towards the sound of hearty, able-bodied voices from along the corridor. 'He'll be along shortly.' The male consultant, this time. His heart dipped, just a little.

Coming round to check on him. For a moment Victor thought of the caravan, its ricketiness, the condensation on the tiny windows in the mornings, the effort to light the little gas stove with its blocked ducts, the effort of being alone, and his certainty wavered. Was it safer here? Hard to maintain the illusion of immortality in a hospital but that wasn't all. The voice was here.

Lisa was turning to go. 'Lisa, would you do something for me?'

Warily, she eyed him. 'Yes?' she said uncertainly.

'You remember those police officers I spoke to – was it yesterday?' Victor felt warm suddenly, the panic nibbling at the edges, and brought a hand slowly up to rest the back of it against a temple. 'I would really . . . I think I need to talk to them again, if . . . could that be managed?'

She put a hand to his wrist, felt his forehead. 'Yes, yes of course, Victor.' She was distracted, though.

CCTV was all over the place here. They would be able to see the man he had heard in the corridor last night.

I don't want to die in hospital, thought Victor.

Stiff after a night on the sofa Nat was woken by Rufus clattering down the stairs. He was talking loudly as he came, a commentary on everything – breakfast, birds, sunshine, garden – and Sophie's soft anxious murmur behind him, 'Watch out, darling, it's so . . . hold on to the banister.'

The house felt quite different with a kid in it. Nat yawned. He was staring at her with interest and she put up a hand to feel her hair, stiff and sticking out to one side.

Shit. It hadn't been a dream. Or had some of it been a dream? Jim had come over, he had, they had . . . She sat up on the sofa, her hands on her abdomen, feeling sick. Ah, shit.

Sophie was watching her and she felt a sudden pulse of longing, for him to still be there. No. That would be a mistake.

They'd had a conversation, a muttered conversation, somewhere between sex and sleep, or had that been a dream? She had been pressed against him on the sofa, her face in his armpit, the familiar smell of him but with an extra, sour note, the smell of someone stressed, the smell of growing up and having to deal with shit. With lies and hiding stuff from each other. What had they said?

Sophie had led Rufus to the kitchen and they were peering into cupboards. Nat shoved it all out of her mind and got up. 'There's eggs,' she said, uncertainly, and Rufus's face turned up to hers, bright. 'And . . . pitta bread?'

She had been expecting stroppiness, after the late night, but Rufus seemed excited by everything, said yes to everything. He ate boiled eggs and pitta bread soldiers and a yoghurt one day past its sell-by and drank some hot milk. He kept hopping off his chair to look out of the back door at the garden, then hopping back again. Nat watched Sophie deal with him: she saw how gentle she was, how anxious, how patient; she saw her intense happiness with her kid.

Of course, Sophie had Victor for a dad. And it came to Nat that her own mum had been like this too, Patty had, at moments, when she had been allowed. When he'd gone.

For so long all Nat could remember was the feeling of panic at home, Patty's stress at trying to hold it together, losing it regularly, *If you don't, I'm going to.* But watching Sophie some of it was familiar, after all. Things came back to her. Mum behind her when she was very small, bending without complaint to pick up something she'd dropped. Rabbie? The filthy cotton rabbit, Jesus, where did that come from? It had been a long time since she'd thought about Rabbie. She'd left him behind somewhere one time, some field where they'd had a picnic, and Mum had driven back to get him and it had taken her an hour to find the field and then him in the dark, Nat sitting quiet in the car, not daring to say anything for fear she'd lost him.

It was like light getting through a crack in a door: her own childhood. Not so fucked up, then, not always, not for ever.

Setting down his milk with a clatter, Rufus ran out

through the door, arms pumping. Sophie began to clear his things from the table and Nat came to help.

She'd been a parole officer before she had Rufus, Nat knew that from Victor. So she hadn't been sheltered, she can't have been naive. But she'd married Richard: could it be that easy, to make such a big mistake?

Rufus, though. What was the opposite of a mistake? She must have been almost fifty when she had him. Something stirred, a question, but it wouldn't come into focus.

'Your dad's worried about you,' said Nat.

Turning from the sink Sophie smiled unhappily. 'He's the one in hospital,' she said, trying to laugh. 'I'm fine. You can see. Nothing wrong with us.'

'There's the wrist,' said Nat, reluctantly. 'That wasn't an accident, was it?' Sophie turned back to the sink. 'Did your husband do it?'

'Does . . . my father . . . has he . . .' Sophie stopped, swallowed something. 'We can manage,' she said, her voice low. 'Marriages go through difficult . . . Richard has a very demanding job. He has to provide for us, there are . . . he loves me. Us.'

'My dad hit my mother,' said Nat, levelly. 'I know what that looks like. Is that how your wrist got broken?'

Sophie's head was very still, then she turned it just a fraction, Nat could see the curve of her cheek. 'What did she do?' she said. 'What did your mother do?'

'What do you mean?' said Nat, and for a moment she really didn't understand. 'What did she do to deserve it?'

And Sophie's head turned fully then, she began to say, 'No – I . . . no—'

But then Rufus called from outside, a high squeal although

it wasn't clear if it was excitement or something else, and Sophie was moving, round and awkward, towards the door, dropping a tea towel as she hurried out into the garden.

Nat stood, looking at the crumpled cloth lying there in the empty doorway, and it came back to her. Jim had talked to her: it hadn't been a dream. Muttering his confession into her ear, that slight sourness on his breath that hadn't been there before. Perhaps he was drinking, perhaps he wasn't sleeping, wasn't eating. Perhaps all three.

'Funny thing was,' he'd said, and Nat had been half asleep by then, inclined to forgive, to think, all right, all right, whatever, Jim. 'Funny thing was, I had this feeling, this feeling.'

'What feeling?' She had made an effort but the words had drifted from her in a mumble.

He shifted beside her, up on an elbow in the dark. 'That there was someone else there. I was in the garden, I was watching, but there were no lights on in the house. I wondered if there was someone inside hiding, then I thought he – it – was in the garden with me, only watching me, watching me watching you.'

'A feeling.' It had arrested her, on the brink of sleep. Jim had sighed then, as if he had done the confessing and this was him being forgiven, and sank back down beside her. 'Am I losing it?' he said, sadly, murmuring into her hair. 'I never . . . I didn't see anyone. I just . . . perhaps I heard something, perhaps I heard something.'

'It was you, though,' she had said to him, and she had heard her own sadness. 'It was you got inside and laid the table. There wasn't anyone else in here.' And his arms had tightened around her from behind, spooning as they always had done afterwards, two hands on her breasts and his breath warm on her neck and eventually they had gone to sleep like that.

On the kitchen table now a mobile shivered, not Nat's. She saw the screen light up, *Richard*, it said. She picked it up and took it outside, holding it out and away from her like something that had caught fire and Sophie, kneeling and with an arm round Rufus, looked up and Nat saw she was afraid, just at the sight of his name on a screen, her face turned white. She stood abruptly and took the phone from Nat. Then turning, edging away, she said in a low voice, 'Hello, darling.'

Nat saw Rufus hunch tighter on the ground, keeping still.

She could hear Richard's voice herself, not pausing, a level monotone that didn't let Sophie get a word in, though she did nod, Nat saw her catch her lower lip between her teeth. 'Yes, darling,' she said in the end. 'Yes, I will, I will. I will.' Silence, and then Sophie thrust the phone into her pocket.

'I expect you've got to get to work,' she said to Nat, still pale, so pale her eyes stood out green. 'We'll pack up our things.'

'You can stay here,' she said. 'Do you . . . did he—' but Sophie just gave a tight little shake of her head. Her eyes were on Rufus still crouched there, unmoving, staring down between his knees.

He knew he had to be careful: he was capable of being careful. His hands looked gentle.

Having to work was an annoyance: he would have rather been able to concentrate on her. There were times when there had to be geographical space between them, when her whereabouts were unknown. Natalie. Nat. Natalie.

He felt though that there was a connection, a wire between them, he only needed to tug on it, gently.

The old man, of course. The old man was safe enough, gaga or close to it. That place would shut him down, he would die in there and no one would pay any attention to what he said. A shock to see his bed empty, all the same. Hospitals – he knows there is surveillance. Where to walk, how to walk.

Now he had the feel of it in his fingers, he felt it draw him, each knuckle, each sinew. A lovely peace descended at the thought of it, something flooded his system at the thought of the body dying – ecstasy was the word that came to mind. His hands that did it, charging his body up, pumping him up.

He had to be careful, though. He had to keep the tugging gentle, give her nothing concrete to take to the police, not yet, not until he could spread it in front of her, what he had done – and stop her ever telling anyone. A clever balance because he liked to watch her, looking this way then that way, thinking she was after him, when really it was the other way around. He wanted to draw her closer, closer, until when she turned, his breath was in her face.

He needed to wind it round and round her, get her where he wanted her, helpless, immobilised. Between his hands.

Work. Someone called him, and he had to turn and not show what he felt.

Chapter Twenty-Four

Owen Wilkins' office in a mobile unit on the caravan site was hot and untidy. There was a filing cabinet, a shelf full of box files, another with books of various sizes. Wilkins was standing behind a desk with a battered computer on it, his head almost knocking on the low ceiling. Sophie and Nat had been herded the other side of the desk: they'd left Rufus outside, sorting through the pebbles arranged in a border around the unit.

'My main concern is that Mr Powell's caravan should be adequately maintained,' said Wilkins, frowning down at his desk, his big, square-knuckled hands. He seemed ill at ease with them in his crowded space. Nat wished he would sit down.

'The place needs to look cared for,' he went on, staring sternly past them. 'If . . . well, kids are kids. If they see there's no one there they'll try to get in, pinch things, make a mess.'

Covertly Nat looked at the books on his shelf: one had a bird on the spine, the word *calculus* on another, and a fat history book about Russia. His gaze shifted in her direction, irritable, and she stopped looking.

He had seen them come in through the site gates and marched over to them.

Now Sophie launched a charm offensive. She was good at that, Nat observed, not least because it seemed to come naturally, not servile, but apology hedged with willingness, all of it humble and tentative. *Yes, yes, of course, it's so kind of you.* Would it drive you mad, after a while?

Nat checked her out: she looked quite different this morning, her cheeks were pink, her candyfloss hair had blown about on the walk up. She was wearing a loose blue dress to her knees, and sandals, but she didn't look frumpy, more like a kid on the first day of holidays.

It didn't seem to drive Owen Wilkins mad: he went still, stopped fiddling with his big hairy hands. He didn't quite smile but something about him shifted down a gear and Nat marvelled.

'Yes, well,' he said, clearing his throat.

Sophie bobbed her head, darting a look out to check on Rufus. It was mostly nerves, Nat could see – underneath there was a version of Victor, sharp-eyed Victor, brave Victor, managing the beast with kindness. How far did that get you?

'I've visited him once or twice,' the site manager said stiffly. Nat had forgotten that Owen Wilkins was the one who had come in to hospital with Victor. 'He's . . . well. He's under my care, if you like.'

Sophie with a handkerchief up to her mouth. 'Really,

that's so . . ..' she said, 'so kind. I didn't know you were such friends.'

Wilkins waved a hand, looking away. 'I wouldn't say friends,' he said, clearing his throat. 'He's a good tenant. He keeps himself to himself. And of course, he's an intelligent man.'

Warily Nat examined him. How old? Forty, maybe. Funny job for a man who liked maths and Russian history – or maybe not. The kind of job that would get you called a loser in some circles, not that she could talk. Wilkins was a loner, for sure. He'd hardly been in the pub but she'd seen his type before, abrupt, impatient, the odd inappropriate laugh. They wouldn't chat while you pulled their pint, not because they were shy but because they thought everyone else was stupid.

'What did you do before you came here, Owen?' she asked, blunt, wishing briefly for one or two of Sophie's soft skills when he stared at her. She probably should have called him Mr Wilkins.

He stared at her. 'I was a teacher, as a matter of fact,' he said eventually. Mr Wilkins, for sure. Then with a flash of arrogance. 'Five years then I couldn't stand it any longer. Stand them. The other teachers.' Scornful. 'The staffroom.'

Then he glared at her, as if she'd forced it out of him. 'Let me know, anyway, if there's anything more I can do. Clearly Mr Powell can keep his pitch as long as' and now he was arrogant, that laugh, 'as long as he pays for it. But if you don't mind . . .'

Pale now, Sophie bobbed and murmured, and then he did turn away from her – from both of them, with irritation. 'Sorry,' he said, blunt to the point of rudeness, and Nat and Sophie reversed out of the door into the warm morning.

Rufus ran after them headlong, weaving and stumbling between guy ropes and tow bars as they walked down the green slope towards the estuary. The tide was halfway up, soft grey glittering in the sun, and there was the fresh smell of the water in from out to sea. Rufus dodged and ran out in front of them. As he tripped and righted himself immediately, down up, you could see how recently he'd been a baby, his body still learning stuff like balance.

'Patrick said would I like to bring Rufus down to his little boat,' said Sophie. 'He said he might take us out for a row or something, after I've seen Dad.'

'Patrick?' For a moment Nat didn't know who she was talking about. She stopped, and Sophie stopped too. 'Paddy. Sure, yes. He must have liked you.'

Ahead of them Rufus had come to a halt as well, because he'd spotted a black and white cat. He squatted, head on one side, at a level with it.

Sophie darted a look at her and the pink in her cheeks deepened. 'I – I mean you wouldn't . . . Richard wouldn't . . . he was being kind. I think Patrick was being kind.'

'He is very kind,' said Nat. 'He lets me have his boat whenever I want to go for a sail. *Chickadee*, she's called.'

'Oh, well I wouldn't . . . if you need to use the boat.'

'Stop it,' said Nat, impatiently. 'Paddy's just being a friend, of course no one's going to say anything to Richard, but even if they did—' Sophie's head jerked round in panic, the pink all gone from her face. 'No one will say anything, people mind their own business and they know Paddy, what he's like. Hardly the predatory type, is he?'

Even as the words came out of her mouth she wondered, though. What was the predatory type, did you always know?

Not Paddy, with his shambles of a shed and his dusty hair and his soft quiet voice? Not prickly Owen Wilkins? Friendly Bill? None of them really looked like predators. Stalkers, maybe? Jim, climbing through her window to lay the table, so they could be a couple again.

Sophie stared and Nat sighed. 'It's a natural thing to do round here, it's for Rufus, anyway. And I'll get plenty of sailing, don't worry about me, there's still a month of summer left.'

Although she wasn't so sure, suddenly. There was a change in the air, or had it been coming a while? It was humid, a heat haze hung over the water, but under it, when the wind shifted, you could feel cooler air coming in from somewhere. The feeling – and the thought that came with it – made her anxious. Get Victor back, before. Before Richard came. Before something happened to him. People died in hospital.

They were at the caravan now, and Sophie had extracted the keys from her big battered handbag that seemed to hold any number of things: a water bottle, half a chocolate bar, a book. 'Rufie?' she called, and Nat heard consternation in her voice.

Find him, before he finds you.

Then Rufus's little shaggy red head appeared from around a caravan a couple down the hill, clutching the cat against his body, its legs splayed. 'Up here, Rufie,' Sophie said and the cat wriggled in his arms and got free, escaping light-footed back behind the caravan. Rufus hesitated a moment, torn, but then began to plod up towards them.

As they came inside Nat could see the tears coming in Sophie's eyes that never seemed far away. 'Oh,' she said, looking around the little dim space, the frames beginning to tarnish already, Sophie's overnight case open on the narrow double bed. The air was stale and stuffy. Rufus barrelled between them and jumped on the bed, bouncing. They had a look around.

'No one's been in here,' said Nat.

Sophie bit her lip. 'I should have stayed, looked after it for him,' she said.

'Stop finding fault with yourself,' said Nat. 'I wanted the company last night, to be honest. And it's all OK here, isn't it?'

Sophie nodded slowly. Rufus went on bouncing, the little suitcase moving closer and closer to the edge and Sophie moved to pick it up. 'I would love to have him with me,' she said. 'My dad, I mean,' the longing welling up. Nat crossed the small space and the caravan shifted. With an effort she prised open one of the small windows and turned back to Sophie, still standing there.

'Rufus would too. We'd love it, there's another two years before Rufie goes to school, we could make him breakfast every morning, when Richard's—' She stopped. 'But it's just not possible.' She folded her hands across herself, clasping each elbow tightly.

'It's Richard, isn't it?' said Nat, and Sophie opened her mouth to protest, closed it again. Rufus was on his back on the bed, pedalling with his legs and she reached to take one of them in her hand.

'It's his home,' she said, flatly and sat beside him.

Nat pounced. 'Is it? Actually his?'

'Well, I . . . he's taken over the mortgage. ' Sophie looked tense at the direction the conversation was taking. 'He says it should—'

‘Let me guess. He thinks it should be in his name?’ Nat interrupted as thought of her own future, homeless and insecure, knocked against her. ‘But it isn’t yet?’ Sophie shook her head, a tight little movement. Nat went on patiently. ‘But he only took over the payments because you gave up your job to look after Rufus?’

Sophie was pale. ‘Richard loves me,’ she said. ‘He loves us.’

No he doesn’t. Nat didn’t say it. Or if that’s love, better to leave it alone. She hesitated, shifted her approach. ‘If he loves you he’ll understand. That you need to be with your dad, here if you have to, that might even be better. Victor might not exactly thrive if it causes . . . if he and Richard don’t get on.’

The flush was back. ‘It’s not my dad’s fault,’ said Sophie, and let go of her elbows, a hand down each side of her as if bracing herself.

‘I’m sure it’s not,’ said Nat, more forcefully than she intended. ‘Look, I’ll help you.’

To leave him: better not say that either. Not yet. Nat knew what they’d say, Richard would say, you’re letting your own stuff get in the way. Then again, having a dad like hers meant she knew a bastard when she saw one.

‘It’s just for a bit,’ said Nat. ‘Getting Victor back on his feet.’

‘He said you’d help me.’ Sophie was uncertain. ‘My father did.’

‘All right, then,’ said Nat, wary, because she could see Sophie’s agitation.

‘It’s not what you think,’ said Sophie, avoiding her eye, fiddling with her handkerchief, out again. ‘I love him.’ She was frantic, frightened. ‘Of course I do, we’re married. He used to be different. If he thought, if he knew I was going to leave him . . .' Rufus had gone still beside her, his legs flat on the bed.

'How would he know?' Sitting carefully beside her on the little bed Nat was curious now. Sophie seemed suddenly deeply ill at ease.

'I – I don't know,' she said finally. 'He looks after me. If I buy something on the credit card, he knows. If I make a phone call, he knows. He's . . . responsible.'

'You don't have any money of your own? No bank account?' Patty came into her head then, sitting at the table while he swayed over her, fumbling in his pockets for what cash was left after the pub. It was called the housekeeping, that fistful of crumpled notes and pennies. Sophie just shook her head, flushed deep red. She didn't answer.

'All right,' said Nat, and she felt a guilty pulse of triumph, at getting that out of her, at the image of her own blue bank card, for all there was barely a grand in there, stashed over three years at least. 'All right, then.' And tentatively she took Sophie's hand in hers. 'We need a plan, that's all.'

Beside them Rufus began to bounce and as she watched him Nat thought again. So lucky, at her age, that he was born so perfect.

And then it hit her, winded her. Clinic 1A, Obs and Gynae and a list of other services, Fertility Clinic. Genetic Counselling. Beth's brother with Down's.

'Hold on,' she said and Sophie turned but Nat wasn't talking to her, she was talking to herself. No, she thought, no, no, no, no.

* * *

You had to leave a message, of course. '*She'll call at the end of surgery, is it a medical emergency?*'

Nat slowed, just as she came to the junction with the little close where Beth had rented, looked across automatically and there was a police car parked out the front, there was Mo Hawkins standing beside it. She was talking to the DS, Donna Garfield. They turned to look at her but no one called, no one waved. She walked faster, getting out of sight. And then her phone rang. Dr Ramsay obviously knew an emergency when she heard one.

'Natalie.' She sounded genuinely worried. 'What's the—'

'She was pregnant, wasn't she? Beth.'

Because there was no point in pissing about. Beth pregnant, and couldn't tell Nat, thinking it would bring it all back, thinking she'd be angry, or jealous or . . . Nat almost wanted to howl. She was pregnant. Was. Not just her he'd hurt, not just Beth.

An intake of breath. 'Just *tell* me,' said Nat, almost sobbing. 'For Christ's sake. Mr Sarafidis is fertility and genetic counselling. I googled him.'

'I can tell you . . .' and she heard Ramsay hesitate. 'I can tell you that I don't know.' Defeated. 'Please, Natalie—'

'Was she trying to get pregnant?' said Nat, and silence was her answer. 'Thank you,' she said grimly, and hung up.

A baby to keep her here, Beth settling down. She wanted a baby. She could have been already pregnant. With Dowd? Did he even know? Had that been why she wanted to see him?

Nat walked on in a daze and all she could see was Rufus, on his knees in the earth, grubby and beaming, his mother opening her arms. Happy for you: I would have been happy for you. She pulled the pub door open.

She must have been early because Steve and Janine looked like she'd taken them by surprise. They were standing behind the bar in mid-conversation when she walked through the door, bar towels hanging over the pumps and cleaning fluid in the air and they stopped abruptly. Not shouting, she would have heard that, but Janine hadn't got her make-up on yet which was unusual in itself, she hadn't come down the stairs without full slap since Nat had known her. She looked strained, ill at ease.

It was Steve told her, calm as usual, but she was beginning to wonder what *would* upset Steve, if an earthquake would do it. 'The police have been in,' he said. She thought of the look Donna Garfield had given her across the roof of the police car.

'In here?'

He shrugged. 'I suppose it was nice of 'em to come before opening time,' he said and Janine snorted.

'Did they talk to you?' Nat asked.

He jerked his head. 'Janine,' he said, gathering up the damp bar towels, swiping the spray cleaner off the bar. 'Seems like they are looking into Beth going missing, after all,' he said.

'I knew that,' said Nat, quiet, and Steve paused, nodded.

'Yeah, well,' he said and there was a hint of something underneath the calm, a wounded note. 'Bit of warning might've been nice.' Janine was grim-faced in the doorway to the kitchen. 'It's looking serious,' said Steve, unmoving. Watching her.

And then Nat was on alert. 'Have they found her?' she

said, and for a moment her breathing stopped, images flooded into her head. Another body, in the water, in the weir, bobbing, tangled.

'No,' said Steve and his voice was thick, choked, he had to clear his throat then it was normal again. Normal Steve. 'Coppers never very forthcoming, are they?'

Then abruptly he handed his load – cleaning fluid, wet towels, two dirty glasses – into Janine's arms. 'Anyway,' he said, 'I've got a job coming up, this next couple of days, I'll get out of you girls' hair. Got to be in Ipswich for four.'

Nat thought of the big container port an hour away. With the image in her head of those big rusting metal boxes stacked on the wharves it felt like everywhere now was just somewhere a body could be found.

White-faced Janine stepped back automatically to get out of his way. Nat stared. Steve seemed unconcerned but at the foot of the stairs he stopped. 'They've got my number,' he said. 'The copper's got it.' And he was gone: up the stairs then back down again in two minutes with a holdall slung over his shoulder. It must have been already packed.

His rig revved in the car park and was gone, in seconds.

'They talked to him a long time,' said Janine, as the big vehicle's thundering in the lane died away.

Nat had never seen her like this. Usually when she was upset, when she was angry, it just burst out of her, she ranted and raved. Now she just stood there, stiff. Stupidly, all Nat could think of was that it was ten minutes till opening, she wanted to tell her to go and put her face on, to shake her, say, what? *What?*

'I thought he said— What did they ask him?'

'They wanted to know about his relationship with Beth.'

'Steve? *Steve?*' Nat was flabbergasted.

'I wish you'd just left it,' said Janine, turning her back but not moving.

'But you talked to them too?' Nat was confused.

And then Janine did turn back, pale and puffy. 'I had to,' she said wearily, avoiding Nat's eye.

'What?' said Nat, urgency rising. 'What have they said?'

Unwilling, Janine met her gaze. 'They do seem to think—' She swallowed. 'The police . . .'

'Beth—' But Nat ran out of breath. Janine folded her arms across herself, white-faced.

'They have decided someone *has* done away with her now.'

The words pattered, horrible, in Nat's head. *Done away with her.* In her head she saw Beth curled to protect herself, to protect her belly. Janine was hunched, avoiding her eye again. 'Or something's happened to her, anyway. And they've got all sorts of ideas.'

Nat couldn't speak, she only stared at Janine, and saw a bit of colour, at last, rising up her neck into her face, squaring her shoulders.

'Fucking cheek of it. I told them, get me down the station if you like. Don't talk to me like that in my own pub.' She hugged the armful Steve had loaded her with, looking down at it as if she didn't know how it had got there.

'Like what?' said Nat, her face felt stiff, her lips numb.

'Like we might have wanted rid of her,' said Janine and then quite suddenly she was set in motion, agitated, clattering, launching herself into the kitchen. Nat followed her. 'Like Steve might have tried it on with her.' Dumping it all into the stainless steel sink.

'They said that?' Trying not to show what she was feeling, wanting to take hold of her and shake her, to shriek in her face. *Steve?*

Janine was leaning against the sink now like she might throw up in it, or it was stopping her keeling over. Taking deep breaths. Nat came up beside her, and set a hand tentatively on her shoulder, feeling it drop.

'Not in so many words,' said Janine, and she raised her head just a fraction, turned it, still not looking at Nat but her hair fell back and Nat could see fine lines, the little wobble under her chin as she spoke, shaky.

'But I could tell it's what they're thinking. Desperate old woman, hanging on to her man, covering up for her man.' She swayed and Nat took hold of her arm. 'He wouldn't have touched her. Not with a bargepole.'

'What evidence do they have?' said Nat quietly and then Janine, Janine who would rather top herself than cry, was gone, she was lost, she dissolved in tears, her face was red and sodden.

'I don't know,' she sobbed. 'I don't know. He won't talk to me.'

Jesus, thought Nat, *Jesus*, and stiffly she put her arms around Janine. It felt wrong: Janine, who never needed or wanted comfort, or at least not from Nat, her junior, her employee, a younger woman. She didn't know what, exactly, she expected Janine to feel like, soft, shaking, frightened, but there was something wrong about what she did feel like. She was rigid.

'What did they tell you?' she said.

Janine muttered it. 'What if he leaves me?' Nat took her shoulders firmly and moved her back, so that she could look in her face.

'What did you tell them?' She could hear the warning in her own voice.

Janine wouldn't look at her.

There was a trick to the walking frame: it was to do with balance. A matter of shuffling, and of disregarding the associations, not thinking what he must look like. Old, old, old and close to helpless. Concentrate: never risk falling.

The male consultant – Victor had wished fervently for the woman to return with her thick curly hair, but perhaps, in this day and age, she had a family to be with – had peered at him over his glasses, kindly. Forty years younger than Victor.

'A small bleed to the brain,' he had said, nodding, satisfied. 'That was really rather efficiently contained. Of course you aren't out of the woods yet.'

Victor had concentrated on holding himself very upright on the bed, one hand still on the zimmer. 'Did you see anything else? When you did the scan. Whatever they are, lesions, plaques—'

The consultant had looked faintly surprised. 'Nothing out of the ordinary for a man of your age,' he said, wary.

'My age is ancient, though,' said Victor, smiling, receiving no smile back. 'Anything that could cause me to forget things I've heard, people I've seen?'

'No signs of any underlying condition.' The consultant frowned slightly over his glasses. 'It was slightly more serious than a TIA, which can leave no effects at all, as the name would suggest, transient. You had a small bleed in your brain that stopped of its own accord: small, but close to the centres of speech and memory. So both of those things could be affected, we hope only briefly. Your speech, for example, is almost back to normal, which is a good sign.'

Hope, thought Victor, is all I have, at my age. 'When can I go home?' he asked, meekly.

'We need to keep an eye on you for a bit longer,' said the consultant. 'I can see you're doing well. You're mobile, that's extraordinary. As soon as the various agencies have signed you off. But why don't you take advantage? Stay a little bit longer. Treat us like a luxury hotel.' Bluff and expansive now, and eager to be off.

Victor had let him go, shaking his hand, but as soon as he was out of sight Victor was leaning, rocking to get upright again and back on the move. Shuffle, shuffle. At the nurses' station he saw someone lean back, sharp-eyed, to monitor him.

Why not take advantage? Because it isn't safe here. There was danger everywhere: in the corridors, in the padding of soft feet at night, in the drip hanging at his bedside. It would be safer in the caravan, with Sophie, with the little boy, Rufus, who liked to place his small warm head under Victor's hand, already.

Victor was approaching the sun room, the big windows that needed a clean. Someone sitting in a chair at the far end raised his pulse, he could feel it, patter, patter, but the someone was old. A patient barely moving, barely breathing, mouth a little open and asleep. A man, though not much difference at our age.

We have until Friday. Richard would come back to get them on Friday.

Was Friday tomorrow? Was he getting muddled?

Victor looked out over the car park, breathing carefully

to slow everything down. A woman climbed into a car, a taxi pulled up at the entrance, an ambulance moved off.

Beth. And suddenly there she was in his head, as though she had just been waiting for him to get strong enough, to get back on his feet. Victor looked at her as though far off, down the wrong end of a telescope.

Beth. When it got quiet in the pub she would come and settle herself at his table while he told her about Sophie, settled, with her baby, her nice house in London. Her husband. And after listening to him she would talk, quietly, thoughtfully, not the way she talked to the men at the bar.

'Do you think even someone like me can settle down?' she'd said, not so long ago, a beermat turning between her pretty painted nails.

'Why not?' he'd said, gently. 'Why on earth would you think you couldn't?'

'I don't set out to hurt anyone,' she had blurted out, angrily. 'You got to look out for yourself, though. You got to.' He'd murmured agreement to that, something meaningless, and she had nodded, still angry, barely listening because the young never did. Restless Beth who couldn't sit still. She had jumped up from his table as quick as a cat and back into the kitchen.

Leaning so gently against the glass he felt himself sway. Whom had she hurt? Who wanted to hurt her?

Victor watched a man walk across the car park, chilled by the set of his shoulders, the sight of his bare forearm in a T-shirt. Would he have the same thought whenever he observed a young man? He felt the darkness.

And feeling it rise he called for someone, not even knowing what sound he made, panicked, but it was Lisa who came. She appeared in the door, half out of a light coat – she must have been outside. 'Victor, Victor, really, what have you been up to?' Anxiously she peered into his face.

'Did I ask you,' he said, genuinely confused, 'to contact the police?'

Her shoulders dropped, she sighed. 'I left a message,' she said. 'I think they're very busy, Victor. There's been a . . . well you know. The boy who . . . died.'

'I would like to go home,' he said.

Lisa almost laughed; she set a hand on his shoulder, patting kindly. 'I don't think so,' she said.

Chapter Twenty-Five

The lunch hour was brief but furious: Janine had her in the kitchen making sandwiches for most of it, because there was no sign of Craig.

Coming back into the bar Janine barely gave her a glance. She could have told punters no food, what with being short-staffed, but Nat had the distinct impression Janine didn't want to meet her eye. She'd been dumped before and Nat had been there to see it, but this was different. It had been on the tip of her tongue to say something like, he's just taking some time out, but she stopped herself.

The bag he'd slung over his shoulder hadn't been much more than a holdall, though. He had suits, upstairs in the wardrobe. He had cowboy boots, for Christ's sake, even if Janine had bought them for him and he'd never worn them. He'd be back. She couldn't say any of it to Janine, though – a single warning flash from her eyes when she walked back through had been enough to tell her that.

It was at the back of her mind that she hadn't seen Bill the cameraman in a couple of days now. Not since the message that she still hadn't answered. It nagged at her, wouldn't it be only polite to say, thanks but no thanks, you're a nice guy, that kind of thing? She'd already said that. And the truth was, she didn't know what she wanted to say to him. He was keeping his distance, which was good.

The crew weren't far away, though. The three fangirls from the caravan site had breezed in at the height of the lunch hour, rum and Coke and making a big thing out of producing their ID before shoving their way on to a shared table and getting out their mobiles, showing each other photographs.

Craig came in.

Their heads all turned. He had a motorcycle helmet slung over his arm and he looked unkempt, older by the day, a kind of new glamour hanging over him. His face was dark and grim. Janine jerked her head towards the kitchen and he stalked past them and disappeared. The girls were still looking at where he'd gone when Nat came over to collect their empties; they barely registered her as she leaned in for the glasses and she caught the flash of something on the nearest illuminated screen, a little gallery of shots.

'Hold on,' she said, and without thinking put out her hand to grab it. The girl holding the phone – the leggy one from the caravan site, long painted nails with diamanté on them – squealed and tugged it away.

'What d'you think yer doing?' she said indignant.

Janine looked over sharply. 'Sorry,' said Nat, tucking the glasses under her arm, holding out a hand. 'It's just that . . . that's . . . I think that's—' The girl turned the screen so she couldn't see it, protective. 'I thought I saw my friend in one of those pictures,' said Nat trying to sound calm, trying to smile. 'Could I . . . would you mind if I had a look?'

The girl stared up at her, trying to read her. 'F'you wash yer hands first,' she said eventually.

'What?' said Janine as Nat leaned round the bar to stick her hands under the tap: behind her she could hear the girls whispering.

'Beth,' said Nat. 'She's got a picture of Beth on her phone.'

From behind Janine she saw Craig lean back to see through the kitchen door, just at the sound of the name.

Janine stared. 'You what?' she began but Nat dodged back to the table, rubbing her hands dry on her jeans. Craig was standing in the doorway and when she glanced at him she saw he wasn't quite steady on his feet. Grudgingly the girl handed the phone over: she and her friends sat there, arms folded, staring at Nat as if she was another species.

'You ain't looking too far back, mind,' said the girl sharply and they tittered in unison. It was a fancy phone and the photo galleries were grouped according to times and places. Where did they get their money, these girls? was the stupid thought that went around in her head, or was it knock-off? The photos were indiscriminate, badly framed, the backs of people's heads, a big piece of camera hardware blocking one shot. She didn't see Bill but she wasn't looking for him, there'd been a church spire – and there it was. There she was.

The pale oval of her face and the arched brows, the long straight dark hair with a sheen of something, the purplish colour she'd experimented with still not grown out but it was the pose as much as anything that tugged at Nat, that made her unmistakable, one elbow up on a tree and leaning, nonchalant, the sheet of hair hanging sideways. Beth. She looked as though she was on her own. The real Beth.

A village green, church spire in the background, a girl with a clipboard and a man she didn't know in a baseball cap holding his hand up for quiet. Cars parked further back up the street.

The girl nudged her side. 'Oi,' she said. 'You finished?'

Nat looked down, keeping the phone out of reach, then slowly she lowered it to show her the screen. 'Do you know her?' she asked. 'That girl?'

The girl made a face, shrugged.

'On the set?' Nat persisted. 'When was this?' Another shrug.

'You see her there a lot?' Wanting to slap her, Nat tried to sound reasonable.

'Don't remember seeing her at all,' the girl retorted, and plucked the phone out of Nat's hand, held the screen out for the other two to gawp at. Nat had to resist grabbing it back.

'How old is *she*?' said the plumper girl, incredulous, and the third shoved her, laughing and putting a hand up to her mouth. 'Too old. Too old for them.'

'Can I just have one more look?' said Nat, trying not to plead, smiling, and crossly the girl held it out, clasped in the diamanté-studded nails, not letting it go. Nat tried to see where Beth was looking, but it was hard to tell; at the actors was all she could see, a bare-chested man, a girl in a bonnet, a cluster of equipment.

Then she spotted him: Bill. Leaning on his camera, big hands, in the far corner of the shot, concentrating on his job. Handsome: it took Nat by surprise how handsome, and not even looking at Beth. Nat put her forefinger to the screen to enlarge it – but the girl snatched the phone away, losing patience.

'Thassit,' she said, her chin sticking out defiantly. 'Mind if we get on with our dinner now?' On the table was a bag of crisps, split open.

Nat retreated, her stomach churning at the sight of Beth, large as life on that little screen. She'd been so real.

They clattered out half an hour later, leaving the room almost empty, their table a litter of peanuts and dirty glasses, a single false nail with glitter in the ashtray. In the Bird they went on setting out ashtrays, though no one smoked any more. Janine was in the kitchen giving Craig a piece of her mind about something in an undertone, and then suddenly he was storming out, through the bar, staggering as he ducked to get outside.

Janine was in the doorway, shrugging, her face blank and obstinate. 'Pissed,' she said. 'Can't have him here like that.'

Nat held her breath, then let it out. 'Back in a minute,' she said.

She found him in the car park, fumbling for the bike's keys. 'You're not getting on that thing,' she said.

He swayed. 'I – I – I miss her too, y'know,' he said. Mumbling.

'You slept with her,' she said.

Silence.

'Did Ollie know?' she asked, quietly. His face looked flushed with booze in the golden afternoon light.

He shook his head. 'I wasn't going to tell him, was I?' he said. 'It was just a couple of times, then she said no.' His eyes were dark. 'My DNA,' he said dully. 'Gonna be all over, isn't it? All over her place.'

'She wouldn't have told him.' She was quite certain about that.

'He'd have found out, wouldn't he?' said Craig. 'Nosy little bastard, I told him, you don't want to know who else a girl's been with. Drive you nuts, that will.'

'He knew who she'd been seeing?'

'Following her on – whatever. Facebook.'

'She hardly did Facebook,' said Nat, unhesitating. They'd had conversations about it, Beth posted once in a blue moon, she thought it attracted the creeps.

'Whatever, whatever . . .' He shrugged and she took hold of his arm. 'I told him,' shaking her off, 'I tol' him, what you don't know won't hurt you.'

'What did he find out?' she said, urgently. 'What? Didn't he tell you?'

He took a step towards her and she smelled the beer on his breath. He shook his head, slack-jawed, side to side. 'Didn' get a chance, did he?'

'Look,' she said, urgently, 'this matters because he's out there. Whoever it was killed Ollie, even if Beth turns up safe and sound—' She broke off, feeling her throat close, knowing it would never happen. 'You know what? You know old Victor? In the hospital, scared to death. He saw someone. He saw someone coming up from the river with blood on him weeks back, around the time Beth disappeared, saw the man again, last week. He's . . . blanked it out, the man's face. He's frightened to death of remembering. What if it's the same man?' And as she shook Craig's arm she thought, did the man with blood on him know Beth wanted a baby? Was that why . . . She faltered. 'What if he comes after Victor?'

He's already after me.

But it was Victor's name that shifted something, behind Craig's eyes. 'Victor,' he repeated, and he focused, briefly, looking at her then away. 'Someone,' he said, uncertain, 'Ollie – he – it wasn't Facebook where he saw it then?'

'I don't know, do I?' She shook him, harder. He stumbled away.

'I – I'm trying to think, aren't I?' he said, swaying, irritable, reaching for the bike.

'You're pissed, Craig. You'll kill yourself, or someone else.'

He hunched his shoulders, refusing to look at her. 'Mind y'own fucking business,' he said.

A wild, pointless fury rose in her then but before she could grab him and shout in his face, he aimed a kick at the bike and wandered off, the helmet swinging from his arm. Nat forced herself to let him go.

Coming round the side of the pub with her fists still clenched she could hear Janine's voice, a low murmur at the end of the narrow garden. Her blonde-streaked head was visible moving to and fro beyond the straggle of the unpruned rose arch. Nat didn't want to creep up on her so she walked straight on.

At the sound of her footsteps Janine's head jerked round, she looked shocked. She looked guilty. Her hand went straight to the receiver, covering it. 'Yes?' she said, sharply, then spoke softly into the phone. 'Hang on a bit, will you, Steve?' A murmur answered her and she said, submissive, 'No, but . . . no, all right, no. Sure.' She hung up, grim-faced when she turned but Nat saw her trying to soften it.

'Look,' Janine said, cautiously, 'you look shagged out, all this . . . going on. I can manage the evening shift. There's a new girl came in yesterday, asking if there was any work going. I could give her a call.' Avoiding Nat's eye, and her clenched fists.

'A new girl?' Nat stared, trying to process this information. 'Just like that? You're replacing me, because of this . . . this . . .'

'Nothing to do with that,' said Janine stiffly. 'I'm not replacing you. It's a trial day.' Evasive though. 'Just be grateful, all right? You need a break, take it from me. See you in the morning bright and early.' And she frowned down again at her mobile, conversation over.

Nat tried not to think of the money. Another shift gone. There was stuff she needed to do though. An opportunity presented itself.

'All right then,' she said, fighting the anger, and the fear. 'Bright and early.'

In a home, Victor supposed – by home meaning not really a home at all, but he couldn't even frame the words '*care* home' to himself, especially not at this point in his life, the words had become terrifying to him – supper would be served at this time every night. Six o'clock, with the sun still warm on the windows, the day still bright.

Warily he looked along the row: only he of all the patients in his bay was capable of sitting up and watching for the meal-trolley's arrival.

Was it a promising sign? When he had been wheeled in here he had not cared about mealtimes or anything else, so grimly had he been hanging on. When he had first been parked in this bay, flat on his back and incapable, he had clung to things more basic, more primitive, as primitive as totem poles or Easter Island statues, the face of his beloved

Joy, long dead. The feel of Sophie's hand in his, from long ago. He eased himself upright in the bed.

The tray was set in front of him: a sandwich, a bowl of soup, a yoghurt. That at least comforted him: the clean cutlery folded in a paper napkin, the neatness of the tray, someone's careful hand and a welfare state he recognised from his youth paying for it all, looking after him. As long as he could get back to his own little kitchen that tilted when he stepped from the refrigerator to the hotplate, his own elderly kettle.

Pulling the tray towards him a little, carefully Victor began to eat. He was on the alert, from now on, and he needed to stay as sharp as he was capable of being. He would have to manage another night.

Lisa had been quite firm, the consultant had to sign off on him, and consultants only came around in the morning. Mornings during the week, elaborated Victor in his head, no one was discharged at weekends. Tomorrow was Friday.

'Then we'll organise everything: medication, a follow-up appointment, a taxi home. Like royalty,' she said. Victor didn't want to be ungrateful.

'You're so kind,' he said and she turned to go, giving him that last pat, where the bones of his knee raised the cellular blanket.

'And . . .' He hesitated. He took courage. 'The police? Did you . . . ?'

Lisa turned back, he saw her pained look.

'Oh, Victor,' she said, tiredly. 'Mr Powell. What *is* all this about?'

'I think I have evidence,' Victor said stoutly, wounded. 'I've seen someone I recognised, who may be connected with that boy's death—'

'Here?' she said, incredulous.

'Well I . . . no . . . yes . . . outside, in fact . . .' He felt himself getting anxious, flustered, why?

Lisa held up a hand. 'Don't get upset, Victor,' she said. 'That's the last thing any of us needs. I'm about to go off shift but I'll try them again.'

He didn't see her again, though. She didn't come in with her coat on to say goodbye as she had before. The next person he saw was a porter he didn't recognise, a middle-aged man with stubble and baggy eyes. They were moving him into a side room.

'These ward beds are for 'igh dependency patients, they need yours back, incoming heart patient,' said the porter, whose belly bulged under a uniform polo shirt. 'It's good news. It means you're going home soon.' The words came out a little too cheery for Victor: he let them settle in his head, listening to their echo.

The side room was cooler than the ward, it was quiet, the lights could be turned off completely. The nurse who settled him – he hadn't seen her before – was encouraging, bustling around, showing him light switches, pushing the water jug within reach. There was no window.

The significance of his being moved ticked away at Victor as he moved slowly around the room after she had gone, resting a hand on the cabinet, testing it for stability, shifting the zimmer so he could get to it if he had to. Was it true that they put those about to be discharged in side rooms? Victor's only knowledge on the subject was that those known to be dying were moved into them, but it would be very stupid indeed to dwell on that: the porter knew, Lisa knew, the consultant knew, he was getting better.

He held out a hand and looked at it, the old veins, the pale skin; he made a fist and released it.

Making sure the door was closed, Victor located his shoes, his socks, his trousers neatly folded, a plastic bag with toothbrush. The jersey he had been wearing when he came in. He spread it out on the bed. It was a wonderful peacock blue, Sophie had bought it for his birthday and sent it in the post knowing that he liked to be warm, knowing that he liked colour and when he'd opened it he had felt quite overcome, suddenly. Only a little stab of wishing, for her to have brought it in person, of course. Perhaps— He stopped himself. He thought he might put it on now: he turned carefully and sat on the bed.

Feeding his arms into the sleeves, he then raised them over his head and inside the blue cocoon felt himself unbalance, just fractionally, in the dark but he kept going stoically pulling the jersey down, his head back out again.

Victor panted. Of such triumphs is victory made. His jumper safely on.

One could never be too warm, when one got old – when had that thought come to him before? Many times, but most recently when sitting on the bench near the telephone box in the sunshine, his last morning in the outside world.

Down by the water the sun was still bright.

Sophie sat on the campsite's jetty with Rufus, holding on to his hand as he stretched his legs down, toes paddling in the warm brown water and a bucket and crabline beside him. She'd had the same equipment herself, aged three, along with a piece of gristle on the hook, her father patiently attaching it for her. She thought of Richard and the questions Natalie had asked her about him.

Richard would never have got his hands greasy wrestling with a piece of fatty bacon just so that Rufus could have a few hours of fun crabbing. How had they met, when had she decided he was the one? At what point had she committed herself? She couldn't think of the answers, it was all muddled, she could not in that second identify one single moment in which she had been sure Richard loved her. All she could think of was his anger, when she had refused to abort Rufus, her turning red when he laughed at the way she held her knife in front of his boss, when he disparaged her cooking. She searched and searched through her memories, increasingly frightened.

Would she know another Richard, if he crept in the same way, smiling? Crept in under her skin.

And in that moment Sophie felt that someone was behind her – it was as though the sun had gone behind a cloud, or as if Richard was there, he'd come to get her – but when she turned, she could see no one. A gaggle of girls climbing out of a car, and Wilkins the site manager closing the gate behind them and the sound of a motorbike through the trees.

Chapter Twenty-Six

The pressure in the cottage's shower was feeble, and Nat felt the need to stand under it a good twenty minutes before she felt clean. The water trickled down her back as she scrubbed savagely. *Beth would have told you, eventually. She didn't want to hurt you.* That didn't make it any better: she wanted to cry.

Walking out of the flimsy cubicle that didn't belong under the low ceiling she felt a sudden urge to just get out and leave it all, just for a second, until they crowded back, all the people she couldn't leave behind. Victor, Sophie looking at her reproachfully, Rufus beside her, Craig.

Janine and Steve? She'd have thought so once, but things had changed, things kept changing. The pub felt shaky on its foundations, its angles all wrong.

Victor. Mostly Victor.

When this was over, what would she do? This horrible endless summer. Where would she be? She couldn't leave. She had to find him. She had to know.

The cottage, like it or not, felt like someone's focus: she needed to be sure it was only Jim, only poor miserable Jim, got so skinny he could climb through a bathroom window and lay the table for her. Jim trying to pretend they were still together.

It had been Jim who'd said it, in the middle of the night – he'd had the feeling there was someone else there, outside the cottage. Just Jim, paranoid, thinking there was someone else in her life? Or like Nat, huddled in Beth's place, knowing there was someone sitting outside in a car, his engine idling?

She put on jeans and a clean shirt – she even ironed, she couldn't remember when she'd last had time to iron anything but it felt better, it felt good, she should do it more often – and went out into the garden. It jumped out at her straight away, stopped her dead.

A strip of turned earth among the overgrown roses. Bigger than she could imagine Rufus doing on his own, a long rectangle, it was the size of it that dropped down somewhere in the back of her mind, too preoccupied this morning to register it but it had sat there. Two metres long by one wide? Had she wondered if Janine had decided to employ a gardener, some dopehead who'd started on the rosebed before getting bored? Not for more than a millisecond.

Nat knelt and, hesitating, put her clean hand down to the turned earth. She pushed her fingers in, down, it was soft, down, then down further. She felt sick. Her ears ringing suddenly she stood, went back to the cottage, located a trowel she knew she'd seen just inside the back door, where she took off her boots.

There was a kind of buzz in the air, Nat couldn't work out if it was in her head or outside, and her body felt horribly heavy as she walked back towards the long patch of turned earth: a flat mound, six feet long. She knelt, and began to dig.

Half an hour later she was bathed in sweat and the knees of her jeans were dark with dirt, the shirt was crumpled and filthy, earth was heaped and scattered around her and she had found nothing. Stiffly she got up and went inside. The first thing she did was to lock the door behind her. Then standing with her back to the kitchen door she called the police.

She was aware that she sounded nuts. *Someone's dug a hole in my garden.* She had asked to speak to Donna Garfield but she was out and Nat was put through to a male officer, a PC something whose name she already couldn't remember.

'You need to see it,' she said urgently. She couldn't quite make herself say what it had looked like to her as she walked out of the back door towards the rosebed. And of course it didn't look like that any more, did it? It looked like a badger had gone wild among the rosebushes.

The PC was talking, she had to work to listen. ' . . . the other night,' he finished wearily and then she realised, feeling sick, that he had been to the cottage before, he was one – the younger, by the sound of his voice – of the two officers who'd come round when she found the table laid. That had turned out to be Jim only she hadn't told them that yet. Nat could picture him straight away. She felt her heart pound, he's not going to believe me.

'Yes,' she said pleading. 'That's me.' Her clothes felt damp and heavy on her suddenly, her hands were caked with dirt, she needed to get clean. She was sweating: the fear wouldn't leave her.

'We were going to come and see you anyway,' he said and at that point she heard sounds in the background, a door banging, a woman's voice, his hand went over the receiver but she still heard him say, *It's her.* There was a scuffle, an exchange and Donna Garfield was on the line.

'Natalie,' Garfield said, and there was a heaviness to her voice that set off alarm bells.

'It's important,' Nat pleaded, not wanting to hear it suddenly. Whatever it was. 'You've got to come and see.' Should she have started this, digging, digging, digging and where did it get you? She had to fight the urge to hang up – and run.

'We wondered if you'd like to come in to the station.'

She felt winded. 'What? But it's here. There's a hole in my garden, someone's come in and dug it up, it looks like a—'

'Someone's dug a hole.' Donna Garfield repeated her words with dry disbelief and Nat's gut churned, sick with panic. They didn't understand.

'You don't—'

Garfield wasn't listening. 'We can bring you in tomorrow morning, how about that?'

'Bring me in?' said Nat. 'What for? What is it?' Dreading the answer. 'Have you found her? Have you found Beth?'

Not in my garden, under the long mound of turned earth that looked like a grave, not there.

Nat was standing at the little window by the back door that looked out into the garden. She had had her back to it but now she turned. She could see the mess that looked like a wild animal had made. At the end of the garden something moved. She turned away again, she sat at the table with her back to the window.

'We haven't found her,' said the woman, her voice leaden.

'So what—'

Donna Garfield went on talking, over her. 'We've searched her place, though, Forensics have taken samples. We've got a certain amount of evidence and we'd like to talk to you . . .' She hesitated and in the pause Nat thought, What, what, then something Janine had said stopped her in her tracks. The shy plain friend, and the girl who gets all the lads. Always ends in tears. What did they suspect her of? Stealing one of Beth's boyfriends – then murdering her, out of spite, out of jealousy?

'We'll be there in the morning,' said Donna Garfield, shortly. Ending the conversation, there and then. Dumping her. 'It's getting a bit late now, isn't it? For looking in holes.'

Nat didn't even know if Donna Garfield didn't hear her begin to beg 'Please—' or if she heard and just hung up anyway.

She stared at the phone, feeling it all boiling up in her. 'Fuck you,' she said, squeezing the mobile till her nails dug into her palm, wanting to feel it, the rage, the frustration. 'Fuck you too.'

But it sounded hollow: all she heard, all she felt was terror. Nat stood.

She wasn't going to stay here. She wasn't going to sit around and wait.

As there was no window in the private room, when Victor tentatively pushed open the door he was startled to see how light it still was in the wide hospital corridor.

There was a figure in his old bed, motionless beside the window. The nurse who'd settled him in the room an hour earlier frowned when she saw him go past on his frame, she might even have sighed. But she didn't say anything. He had his sights on the payphone in the day room and he kept going steadily until he was there.

Money: Victor had a coin purse for this very purpose and he was always careful to stash two-pound pieces there, whenever he got one, because a call to Sophie should never be cut short for lack of funds. Now she had a mobile phone at least, it wouldn't be cut short because of Richard, either. There was no chair but he could lean against the wall-mounted machine a little for extra support.

Rufus answered, halfway through an unintelligible sentence about a boat.

'Rufus?' But the sentence ran on oblivious. 'Rufus? It's Grandpa.'

The babble stopped abruptly. '*Mpa.*' Repeated solemnly, wondering.

'Grandpa. Victor. Where's Mummy?' asked Victor, as gently as he could. 'Is she there?'

'She's with the man,' said Rufus. 'The man's going to take us on his boat.' And for an awful moment a wave of panic lifted Victor. In his head he glimpsed them, far out to sea, he saw a man on a deck lifting a strong bloodied forearm.

Then Sophie had the phone. 'Daddy!' and he felt himself breathe at the cheerful sound. How long since she'd called him that? All these other presences that forced her to say 'my father'.

'Darling,' he said. There were other voices in the

background, Rufus's babbling to someone. All right, it's all right.

'It's so lovely here,' she said. She sounded like a different person, she sounded happy, she sounded relaxed.

'Where are you?' he said.

'At . . . well . . .' She was confiding, excited. 'There's a man called Patrick, a friend of your friend Nat. He's been so kind! He's got two boats, one he lends to Natalie and another he . . . he's taking us out for a . . . he has even found lifejackets.'

'Patrick,' said Victor. 'Paddy.'

They had had conversations, he and Paddy. They had talked once about history, the Crimea, a conversation in which he had understood that Paddy was an intelligent man. A thoughtful man. A quiet, private man. And he was taking Sophie in his boat? Victor tried to put the pieces of this puzzle together. Natalie liked Paddy. Therefore Paddy was safe.

'Lifejackets,' he said, helpless. 'Isn't it getting a bit late? To go out on the water?' It was after eight, by the clock on the day room wall, and the sun was low over the suburban rooftops and dark trees to the west of the hospital.

'Just a quick row,' she said, 'maybe a little sail. Patrick says the wind does sometimes get up a little at sunset, we won't be out long. Half an hour.' Her voice was so bright and happy.

'Well . . .' This was entirely his trouble, Victor thought, he only wanted her happiness. He had never been able to intervene. 'Just be careful, darling,' he said. 'Be careful.'

'We've been to his little cottage, Daddy,' she said, as if she hadn't heard. 'He made us a cup of tea, the cottage was so pretty, it was charming. He even seems not to mind all the questions Rufus keeps asking him.' There was a muffled sound and he heard her laughing, then she was back.

'Can I speak to him again?' Victor asked timidly.

'Patrick?' she said, sounding bewildered.

'Rufus,' said Victor but even as he said it he thought it was indeed Paddy he should have been talking to.

'Well . . . just a minute.' Again her hand went over the phone but the next voice he heard wasn't his grandson's, it was hers.

'Oh, he won't come,' she said, but unembarrassed. 'He's just climbing into the boat.' There was more laughter and a low rumble he recognised as Paddy's voice. 'Patrick says we have to get a move on or it *will* get dark,' she said and he heard the beginnings of anxiety.

'You go,' he said, hurriedly, the last thing he must be is the cause of anxiety. 'Yes, go on. I'll see you tomorrow.'

'Yes, yes,' she said, distracted, his Sophie. 'It could be your last night there, who knows, sleep well. Sleep well.' And she was gone.

On the walking frame he edged his way back past the nurses to his room and once inside stood a moment against the door. The room's cool began to creep up on him.

If necessary he could call his own taxi, in the morning. He only had to get through another night.

Nat was going to the weir.

She hadn't even been sure she would remember how to get there. Since the discovery of Ollie's body the geography of it had hung in her head, frightening. She hadn't come down here in a long time. Water trickled and gushed somewhere out of sight, and as she left the road to head down towards the river Nat could smell mud and rust.

The estuary dwindled after the caravan site and there was an ugly single-track road bridge, a Victorian warehouse building someone had planned to develop and given up halfway through leaving it with empty window-sockets. It was getting dark. A track led off parallel to the muddy river with a faded sign that said PRIVATE ROAD. The path was narrow now, steep downhill, and knotted with roots. At one point Nat tripped, painfully, and had to grab for a thorny bit of branch. Listening to her own heart pound, she stopped where she was, suddenly unwilling to move.

All the windows in the private road had been dark, mostly curtained, mostly thick with dirt. One of them had five or six abandoned cars outside it. People must live there, but she'd seen no one. People didn't come here.

Down there waiting below her, the weir wasn't a beauty spot. Densely overgrown to either side, there was nowhere to sit in the sun: it was marked with rusty signage warning people off. DANGER, DEEP WATER. A low long wall the water trickled over, a sluice it rushed through, a dark swirling pool. She couldn't imagine Ollie coming even this far alone, unless he had good reason. *She'd* come, her reasons tangled and painful. She wished she hadn't.

Hanging up on DS Donna Garfield, the desire to walk out of the front door and up the lane and not look round had become too great. A quick look, out of the corner of her eye, through the kitchen window, it was nothing, Nat told herself she wasn't even sure if she'd seen it. Something white, moving in the trees, something that could have been the pale leaves in the wind. It wasn't till she got to the turn in the lane, it seemed, that she had even let out a breath.

She wasn't going to shut herself into the cottage and wait, frightened by every snapping twig. She had to do something real: go where she knew for sure something had happened. Since the picture in the paper of the discovery of Ollie's body it had been there, waiting, down the lane, turn inland towards the water and the empty windows of the warehouse. How far had she come? Three miles, maybe? The closer she got though, the less she wanted to arrive. But if the police weren't going to do anything, she had to. Scene of the crime – or at least the discovery of the body. Something real.

But the faster she walked the more Nat knew she hadn't imagined that strip of dug earth, and Rufus hadn't dug it, so neat and rectangular; she couldn't even imagine putting the question to Sophie. Rufus had been out there ten minutes at the most, messing about: the earth had been dug deep. It would have taken an adult a good hour. Maybe more.

At some point there had been a man out there, digging methodically, taking his time. Knowing she was inside.

Could it have been Jim? Had it been a kind of diversion from the weirdness of his own behaviour, for him to imagine another person there that night? A way of saying, not me, I'm not the real stalker, that's someone else? Or thinking that last time he had been rewarded with a night on the sofa. Why not scare her again?

It didn't make sense. Not the Jim she knew. Jim didn't have the focus. Jim was lost.

Still hesitating at the junction of the paths she got out her phone, and dialled. She could hear her heart still thumping: it didn't want to slow down. Sunset was a long way away, she told herself. It was only just gone seven. But where the field dipped down towards the reedbeds it was dark.

'Nat!' She closed her eyes involuntarily at the excitement in Jim's voice when he answered.

'No – Jim.' She was firm. 'I want to ask you a few things.' She heard him subside at her businesslike tone. 'That night,' she said, then quickly, so he wouldn't think about last night instead, 'that night when you broke in, when you laid the table.'

'Yes.' His voice was flat.

'You said you had a feeling. That someone else was there.' He said nothing. 'Jim? Was it just a feeling, or was there anything concrete?' Still silence. 'You do know why I'm asking, right?' she said, getting angry. 'You think I'm just making this all up, about Beth? You know me, Jim.' Better than anyone, probably. The thought made her angry. 'Do you think I'm the type to get hysterical, to imagine things, to think the worst?'

She was on the point of telling him about the dug earth but stopped herself. She pushed through the hedge and set out across the grass – down at the bottom of the slope something moved. A rabbit, two rabbits, scooting for cover, low and urgent.

'I don't know,' said Jim, dully sad. 'You might have . . . you might . . .' She could almost hear him thinking. The abortion might have sent her nuts. But what had it done to him? *What about you, Jim?*

He sighed. 'It was more than a feeling,' he said. 'There must have been something.' She waited. 'I think I heard something in the trees at the end of the garden,' he said finally, but distracted, unsure. 'I mean . . . I did hear something. But I thought it was an animal, a badger or something. Noisier than a cat.' He was thinking harder, more carefully now.

She kept walking, stumbling on the uneven tufted grass, hearing her own quick breathing as she waited for him to answer. 'Anything else?'

'Maybe,' he said slowly. 'Maybe. There was a car parked up the lane a way, but that could have been anyone.' He was unsure now, wary. Was he frightened? It was a frightening thought, him slipping in around the back of the cottage and all the time someone else was there watching.

Something occurred to her. 'Have the police been in touch with you?' she asked, feeling the flutter in her chest. 'About Beth?'

'No,' he said. Something in his voice. 'Nat?' He sounded odd, ill, feverish. 'Can I see you again?'

'Not now, Jim,' she said, very quietly. She hardly the heard the click, it was so softly done. 'Jim?' he had hung up.

In the sudden silence then Nat thought she heard something and she stopped. She hadn't been paying attention and she was surrounded now, the path squeezed between high tangled mounds of brambles and whispering dry reeds. There was the rush of the water, somewhere ahead. She thought there was something else, though, a murmur, a human voice. She swallowed, and the sound of her own blood filled her ears.

Was there anyone, *anyone* she would be glad to see, here, now? Ollie might have thought he was coming to meet Beth. That would have got him down here, the thought of her wide smile, her warm strong arms open. Who did Nat have? No one.

It came back to her, forcefully, that Janine had wanted rid of her, this evening, the two of them standing there in the pub's back garden, Janine with her hand over the mobile phone, trying to sound friendly, trying to sound casual. Giving her the evening off, when she'd been rushed off her feet, Steve was away, Craig out of his head? Some teenager recruited at the last moment to fill in, some . . . some girl. And she'd sent Nat away.

Janine had been talking to Steve about something she didn't want Nat to hear. And then she had told her to go, not looking her in the eye.

The voices were still there, mumbling, indistinct, urgent. Hesitantly Nat started walking again, towards the sound, when all she wanted to do was turn around and run, tearing the brambles off her, running up and away. She kept going. The roar of the water through the weir filled the air and then she saw it, a stretch of railing that led out across the concrete slope where the water rushed. In the grey uncertain light she saw a bunch of flowers, bleached and wilting, tied to the railing hanging at an angle, and then she saw two people. An older couple, a woman with thin wild hair clinging to a bulky man who was standing with both hands on the railing stiff and upright. They turned and looked at her.

His parents. Ollie's parents. Mr and Mrs Mason.

It seemed to Nat that they looked as if they wanted to

run away when they saw her – or throw themselves into the water. Nat retreated, suddenly shaky, reaching out with her hand to support herself. She wanted to hide, the look on their faces was so awful. The woman called after her. Her voice was angry, distressed. 'Don't!' Nat heard, distinctly and she made herself stop. She turned back. The man had his hand on the woman's arm, he was trying to pull her into an embrace but she wanted Nat.

Nat set out across the walkway towards them, one hand on the railing. She stopped a few feet away.

'You're her friend.' The woman's face was wild and haggard. Nat could see Ollie's eyes in it, though, bright washed blue.

'Her friend?' Though she knew with sinking certainty that she meant Beth.

'It was her fault,' the woman said and her husband looked away, agonised.

'Beth,' said Nat. 'Beth didn't do anything. She didn't.' She didn't know how she knew that or why she was defending Beth, any more. This was so terrible.

'It was her fault. He never used to be that kind of boy. Pubs, drinking. He was a good boy.'

'Ange,' said the man, pleading.

His wife – Ange – shook him off. 'You think I don't know what girls are like?' she said angrily, without looking at him. 'She was a prick-tease, he would have done anything for her.' Staring at Nat, as if she was Beth.

'He was . . . he was just a normal lad, Ange – hormones and that.' He grabbed for her uselessly.

For a second the gulf between men and women seemed vast, as they stood there with the roar of the water in their ears. Nat saw the father as his wife did, he was a man, all men the same, driven by sex. And then he let his wife go and he was just a grieving father.

'She didn't care about his feelings,' said Ange Mason, her face tight now, and focused. On Nat.

'How do you know all this?' Nat said, faint. 'Did he talk to you about it?' Looking into the woman's face.

'He had a diary,' his mother said, drawing herself up. 'They never found his phone but he had . . . just a notebook, he scribbled in it. I gave it to the police. Saying how he knew there were other men, he'd seen her with them but he didn't care. They were going to be together.'

'Seen her with other men?' Nat got in swiftly, to catch the straw in the wind. 'Where? Did he say who?'

Ange looked at Nat, her eyes wild, empty. 'You know boys,' she said, hollow, more to herself than to Nat. 'He wasn't one for writing, he was just scribbling, he was upset.' She was holding herself, a straitjacket of her own arms across her body, and the husband stepped in front of her.

'The police think that barmaid had something to do with . . . Ollie's death,' he said, not quite looking Nat in the eye. 'Your friend.'

'But they think she's dead too,' said Nat. 'What have they told you?'

'I don't care,' said Ollie's mother, mumbling from behind her husband. 'I don't care about her.'

He turned, and all Nat could see was his broad back, as he wrapped his arms round his wife, rocking her, very gently.

'It's getting dark,' she heard him mutter. 'Let's get home, Ange.'

They came past her then, Ange's hand groping along the rail like a blind woman's and Nat could only watch them go, thinking of their empty house, getting dark.

The water went on roaring, after they'd gone, and she stood there, leaning against the railing. Someone had killed their son, because he knew something he shouldn't. Seen something – like Victor? Had he seen the murderer, like Victor had, early one morning? Ollie had *seen* her with other men, and perhaps he'd seen one man in particular, in the wrong place at the wrong time.

She took a different path from the one they'd taken, not knowing, not much caring, where she would end up as long as it wasn't with them. At least it headed uphill: she had to scramble at one point, the dusty hard-packed earth giving her no purchase, and for a panicked five minutes there was nothing resembling a path at all. Then she was out, panting, on a narrow tarmacked lane she didn't recognise, just as a car came past.

She glimpsed a profile in the driver's seat, a head turning with something in it that she had seen before then the car came to an abrupt stop a couple of yards ahead of her. The door opened as her scrambled brain tried to process it, a leg, a muscled forearm, a broad hand on the rolled-down window.

Him. He climbed out. It was Bill Sullivan.

Chapter Twenty-Seven

Friday

An alarm had gone off as Emile, the porter, brought in the trolley, closing the door behind him. Victor lay there, listening to footsteps hurrying to and fro in the corridor. There were always alarms, he had adjusted to that, alarms that sounded when a drip finished or a battery was dying, but this one generated more commotion. Voices whispering.

Today was Friday: today Richard would come.

Emile knew nothing, or professed to. The nurses had not yet come round to take his observations, although usually they would have done: Lisa should be back on duty.

He asked Emile for cornflakes and made himself eat them, methodically. Beyond the door it fell quiet. When he was finished he set the bowl carefully on the side table and got up. As he got to the door and peered around it he saw Lisa, kneeling, tutting over something. He edged out and she looked up. She got to her feet and he saw what it was she'd been looking at.

A small scattering of brown: it looked for all the world like earth to him, a little dusting of the outside world although perhaps it was only compost, from a plant brought in.

Now Lisa was leaning across the nurses' desk saying something, reaching for something. A dustpan and brush – she had it in her hand when she returned to him.

'Has something happened?' he said, leaning carefully on the walking frame to get his breath back and her head turned, just enough. He followed her gaze. The curtains around the bed he'd slept on every night until last night had been drawn.

'Nothing you need to worry about, Victor,' she said, although she looked worried herself.

Feeling himself under a compulsion he didn't quite understand, Victor shifted his position to face the curtained cubicle. He pushed the frame, one small movement towards it and then Lisa's hand was on the frame.

'No, Victor,' she said. 'You can't—'

'Did he . . . did he . . .'

The porter who had moved him the night before appeared at the far end of the corridor with another man, ambling. They were talking about football results but when they reached Victor and Lisa they fell abruptly quiet – the one Victor knew gave him a quick glance, almost sheepish. Lisa nodded and they headed towards the cubicle.

'These are high-dependency beds,' said Lisa in a low voice. Her face was strained. 'Patients sometimes . . . there are sometimes limits – sometimes there's nothing we can do.'

'Was he old, like me?' said Victor, faintly.

She frowned. 'I don't know what—'

'Did he look like me? With the lights out, could he have been me?'

'He was an elderly gentleman, yes, Victor, but you mustn't worry, he . . . you're doing so well. There's no comparison.' She looked alarmed.

Victor leaned back a little and she put her hand on his elbow to steady him. She would think him mad, if he said any more. The two men were behind the curtains and he could hear the mumble of their voices. He could see the outline of their bulky bodies through the thin fabric as they leaned across the bed. 'I – I . . .' he said, feeling his heart flutter, uneven, and Lisa gently steered him away, back towards his own room. They were behind him now, and he didn't want to turn and see what they were doing. He didn't want to see them wheel the body away.

She stood inside the door, waiting for him to get back to his bed. She took his observations in silence. He could see – he could feel – that his pulse was high, but she didn't say anything.

Twenty minutes later, as Victor lay there trying to return himself to quiet, the door opened softly and the porter's head came around it.

'You all right, mate?' he said. He looked pale. He took a step inside but the door stayed open.

'He died,' said Victor. 'Is that right? The heart patient.'

'Yes, but it's still a shock,' said the porter. 'You sure you're all right?' Victor tried to nod, but it was feeble. The porter grimaced. 'Get used to it in here,' he said. 'Quicker than they thought, but sometimes hospital does that. You're a tough one, you're going to be all right.'

'What happens now?' asked Victor. 'What happens when you die in hospital?

'You what?' The porter did a double take. Perhaps he thought Victor was past curiosity about dying. 'Doctor comes to certify him, look at what happened.' He leaned against the door jamb.

'Is there a post-mortem?' asked Victor, whispering. He felt something ebbing, strength or . . .

The porter looked dubious. 'I doubt it,' he said. ''E was ancient, he'd been brought in with heart failure, no one's gonna question it.'

I'm ancient, thought Victor. Would they ask questions if I died? The consultant, the nurse. He nodded, and the porter looked briefly relieved, then he was gone, leaving the door ajar.

Victor thought of the earth the nurse had swept up, the outside world, and it made him shiver. Turned earth from a garden, not compost. He heard a sound, a soft click, and when he looked someone had closed the door.

The room felt strange even before Nat was properly awake, there was more heat in it, in the air, under the sheets. And it wasn't her room. Nat lay very still, eyes shut, fighting panic.

She opened her eyes and turned her head. Bill lay on his back and his eyes were closed, his hair stuck up off his forehead, the fine brush of stubble on his chin, some of it white. He had slept in his T-shirt, a nice T-shirt, she registered, aware that she was grasping at straws. Then he turned, opened his eyes and smiled, a broad, sleepy smile, into her face and his arm came across and rested on her and he closed his eyes again.

Last night: and with a lurch she was back there so abruptly she had to close her eyes.

Wouldn't it be nice, shit, wouldn't it be nice, to actually choose to fuck someone, instead of just falling into it? An old expression popped into her head. Falling pregnant. Like you trip and tumble and whoops, there it is. There you are. Fucked.

Nat realised she was talking to herself in her head as if she had been in the Ladies at the Bird with Beth, leaning back on the basin, spilling the beans, going off on one. Who was there she could say any of this to? Now Beth was gone. And it rose up in her, a great sloppy gush of grief for Beth, mixed in with terror. Mixed in with self-pity, more like. She blinked. What would Beth say? It happens. *It's what we're designed for, ain't it? Boy meets girl.*

There'd been a time – a month, maybe – when Beth went more or less celibate, an experiment she called it. She had moaned about her skin, how it gave her spots, made her bad-tempered. Then she'd disappeared on a three-day lost weekend with a band she went to see in the town and she was back on track. 'Life's too short,' she had said cheerfully, breezing back in and ignoring Janine's black look. True enough.

Had Steve been around then? Tick, tick, tick they went, the questions starting up again. Yes he had, because she remembered him on the stairs at the sound of Beth's voice, thundering down. He'd been around, shaking his head over her.

Party girl. For a flicker of a second Nat wondered if she was turning into Beth. No chance – one Beth was enough.

But you don't have to feel bad. Boy meets girl.

Not pregnant, though; not this time. An advantage of both being sober enough for that considerate exchange, kind, even – at least it had felt kind, him setting two hands on her forearms to hold her there and saying, *We'd better . . .*

There. She heard Beth's voice, encouraging her. Comforting her. *So: no harm done, right?*

He had climbed out of his car on that twilight road and come two steps towards her before stopping, holding up two palms.

'You all right?'

Of course it was only natural that he should stop, that he should ask that, seeing her stumble out of the undergrowth with twigs in her hair, panting and wild-eyed. He was hardly going to drive on. She had staggered and straightened up, brushing herself down.

'Jesus,' Bill had said then, and began to laugh, and with the sound the question that had hovered when she saw it was him, something to do with coincidence, and what had he been doing there, and was he . . . was he . . . that question evaporated.

In the car she had begun to tell him about Ollie's parents but he had just frowned and she realised she wasn't saying what she meant, and he probably wasn't the person to say it to anyway. The difference between men and women, mothers and fathers.

'Perhaps you should get out of this place,' he just said, mildly, 'when this is all over.' So he knew, all right, about Beth. 'Don't you . . . have plans?'

'You mean a holiday?' She didn't mean to sound so scornful. She just couldn't imagine it, a beach or a foreign city. He was driving carefully: his car was anonymous, a rental firm's sticker in the window and a pine-tree air-freshener hanging from the rear-view mirror, clean and empty. The room was like his car, a short term rental in the next village, inland, the end unit in a converted stable. She could see a couple of things hanging neatly in a fitted wardrobe: dark trousers, a jacket.

Was this his life? Everything temporary, three months here, three months there. Girl in every port, and was that her, here? He'd be off soon. None of the arguments got through, though, she was just liking it, sitting next to him in his car, his broad clean hands on the steering wheel. The thought of Ollie's parents receded, although it didn't disappear: it sat in darkness, where the chaos was, beyond the neat interior.

'No,' said Bill, patient, leaning forward to check his mirrors, indicating. 'I meant, you know. Moving on, working out what you want to do with your life.'

If someone else had said it – and punters did, sometimes, beerily, by way of a let-me-take-you-away-from-all-this conversation, she would have had a smart reply. As it was all she said was, 'Maybe.'

And as she said it he turned out of the top of the lane and she saw where they were, the estuary spreading out dark ahead of them, a few lights coming on across the distant dark velvety sweep that was the caravan site and she sat up in the passenger seat to gaze. 'How long did you say you'd been here?' she said to Bill. 'You and the crew?'

'Since June.' Was that impatience? He wasn't looking at her, indicating to turn into the lane. He was taking her home and without thinking she put a hand up to the wheel and said, no. The cottage was the last place Nat wanted to go to.

'You hungry?' she said. 'I mean, I've got the night off. We could . . . or . . .'

He'd sat back in his seat, the car waiting at the junction, and looked at her, not quite surprised. Then reversed, and turned the other way.

'I mean, I can see why you like it here, though,' was all

he said, as the trees flickered overhead, a green tunnel swooping up to a ridge and the darkening blue of the evening sky.

More than that, she thought, it's more complicated than that, but she sat quiet, barely registering where they were. The edge of a village she didn't know, a row of big chestnut trees, a post office, then he came to a stop outside the barn development, switched off the engine and he turned to her and kissed her, soft and warm, and she tasted the inside of his mouth and felt his hand move quick and sure under her shirt to her breast, and her train of thought was gone, elsewhere.

He had had the condom in his pocket. It had been a small shock, him being one of those men who carried one with them at all times. Now lying still with his hand on her in the high-ceilinged room with the warm green light of day filtering through the blinds, she let herself think, It's just normal. Practical. He had moved a pillow for her without needing to be asked, shifted his hip to make her comfortable. He had stopped for a second at the quickest indrawn breath from her to make sure he was doing the right thing. It had seemed like she knew him already.

And then, of course, the questions tumbled back down.

Had Beth woken up this way, how many times, a hundred? Two? Rationalising, rearranging her fears. He could have said, we can wait. Tomorrow, I'll be prepared. Can I see you tomorrow? Nat could feel her heart patter, she could feel chemicals running through her. You haven't hurt anyone, you haven't lost anything, no one owes anyone – *It's what we're made for, ain't it?* It's only sex.

He'd known what he was doing, with the condom too; he was practised, everything about him had been practised, and she had only to enjoy it: his mouth, his hands, the diagonals of muscle running down either side of his abdomen. 'Let me,' he'd said, a finger to his lips, his face over hers, and she had let him. Stop thinking. Stop thinking.

But then suddenly there was movement beside her and with a yawn and a stretch and a quick smooth movement that lifted his T-shirt and showed her that line of muscle again Bill sat up, tugged at the pillows behind him and was looking down at her, smiling, perfectly at his ease. Nat resisted struggling upright beside him, she just turned on her back, arms over her head. Don't think: look. Work it out. Talk.

A big metallic case sat on a table, more like a toolbox than a suitcase, and she could see black plastic and metal inside it, the curve of a big lens. His jacket – multipocketed, outdoor, waxed but worn in – hung over the back of a chair. He was used to being alone.

'What's it like?' she said. 'Your life.'

He laughed abruptly. 'That's deep,' he said, and an eyebrow went up.

'No, I mean, day-to-day,' she said, calm. 'The work, living like you do. No home to go to. You must get to like places, don't you ever want to stay? How long are you on location for?'

'I've got a home,' he said, and she wasn't sure if he was pretending to take offence. 'I've got a flat in Kilburn.' Laughed. 'At least, that's where I left it.' He set his head back against the headboard.

'This place has been . . . not like the rest.' There was something in his tone, thoughtful. And he turned his head to look at her, not smiling. 'There's you.'

'What else?' said Nat, tougher than she felt.

'Well,' Bill said, swinging out of bed and crossing to the window, tugging the blind open and looking out, 'I've done a couple of detective series, five years one of them, five years on and off in the same village, filming, faking it – the atmosphere, you know, looking for the right light – and all the time all you can think is how safe those places feel, you have to work really hard to get the . . . the fear in there.'

She did sit up now, watching him. He leaned down and pulled on some boxers, intent, thinking.

'And actors, dressed up as cops.' He raised his head and laughed. 'If you could see them. The way they stand, even, the way they talk, it's nothing like the real thing. The real thing . . . well, they're different. They're . . . you know, cheery and all that, but underneath . . .' He shrugged, three steps and he was back in the bed with her, he was leaning up on an elbow, looking into her face. 'Underneath they're cold bastards.' His finger came up and touched her cheek and then he took it away again.

'So,' he said, musing, 'five years' filming and the first time we see real police is here, and we're filming some ancient historical. A real murder. A body.' The smile was back, but distant. 'You were down at the weir,' he said. 'Last night. Where his body was found.'

'You've been following the case,' she said, feeling a tremor of something. Bill shrugged, still at his ease but an edge to it, a readiness.

'So have you, though,' he said.

'She was my friend,' said Nat without meaning to shift it to Beth, but once she'd said it she saw his eyes change and darken. 'You knew her,' she said, quick and soft. 'You knew Beth.' Not another one. Not him.

'Oh no,' he said, half laughing. Half warning her. 'Not in the biblical sense, I didn't.' She shifted, turning against the headboard to get a good look at him.

'In what sense, then?' Nat was stubborn, she could feel the danger.

'No,' said Bill, quite calm, watching her.

Stupid, thought Nat. I've been very stupid. This hadn't been about him fancying her, that wasn't what this was about. And she didn't even know where he'd taken her. Had it been his car parked outside her cottage? The anonymous rental hatchback. 'You knew her.'

Bill sighed. 'I think I saw her once,' he said, still calm, but with a hint of edge now. 'It's how I heard about the pub. We were out in the town, some club. She was dancing. Everyone was looking at her. Nice-looking girl.'

But? Nat waited for him to say, to even hint at it. She was a slapper.

'Good dancer,' he said. 'You could tell, though.'

Tell what? She said nothing, but felt her hands clench into fists.

But he didn't say what she expected, not exactly. 'The reckless sort.' Bill looked tired suddenly, then he looked sad. He put out his hands, examining his palms, and she looked too. They were rough: they showed he wasn't young. 'It's a risk,' he said finally. 'It can pay off – curiosity. No boundaries, no fear, no regret.' He sighed. 'It's exciting, sure. I've had girlfriends like that. I'm too old for that kind of fun. The bloke she was with looked like he was, too.'

'What bloke?'

'What bloke? Just a bloke,' Bill said, then, frowning, 'Perhaps I've seen him around, somewhere. Not sure.'

'Jonathan Dowd?' She tried to describe him but Dowd could be anyone. The invisible man. 'Or a skinny guy, dark?' She was talking about Jim: Bill just shrugged.

'So.' She shifted on the bed, and reached for her shirt. It was lying on the floor. He watched her put it on: lifting her arms, it went over her head and she was uncomfortably aware of her breasts exposed – she felt him tug at it gently to help her. She pulled the sheet up to her waist. 'You knew where she worked? You asked?'

'The barmen were talking about her,' he said. He was patient, but it just told her, his patience could run out. 'Her gay best friends. I didn't ask . . . well, I asked about the pub. But only because I wanted somewhere I could get away from the crew.'

'What was the club?'

He told her; she knew it, and Nat dimly remembered Beth talking about two gorgeous gay guys who worked the bar. Nice for Beth, she remembered thinking that, to not be hit on for a change.

'And you came to the pub looking for her?' She could hear her voice, jealous, petulant: she told herself she didn't care.

'They said it was a nice pub,' said Bill mildly. 'And actually they *did* say it had the best-looking bar staff in the county. Which turned out to be true.' She looked at him. He wasn't smiling.

'She came to your film set, once at least,' she said.

He frowned. 'When? I never saw her there.'

'Oh no? A girl like Beth?'

'Lots of girls on film sets,' he said wearily, 'and I would have been working. Looking through a viewfinder.'

Nat stared, not sure if she believed him, then she remembered. Shit.

'I've got to be back,' she said urgently, out of bed and scrabbling on the floor for her jeans. 'Where . . . Shit, shit, shit.' She couldn't find her knickers: she felt herself get hot, all up her back, armpits, at the thought, this isn't me, looking for my underwear in a strange man's rented flat. 'It's the police,' she said, head under the bed. There. She hauled them out, dusty, shook out her jeans. Dirt from her sandals on the floor. He was beside her then, holding her by the elbow as she teetered on one leg trying to get her clothes on, all of them at once.

'I've got to be back for the police.' She felt the strength of his grip on her then he let go and was swiping his own clothes from the chair, picking up his keys.

'I'll get you there.'

He drove fast, without talking, the only sound the air rushing past the open windows. At one point he glanced to check on her then back to the road and for a quick second as her eyes travelled over his hands on the wheel a whole other life flickered in front of her. Her beside him in a car, the two of them going somewhere together, some other time, some other place. A lift to work, off on holiday. Heading home together.

You hardly know him. She looked away, out of the window.

It was early but it was hot: a different kind of hot. When they came out at the top of the slope that would take them down to the village before they turned, Nat saw the weather front, coming in from the west, a line where the blue was blurred grey, a thick ridge of cloud spanning the horizon.

Bill saw it too. 'Looks like the weather might break,' he said.

You hardly know him.

'Is that going to stop filming?' she said, feeling herself allow uneasiness to creep between them.

He shrugged. 'Depends,' he said, turning into the lane. He came to a halt outside the cottage and applied the handbrake. There was no police car. It wasn't even eight thirty. He turned to her. 'If it pisses down, yes. Up to that point it's a sliding scale. It's to do with continuity.'

'You might get the afternoon off, then?' she said, then wished she hadn't. Did he think she was . . . She let out a breath. Shit. Shit, shit, and shit again.

'You never know,' he said, amused, and in an agony of embarrassment she shoved the door open with her shoulder and practically fell out on the tarmac.

'Thanks for the lift,' she said, leaning down through the window, almost too late. 'Just . . . well, thanks. Sorry.' He nodded, already engaging gear.

As Nat watched him go the thoughts fell down one after the other, clunk, clunk, clunk. That's that, then. He's fed up. He doesn't like you. And: what were you apologising for, exactly?

In a kind of daze she walked in through the low front door and straight through to the kitchen sink, ran herself a glass of water, listening to the tap, trying to blot out the other sound. Looking out of the back window with a glass of water in her hand. The tap turned off and there it was, buzzing in her ears again, like electricity, and focusing she saw it. The white in the trees again, not a carrier bag caught in the branches, not leaves in the wind. Too long for that, too much of it, as long as a human form.

She didn't know how long she stood there, frozen. Then she set down the glass and opened the back door and walked out.

It was hanging in the trees: Beth's favourite dress, her favourite ever, white, like a Victorian nightie with lace, she used to haul the front down to show her boobs, the one item of hers Nat would have liked for herself, in her dreams. The grass was soaking under her feet but the cotton of the dress was barely damp, as though it had been hung there as dawn broke.

She reached for it, wanting to wrap her arms around it, her whole body bathed in sweat – *It was hot, wasn't it? It was so hot, even though there was no sun, the sky was grey, grey as a tin lid* – and stopped herself. Just in time, because it was evidence, *Remember that, evidence* and then she heard the sound.

He knew she would find it, and then the police would arrive. But there would be an interval. He gauged the interval. He put a forefinger to his pulse and felt it: slow and steady. If he remained motionless, he would be invisible, it was a trick he'd pulled off a good few times.

The police would look at the empty grave he'd dug and shake their heads. They'd look sideways at each other and when they got back in their patrol car one of them would tap the side of his head and say, 'Loco.' Another hysterical female.

She knew, though, the girl knew what it meant. He

wanted her to put her hands down into the empty earth, fearful, wondering if her fingers would, searching, encounter cold dead skin, a hand, lips, teeth.

He swallowed, savouring the moment. She had found nothing, but she knew, the grave told her, it was waiting to be found.

The problem with the old man had been that when the man had seen him he had been moving, not motionless. And that leaning down into the water to wash her blood off him he had missed it, that great streak under his forearm, the streak he had been looking at when – sitting on the bench, eyes closed in the sunshine – the old man had chosen that moment to open his eyes and turn his head. That was a question. Why had he known, why then? Under his finger the pulse quickened, a tiny itch of annoyance mocked him and carefully he took his finger away. He didn't make mistakes, think of it as a practice run. Surprisingly easy, a pillow held over the face in the dark, two minutes, make it three and a weak heart gives out. The wrong heart, as it turned out. But now you're on borrowed time, old man.

No one had seen him meet Oliver Mason, nor return from the weir, his hands in his pockets, still warm from what he'd done. He'd chosen the place well, though somewhere inside him he would have enjoyed stopping to talk to a dog walker. Hands in pockets.

He willed her to look, to raise her head and look. Look for me. I am closer. I am closer.

She was reaching for the dress.

He had not had to look for it, it had been on the floor of her bedroom, under his feet as he hauled her into the bathroom. Her in that dress. So many men watching her in it. Slipping into the back of the pub just to let her know he was there, he could see. She had liked that, in the beginning.

The white dress hanging in the tree all night, it didn't matter how long it hung there because eventually this moment would come. She had her face against it now. Spunk on that dress. The cool fabric against his skin, the smell of her and all the while knowing where she was now, what he had changed her into. He had come in a white light, three seconds. Washed it after.

For a second, as she stood in all the green garden and gathered the dress into her arms, by some trick of the light he saw her again, alive, and a rage jumped inside him. Alive? And with the thought he considered that there may have been thoughts that body had had, that he didn't read. The rage ticked, he slowed it, like his pulse. No: he saw things other men don't see, even if they could never know that. He had been inside her head. He had cut her open.

Behind him a branch cracked and his head moved before he could prevent it. An animal, ugly. Muntjac. He saw her change, her body changed, her head was still. She stared straight at him for one second, two, then the animal. It jumped away, half pig, half deer, it bounded off behind him into the light and her gaze shifted. She didn't see.

And then she was turning because she heard it before he did: the sound of a car door slamming. The sound of voices. And he was gone, the same way as the muntjac, skirting the tangled hedge. Gone.

Chapter Twenty-Eight

As she walked away from the Bird in Hand – at close to eleven, when she should be starting her shift, a busy Friday lunchtime and a handful of punters already clinking glasses out front under the uncertain sky – Nat thought, on balance, that she had been fired.

Beth had pushed her luck far and often, and although Janine had made threats she'd never fired her. A month or so ago Craig had turned up so hung-over he couldn't turn his head and had served a portion of whitebait smelling so far gone the punter had simply draped her paper napkin over it – but Janine had just told him to come back when he'd had a bit of kip and a fry-up.

And now, although the words hadn't been spoken, and although Nat hadn't been late or pissed or talked back, she had the definite feeling there was no going back.

The police had been at the cottage twenty minutes after she made the call: they had already been on the way, said

Donna Garfield as she stepped out of the car, when they got the message. The younger man climbed out after her.

Garfield looked pale when she saw it – that hadn't been Nat's imagination. Nat concentrated hard on looking calm, holding her arms tight across her body to stop the shaking. 'I stayed with a friend last night,' she said quickly. 'I didn't want to be on my own in the cottage.'

Garfield frowned, uncomfortable. Guilty? So you fucking should be, thought Nat. But she said nothing. Telling them they were useless bastards would get her nowhere.

'It was there when he dropped me off,' she said stiffly, and then she realised something, not him. She was Bill's alibi, he couldn't have anything to do with this. He'd been with her. 'I called you straight away.' Feeling something ease, just fractionally, just for a second.

Garfield had cleared her throat then. 'And the . . . disturbed ground.' The man she'd brought with her – the younger policeman who'd been round the first time – was standing at a respectful distance from the oblong of turned earth. He was grimacing as he looked at it. Despite her frantic excavations you could still see its shape. Or was that just her? Losing it.

What do *you* think it's supposed to look like?' Nat tried not to sound as angry as she felt. Or as scared.

'Yes,' said Donna Garfield and Nat saw her swallow. 'It's nasty.' So police officers could be freaked too. Garfield's eyes kept being drawn back to the white shape shifting in the tree.

'We'll get it taken down,' she said, lips compressed, and put her arm out to Nat's elbow. 'Let's have a cup of tea, all right? While we wait for the team.'

In the cramped kitchen, jerky with suppressed anger Nat told Garfield she'd make the tea. Her place, her kettle, her mugs.

'You wanted to ask me questions,' she said, setting the mugs down. Pushing one across to the man. And DS Garfield sighed.

'We've identified the blood we found on Oliver's body as hers. It matches DNA from her hairbursh. On rags used to tie his hands and feet. Looks like strips torn from a dress.'

Despite herself Nat found she had a hand to her mouth, her eyes filling. She strained to keep it all back, inside, but she couldn't. 'She's dead,' she said. 'I was right, I was right.' Hollow. She didn't want to have been right.

Garfield leaned forward across the table, chin resting on her knuckles. 'You were the one that knew, all along,' she said, softly.

And then the questions. It was as if the earth hadn't been dug, the dress not hanging there.

Or as if they thought she'd done it all herself.

'Did you fall out?' Still speaking softly and the male officer smirking across the table. Nat had stared: she knew where this was going but she couldn't believe it.

'Your boss – Janine – she said she thought you were a bit too close, for all you were chalk and cheese. You were the home bird and Beth was never going to stick around. She was a bad influence and she was going to let you down.'

Garfield's face was pleasant but stupid. Nat wanted to push it in.

'Too close?' Nat heard the dangerous edge to her voice.

'Beth was my mate. She didn't let me down. Everyone said she'd be off sooner or later but she didn't go anywhere, did she?' As the words left her mouth she knew what Garfield was going to say next, leaning even closer over the table.

'Looks like she didn't, no.' Thinking she was clever, with her flat smile. 'Looks like someone stopped her before she could.'

'She wanted to settle down,' said Nat, blurting it out before she could stop herself. 'She wanted a baby.' Garfield's small stupid eyes widened. 'You didn't know that, did you?' Nat went on. 'The appointment she had at the hospital was with a fertility guy. She could even—' and her voice broke, she had to stop before she said any more. 'She could have been pregnant.'

'Pregnant,' said Garfield sitting back, and Nat saw something in her eyes. She knows about the termination. She thinks I could have hurt Beth.

'She was my *friend*, you fucking moron, do you know what a friend is?'

And she saw Garfield nod, just once, satisfied. Hard as nails now, against her.

Donna Garfield had started talking about Jim.

She had got to work in a state of shock, and there was Janine behind the bar, wiping her hands on a tea towel, avoiding her eye as she started to say it – *Look* . . .

And now in the lane Nat's phone rang and she stopped, feeling sick.

Could it be true, what she'd said. They'd said. Garfield, Janine?

Jim. Jim.

'Look,' and finally Janine raised her head to look her in the eye, 'I think all things considered . . .'

Far off somewhere something rumbled as Nat answered and it took her a while to catch up with who the woman was that she was talking to, and what she was saying, she felt so sick. Don't.

I think, all things considered, it would be best if you didn't come back. Dropping the tea towel.

'Sorry?' she said into the mobile.

The woman was patient on the other end of the line. 'Yes, Sam would be happy to see you.'

It was Walters. The supervisor from Moorsom House. The woman who ran the care home where Beth's brother was living. Sam.

It wasn't until she'd hung up that Nat realised she hadn't said anything to the police about Moorsom House, or Sam, and if they were actually looking into Beth's disappearance they hadn't got as far as finding him themselves. She stood in the lane, hesitant. The air was warm and heavy and she kept thinking she felt rain. She didn't know if she should tell them. It was her Sam wanted to talk to, though, it was her. She was his sister's friend.

She dialled the taxi firm. At the back of her mind it beat, *Jim, Jim, Jim*, it drummed, it circled. Janine was lying. The only explanation. She stuffed the thoughts away, stick them in a bin bag, throw them in the river.

There was a droning Celtic music track while she waited, and when she got an answer, the line crackling and cutting out, she was told they wouldn't have a driver for half an hour. Impatient, she hung up. Shit. She could wait half an hour. But she felt itchy with something, the need to do something. Had a thought, and dialled Paddy.

'Hey!' She'd never heard him so upbeat. 'How are things? This weather . . .' and he was off, so uncharacteristic that it took her a while to work out how she might interrupt him. He was talking about rain coming, about Sophie, meandering, the kid Rufus and something he'd done with his lifejacket, there wouldn't be much more sailing this season, lightning strike in Lincolnshire, the caravan site was going to empty out and would Sophie be able to stay with Nat—

'I phoned to ask for a lift, Paddy,' she said.

'Oh – right,' he was thrown, not quite wounded but he faltered.

'I need to get to the care home where Beth's brother is.'

'I didn't know she had a brother,' said Paddy, quiet.

'I'm sorry,' said Nat, and she really did feel it.

'No, no,' said Paddy, 'it's all right, I'm sorry, it's me . . .' His voice receded as if he'd taken the receiver away from his mouth then he was back. 'I couldn't get my car started this morning.' Apologetic, humble. 'I'd been thinking I really should get a decent—'

'It's OK,' said Nat, unable to be patient. 'It's fine, Paddy, see you.' She hung up, feeling guilty at having cut him short, not listened, at the shame in his voice at having only a dusty old banger. Perhaps Sophie had seen it, and laughed, perhaps Rufus had.

She stared at her phone, about to dial the taxi firm again, thinking.

Bill. Would he be the natural call to make? The man

she spent the night with. No. In her head that bin bag bobbed and floated in dark water. Sink: she willed it to go under.

She called Jonathan Dowd's number.

He was there by the time she got to the top of the lane. She had lingered at the turning to the close where Beth had lived, at the dull curtained windows all looking in on each other, no one moving in the heavy midday air. There was police tape across the door now and at the thought of the police she felt angry. She hadn't thought they wouldn't believe her; she hadn't thought they would keep information from her. Such as what it was exactly they suspected her of. How was this supposed to work?

Dowd was unshaven, he smelled like he'd been up all night, and she said so as she climbed in.

'It's the weather,' he said. 'Up processing samples before it breaks. I didn't get in till around eight this morning.'

'Sorry,' she said and he darted a glance at her in the passenger seat.

'Also it's hard to sleep at the moment,' he said. 'I keep thinking – I think about her body.' He stared ahead, stony. 'I think every time I turn on the radio, search for news stories on my phone, there'll be something, they'll have found . . . remains.' His profile was grim. 'Where are we going?'

The sickness was back, souring in her throat. Remains: that bin bag drifted and circled, it wouldn't go under.

Whoever killed Ollie hadn't hidden his body, he hadn't weighted it, he had tied it up with bloodstained rags and let the water carry it. Just chance it had taken so long to surface. No shame, no need to hide. Did they think a woman had done that? When she lay next to Jim on that sofa he had oozed shame from every pore, or had she just been projecting her own on to him? She blinked, trying to scatter the thoughts, of what Janine had said, of the accusations she had made.

'We're going to the place Beth used to get dressed up for every Tuesday night.' Dowd stiffened, hands on the wheel. She told him, 'Brandon. Moorsom House. You know where that is?'

'The rehab place?'

Of course, that would be what it was known for. 'There's a residential home,' she said, hesitating. 'Beth used to go there to see her brother. He's got Down's.'

'A brother,' repeated Jonathan Dowd, blank. 'I didn't know that.' He swallowed.

'He's agreed to talk to me.'

Wordless, pale, he started the car. When they got to the big gates at the foot of the drive Dowd didn't turn in but pulled up on the verge. 'I can come in with you,' he said. 'I—' He cleared his throat. 'I'd like to meet Beth's brother.' She couldn't tell if he was grieving, somehow, or in a kind of trance.

'They'll only let me in,' she said gently.

He nodded, and leaned across her to open the door for her. 'I'll wait for you here,' he said.

'I can get a cab,' she said lamely, but he shook his head. 'I'll wait.'

Sam was a nice-looking boy. Nat hadn't expected to see Beth in him, she hadn't known what to expect, but there she was even if Nat couldn't pin down where. In the eyebrows, the cheekbones, the colouring. He was slighter than she expected too and Nat felt herself uneasy in her skin at having thought she knew what Down's kids were like, that they might be all the same.

Walters the supervisor had escorted Nat down a carpeted corridor. She stopped halfway and turned to her.

'Sam's condition isn't severe,' she had said, quietly. 'He's a bit above the middle of the spectrum, some cognitive difficulties, speech problems. But he's a bright lad, he can cook, he's done acting classes, and as a matter of fact he's got a girlfriend in the unit so you won't find it hard to get through to him. He's still vulnerable though. Things frighten him. So please don't frighten him.' She held Nat's gaze a moment to make sure she'd understood, and then walked on. When they got to the door she knocked.

Sam had opened the door immediately and Nat saw a short shock of hair that stuck up at the brow line, a shy smile, long delicate fingers. A short-sleeved check shirt open over a dark T-shirt.

Behind him was a small self-contained flat, a kitchenette visible through a door and French doors opening on to sloping grass. 'You all right for me to leave you with Miss Cooper, Sam?' said Walters, gruffly. Nat could see how much she liked him. He nodded.

He offered her a cup of tea and she watched him make it painstakingly. 'I make it strong,' he explained, and his slight speech impediment was there, the fluffing of the consonants. He handed her the cup, with a saucer, reached down from a cupboard, carefully. He sat on a chair, elbows on his knees, leaning forwards and examining her. 'I've got a girlfriend,' he offered, watching her drink. The tea was very hot.

'Do you think she'll mind me talking to you?' Nat said

seriously, and he squirmed a little in his chair, smiling. 'I won't be long, Sam,' she said. 'I'm trying to work out where Beth has gone. I'm trying to find her.' *She's dead.*

It came to Nat that she should be the one to tell him. When the time came.

Sam nodded, brightening. 'Tell her I need some more cool T-shirts,' he said and he opened his check shirt to show her a Japanese anime figure underneath. 'She always brings one when she's been somewhere.'

Nat nodded, smiling. Don't frighten him. She went on, quiet. 'She didn't say anything to you? Goodbye, or when she'd be back, or . . . a new relationship, maybe?' When he said nothing she rephrased. 'A new boyfriend?'

'Someday my prince will come,' he said. 'Beth said that all the time. If she'd found her prince she'd be back anyway, though. She promised me she would.'

'What about your mum?' she said, and Sam frowned, uncomfortable. 'She came once,' he said. 'She came before Christmas once.' He shifted agitatedly on the chair, shit, shit shit, thought Nat. 'She brought me a calculator.' He's only got Beth. Of course she wouldn't have left him. The tea had cooled enough, and she drank it while he watched, still frowning.

'Can I come again?' she asked. 'Just to . . . just to, you know, say hello? You could introduce me to your girlfriend.'

'All right,' he said, uncertainly.

'Is there anything . . . could I bring anything? Take you somewhere?'

Sam chewed his lip, hesitating, then sat up straighter. 'Fish and chips,' he said triumphant. 'Beth brings me fish and chips sometimes.'

'Yes, I—' Nat began but he hurried on.

'Got to be from the Seashell in Litton, though, Beth only goes there, she says it's the best.'

'Litton?' She was taken aback. 'It can't have been too warm by the time she got it here, can it?'

'She said her knight in shining armour took her,' said Sam, smiling, just a slightly worried look to him, as if he wasn't sure, as if he was beginning to understand. 'He flies like the wind, she said that.'

Nat thought of Dowd, waiting in his pickup for her at the foot of the hill now. 'Right,' she said slowly, and got to her feet. 'Well, I'd better get myself one of those, for next time.'

Sam stood up, taking his cue, shifting from foot to foot, trying to be polite, trying to get it right. 'Maybe Beth married him,' he said, uncertainly, at the door. 'I asked her if she was going to marry him, but she just laughed.'

Nat didn't know what to say so she put her arms around him: she smelled boys' aftershave and washing powder. 'Don't worry, Sam,' she said, holding on tight. 'We'll sort it out.'

She was glad he couldn't see her face.

Dowd was waiting where she'd left him in the driver's seat of the pickup, staring straight ahead.

'All right,' she said, climbing in. 'I fancy some fish and chips. You know where Litton is?'

The woman behind the fish counter frowned down at the picture Nat showed her, on her phone. She shrugged. 'Might have,' she said. Something a bit sneering about the way she said it. She had thick fingers, a broad gold band embedded in one of them.

Dowd *had* known where Litton was. He had cleared his throat, nodded, engaged gear. ('You ever bring Beth here?' He shook his head, not looking at her. But he knew where to find it.) He might just think she was hungry. They took a turning and got a flash of the estuary gleaming brown between the banks, a roof that might or might not be the Bird in Hand, and she had to blink.

Donna Garfield's stupid face: she didn't understand Beth. She just thought Beth was a party girl, like party girls didn't have brothers they loved, like they never had to make hard decisions or went to see genetic counsellors or stuck by their female friends, chalk and cheese or not. She wasn't going to find out who killed Beth, because she didn't understand, and she wasn't listening.

Jonathan Dowd had shot her an anxious glance. 'What?' he said, torn between her and needing to keep his eyes on the road. She just shook her head, flapped her hand. 'Nothing.'

It wasn't just Nat who was sure Beth was dead, was it? They hadn't listened to her say that.

'What do you mean, might have?' From behind the fryer cabinet where a slab of fish in batter lay alongside other, less identifiable items the woman gave her a level, heavy-lidded look from under her plastic mobcap and Nat felt something flare inside her. She controlled it. 'She might have looked a bit dressed up, you know, for the fish and chips?' she said. 'Heels on, that kind of thing?'

The woman's head tipped back a little, and taking the phone, she held it out to focus. 'All right,' she said grudgingly. 'Yeah, now you come to mention – I seen her. Every few weeks, once a month maybe.' A jeer just below the surface, at Beth flying in, Beth clicking in and out in her heels. Jealousy. 'Not for a while.'

'Was there ever anyone with her?' Nat tried to sound casual. The woman handed the phone back.

She shook her head. 'Not that I ever seen.' Jerked her head. 'I wouldna' seen anyway,' she said. 'Car park's out the back.'

And when she came out with the hot greasy vinegary bundle of cod and chips, that was where Nat found Jonathan Dowd waiting for her.

Sophie bounced in through the door to Victor's room, full of a secret pleasure, and Victor couldn't spoil it for her. He wondered if she had forgotten that Richard was coming for them. Richard will kill me, was the thought that popped into Victor's head. He'll find a way.

Imagine, if Sophie had wheedled Richard into letting Victor come and live with them. The supper table with Victor's eye on him, Victor peering round the door without knocking. Sophie fretting, anxious.

This was the Sophie he remembered, sunny, trusting. He should perhaps have taught her to be different, though he couldn't imagine how one went about doing that. She hauled one of the old-fashioned heavy chairs with padded leatherette seats and armrests up next to Victor's.

There was so little time, so little room for manoeuvre. Victor felt his heart jitter with the prospect of getting all things to the right place at the right time.

There was the possibility, of course, that he was wrong. That he was safe in here; for a moment he wanted so much to believe that. After all, what evidence could he present – to those policemen, with their dubious looks, their exchanged glances, their book of suspects? To poor weary Lisa, all too used to silly old men. The sound of a voice in the corridor, the sick patient who'd been given his bed, dead in the night. A scattering of earth, still damp, outside the side-room he'd been moved to. That had been real, earth from a shoe, not a nurse's. But it was hardly conclusive, was it? It was hardly anything. All that Victor knew was, if he had trusted to an instinct, long ago, he might have saved Sophie from Richard. If sitting on that bench in the sun he had held his nerve and waited for the man with blood on his arm to take a few more steps into the light, he could have said to the police, *not* my imagination.

But the one thing Victor knew with certainty was that the man with blood on his arm had seen *him*.

The understanding made him quiet a moment. All right. And then he set that to one side. What was important was that he should be out before Richard came. That Sophie should be in place and holding her resolve.

'Where is Rufus?' he asked, heart sinking, surely, surely Richard hadn't already come? The next person to come through those doors.

'Oh, I left him with Paddy,' she said, blithe.

'Paddy,' repeated Victor, ruminating, anxious. Paddy was certainly better than Richard. But what, after all, did one know about people? Paddy, quiet and tall and thoughtful, carrying Victor's sherry over to him in the corner of the Bird in Hand. Could one trust him with something as precious as Rufus?

'He was desperate to go out again on the little boat,'

said Sophie, leaning forward to take his hand. He felt her gentle presence, just like her mother, only sees the good. 'I thought it would be a good argument, you know, for us staying, just a little longer – when Richard, if he . . . if Rufus is adamant, enjoying himself . . .' She faltered. 'Of course it might . . . Richard might get—' Victor put up a hand and seized hers.

'I'm going to be discharged today,' he said.

Immediately she looked alarmed. 'Are you ready, Daddy?' she said.

'It's in hospital that people die,' he said, trying to pretend it was a joke. 'The consultant said it would be fine.' He was well aware that this was not true, that there was the risk he would be found out, but the deception only needed to last a certain length of time, to convince a certain small number of people. He changed the subject. 'So Richard *is* coming to take Rufus home? Today.'

'That's why I left him with Paddy,' said Sophie, low-voiced. 'Richard will come here.'

'If I'm discharged, you will have to stay,' he said bravely. 'You and Rufus.'

Sophie opened her mouth, and closed it again, thoughtful. She knew now, at least, that he wanted to get her away from Richard: he hoped it gave her strength. He hoped he hadn't misunderstood, that it really was what she wanted too. 'Cup of tea?' she said, jumping up.

When Sophie came back, Lisa was with her, walking her back to Victor so briskly the paper cup of tea was jumping in her hand.

'I was telling Lisa,' Sophie said, looking worried, 'that we're hoping to get you home today.'

Lisa sighed. 'I think we'll decide when you go home, Victor,' she said, frowning.

Sitting as upright as he could in the chair, Victor held his nerve. Leaning forward, he opened the door to his little cupboard to show the neat pile of his things. 'I've got everything ready,' he said. 'I just need the drugs the consultant prescribed. I really only need him to sign me off.' He had to concentrate very hard to get all the words out fluently, no faltering or slurring. And smiling.

'Oh, Victor,' said Lisa, glancing to Sophie for support then back to him, a little smile returning his. 'It's not quite that straightforward. We're not letting you go back to an empty home.' Spreading her hands. 'There has to be someone there, social services will insist. A care package.' She sighed. 'It's very complicated.'

And oddly, as she spoke, as she turned again to Sophie for backup, Victor had a flash of understanding out of nowhere, a profile, a face, the man walking up from under the trees raising his face. He saw the face.

And he felt his heart gather and race, faster and faster in the frail cage of his chest.

He was watching Lisa when Sophie spoke.

'I'll be living with him,' she said, and her voice was quite firm, her head was high. His Sophie. 'My son and I. We'll be there.'

Chapter Twenty-Nine

The pickup rattled down the hill, swung around the corner, past the Bird. They were busy: she saw a girl she didn't recognise, young and harried, coming out of the door with plates along her arm.

They had hardly got halfway through the fish and chips, parked up in a lay-by, neither of them hungry. They could have sat and eaten it in the shop's car park, but Dowd had started up the engine the minute he saw her. She wondered if he ever ate – he was so thin. Wrapping the greasy bundle back up she climbed out and put it in the lay-by's bin. Turning to come back she saw him gazing at her.

'Did you find anything out?' said Dowd, fastidiously cleaning his hands with wipes he extracted from the door pocket. He handed her one. 'From Beth's brother.'

She shook her head, rubbing at her greasy fingers. Held them to her nostrils: the smell. 'She had a boyfriend, Sam never saw him,' she said. 'Well, a special boyfriend, maybe.

She called him her knight in shining armour. Is that you?'

'I doubt it,' said Dowd stiffly.

And then, because it had been sitting there since she walked out of the Bird this morning with the words ringing in her ears, before she could stop herself, or think of the effect the information would have on him, she told him. What Janine had said.

'I don't know if you know,' Nat said and Dowd turned his face to her, pale and tense. 'Who Jim is? My ex.' He shook his head, waiting. 'We broke up months ago.' She swallowed, knowing the date exactly, the day, the hour, the light spring evening and the hollow feeling inside her. 'April.'

Janine, standing behind the bar with both hands flat, palm down on it, watching her come through the door. No sign of Steve.

'There's something you've got to know,' the landlady had said, sounding like she knew it was wrong but she was going to say it anyway. Angry, defiant.

Nat had stopped, right there in the middle of the public bar under the low ceilings, gunfight at the OK corral. Said nothing. And when Janine said, 'Perhaps it's for the best. We all need to move on,' Nat had just turned and walked out.

'Jim and Beth had a . . . well. A . . .' Dowd was staring at her but it wasn't his face she saw, or Beth's, it was Craig's with that ghost of Beth in it. 'I don't know what they'd have called it,' she said. 'A fling, a one-night stand.'

Dowd had patches of colour in his cheeks.

'But you get the gist.' She felt abruptly sorry for him.

Janine was waiting for Steve to come back. Hoping. Had

getting rid of Nat been part of that? Because she was stirring things up about Beth. Because there were things Janine didn't want her to know.

'Come *on*,' Janine had said. 'You dumped him. Want it both ways, do you? Wasn't he allowed to move on?'

'Move on to Beth?' Nat had been contemptuous. 'That wasn't going to happen.' She felt something dangerous stir, something she didn't want. Anger.

'Well, to have some fun, then,' Janine said, smoothing bar towels, not looking her in the eye. 'Maybe he was feeling bad, maybe she looked after him.' Smoothing her own comfortable aproned front with manicured nails, Janine who knew how to look after her man. Janine who had told the police Jim had slept with Beth to take the heat off her and Steve.

Poor Jim, was all she thought now. Poor Jim.

Dowd was looking at her, in the pickup in the lay-by, the smell of fish and grease in her nostrils and she wanted to be sick. Poor Jim, poor Beth.

Blindly, she looked back at Dowd, she took in the rawness of his face, his staring eyes.

Janine was protecting Steve. What from? The police had asked about his relationship with Beth, Janine had admitted that. But Nat had never seen Steve touch Beth, nothing but cool air between them, never seen Steve make a false move.

Was that suspicious, of itself? Steve was nowhere now. Steve had gone off the radar.

'I'm worried about you.' The voice broke in on her thoughts, Dowd's voice, hesitant, rusty. 'You need a cup of tea,' he said, randomly. Did she hear panic? Poor old Jonathan, never knew what the right thing to say was, or the right thing to do, she was beginning to get the measure of him. He turned the key in the ignition.

Don't go with him. She heard the voice in her head, she knew the danger. But she had to know.

'I'm taking you to my place.' He looked at her, waiting for her to shake her head.

'All right,' she said.

His camp was as neat as when she'd last seen it, the tent zipped, the sample fridge padlocked. 'Did you ever bring Beth here?' she asked and she saw something in his face she hadn't seen before, the delicate bloom of something soft.

He blinked. 'Once or twice,' he said, and Nat could hardly hear him. 'She liked it.' He ducked to unzip the tent and reached inside.

Nat looked, through Beth's eyes. They were in young woodland five hundred yards from where the sloping bank dissolved into samphire and mud and water. It was very green, the canopy only thirty feet or so, and the dull light fell, slanting through the foliage in patches. There was a clump of silver birches where he'd set a folding chair and from there you could look out to the water. Brown now, under the low sky, and a bit of wind whipping up wavelets, dashes of white. There hadn't been wind in weeks, it seemed, and for a second Nat almost felt the *Chickadee* under her, picking up speed, hissing across the water. Without knowing she was doing it she turned to look upriver, past the trees, to the low clump of boatyard and houses.

Dowd came out from behind the tent with two mugs:

he held one out to her awkwardly. It had the logo of a pharmaceutical company on it.

'When would this have been?' he said quietly. 'Beth and your . . .'

She blinked at him over the tea: it smelled unfamiliar. Some herbal stuff; gingerly she sipped. 'You mean – when did Beth sleep with Jim?'

They were both in the same boat now, of course, her and Dowd. Misfits, losers, the ones that get cheated on, the ones on the outside.

She shrugged. 'Janine wasn't specific,' she said drily. 'Although she did say it was after Jim and I split up. Not long after.'

It was Beth all over, a bit reckless, a bit impulsive, conveniently forgetting that to some people, sex was a dangerous business.

Getting pregnant was, too. She hoped, hoped, hoped, that Beth had decided she wanted a baby after sleeping with Jim, not before.

Dowd held his tea in both hands, feet slightly apart, head low. There was something about his stance, the way he was swaying, as if he was trying to stay calm.

'Might he . . . might he . . .' Dowd couldn't quite get the words out.

'Might he have hurt her?' She made him look at her, staying calm. She couldn't make it ring true. Jim was so patient, Jim was so kind. 'I . . . not the Jim I knew,' she said. 'No.'

'If she laughed at him?'

Nat looked at him, uncomprehending. 'She wouldn't.' Slowly, she tried to think. 'Not unless someone was cruel to her. Then she'd get in there. Get in first.'

She'd seen that. Beth kicking a chair from under a punter needling some girl. You couldn't touch her. *We're all free*, Beth's mantra. Free. And something occurred to her.

'Did she laugh at *you*?' she said, but slowly Dowd shook his head.

Dowd wasn't free: look at him. A man in a prison. So as not to look she sipped the tea: it tasted weird.

She thought of something else. 'There's a club,' she said warily. 'In town.' Even as she named it she thought, uh-oh. No way. Clubs and Jonathan Dowd didn't go together. But it was too late and so she blundered on, retelling the story Bill had told her.

'Sorry, who is this guy?' said Dowd sharply.

'A cameraman from the TV set I met. He came into the pub . . . he . . . just a guy. I hardly know him.' But Jonathan Dowd was looking at her as if he knew exactly how well she knew him. And again she had that fleeting sense that she and Beth had got confused: Nat wasn't the one who slept with guys she hardly knew. Was this how men looked at Beth? It felt dangerous.

She went on, bravely. 'I don't know if he was telling the truth. He didn't know who the man was, that she was with. The club – it was that one beyond the station.' He was still looking at her: he hadn't touched his mug of tea. She set hers down carefully. 'Pink neon sign.'

There was a long quiet moment during which she heard something, far off, a soft crack and rumble from somewhere inland, beyond the stand of trees. She turned to look out to the estuary, where it widened to the sea. The water was dark at the horizon, a line of steel.

'It was me,' said Dowd, and his voice was low. 'She

dragged me there. I don't know why, she said something about wanting to broaden my horizons.'

Was that nasty? thought Nat, unable to stop herself, maybe it was, maybe thoughtless was cruel, maybe . . . Then that thought was interrupted by a sudden realisation: this could have been worse. What if it hadn't been Dowd there? If she'd rubbed his nose in Beth's social life, that didn't include him, all over again. And he'd confirmed Bill's story: that mattered to her, she realised.

'I don't drink,' he said. 'Don't do drugs. I don't dance. I . . . can't.'

She sighed. 'Beth, well, maybe she really thought you'd like it.'

'Like me watching her with other men?'

He was staring down at his big hands. 'Don't . . .' she said, but she didn't know what she was asking. Don't get angry. Don't lose it. There was something about Jonathan Dowd – and maybe it was what had made Beth take him to some dodgy club she knew he'd hate – that was wound up too tight and small; you had to wonder. 'Don't torture yourself,' she said, and put out her hand to his arm. He flinched.

'I've got to go,' she said gently.

His head tipped up, his pale eyes suddenly very large, long-lashed. 'Let me give you a lift,' he said.

Nat nodded: what choice did she have, after all? She could hardly call the taxi firm, get them to bump off the road into the woods. She looked around, it seemed important to look hard before she went. The tent, perfectly pegged, each guy rope straight and symmetrical. A rack of tools, a stack of metal boxes. A spade, leaning against a fold-out table.

'Were you her knight in shining armour?' she asked again. 'Would you have done anything for her?'

She realised that what she wanted more than anything else was for it not to be Jim, but where did that leave her? Alone with Jonathan Dowd in the woods, because she hadn't listened to that voice. Earth on the spade.

He was pale. 'I was the one came to ask about her,' he said, standing quite still with those luminous eyes on her. 'I was the one that was worried about her.' He had his car keys in his hand, and he looked down at them.

'Have you talked to the police, though?' she said and his head jerked up.

'So they're interested now?'

Nat hesitated. She could tell him, about the digging in her garden, about the white dress hanging in the tree, part of her wanted to see his face when she described that dress and how it looked on Beth. When she let him know how frightened she had been. And part of her was afraid.

Jim said he saw a car, waiting in the lane. Wouldn't he have said it was a pickup, if that's what it had been, if it had been Dowd's? And maybe she couldn't believe anything Jim said any more. 'I need to go,' she said.

And Dowd was putting out a hand to her elbow, pulling at her. She felt alarm spark as she heard the rumble again, closer now, when she looked up the sky was still pale but thickening.

He felt her resist him and stopped. 'I could take you,' he said, 'Wherever.' His eyes big in his gaunt face.

She looked from him to the pickup: all she knew was, she didn't want to be here.

'All right,' she said slowly.

Pulling open the passenger door she climbed in, unwilling, what choice, what choice did she have? To shake her head, tell him she'd walk? Feeling herself scan the small space. Looking for a strand of hair, a clump of earth. She couldn't see anything.

As they turned on to the road briefly, far ahead she heard the high whine of a motorbike, she saw a low crouched outline hit the bend fast and disappear.

'I want to go to the boatyard,' she said, her heart in her mouth for knowing she was running out of options. Knowing she was so close to feeling the way Beth must have felt, when it happened. 'Please.'

He stared at her.

'I want to see Jim.'

There was a boy sitting in the corridor outside Victor's ward, with a motorcycle helmet in his lap. He looked like a boy when Victor saw him sitting there, as he said goodbye to Sophie on the open landing.

It was the first time Victor had been beyond the doors of the ward, and it smelled different, cars and fresh air coming up from below. The outside world was tantalisingly within reach. 'Please,' Victor said gently, patting her hand, but as he spoke to her he was aware of the boy in the corner of his eye, sitting there as he spoke to her. His young head was bent over the helmet and a shaggy lock of dark hair was obscuring his face. He didn't seem aware they were there.

'You should get back to Rufus.'

Sophie was searching his face. 'Rufus is fine with Patrick,' she said, anxious.

'Yes, but . . .' But when Richard comes for him. He didn't want to say it, to alarm her, he wanted Sophie feeling certain, not dissolved into nerves and panic.

The boy stood up and suddenly he was a man. As boys do, they grow – Rufus would grow, too, he would turn into a man. Did boys turn into their fathers?

Someone came through the ward's doors behind them and the boy slipped past them, the helmet dangling from his arm, and inside.

Sophie was on her way down the stairs: leaning on the rail he could track her progress, the small fair head, strands of grey in it, her small hand on the banister. Victor turned slowly and made for the door where he pressed the buzzer for admission, a crackle and he was inside, because they could see who he was through the long strip of reinforced glass. He had a joke on the tip of his tongue, something about the great escape, was wondering, almost melancholy, if Lisa was even old enough to know the film or indeed anything about the war it referred to, but in any case as he approached the desk, she was busy.

The boy was in front of her and she was telling him – with just a hint of sternness – that he would have to come back. 'Two till five, seven till eight, only relatives in between.' She did lift her head, though, as Victor came into view, a half-smile hovering, a half-smile but something else, not quite impatience, but perplexity – and the boy turned his head to see where she was looking.

I know him, thought Victor, I know him, and the understanding, that old feeling of knowing a face but not being sure where he knew it from set up a palpitation inside him that radiated to his hand trembling on the walking frame and down to his legs, the old skinny shanks he needed now more than ever to support his weight. Think, think, think.

There was a warning in the boy's eyes. A warning from a ghost. Ollie?

Think.

Not Ollie, and as he remembered Victor had to concentrate to stop the trembling that passed through him, so that Lisa of all people should not see it and keep him there. Not Ollie because Ollie was dead.

And then with a rush of relief he knew the boy, of course he did. The one who worked in the pub. What was his name? His name was Craig. Shy young Craig, half glimpsed through the door to the pub's kitchen. He had changed, grown taller, thinner even since Victor last saw him. Did boys still grow, at eighteen, nineteen, twenty? This one had aged, grown gaunt and hard.

'Cr—?' But as he began to form the name the boy moved his head, a quick sharp shake that not only stopped Victor saying anything but almost physically shifted him, set him rocking a tiny bit back on the walking frame and steadying himself. Come to tell me something. Come to warn me. Moving on and away back to his private room and leaving them behind him. He didn't turn around until he got to the door and when he did he saw that Lisa had come around the desk and was standing there physically blocking the boy's path. Shaking her head.

A metallic ringing was coming from somewhere. As he pushed the door inwards Victor realised that it was coming from inside his room, from the contraption suspended over the bed to which he had paid no attention because it alarmed him, with its schedule of prices for streaming films or watching satellite television. How many shuffled steps to get there? Three, four, five, *there*. Victor slid sideways on to the bed and reached for the receiver that hung alongside the screen.

The voice: familiar but not familiar, again it set his heart pounding. And talking without giving his name nor waiting for him to recognise . . .

'Owen,' he said, faintly. Wilkins.

There was a pause. 'Right, sorry,' said the campsite manager stiffly.

'I didn't quite catch that,' said Victor. He felt slightly faint. Breathe. 'Would you mind . . .'

'Your daughter's husband is here.' Wilkins' voice was full of dislike. 'Reading the riot act, asking where she is, where she's taken his son.'

'His son.' The boy Richard never wanted in the first place if Victor's interpretation of Sophie's painful skirting of the topic had been correct. Rufus, for whom she had had to fight.

'I told him,' Owen enunciated carefully, 'that I didn't divulge information on my residents' whereabouts.' Inside Victor something recalibrated, reset. His heart slowed, grateful.

'She's on her way back,' Victor said. 'Richard . . . well. He doesn't necessarily need to know that. Please – you haven't told him where Rufus—'

'None of my business,' said Owen. 'I don't know where the boy is.'

Victor looked around at his things, stacked ready, a plastic carrier brought by Sophie for them. Toothbrush.

'Owen,' he said, 'distract him, will you? Until I get there.'

How though? How on earth? 'Keep him there, stop him. Don't . . . don't—'

'It's all right, Mr Powell,' said Wilkins gruffly and Victor thought of the shelf in the man's portakabin with books on birdwatching, his irritable, awkward manner, his exile, with Victor, to a caravan site on the grey edge of the country.

'Don't let him take her,' he said.

'Leave it with me, Victor,' said Wilkins. And he was gone.

And Victor sat, the receiver still in his trembling hand, on the edge of the bed in the windowless room. Now is the time. Now.

Stroke of luck, that.

Stroke of luck, and no need to find an excuse, no need to wheedle her, no need to work around to it, direct access. Of course, what's the phrase, there is one, fortune favours the brave. You make your own luck. Not luck but skill, right place at the right time. That and the nerve to just walk straight in and take what you want.

So few of them even know what they want. Out there, walking the pavements, choosing what to put on, calling to their children, cruising the supermarket aisles. They're just going through the motions, might as well be dead as alive and barely worth the living.

A tiny thing snagged at him then, a tiny sense. Her though. Her. She had been alive. The boy? Too young to tell with him. Her. With her clothes he'd looked through, the smell of her on them, her place full of her, hairs in her hairbrush, make-up bag, she got in everywhere, under his skin. Was she gone, even now? She was gone, all right, and he knew where. He had her where he wanted her.

The old man, on his last legs, but refusing to die. It was going to be so easy, to kill him now.

He leaned back, closed his eyes, roaming. Her. That I can do again. Another one like that and she was on his radar, alive and pulsing, better than that. He could reach out his hand and take her.

Natalie.

He knew where she would go. Out on the water, where she thought she was safe. Sooner or later, that was where she would go.

Chapter Thirty

It was getting late: four, five o'clock. The tide was coming up under low cloud as the pickup came out of the trees and turned down along the road that ran parallel to the estuary. It was going to be a very high one: the grey-brown water lapped on the mudbanks, the channels were already disappearing. The heat lay on everything like a blanket, and the land was very still, birds had gone quiet in the hedges as they passed as if they knew a storm was coming.

Dowd drove in silence. Nat held herself very still, as if any quick movement, any word, would spark something in the small space they shared.

Nat's phone rang and Dowd's head turned at the sound. She answered it in a hurry, feeling her body stiff with tension.

'Steve?' The last person she had been expecting, probably. She bent her head over the receiver, not wanting him to hear, and then Dowd was looking back at the road, she could see his jaw set and working. Steve's voice came to her as though from far away: it seemed suddenly a long time since she had heard it. Out of the corner of her eye she saw Dowd's knuckles on the wheel.

Laidback Steve: she realised she had expected him to be gone, over the horizon and away from all this shit. Police, Janine, Beth – the lot. He was still slow, measured, but there was something else in his voice. Concern, or unease.

'She's told me,' he said, clearing his throat, 'what she said to you. About Beth and Jim.'

'Janine.'

'Listen,' he said, and there it was, the strain, 'don't be too hard on the girl.'

Janine: his girl. That softened Nat, just a bit. Was he relying on that?

'It's the whatsit,' said Steve heavily. 'Menopause. She can't really hack it and having coppers tell her I fancied Beth sent her off on one.'

'Did you?' asked Nat. 'Fancy her?' Dowd was watching her. He was listening.

Steve sighed. She wondered where he was. He'd spoken to Janine, but that didn't mean he was back. For some reason she saw him leaning against his rig in a lay-by. She thought of some case there'd been in the news: a truck driver who picked women up and murdered them, or had that been kids? No, that had been another one: a delivery bloke in a white van, abducting ten-year-old girls.

'It was a bit more complicated than that,' he said.

'Complicated?' said Nat, and the word hardly got out, her throat was constricted, she saw Dowd flick a sideways glance at her.

'She were mine,' he said, and his voice fell away.

'Yours? Was?' *Past tense, past tense, past tense, she were mine.* 'Do you know what's happened to her, Steve?' Without realising it she was bent forward, almost in a foetal crouch, and she detected Dowd slowing the car, what was he doing? She caught a look from him, a frown, and made an effort to straighten up.

'What do you mean, she's yours?' she said, levelling her voice.

Steve's voice was patient, careful, but still the words didn't make sense. 'She didn't know . . . Well, I didn't know myself till, what, six, nine month ago when her mother told me, just like that,' he said. 'It were Facebook, my picture must've come up somewhere and she wanted money off me, after all this time. She was mine. Beth was. Beth. I was sixteen or summat. I came to look for her, and I fell for Janine.'

'She . . . you're her father? Her father?' What had Beth's mother said? Something about her dad. No: she'd just laughed. As if Beth's dad was nothing, of no use, no interest.

'I was sixteen,' he said, sounding as if he was in pain. 'I give her money. I give her a grand and asked where I could find her. How were I to know?'

'Your daughter,' said Nat, wonderingly. 'She was yours. Did Janine know?' Something had changed. Looking up she realised Dowd had stopped the car. They were under some trees. Steve was still talking, his voice low.

'I told the coppers,' he said. 'I never told her, but I told them, can you believe it? I hardly knew her, did I?' Beside her Dowd was sitting quite still in the driver's seat, staring ahead. 'I just wanted . . .' and she heard his voice break. Tough Steve, kind Steve, Nat leaned in his favour, she couldn't help herself, big silent Steve. 'I didn't want to bother her. I just wanted to keep an eye.'

Beth never knew he was her dad. For a second protest rose inside her: this was all wrong. Beth never knowing she had a dad, a decent bloke looking out for her?

So wrong that for that moment, it was like a tidal wave, washing everything she knew away. Couldn't Beth just be alive, please, please, please? Lost somewhere for a month, with the love of her life, just walk back in with your wide smile and your pvc backpack and meet your dad, Beth?

And then it all crashed back down.

'Didn't do much of a job, did I?' he said quietly.

She thought of how Steve had been around Beth, keeping all this quiet. And very successfully: none of them had guessed. Not her, not Craig, not Jim, not Ollie who had watched her like a hawk.

'Does Janine know?' Because he hadn't answered that question.

'She does now,' said Steve and his voice was low.

'What about her brother?' she said, glancing at Dowd. He was pale and she felt a sudden access of pity. 'Is he yours too?'

'I was long gone by the time he came along,' says Steve, his voice flat now, drained. 'She told me she had him, when she told me about Beth, saying she was strapped for cash, weren't cheap having a disabled kid, she said.'

'She doesn't pay anything for him,' said Nat. 'Didn't even visit him. Beth did that.'

She heard him sigh.

'Where are you now?' she asked. 'You're not in Ipswich, are you?'

'I'm on my way back,' said Steve. Then, 'Don't worry.

You be careful.' Dowd was frowning, hands on the wheel. She said goodbye to Steve and put the phone carefully in her lap and turned to Dowd.

'That was—' but Dowd shook his head, not looking at her.

'I don't want to know,' he said and his voice was low and level, correcting himself. 'I don't *need* to know.' He leaned to turn the key in the ignition again, his profile gave nothing away. He seemed to have become calmer, as if something had been taken out of his hands.

He didn't open his mouth again until they pulled in at the boatyard, the pickup crunching on the wet gravel where the tide lapped: it would be coming up another hour and it was already high. The *Chickadee* had been pulled right up on the hard and she was lying carelessly, tilted. There was something unusual about her, she looked unkempt. An oar lay across the thwart, the sail unstowed. Perhaps Paddy had taken Sophie and Rufus out in her and just got back. There was no sign of them, though: no sign of anyone. The big flaking double doors to the boat shed were closed.

'I've got to get back,' he said, gesturing towards her door without looking at her. 'I've got to get on with the sampling. The tide.'

She could tell that he would have liked just to lean across her and open the door. To get rid of her. The thought, of his body moving across hers, getting inside her space, had a curious effect. It frightened her. Nat went for the handle but it was stiff. She hefted the door open with her shoulder and all of a sudden she was out, standing on the wet stones and her bag swinging against her.

'You don't have to wait,' she said stiffly.

He didn't answer but in a smooth movement he leaned across for the door and tugged it to behind her.

Nat stood there, surprised by how much the sound of the door closing shocked her. The sound of him shutting her out. He was inside, a dark shape unmoving, and she turned away. There was the hard, the boatshed with its concrete dry dock, Paddy's shack on stilts across the way. A spade leaning against the wall, a bucket, a small faded lifejacket. This place at the end of the road, nowhere beyond it and the water still creeping up.

Behind her Dowd still hadn't turned his engine on, but she didn't look round.

The big wooden double doors to the boatbuilding shed were nibbled and slimy with algae at the bottom where the water got them. They were padlocked. Jim should be at work, even if it was a Friday afternoon. The hasty drumbeat of panic set up, it was her fault, Jim was her fault. Jim drinking too much . . . if that was all it was. Jim hanging around the cottage at night.

She heard voices.

They weren't coming from inside the boatshed, but from further off. Round behind the cottage. Carefully she walked away from the lapping water. With the estuary behind her she could see how dark the cloud was inland, and how high it went, a tower block of storm cloud. The weather always seemed to come from there, blown across from Wales, from Ireland. From the big Atlantic, morphing as it moved, depressions coiling up ready for the thin grey strip of the North Sea.

The wind was moderate still, though: she calculated that it would be a while coming.

Now Nat recognised the voice as Paddy's. She slowed, coming around the side of Paddy's shed, not wanting to startle anyone, and there he was at the shed's little worn down steps with his head down and attentive to Rufus, whose hand he was holding. Paddy must have heard her because he looked up, and his expression turned sheepish. Then she saw that both he and Rufus had bare feet, and mud slicked up to their knees. Rufus gazed at Paddy with adoration.

Paddy stopped, tilted his head, enquiring.

Rufus distracted her. There was something in him that made her eyes burn, made her want to crouch and take his hand so that his head would turn to her. His smallness, his hand in Paddy's. She cleared her throat. 'I'm looking for Jim,' she said. Rufus was swinging the hand he held, tugging.

Paddy sighed. From the other side of the shed she heard the sound of Dowd's engine turning on, the slow crunch of his tyres on the gravel, the noise receding.

'Jim was here an hour ago,' Paddy said, clearing his throat, and the frown deepened. 'I'm not sure he was . . . himself, if you know what I mean.'

'Had he been drinking?'

Paddy shrugged, uneasy. 'Maybe.' He nodded towards the sound of Dowd's engine. 'That the bloke camping upriver? You seeing him?'

'No! He's just . . . he was just giving me a lift. Jim doesn't think . . .' She stopped.

'I dunno what Jim thinks.' Paddy hesitated. 'I just saw him walking down the lane and he was weaving all over the place, side to side. Pale, like he's not well. He's been like it a while though, hasn't he?' Nat felt her mouth turn down, stubborn.

‘At least he didn’t drive,’ said Paddy. Rufus had gone quiet, as if he heard something in their lowered voices that he recognised.

The tinny sound of music came from somewhere: Paddy’s pocket. He fished out a mobile. Nat hadn’t even known he had one. His face screwed up in concentration as he answered: she heard a breathless stream of words on the other end.

‘No,’ he said, interrupting the stream, ‘no don’t— Please don’t, S-Sophie. Please don’t worry.’ At her name Rufus’s head jerked up to listen. ‘He’s safe, Sophie, no— I won’t let— No.’

He turned a little bit, still talking softly into the receiver, calming her, and there was something in the way he stood, or talked, that was different. He seemed taller, the quiet nervous movements had gone and instead there was an energy she didn’t think of as Paddy’s. He hung up and turned back.

‘That was Sophie,’ he said. It was, it seemed to Nat, just that he wanted to say her name again. ‘She’s just left her dad, she’s on her way to Sunny Slopes.’ He released Rufus’s hand and said, ‘Get yourself a drink, Rufus, your mum said, didn’t she? Make sure you drink plenty?’ After a second’s pause Rufus nodded and dashed for the shed door. They heard the tap splash on inside, she could picture him stretching for it.

‘His dad’s turned up,’ said Paddy quickly. ‘He’s come to get the kid.’ He stepped to one side to look past her out to the water: scanning the horizon there was something fierce and bright about his expression. ‘I’ll keep him with me,’ he said, talking to himself. ‘We’ll go and get something to eat.’ The tap turned off inside and Rufus was coming out of the shed with a full pint glass held out in front of him with both hands. They both turned to look at him and in that moment a sound came, distinct and clear, from inside the boatshed behind them.

'What the—' he said but then Rufus let out a little sound as the glass tipped and trembled in his hands and Paddy was down on his knees taking it from him.

'It's . . . I think Jim's in there,' said Nat and Paddy just looked up at her from where he knelt, one hand shading his eyes from the sky's white cloud-glare.

'You want me to stay?' he said, looking defeated. 'You want me to come in with you?' She looked from him to Rufus and slowly she shook her head. She had a feeling. A bad feeling: she wanted them gone, out of this.

Paddy stood back up. 'Come on then, sailor,' he said to Rufus, taking the half-drunk glass, holding out a hand. 'Let's get your shoes on.'

She took a step: the distance between her and the big double doors seemed to extend. She willed Paddy and Rufus to go before she reached them and when she did get there and turned they were fifty yards away, up the lane. Up close she saw the doors weren't padlocked at all, the chain was hanging loose. Gingerly she pushed.

It was dark inside, the long space filled with the hull of an old oyster smack that loomed over her on its props and trestles, the smooth-bellied sides half sanded, gleaming with a dull sheen in the near-dark. There was light coming in from some chink in the shed's neglected weatherboards: if you looked you could see cracks everywhere in the old wood. She couldn't hear anything: she couldn't see Jim. She stopped, put up a hand to the curve of the boat, and listened.

The wood felt warm to the touch. Jim had been recaulking the thing for months now, he'd taken the job off Paddy, insisting on doing it himself, and it was taking longer than it should. A lot longer. She'd heard the owner – a Londoner – in the pub complaining, and she had tried not to listen. In the water these boats looked feather-light, effortless and natural, but in here she was only aware of the weight beside her, over her. Of what would happen if one of these chocks on which it rested was knocked out and the tonnes of wood and brass were to tilt and fall – she could almost hear the crash.

'Jim?' she said, and then there was a sound, of someone trying to stay silent, a gasp of something held in. She took a step. 'Jim,' she said again, pleading, soft, and the gasp became a gulp, a sob, an awful hoarse noise.

Hands against the boat's hull she felt her way around it, following the sound. For a moment she couldn't see him, he was crouched so small, a darker patch of dark, but then she saw his dirty white canvas shoes, pale against the littered dark concrete of the floor and the toes turned in, the feet of a kid waiting to be told off. Waiting to be found out. Nat came closer, kneeling, she came right up against him and she almost closed her eyes at his familiar smell, his sweat like no one else's, and the daily cocktail of diesel and paint and linseed the job left on him. She put her arm around him, helpless to do anything else, she put her cheek against his.

'Jim,' she said, hopeless, and then this close there was a different smell, a different bitter chemical sourness. He felt strange under her arm, too: he swayed and she said it a last time, this time sharply, 'Jim!' She shook him. 'What have you done? What have you done?' His head lifted, his shaggy head, the hair falling back and she could see the planes of his face, his mouth slack, his eyes not looking.

'You've taken something.' She could hear the anger, the bitterness, the frustration in her voice, all of it pouring out now, when she needed to be kind. 'Tell me what it is. Tell me.'

He whimpered, his head came down as he tried to hide from her, to escape her. 'I know you slept with Beth,' she said, but it came out odd, wondering, as if she didn't know what the words might mean.

He was crouched inside her arms, and then he spoke. He mumbled. 'I didn't,' he said, 'She didn't—' And his head fell into his hands. 'You wouldn't talk to me,' he said and it was almost a moan. 'She let Janine think we had,' he was hoarse, 'but all we did was . . . she just let me stay. All she did was lie next to me, put her arms round me a bit. She wouldn't have . . . she was your friend. She said it was none of Janine's business, let her think what she wanted.' His head lifting up and his voice rising, but all Nat could hear was the past tense. 'I only wanted you back.'

'I'm not coming back, Jim. I can't come back.' She wished it was different. She wished . . . she wished she could go back, and change it all. From when? From the day Beth dropped her shiny backpack at Nat's feet in the doorway of the Bird? From the day Nat walked into the dusty anonymous clinic on the other side of the town and signed her name, turning her face away when the woman leaned in to the screen to see was it there, was it alive, inside her, was it true, was the baby real? It had been real.

It seemed to her that Jim was telling the truth: she could

hear Beth saying it, contempt for Janine, *none of her business*. If she had wanted a baby, it wouldn't have been Jim's.

My friend. She *was* my friend.

Jim had gone still now, tensed and waiting. He was stronger than her, even like this, even thin, even sick. She could feel the sinews on him but she wrapped her arms round him. 'I know it wasn't you, Jim. I know you didn't hurt her.' His head drifted side to side, she could tell he was trying to focus on her. There was something he was trying to understand. 'But someone did. Someone dug in the garden. Someone hung her dress in the tree.' Whispering, to herself, 'I need help here, Jim. If you know anything—'

She wasn't even sure if he heard her. He swayed against her arms.

'What have you taken?' she asked again, gentler this time.

Consequences. She didn't even want to think about Bill. She'd done nothing wrong. Sort Jim out first, that was the thing. Bill could wait.

'And Ollie. That poor kid. He saw something, he knew something about who Beth was seeing.' Persisting. Jim just stared, big eyes in the dark, like a kid. 'Did she say anything to you, about who else was on the scene?'

'Why would she have?' He shook his head, she could see his bewilderment at what she was saying. 'She was private, wasn't she? Beth was. I didn't even know about that guy, that guy that's been hanging round, him with the pickup—'

She heard his voice rise, wavering, she shushed him. 'Nor did any of us, it's OK, Jim. Forget it.'

That panicked drumbeat started up again, and she knew somewhere there was truth in it. Maybe the world shouldn't be like this but this is where it got you. This was dangerous shit. No such thing as no strings, no such thing as safe sex, these are consequences. Once you get inside someone's space, into their head – sometimes you're lucky, and all there is in there is flowers and sunshine. But sometimes it's got claws, sometimes it's a lake of tar; sometimes you don't get out again.

It was a gamble, and Beth liked the gamble. Maybe she thought she had the eye, she could tell who was a big risk.

'Ollie died, didn't he?' mumbled Jim. 'I don't know what he knew. She never told me anything.' Desperate; overwhelmed. Nat sifted her position, she took hold of his hands. They were very cold. 'I miss her, too,' he said. Mumbling.

'Have you taken pills?' she asked again, a last time. 'Have you overdosed?' She was holding on to him, holding his hands tight, but she didn't know what it was she was feeling. Something huge and painful and frightening.

'I'm phoning an ambulance,' she said, and then she was on her feet. She blundered back through the dark space, her shin knocking painfully into a trestle, feeling her way along the big silent hull. She got to the doors and pushed them open. As the flat white glare from outside hit her she was aware that he had made no sound, he hadn't moved to come after her.

Shielding her face she got out her mobile phone, and was about to dial 999 when she saw the car, boot open, parked up on the hard.

Just an ordinary silver car and she knew it from somewhere but her brain didn't seem to be working at all. Then in the same moment she saw the white plate advertising the taxi licence, she saw a man leaning to look in through the glass of Paddy's shed.

He's come after her, was Nat's thought. Sophie's husband, Richard. But then the man turned, and she saw it was the taxi driver, the same one who had taken her and Craig to Brandon. Don.

'They've gone,' she said. 'You've come for them, haven't you?' She couldn't stop the anger in her voice. 'He sent you. For the kid.'

Don stepped back – alarmed, perhaps, by the sound of her voice.

'They're not here,' she said, just wanting him gone. Something I've got to do.

'I can't leave without him,' he said, his smile steady. 'I've come down here. Who's going to pay me?' He turned to look at the car, boot open.

'You want money?' Nat felt in her bag, scrabbling for her purse in stupid pointless rage. She felt like she could kill someone herself in that second. A tenner, twenty. And then she heard the creak of the boatshed's door and saw the taxi driver's head turn to look.

Jim came through the doorway. Nat grabbed him to steady him: he was very pale. She held him upright with one hand.

'Take us to Casualty,' she said. Trying not to sound too desperate. Pulling money out of her pocket, twenty. 'Could you, please? It's an emergency. And you get paid.'

Don looked from her to the money to his car and shrugged. 'All right, then,' he said, and walked round to shut the boot.

For a panicked moment, seeing the boot open and wondering why, what was he expecting here, she thought,

Richard's in the back seat all along, they were going to abduct the boy.

He stood at the driver's door, frowning.

'Please,' said Nat. Jim mumbled into her neck: skinny or not he was a deadweight against her, and his breath was sour. Don sighed, and bent to open the rear door. Coming over, he took hold of Jim's upper arms in both hands and she transferred the weight. Jim's head went up and he looked around, dazed, then leaned sideways against the car, his mouth opening and closing.

'He's taking us to hospital,' sad Nat. He looked clammy and white.

'Not you,' Jim said, with an effort.

'What?' She held him away from her, his head flipped up and he looked into her face. 'I don't want you to come with me,' he said distinctly. 'I can . . . can do it on my own. 'S enough. You've done enough.'

'Don't be—' she began exasperated, but he pulled away from her, lurching against Don.

'I don't want your pity,' said Jim. Then, his shoulders dropping, swaying. 'Let.' A heavy breath. 'Me go.'

Don looked at her across his drooping head, shrugged. 'You heard him,' he said. 'Come on then, son,' he said and surprisingly easily – or he was strong – Jim went to him, allowed himself to be deposited on the seat. The door slammed and the driver looked down at the money in Nat's hand. He smiled and as if from a distance Nat saw how that changed things, all you had to do was give out that open smile and she was smiling back, she was thinking, *fine.* Why had she never learned to do that? *Cheer up darling, it might never happen.*

'Just get him there quick,' she said.

'Before he throws up?' He'd have seen all this before. Blokes pissed and crying over women, swallowing pills by the handful and the girl always caves, gets in, *All right, but this is it. This is the last time.*

Don looked at her a moment, and for a second she thought he was actually amused. Then he shrugged, pocketing the cash and tugging on the driver's door. Climbing inside and the matt silver car was moving away, a careful three-point turn on the wet stones, and it was in the lane. As it hit the bend there was a quick flash of the hazards – cheeky, cheerful.

Almost immediately, as the anger receded, her mistake overwhelmed her. Shit, shit, shit: she should have just shoved her way into the car after him. What was she doing here alone by the water, twiddling her bloody thumbs? And it wasn't just Jim. There was Sophie, Richard – and Victor about to be discharged.

Dowd, too. The only one of Beth's men to have come out of the woodwork. Think. Think.

She got out her phone: three missed calls, from Craig, no signal in the boatshed. Impatiently she scrolled back, looking for the taxi firm's number, dialled and got put on to a tinny music track. Hung up and called Craig, it went to answerphone, then hanging up again she saw he'd left a message on hers.

She stamped across the wet gravel, listening, *press one to listen to your messages*. But when the message finally came it was indistinct, she could hear traffic noise, and at one point the signal must have cut. *I saw him on her Instagram feed, Ollie must have . . . I know*— Then nothing.

Saw who? Shit, shit. Nat had always known Beth was on Instagram, hadn't she? Posting pictures of trees and birds and food – and people, she supposed. Nat hadn't ever bothered with it, she worked with Beth, after all. She brought up the page on her phone.

Sign up to see photos and videos from your friends. Her battery was low. Had Craig really seen something?

Where was Craig? She needed to get to the caravan site. Paddy wasn't going to be any use, between Sophie and Richard, was he? How long would it take her to get up to the caravan site on foot?

There was the dinghy, the *Chickadee* in front of her, her gear loose on the duckboards. The tide was lapping close to her tilted hull and without stopping to think Nat was leaning down and setting her shoulder against her stern – just to see.

Over the boat's wooden flank she saw something that didn't make sense, sitting in a puddle. A suitcase – Sophie's suitcase? – already beginning to stain up one side. Was she moving in with Paddy?

Who had left that there? Dowd?

She kept shoving the *Chickadee*, thinking, thinking. Just to have it confirmed that there was too far to push her and the weather was turning anyway and . . . but the hull shifted, her bow was already in the water and before she knew it Nat was knee-deep in the tide too. And then with a quick movement she didn't even need to think about she had one dripping leg over the side and was hauling the sail up.

Centreboard down, sheet in, she scrambled back to the tiller and felt the boat quicken. The wind had picked up, it surprised her: she could get to Sunny Slopes this way. Upriver. How long: half an hour? The wind was stronger than she'd thought, offshore and picking up all the time. The exhilaration was mixed with something else as the land slipped past. Calculation: how strong was too strong? And she'd lost track of the tide, it must, she realised, be about to turn.

Something else was wrong, too, but she couldn't put a name to it. She turned to look back and was startled to see how far away the boatsheds were. The suitcase: a big suitcase. A dark rectangle standing there, waiting. Had it been there when she was talking with Paddy? When they came out again and saw Dowd, leaving?

She looked back out to sea, trying to put things in their right place. The horizon was blurred and to either side of her she saw the unnatural height of the tide, the mudbanks submerged, just a roughening of the grey water here and there where the sea lavender still broke surface. The caravan site just visible. The *Chickadee* was moving so fast it must have turned.

There was something else changed, too, a small creeping feeling, a low feeling though whether in the pit of her own stomach or beneath her feet in the boat's hull, the wind and tide beneath it, she was no longer able to tell. And then she was at the mouth of the creek and looking across the water to the woods where Dowd's camp was, seeing his little tender at the jetty, this side of the caravan site. The line of heavy cloud inland was coming up fast, it had overtaken her.

She heard a sound, distinct from the wind's rush in her ears. A tiny trickle. And then, somewhere far off, a rumble of thunder.

Was that why the dinghy had been hauled up out of the water? The weather was going to break. She should have asked him.

A suitcase, sitting on the hard by Paddy's shed, stained from the tide.

Staring up at the canopy of trees as he moved beneath them, he felt light as air, euphoric, high on triumph. He had arrived at the perfect moment, the conjunction. She moved towards discovery, he had been there to show her. She only had to look. She was gone, or almost, she would be gone. It was the moment of panic he enjoyed. If he closed his eyes he could visualise it perfectly, he could superimpose the one face over the other. Beth, her head tilted back as he had tightened his grip and watched her eyes widen. He could still feel the soft parts under his thumb, feeling for the artery, the windpipe, feeling lovingly, gently.

And then the tendons go taut as she struggles, her hands flapping, a nail catching him.

The sky was grey overhead, he could feel the wind picking up, he shifted as something snagged, caught, irritated him. That fingernail: he had cleaned beneath it, he had had hours to do that, and other things, inspecting her secret places that were his now. Inside out.

Had she got away from him, out on the water? It had been his impulse, seeing the boat lying there, a flimsy contraption of wood and rope and – because luck was on his side, it always was – the weather breaking, and then knowing that was where she thought she was in control. Natalie. Just like Beth in the bedroom, thinking she knew.

And if he got the timing right he could even be there to watch, he could stand there on shore and she would see him and she would know.

She'll be swallowed up, the water will close over her head, and at the thought something rose inside him, joyful. There was a sound, a disturbance, and he wasn't sure if it came from inside himself. He was listening to Bach: he moved to turn up the sound, in case someone heard.

The buzzing of a high-pitched engine, something like a motorcycle engine, disturbed his perfect shiny peace. It came closer, then receded, taking a different path.

Victor was at the window, standing stiffly upright to show them, to show Lisa that he was capable. He had the oddest feeling, as he presented himself with his carrier bag of neatly folded things at the desk, that she was losing patience with him, that she was no longer on his side. She had called her husband: was it something he had said?

He looked down into the car park, the rows of roofs were dull under the overcast sky. He wasn't worried about rain, he had spent enough months listening to it drum on the caravan roof, wind roaring. It was the rest of it that held him upright, on his mettle. Richard, and Sophie on her way back to him. Rufus: Richard had only to get to him first and Sophie would lose the fight, he could even see her with her small helpless hands held out and pleading.

'Victor.' The voice at his shoulder was Lisa's and when he turned he saw she had a small stack of medications.

'Here you go, then.' Lisa was bright now, normal service resumed, but there was a brittleness about it, as if he'd disappointed her, wanting to leave. She folded her arms across her body and leaned past him to look down at the drop-off area.

'He's on his way. He's had a long day, it was crack of dawn when he brought me in. I expect this will be his last fare of the day.'

Victor took the boxes of tablets and carefully stashed them in the top of his carrier bag. Sophie, Sophie, Sophie, he thought. She'll be waiting for me.

Lisa was still scanning the approach road as he straightened up. 'There have to be some perks,' she said, smiling into his face, and maybe it was the flat white light but he saw the lines now, not so much laughter lines as worry lines, her forehead furrowed, her eyes crinkled and small and anxious.

'Perks?'

'Being married to a cab driver,' Lisa said and then the lines deepened, she leaned sharply towards the glass, he heard her catch her breath. 'There he is,' she said. 'Looks like he picked up a fare on the way down.'

Whoever it was seemed to be having trouble getting the door open but the driver didn't get out to help him. Then it was open and the passenger half fell out on the forecourt, righted himself, turned around and around. A paramedic leaning against a waiting ambulance pushed himself off and took a warning step towards the man – but then Lisa had taken Victor by the arm, drawing him back from the window.

'Best get going,' she said. 'Don't want to keep anyone waiting,' and Victor heard the panic in her voice.

The minicab was still there, though, when the doors slid apart to let Victor out, and he took a breath of outside air.

There was rain, rustling in the air, he felt wet on his cheek. The car sat there, waiting, and for a second the prospect of the freedom he had waited for so patiently, had planned for so carefully, only made him afraid. He turned back to look for Lisa but she had disappeared back behind the wide glass sliding doors. Go on, he told himself.

The driver didn't get out for him, either. Victor only saw the dark shape of a head and shoulders as the man leaned back over the front seat to reach for the door handle and the door swung out.

As he climbed in a motorcycle turned into the hospital car park. Victor heard it before he saw it, the insect buzz of one of those trailbikes, with the high seat, meant for teenaged boys to roar up and down dusty hills on. Crouched in the back seat Victor looked up out of the rear window, aware of how small he had become, how shrunken – the rider turned to watch the cab go, only at the last minute did he meet Victor's eye, then they were obscured by a medical van delivering something. Then there was an ambulance moving to meet it, then there was an altercation that Victor heard as they moved past it. Raised voices, the bike's rider a man – a boy – reaching to pull off the heavy helmet with its menacing visor.

Looking for Victor, a message in his eyes, the same boy, the same message. His head shaking. No. No. No.

'All right?' said the driver, picking up speed, not turning his head. 'We know where we're going, don't we?'

Chapter Thirty-One

There was something wrong. The wind was fierce and steady, blowing hard. Nat was fighting the tiller to hold her course – and now she didn't even know if she'd been heading in the right direction to start with.

Jim. She should have gone, even if she had no idea what he'd taken, or when. Could she trust a taxi driver to explain? Of course she couldn't. Couldn't trust anyone.

And behind her on the hard, what bothered her was the suitcase, sitting there, Sophie and her husband. Had he chucked her out? Did he have a plan? Her head ached under the low sky, with trying to make it make sense.

And there wasn't any escape, either. The *Chickadee* was sluggish, low in the water, she wasn't handling properly. The wind and tide were dragging her, and the tiller just wasn't responding and Nat didn't understand why. Her head felt as sluggish as the boat, overloaded. More of the boat below the water, so the wind had to work harder.

And the wind was offshore, the tide beginning to run.

Nat looked back at the land, searching it, the trees dark from a summer of sun, the bleached fields. He was there somewhere: the man who had taken Beth, who had hung her white dress in a tree. Who had dug her empty grave under Nat's kitchen window. Nat hadn't got him, she was only running away from him. And with that thought she had the weirdest, most horrible sickening feeling that he had come after her, he was in the listing boat, he was under the boards, in the tiller that resisted her. She sat up straighter on the stern thwart, trying to get a better view, and as she saw the clump of trees that concealed Dowd's camp and a pale spot appeared, standing there – in the same moment an answer unfolded itself. Stupid: so obvious.

Had he done it while she was behind the shed, talking to Paddy, kneeling to talk to Rufus?

You'd have to know me, that was the thought that chilled her, that curdled her. You'd have to know what I would do, when things get shitty, that I would climb in the *Chickadee*, just fuck the lot of you, I'm going.

'Shit,' she said savagely, to no one.

And he did, didn't he? She'd let him get to know her.

You'd have to have watched me.

She wasn't going to make Sunny Slopes.

Across under the trees she saw the pale spot emerge, become Dowd, and he was walking out towards the sea wall and the jetty. The wind was blowing steadily offshore now and the sky was lowered, bruised cloud down to the horizon. Then to the right, inland, a flash flooded the sky, lighting up inside the cloud and down to the land. Sheet lightning. On reflex Nat began to count.

One thousand, two thousand. You needed to count to know how far off the storm was: every second two hundred yards, something like that. She got to ten before the thunder came, a long rolling crack, deafeningly loud, unfurling across the trees that were tossing now in the wind, black and silver.

And the suitcase. The suitcase.

Dowd had got to the jetty, his arm raised above his eyes. He was watching. Nat half stood on instinct, showing herself, even if it was the wrong thing to do, even if he wanted to see it was her, even if she would be making herself a target for the storm. Standing told her something, though, the way the *Chickadee* slid under her – clumsy, heavy – would have told her if the sickening tepid slosh of bilge water over her feet hadn't, even if she hadn't already guessed. This wasn't a matter of boards opening a bit in the heat.

The suitcase.

It had been stained at the bottom. Nat felt a thump in her chest as she understood. It wasn't mud, or tide. It wasn't Sophie's suitcase. It wasn't stained with mud, mud wasn't that colour.

And then with a lurch and a gasp Nat was on her knees, soaking, groping for the baler, trying to find the source of the leak. Did she even check that the bung was in? No, of course she didn't, too much of a hurry to run away, from Jim, from the taxi driver with judgement in his eyes and his hand out for her cash. She felt under the slimy water: yes. The bung was out but that wasn't all. She was leaking somewhere else. Not just in one place, either, and there had been no leak the last time she sailed, tight as a drum. The size of her mistake ballooned in Nat's head.

Something popped up from under a thwart, jaunty orange plastic, with a handle. The baler.

Right. *Right.*

Nat grabbed it, sat back on her heels in the bottom of the boat, hauled the mainsheet up over the hand that held the tiller, set the bow towards the shore and with the other hand she began to bail, frantically.

When she looked up, Dowd hadn't moved on the jetty except his arm was down now. He had his hands in his pockets.

She waved the orange baler, frantic. Nothing.

The suitcase must have been under the tarpaulin in the back of the pickup. All that time. Beth.

In her pocket her phone rang and in the same moment she felt the lightning as much as saw it, a fork this time, a mile high. Falling back on her arse in the water with the mainsheet tangled round her hand and the tiller swinging free, the baler between her knees, she began to count again, stupidly, pointlessly. The phone was in her hand.

It was Jim. The crash of the thunder – five seconds this time, getting closer – meant she didn't hear what he said straight away but she had already seen his name on the screen. She realised as she spoke into it that she had thought it would be Jonathan Dowd, phoning to goad her, to tell her what, why. To tell her what was in that suitcase he'd kept under a tarpaulin in his pickup.

'Jim,' she said in despair and sitting there below the gunwale of the boat she'd always trusted and feeling its fragility, feeling the surge of the water pressing against it, trying to pull her down, all she could think of was, if this was it, she'd better talk to Jim. She let the mainsheet run. Sod it. Listen.

'You called me,' he said. His voice was slurred with need and she could feel herself losing it, losing patience with him, desperation climbing as she struggled to be kind. 'Jim,' she said again, pleading. 'Have you got to the hospital? Did he get you there?'

Don't give up. Don't give up.

He sounded weak, his voice strained, wandering. He was saying something about the taxi driver. 'Help me,' she said. 'Get the lifeboats out, someone's scuppered the dinghy. It's too far to swim.' Her hands were cold, the phone slippery and Jim didn't seem to hear her, he didn't seem to be listening because he was talking about a car.

'*Please*, Jim,' she said, and then his voice was suddenly clear, certain.

'The car I saw, outside your house that night,' he said.

Noise behind him, an alarm beeping, hospital noise. 'Get the lifeboat out,' she said, but her voice was too weak.

'There's something I remembered,' Jim said and she could hear how hard he was trying. 'Only not until I climbed out of the taxi at the hospital. That was it, you see, I saw it and I remembered.'

'Saw what?' The water was lapping up her back, under her shirt. Nat didn't dare raise her head to see how little freeboard there was left, but the water told her anyway: a wave sloshed in over the gunwale at her cheek. Too low at the stern. Nat tipped herself on to her knees and began to crawl forwards. 'Saw what, Jim?'

She let the mainsheet fly: all she could hope was that the tide wasn't in full flood yet, that she wasn't already at sea.

'Silver car, just like the one brought me here. With that

thing screwed on below the number plate at the back. Licensed taxi.'

'Do you mind?' said the man, leaning down to turn the music up.

Bach, thought Victor, and looked in the rear-view mirror for the taxi driver's face – but his head was down as he reached for the CD controls and all Victor could see was a shock of dull brown hair, a full head of hair, carefully maintained. Dyed, even?

That told you something. Victor felt his thoughts roll on as they had all his life, meandering, remembering, deciding. A man who takes too much care of his hair is vain, narcissistic they call it these days. That is all we are. Thought and memory, that is all we are. Victor knew the end would come. Was it now?

Between the seats in front of him he saw the man's rolled shirtsleeve, his forearm. Victor saw it coming. He saw it even before he raised his eyes to the rear-view mirror again and met the man's eye.

Thought and memory – and love. There's a quote, biblical. *And the greatest of these is love.*

'It was you,' said Victor, on an outward breath. He felt as though he'd come full circle. Even as the worst emerged he knew he shouldn't have said it, shouldn't say anything at all, but it was too late for that.

The man smiled, looking at him in the rear-view mirror. His name tag sat beside it above the windscreen, where Victor's long sight, the old man's gift, could read it, if it meant anything, by now. If it wasn't too late. Don Jason, licensed taxi driver. Remember that, anyway.

He had to keep staring, into the man's eyes. Don Jason. Lisa Jason's husband, who worked nights, the husband, he had finally understood, of whom she was afraid. And then Victor looked away, through the window, seeking the real world, the outside world – it was important to know where he was. Where the man was taking him. He didn't recognise the empty road, the trees, the dark cloud. There was a crack and rumble somewhere close.

'What was that, Mr Powell?' said the taxi driver pleasantly but in that voice, the voice that sounded in Victor's ears down most of a century, the voice of the teacher who wants you to know how clever he is, how much cleverer than you, the voice of the lieutenant on the beach at Anzio, with his heavy gun in his hand. Don Jason. Remember that.

'We're old friends, Mr Powell, aren't we? Old enemies.'

The sound of the music rose, flooding the space, unbearable. Had it taken this, wondered Victor, to know he hated Bach?

'There's something I'd like you to see,' said Don Jason.

And then the driver looked away, and the taxi swung off the road, the ground turning rough beneath it, jolting Victor against the window.

Chapter Thirty-Two

The mobile fell with a clatter into the bilges as Nat stood, cursing, and waved with her whole body into the misted distance, feeling more water slosh in with every movement. Nat couldn't see Dowd, now, she could hardly see the land. The weather had come down, an ominous silent rain driving sideways. Huge drops. She was drenched.

'He picked up someone else.'

The water was level with the gunwales, with her knees, and creeping over every minute. Nat heard something, the high buzz of a two-stroke engine that came and went, maybe a motorbike far off.

'The taxi. The old guy, your friend. Coming down as I was coming in. Took him.' Jim's voice had been tiny at the end of the line, tiny and distant.

That had done it: Nat felt as though her head would burst with the magnitude of her fuck-up, being in the wrong place at the wrong time, following the wrong guy.

Thinking too much about where she stood in all this. This isn't about you, and who you slept with last night. It's about Beth, it's about Ollie – but most of all it's about stopping him hurting anyone else. And she hadn't stopped him.

'Victor?' she said. 'You mean Victor?' The water up her back, salt in her mouth, on her eyelashes. 'Call the police, Jim. Tell them it's him. Ask for Donna Garfield and tell her it's the taxi driver.'

'I don't even—'

'His name is Don,' she said. And that had been it, her last communication with the world and the phone slipping out of her hands in the same moment that she understood that if her survival depended on Jim, strung out on a busy casualty ward and no doubt losing battery or credit on his phone into the bargain, she was fucked. They all were.

The bow was under. The grey water erased it and as the gunwale disappeared the *Chickadee* listed abruptly sideways and forward, nose down. She no longer knew which way the shore lay, and it was too late to think. She was on her knees in the water then, the boat was gone from under her and she was thrashing, kicking off her shoes, reaching for an oar that floated free, she was swimming.

The high-pitched buzz filled her ears, as though the motorbike had driven out across the tide, unless it was panic, it was terror. Nat twisted in the water, and as she felt herself dragged down, the jeans, the shirt ballooning around her, she saw it. The triangular bow wave, a hundred yards away, closer, of a grey inflatable almost invisible on the flat grey water, bouncing and cresting the water towards her and then, above it for a second a head, hair plastered down but his eyes fixed on her, Jonathan Dowd, his hand on an outboard's tiller.

Fighting the tangled weight that hauled on her under the water, Nat strained to lift a hand, a wave slapped her full in the face, and she was under.

Victor kept his eyes on the man as he left the driver's seat and stood up, stretched.

The car was parked on a track that led down to the water. The wind was blowing in through the door the man had opened and Victor felt it cold, cold. There was a patch of wood beyond them, between them and Sunny Slopes.

Sophie, he thought, Sophie was there but he couldn't see her. He couldn't reach her.

'Of course I couldn't take the risk,' said the taxi driver, leaning in to smile at him. Don Jason. 'In the end. How many times have I had you in the back? No more than three or four. And you might not have got a good look at me, coming back up the lane, not enough to know me, not enough to make the connection. But Lisa coming home, telling me about her new model patient, how well you were doing.' His mouth turning down, contemptuous. 'And then she'd say, "At his age, of course, you can't take mental health for granted." Asking to see the police?' Victor's breath caught at the betrayal: he'd thought Lisa had been on his side.

The driver straightened and disappeared again, looking for something out on the water.

Painfully Victor tried to edge along the seat while he was not being observed: every muscle and joint felt stiff, old. Slow.

'There she is, there she is,' he heard the man say, his voice low and throaty.

Crouched in the rear seat, Victor was aware that he must look like a helpless sort of creature, mesmerised, but it had been a long time since he had worried about his appearance to others, an old tortoise in his shell. He knew all about powerlessness and as the man set his broad, strong hand on the car's roof over his head and looked down at him utterly confident in his physical superiority, Victor felt a tiny spark of something, not hope exactly but knowledge. Don Jason could tell him nothing about survival: he was ninety-two years old.

The lieutenant on the beach at Anzio had died thirty hours after he'd loosed off that shot in hatred, his own head blown off as he stood up in the dunes for no reason anyone had been able to discern except arrogance.

'He saw me going inside the house, you see,' said Don Jason, conversationally, leaning back in again, head tilted, to examine Victor. 'Silly kid, hanging around her place.'

'Oliver?' Victor's voice cracked.

Don Jason smiled.

What had possessed her? thought Victor, looking back, seeing the square face, the hair, strong chin, the prominent Adam's apple. What could this man have said to that girl with her hair tangled round her pretty face, her brown legs, the soft arms she swung as she walked, that had led her to put those arms around him, take him into her little room and let him have her? Sadly Victor acknowledged that he knew very little about women really, having had experience only of his own wife, his innocent Joy. Just that they were often more generous than one expected. Kinder.

And that men like this, like Richard, like the lieutenant at Anzio, could always get women – for a while, for their limited purposes. Even lovely girls, even clever girls. And especially kind girls.

'Lads like that, they don't have the control, you see.' There was a hint of nostalgia somewhere in Don Jason's voice. 'Testosterone, is it? He had to come after me, he had to say everything he had in his daft little head, "Where have you taken her, what have you done with her?"' A silly mimicking of a childish voice that sounded to Victor nothing like Ollie. Poor fierce little Oliver.

'What *have* you done with her?' Victor asked, trying, trying, to be brave enough, terrified. I've never fought, he thought, I was in the navy, I've never fought, hand to hand, am I even a man? Shame rose in him, never fought, and now too old, too hopeless. At the question, or perhaps the tremble in Victor's voice, the man came down, squatting in the doorway.

'Ah,' he said, and his voice was low, hoarse with something like pleasure. 'Like to know, would you? She was smaller than she looked. Swaggering around like she did and then – I got her down pretty small. Packed her away nice.' Her blood on his arm.

And then fear did come, in a blind rush, fear that was cold like a drowning, and for a second he was back there, long before Anzio, back on the north Atlantic and pulling men from the water. Tags round their necks, for identification.

'Natalie knows,' he said, out of nowhere, instead. Deflecting. 'Natalie is on her way to the police.' Hearing himself like a stranger with a tight, hard voice.

'Do you know, I doubt that,' said Don Jason, musing,

lifting his head to look again, out across the water. 'You want to watch this, if you think your Natalie is in a position to help anyone. Worked better than I thought, what do I know about boats? You only need to be smart. To keep your head, see?'

'Watch this?' repeated Victor. 'What should I watch?' Feeling his heart quail, despairing, not knowing if he had even a fraction of what was required. But the man still wasn't looking down at him, that was something. Taking advantage of the momentary shifting of his attention, Victor felt along the seat behind himself. Thunder rumbled, not far off, and there was a flash. The sky was low and dark but no rain, not yet. He groped, careful.

There it was, lying along the crease. A crutch, the crutch Lisa, fussing at the last minute, had found for him when he had refused the walking frame. It was light, though, and his hand no more than skin and bone.

Lisa. Had she known? Had she let her husband in at night or had he taken advantage of his familiarity with the wards and the staff, knowing how to make himself invisible? Let him in to pad the corridors. Victor knew now, however much he might wish never to have known, that some men can force women into shapes they can't control, they can make them do things they hate.

The taxi driver straightened a moment so that his head disappeared and as Victor heard the sound again, that high whine, he visualised the motorbike with the boy riding high on it. It grew piercing, it was on the ridge above them, but it kept going, it receded. He slid the crutch carefully forwards and on to his knee and froze as the man's face reappeared in the door.

'Out you get, Mr Powell.'

Victor hunched in the seat, he didn't move.

'Will I have to do it in there?'

The sound. The sound. Something revved, a way away still but not gone, after all. Victor tried as hard as he could not to let the man see how hard he was listening.

'I was seen getting into your cab,' he said, crouched over the crutch in his lap, the old tortoise, the old pacifist. 'I was seen. There are cameras. They find traces—'

Jason laughed, a soft sound. 'I don't intend to tell them any different,' he said, reasonably. 'I tell them, he was taken ill, on the way. I say, I tried to resuscitate him, I might have been a bit rough, if there's bruises, but they're not likely to look too closely, are they? At your age.' He shook his head, the ghost of a frown. 'I'll just deliver you right back to them, there'll be all the DNA you like.' He was half crouching now, peering in.

A revving, then somewhere out down the lane the throttle opened, and bore down on them. Don Jason stepped back fractionally, turned his head, and in that second Victor took his chance. He had no choice. He thrust the crutch out in front of him, aiming, hoping for the gut, but God or history or something – the greatest of these is love, Sophie – was on his side and he got the man's balls instead, he felt the softness slip under the rubber tip and he shoved, as hard as he could.

Then he saw it unfold as if on a screen, the taxi driver bending over and reaching for the aluminium shaft, flinging it away and then staggering backwards just as the high-saddled motorbike roared in past the hedge, bumping over tractor ruts, not slowing. And then it was on its side and the wheels spinning and a helmeted boy stumbling towards them.

Through the door Victor saw the driver crouching, he saw him lift his eyes to Victor, he saw the yellow glare. And then Victor saw him unbending, not towards Victor, or the motorcycle rider, but extending himself like an animal inside the car, scrabbling for something, his hands on the glove compartment. A flash of something, bright.

No – don't . . .' Victor had his hands now on the door frame and he was pulling. He was trying to pull himself out but it felt impossible, his old body was too slow, the car's interior refusing to let him go. He could see the tall boy running, pulling off the helmet and his hair sticking up all in disarray.

'Don't, he's got a—' Victor saw the boy pull up as he saw it too, in the man's hand.

Thunder crashed, above them. The boy, he saw, was drenched, blinded by the rain.

A knife. He's got a knife. The words wouldn't come, and then he heard himself. Shouting. 'He's got a knife.'

It took Jonathan Dowd three approaches before he got her, and she was losing strength by then, choking, trying to estimate how much water in the lungs meant drowning was inevitable. Then he cut the engine, the inflatable drifted and he was in the bow and reaching for her. She was a deadweight in the water, and Nat thought he'd never manage to haul her in – she thrashed as hard as she could. She felt herself slip back in his hands and in desperation launched one last kick just as he found strength from somewhere in his arms that were all tendon and bone and there she was, gasping in the bottom of the grey inflatable. Alive.

She gestured wildly to the land, as if he might be planning to take her anywhere else, and the lightning lit the sky again, all around them this time. The counting was in a kind of delirium, she couldn't make it work, to ten, to twelve, fifteen – and then the thunder came. It was moving away. Dowd turned for the jetty without a word.

The suitcase. Someone else could tell him. Someone else could look. Not her. Not her. Who else, though?

'We need to—' she said, gesturing back where she'd come from, exhaustion hauling on her, flailing her arm. 'There's something . . .'

But Dowd was on his feet, the tiller of the outboard against his knees, swaying in the unstable inflatable. Looking at something unfolding on shore, and she turned to follow his gaze. The low outline of a car against the short marsh grass, on the slope down from a ridge. As they looked she heard the noise she'd thought she heard before, of a trail-bike and it appeared, cresting the ridge. A single figure riding high off the saddle.

The car was dull silver. The motorbike bumped and tilted on the track, down towards it, stupidly slow.

'It's him,' she said, then with urgency, 'It's him, it's him, Jonathan. There.'

And without needing to be told Jonathan Dowd opened the throttle.

Chapter Thirty-Three

As Nat ran, stumbling and sliding, up the muddy bank towards the silver car, they were standing there on the other side of the car in the pelting rain, Craig with his palms face out like he was surrendering, or trying to stop something happening. He swayed, too tall and rooted to the spot. Nat couldn't see what he was looking at but she knew it must be something terrible. She shouted into the wind, '*Stop*.'

Abruptly, both feet slid out from under her and she fell hard, face down. She could taste mud. Seizing clumps of the wiry grass in both hands she hauled herself back to her feet. She didn't look round to see where Dowd had got to. She had left him trying to tether the inflatable, shaking violently, with cold or something. Nat knew she was soaked, she knew it was driving cold rain, but she couldn't feel it. Another ten yards. Five. Slithering, she made it on to the patch of orange gravel and her hand was on the car's bonnet.

As she rounded the vehicle she got a glimpse of Craig's eyes, wide and pleading under the hair plastered down his face, but she already knew, could already see.

Victor's poor face, pressed against the car's door frame, his skin so thin and old, almost transparent, his eyes half closed, *no, no, not gone* beat like an awful drum in her head – and then Nat saw the knife. A knife in the taxi driver's hand, a knife for butchering, big rivets in the handle and the blade so big, big as a cleaver against the soft, liver-spotted papery skin of Victor's old throat. Don held it there, smiling, smiling Don who had looked at her in his rear-view mirror. Following her with his eyes.

Then came a sound – the thud of footsteps as Jonathan finally made it up the slope – that drew Don's eye away. Victor's lips moved, and Nat saw Don's knuckles tighten white on the knife handle, and in that split second, she lunged.

She had to get the blade. As Nat fell back she saw the blood but didn't know where it came from. She only saw Victor slump to one side and Jonathan Dowd's big bony hands on Don's shoulders hauling him off them, off her and Victor, and then the boy moved in beside Dowd, both of them holding him down.

The blood was on her shirt, clean shirt that morning, she thought stupidly, then *Victor*. Forwards on her knees. *Victor.*

He saw the cloth of the car's interior, the paper pine tree dangling from the mirror, the great grey sky over their heads.

It played before him through the frame of the car's door

as though it were a film, a silly film, young men fighting. *I've never fought.* And this was what it was, it turned out – a messy, painful, dirty business, wrestling in the mud while the rain fell. Life so untidy, it escaped you, always. Victor lay, panting like a rabbit, waiting for it to end.

Then Natalie's face appeared, streaked with something, mud and blood and crying, crying, crying, begging him for something he couldn't understand, that was not in his gift. Holding up her hands to him. He saw a deep welling line across them and the blood, and tiredly he raised his old hands to hers, parchment-skinned, liver-spotted, he took her poor fingers in his.

And he didn't know if she pulled him or he her but then there they were, rested against each other in the door of the taxi, and both their hearts still beating.

Epilogue

It was more than a year later that they contacted her. DS Donna Garfield on the phone, tense and wary and, underneath it all, sorry. Nat could tell, in the hesitation at the end of every sentence, looking for the space to say it out loud. But Nat didn't have the time or space or energy to waste on having a go, and she wanted to know, anyway, why Garfield was calling.

'I'm not sure if you were planning on coming back here at all, to the village . . .' There it was, the hesitation.

Nat had sighed. *Back there.*

Back there where the *Chickadee* sat hauled up on Paddy's hard, Jim earnestly working on her every evening under Paddy's eye. Not quite ready to talk to Nat yet, Paddy said, but the time would come. Janine and Steve behind the bar of the Bird, a bit older, wiser, more knackered but still loved-up, or loved-up enough, anyway. That was what got you over it, she guessed. Steve in an alley chain-smoking after listening to a forensic scientist describe how his daughter had been dismembered.

Because against all counsel Don Jason had pleaded not guilty so it had gone to trial. Jonathan Dowd had sat straight-backed – and absolutely motionless, it seemed to Nat who was sitting beside him – until it was over. It was soon clear that Jason had wanted his day in court so he could grand-stand. The Instagram feed identifying him – Don Jason waiting for Beth in a doorway; Don Jason standing in the back of the saloon bar watching her or smiling up at her from the driver's seat of his cab – he had dismissed, freely admitting to the relationship. 'We had fun,' chuckling, then leaning forward and looking across the room at Jonathan Dowd, shrugging, then jeering as he said Beth had ended the relationship – because she wanted to *settle down*.

She had been pregnant. Six weeks.

In a corner of some Victorian backstreet pub in town where they'd all found themselves a week after the verdict, Dowd had said, haltingly, 'She told me she was on the pill.' And Nat had looked at him, not quite understanding. 'The . . . him. Don Jason. She made him use condoms.' All the pub noise, the panelled walls and Victorian tiling seemed to fall away as she tried to process his meaning.

'She wanted your baby.' He was pale, with longing, with grief. 'Jonathan,' she had started to say but he had stopped her.

'It's all right,' he said. 'It's all right. I know now.' His voice steadying, far away. 'I know now.' Steve had come up behind him then, his arm round Jonathan's shoulders, and the two men had turned away.

Even Jason's barrister looked dismayed at the defence

he was obliged to mount – the knife hadn't been his, the baby hadn't been his, Victor was senile, it was Craig, it was Dowd – but in the end even if the physical evidence against Don Jason hadn't been overwhelming, the witnesses for the prosecution finished him. Lisa Jason, trembling and unable to meet her husband's eye, had stood in the witness box and testified to blood on his clothes, that she had washed, the day before the message was sent to Janine saying Beth had gone north. To his coming into the ward late one night, looking for Victor, her model patient. To his patient brutality, night after night, in their own home.

And Victor himself, standing straight in the witness box with both old hands on the rail, answering every question politely and calmly. Repeating Don Jason's words from memory, unswerving until the defence barrister admitted defeat and released him.

Now Garfield's voice came to her as if from the distant past as she sat in London, in her new life.

'Sure,' she said, wearily. 'I'm working weekdays but . . . sure, yeah.' Projectionist in a small cinema under a railway arch, her own little private space and a window opening on to images flickering on a screen. Real life being something she'd had enough of, for a while. She loved it.

'Could be a Saturday,' said Garfield. 'Coroner's office has released some of your friend's things. We contacted her dad but he said you had as much right as he did. We thought . . . if you wouldn't mind collecting them for . . . well, for whoever.'

Nat had walked to the end of her projectionist's booth and called his number. The apprenticeship had been Bill's idea, and the guy who owned the little cinema was a mate of his. 'I'm only asking them to talk to you,' he'd said. 'You get to do the rest.'

He answered on the third ring: she could hear birds in the background. He was working on some historical drama, in a quiet village.

'When do you get back?' she asked him. 'There's something I want you to help me with.'

The clothes had been packed up in boxes and on top of them there'd been a photo in a cheap flowery frame. She didn't know where it had been when she had walked through Beth's flat, because she'd never seen it before. A selfie taken on Beth's phone, their faces pressed close together, Beth's wide, wide smile. She must have had it printed up, she must have trimmed it carefully to fit.

After the guilty verdict Don Jason had decided he wanted to tell the police all about it, every detail. Steve had relayed that he was talking now, Garfield had been in touch – as if it might get the policewoman off the hook. Unstoppable, Steve said grimly: every detail, the texts he'd written to Ollie, his grandiose plans to kill Victor in hospital, under the noses of the doctors. What Beth had said, how he'd taken her body apart, where he'd kept it. It seemed they couldn't shut him up.

In the end it didn't matter what Don Jason had said, not to those who loved her, because that detail wasn't Beth, it was nothing to do with Beth, just like the crammed and oozing suitcase was nothing to do with her. Beth was gone elsewhere, gone wherever we go.

Nat took the picture in her hands, where the scars now

on the inside of her fingers had faded silvery-pale, and held it a moment, pressed against her shirt, pressed so hard she could feel the corners against her breast, and then they turned, she and Bill, and went home.

The summer had ended, eventually, with a sudden flurry of black storm cloud and a wind that blew all the yellow leaves off the trees at once. It ended around about the time Victor moved – Sophie moved him, Paddy loaning her his little car and helping her pile his possessions into the back while Rufus ran excitedly to and fro – into the cottage Natalie had left.

It held some of her still in it: she had left her plates for him, and a drawing she had made of Rufus tacked to a door. But it was that moment when Natalie had fallen against him in the taxi's door, under the rain, that moment, he knew, that tied them together. Holding on to each other knowing that whatever came next, neither of them would be alone.

The divorce was under way. At the first meeting with the solicitors Victor had seen Richard turn instantly savage, raging and threatening, but he and Sophie had sat calmly side by side until he had blown himself out under the eyes of both sets of lawyers. It was not easy to know if he was merely biding his time but to Victor it seemed that he knew he was beaten. As instantly as he had raged, Richard had decided to walk away, and if it revealed how little he had ever really cared for his own child, then Victor and Sophie cared enough, and more. Now and again Natalie phoned Sophie, and Victor liked to listen to them talk as he sat in the comfortable chair Sophie had bought him, or under the apple tree in the garden. Their happy discussions of him, how long a walk he had managed, details of his suppers, apple crumble for pudding. And Sophie – sometimes sitting next to Paddy, sometimes just the three of them, *triangulated* – glancing across at him with that look on her face, fondness was too tiny a word, even love did not seem to encompass it, it had joy in it, it was like a door opening into a bright warm room. Then Rufus would seem to see the look and run, small red-headed arrow, along its path to his grandfather, where he would fling his arms recklessly around Victor and they would twine together under Sophie's eye, safe as safe as safe could be.

Victor didn't think about how long it would be. Time had slowed, anyway, and the world had contracted, to this bright space, these beloved faces, looking back at him. Now, was the thing. Now.